IN ANOTHER PLACE

ALSO BY BRUCE MCALPINE

These Millions of Years

IN ANOTHER PLACE

BRUCE MCALPINE

Copyright © 2023 Bruce McAlpine

The moral right of the author has been asserted.

Apart from any fair dealing for the purposes of research or private study, or criticism or review, as permitted under the Copyright, Designs and Patents Act 1988, this publication may only be reproduced, stored or transmitted, in any form or by any means, with the prior permission in writing of the publishers, or in the case of reprographic reproduction in accordance with the terms of licences issued by the Copyright Licensing Agency. Enquiries concerning reproduction outside those terms should be sent to the publishers.

This is a work of fiction. Names, characters, businesses, places, events and incidents are either the products of the author's imagination or used in a fictitious manner. Any resemblance to actual persons, living or dead, or actual events is purely coincidental.

Matador
Unit E2 Airfield Business Park,
Harrison Road, Market Harborough,
Leicestershire. LE16 7UL
Tel: 0116 2792299
Email: books@troubador.co.uk
Web: www.troubador.co.uk/matador
Twitter: @matadorbooks

ISBN 978 1 80514 086 3

British Library Cataloguing in Publication Data.
A catalogue record for this book is available from the British Library.

Printed and bound in Great Britain by 4edge Limited
Typeset in 12pt Adobe Jenson Pro by Troubador Publishing Ltd, Leicester, UK

Matador is an imprint of Troubador Publishing Ltd

For
Marina

'il miglior fabbro'

PROLOGUE

The Amalfi Coast, Italy. April 1972.

In the night the wind has dropped. The sea is an inky black now, smooth and slicked like oil, but heaving as if some huge submarine creature is stirring itself down there. To the east the sky brightens and, as the dawn comes up, the string of distant lights round the bay of Amalfi begins to fade and the mountains of the Abruzzi show themselves dark and dragon-backed against the whitening sky. Gradually the sea shifts from pewter to palest gun-metal. It is a majestic scene, touched with Homeric grandeur. But the figures in the two small fishing boats appear indifferent. They are working rapidly, focused only on what lies beneath them, unaware of the train of events they are about to set in motion.

Nino Lombardi crouches, legs splayed, brow furrowed in concentration, scarcely feeling the surge and swell of the wooden deck under his bare feet as he feeds the slithering net over the gunwale into the water. He watches it drift and bubble, then sink into darkness. A hundred meters away Giorgio's silhouette is hunched in the stern, his hands moving with the slow, even motion of a woman carding wool. Finally, with a muffled thud, the rope snaps tight.

"*Bene,*" mutters Nino, then gives it one last tug for

reassurance. He rises and stretches out his long back. The sun is a copper disc now, hanging just clear of the horizon. In the east the sky is already bleached and cloudless. It's going to be another scorching day, one of those when even the links of the anchor chain look hot on the seabed.

Nino draws the back of his hand across his ragged moustache and surveys the catch – one shallow box lying on the deck amongst the clutter of nets and roping. He can count the fish without even having to spread them with his hand – just eight small *scombri* and two precious *spigole*. After a whole night in this heaving sea! He spits over the side in disgust. It's scarcely enough to keep him in cigarettes these days, and with all the new regulations and the foreign boats and the fish not breeding properly it's getting worse every year.

A sharp whistle carries clear across the water and breaks into his thoughts. Giorgio raises a hand, followed by the low cough and splutter of a diesel engine starting up. They have decided to use the drag-net now to scour the seabed. It's against the new laws, of course, but out here there's no one to see. He's heard that in Greece the quaysides are littered with dragnets and acetylene lamps for night fishing and no one gives a damn. So why should he? With a family back home to feed, what the hell else is he supposed to do?

Nino bends, turns the small key and prods the black plastic button with his forefinger. The exhaust smokes and bubbles and a shudder runs through the deck. He taps the throttle with his foot. There is a slight thud as the gear engages, then both boats begin to edge forward. As the thin wake ribbons out behind him, the first gulls come tumbling out of the sky. They wheel and shriek in the still air, then gradually settle down to wait with a lugubrious furling of their black-tipped wings. Nino regards them warily. "*Bastardi*" he mutters.

The net is fully stretched now, the ropes pulled taut, straining at the metal cleats. The boats begin to labour. Nino dabs at the throttle. The hull settles deeper into the water and they slide forward again, churning up a thicker wash behind them. Suddenly a high-pitched shriek bursts from the ropes. The boat shudders. The engine stalls and thuds to a halt. Nino stumbles and grabs the edge of the gunwale to steady himself. From the corner of his eye he sees Giorgio stagger and crash out of sight.

"*Santa Madonna!*" screams Giorgio. "What the hell is it?"

"We must be snagged on a rock."

"*A rock? Out here?* There aren't any bloody rocks. It's all sand." Giorgio's head emerges and stares down over the edge, his face just inches from the water. "It can't be a rock. Look! We're still moving."

And it's true, both boats are edging forward again, but listing heavily under some invisible load. Nino can hear the creak and groan of the timbers under his feet.

"We must have caught something," shouts Giorgio. "Something huge like a wreck. Forget the bloody net. Let's cut the ropes!"

"Like hell! Nets cost money. We'll pull it up, whatever it is, then see if we can tip it out."

Nino presses the rubber button and, with a low electric whine, the heavy metal spool starts to turn, slowly coiling the thick rope dripping onto the deck. He holds the tiller tight under his left arm as the load slews them round. Gradually the boats draw closer and the net begins to surface. Its braided edges are thick with slime and weed. The tight mesh is studded with shells and pebbles. They are less than five meters apart now, the end of the net still hidden. Nino takes the plastic, glass-ended tube they use for spotting octopi on the seafloor and puts it to the water.

"Can you see anything?"

"Not a thing. Too bloody dark. Take it very slowly."

The ropes squeak and strain and slip on the steel capstans with a fierce sound like a banjo chord snapping. Both boats are listing heavily now, their edges dangerously close to the waterline. Then, with a sudden glassy rush, the sea begins to pour in over the gunwales. The scattered contents of the deck, the plastic bottles and fenders, polystyrene floats and flags, wooden catch trays lift from the planking and float free, revolving languidly.

"Jesus, if we don't get rid of it soon…."

And then, with one last groan from the winch, the net comes clear and something huge and black breaks the surface. Both men stare in astonishment.

"*Porca miseria!*" gasps Giorgio. "It's a woman!"

In the half-light the figure looks enormous, cradled in the saffron-coloured net. The surface glistens like oil. The head has gone, the feet and legs are whitely encrusted with barnacles; but there is no mistaking the rounded forms of the body. Water slips glassily from her long thighs and powerful hips. A thick clutch of weed clings to one shoulder. A tiny translucent crab scuttles from its green tangle and slides away into the darkness.

"But black!" screams Nino. "She's black, for Christ's sake! It's bad luck. *Brutissima fortuna!* Cut the ropes!" He spins round and thrusts his hands into the water, searching for his knife.

"No, wait!" There's a sudden authority in Giorgio's voice. "I've got a better idea. Listen to me…."

In those days I hardly ever dreamt and I certainly didn't believe that a single dream could alter the course of your life. But, on that particular April morning, as I drove south, there was a strangeness to the day, an uneasy sensation of being touched by something from beyond my normal waking senses. I could, as they say, feel it stirring uneasily in my bones like a lurking premonition. At the time I tried to put it down to the adrenalin rush at what I hoped awaited me. A wiser man might have sensed other forces at work. But that was back then in 1972.

PART ONE

*Why do you stay in prison
when the door is so wide open?*
Jalal al-Din Rumi

ONE

It's a wet and blustery Tuesday morning and, despite my best efforts, I'm twenty minutes late for my breakfast appointment with David.

When I finally arrive I catch sight of him from the doorway of the hotel restaurant. He is on the far side of the crowded room, reading a newspaper. Despite not being a regular here, he has somehow managed to secure one of the coveted corner tables with a curved banquette. David's languid charm can usually get him most places.

David Anselm is one of my oldest friends. We had met at Cambridge where he was on a two-year exchange scholarship from studying Classical archaeology at Harvard. It was David who persuaded me to go traveling with him through Italy and Greece during our first long vacation. At the time, it had occasioned some hilarity amongst my other friends that I would be spending eight weeks alone in the company of someone who was openly gay. But by then my heterosexual credentials had been too well established for anyone to take the rumours seriously. And besides, David turned out to be the ideal traveling companion: sensitive, humorous and with an encyclopaedic knowledge of Classical archaeology. He already spoke a beautiful, precise Italian, having spent a year at the American School of Archaeology in Rome, and made a far better shot at learning Greek than I did in the weeks that we were there.

I have always suspected that it was the vicarious excitement of watching my early years as an antiquities dealer – the wheeling and dealing, the impromptu flights to Rome or Cairo, the shifty, fascinating characters who drifted in and out of my life – that finally diverted him from a potentially glittering academic career. That is if any academic career can be said to glitter. Occasionally I have pangs of conscience about this, for although David may be a formidable scholar, his life as a dealer has been less than successful, at least in financial terms. His cramped apartment in Manhattan's upper East Side looks like a junk shop, littered with miscellaneous fragments of vases and sculpture, which are doubtless of riveting academic interest, but hopelessly uncommercial. David is the only man I know who can pick up a tiny shard of Greek pottery, painted with maybe just an ear and half a collar bone and instantly identify it as being by the so-called 'Elbows-out Painter' (or some equally obscure artist), and recognise moreover that it probably joins another fragment buried in the archives of the Pushkin Museum in Moscow. This sort of thing is, of course, an intellectual *tour de force*, but it doesn't really cut the mustard with the big collectors and museum directors who want something a little more showy for their cash. None of this seems to bother David in the slightest, nor quench his endless enthusiasm and, over the years, he has managed to gather around him a faithful circle of serious-minded collectors, who just about manage to keep him financially afloat.

Despite the early hour, the restaurant, a discrete art world Mecca, is almost full, quietly humming with intense conversation. As I cross the room a few heads nod in casual greeting. When David sees me, he raises a hand and lifts his tall, lanky frame from the banquette. At the same moment a waiter materializes and pulls out a high-backed arm-chair for me.

David waves aside my apologies and leans forward conspiratorially.

"You know, this is where the real art business gets done, not in the fancy galleries in Bond Street. Just look around. It's incredible. All the usual glitterati and old queens are here, busy buttering up their clients so that they can then screw them for millions with their dodgy Rembrandts and reconstructed ormolu commodes."

"You'd think the clients might learn."

"No chance. Being buttered up and screwed is the real attraction. The clients love it. The art is purely incidental."

Before I can respond the waiter hands me the menu. It's a massive, ecclesiastical tome, leather bound and embossed in gold with some kind of spurious coat of arms. Inside I find the usual breakfast fare, plus an array of Edwardian oddities – devilled kidneys, kedgeree, kippers from some obscure village in Scotland. I order scrambled eggs, bacon, toast, coffee. Despite this deeply unoriginal choice, the waiter bends low as he retrieves the menu and mutters conspiratorially in my ear, "An excellent choice, if I may say so, sir."

The Connaught restaurant is the quintessential watering hole for the top echelons of the London art world. Its slightly worn, aristocratic feel – plush mushroom-coloured carpets, faded velvet banquettes, waxed card lamp-shades that exude a glow like a Dickensian gas lamp on a foggy afternoon and dogged white-jacketed retainers who slide silently around as if on rails – is the perfect backdrop to all the ruthless wheeling and dealing that goes on here. Top-flight art dealers are adept at convincing their clients that these cut-throat transactions are just a mildly entertaining, gentlemanly form of sport between two almost equals (the 'almost' is crucial to the success of the deal), which will discretely enhance the social status of the buyer, whilst also diversifying his bulging portfolio of assets.

David orders the stinking kippers.

"Christ, David, do you really like those things? Normal people haven't eaten them for the last hundred years."

"Got to keep your moribund Brit establishments going," he says blithely. "Otherwise you'll end up a gastronomic wasteland of MacDonalds and ice cream parlours just like us in the poor old U S of A."

I laugh. "What on earth are you doing staying here anyway? This isn't your normal territory. It must cost an arm and a leg."

"Worse than that. The place is obscenely expensive. But I'm having dinner this evening with the owner of an old collection of Greek vases from a castle in the icy wastes of Scotland." He obviously catches my look of surprise. "I know, old son, this ought to be your territory, but the Germans have a charming expression, 'Sogar ein blindes Huhn findet manchmal ein Korn.'"

"Meaning?"

"Even a blind hen occasionally finds a corn."

"So you're the blind hen?"

"In this case, yes. I happened across a reference to the collection in an obscure *Festschrift* of the *Deutsches Archäologisches Institut*, published in 1912."

"Jesus, David, how do you find that kind of stuff?"

"I know, it's pretty sad bedtime reading, isn't it? The sort of thing only unearthed by small-minded pedants such as myself and geriatric scholars in places like Leipzig. But it turns out that the vases are all still there in the Gothic castle, presumably mildewed and smothered in cobwebs by now and I'm dining with the kilted laird tonight to talk about it. If all goes well I'll make a foray up north to take a look at the stuff. I think it must be somewhere close to the Arctic Circle."

"But what's that got to do with staying here?"

"Well, I reckoned I could hardly impress him with drinks in some seedy flop house in Bayswater, followed by a take-away pizza. So I booked myself in here for just one night. Tomorrow I'm back to the boon docks." He takes a sip of his coffee. "In any case, the whole thing will probably turn out to be far too rich for my blood. Or I'll screw it up by not understanding some arcane bit of Scottish lore. How *do* you address a Laird of that Ilk, or whatever he calls himself? So if it all goes belly up, shall I pass him on to your capable hands?"

"At a price?"

"We can talk about it," says David non-committaly. This is why he will never be really successful in this business. He doesn't nail people's feet to the ground until they cough up the money. I know that, when it comes to it, he will probably refuse my offer to take a commission.

David leans back and pushes a tumble of unruly blonde hair from his forehead and I'm suddenly aware that he looks uncharacteristically strained.

"Are you all right?" I ask.

"Actually, not great. Have you seen this?" He picks up the copy of The Herald Tribune he has been reading, folds it over and passes it across to me, tapping on an article at the top of page three:

GETTY MUSEUM DIRECTOR INDICTED BY ITALIAN COURT

It takes me a moment to register the significance.

"Jesus Christ!"
"My thoughts precisely. Read on."

An Italian judge in Rome's Supreme Court yesterday indicted Dr. Miriam Gorst, the director of the J. Paul Getty Museum in Malibu, California, on charges of fraud, smuggling and dishonestly handling stolen goods. The indictment lists fourteen items of Greek and Roman art on display at the museum, which the Italian state claims to have been looted from excavations in Italy and illegally exported. The Italian government has formally requested the extradition of Dr. Gorst. Neither Dr. Gorst nor the Getty Museum was available for comment. A spokesperson for the State Department said that they were cooperating with the enquiry and would give all appropriate assistance to the Italian government.

I put the paper down and stare at David. I feel winded, as if someone has sucked all the air out of my gut.

"Did you know about this?"

"Only a couple of days ago. I received a *sotto voce* call from Lorenzo Darzio – or Larry as my uncouth fellow countrymen prefer to call him. You know him?" I nod. Larry Darzio is the legal council for the Metropolitan Museum. I have met him a couple of times at museum functions: short, suave, impeccably dressed, as smooth as silk and – I reckon – as tough as nails. Probably just what the Met needs to keep vexatious law suits off their back. "We're old friends from Harvard days. He's usually kind enough to alert me discretely if something comes up he thinks I should know about."

"If it was so top secret, how come *he* knew about it?"

"Apparently the Getty consulted him when the whole thing first started to rumble a couple of months ago. Larry has a lot of experience in this area and, because he's part Italian, he also knows some of the key players at the other end."

"And what's his take on the likely outcome? Surely the Italians don't really hope to swing this one?"

Before replying David raises his hand and a waiter glides towards us bearing two silver coffee pots. We wait until our cups have been replenished. David is affecting unconcern, but I know him well enough to see from the lines around his mouth and the soft drumming of his fingers on the starched tablecloth that he is unsettled.

He goes on, "Larry's not at all sure what will happen – any more than anyone else is at this stage. The Getty, of course, can afford to hire cohorts of the world's most expensive lawyers and they have a lot of diplomatic clout behind the scenes. Also Miriam is one of our brightest and best and something of a public figure, so he reckons there could be quite a righteous American backlash if the Italians brand her and put her in the stocks – no US tourists climbing all over the Coliseum next summer, sales of Chianti and mozzarella falling through the floor, Italian restaurants in New York empty and shuttered. You know the sort of thing. So one possible outcome is that the US won't give Miriam up and the Italians will have to try her *in absentia* – and will, of course, find her guilty. That way they get a lot of publicity and scare the shit out of people like you and me – which presumably is part of the plan – and Miriam stays free to go about her business, just so long as she never sets one dainty little foot on Italian soil ever again."

It's hardly an ideal solution, but still I can feel the tension that has been welling inside me begin to ebb.

"So, in the end, it'll turn out to be just another minor art market scandal. Pretty soon the whole thing will blow over as usual and ..."

David holds up a hand. "Wait. It gets worse. About half an hour before I left for the airport yesterday, Larry called me *again*."

"About Miriam?"

"No," he sips his coffee and seems to be choosing his words carefully. "You know Arthur Seligman?"

"Of course." Arthur isn't, strictly speaking, part of the antiquities world. He's what we call a 'Works of Art' dealer. This means that he selects particularly choice *objets d'art*, regardless of age or culture, and peddles them to an effete circle of collectors from his elegant apartment overlooking the north end of Central Park. Occasionally he comes into possession of an antiquity, usually a seductive marble torso of a youth, always of great 'beauty' and often of dubious authenticity.

"It seems," goes on David, "that Arthur currently has a portrait of Hadrian's beautiful boyfriend Antinous. I haven't seen it, but by all accounts it's pretty good. And, for once, unquestionably ancient." He pauses.

"So what's the problem?"

"The problem is that the surface is as fresh as this morning's dew. Apparently it even still has earth on it in some places. And the Italians claim that it's been found under a building site close to Herculaneum."

"Can they prove it?"

"They say they have witnesses. Whether genuine, bribed or blackmailed wouldn't make much difference in an Italian court of law. And photographs. They've also arrested the builder."

"Christ!" I sit back trying to hold down the swell of anxiety that is rising again in my stomach. This is getting far too close for comfort. "How does Larry rate the outcome of that one?"

"Well...." David draws in a deep breath and then expels it slowly. "That's the problem. Not good. Obviously he's cautious, but he also has good contacts in the State Department and his prognosis is not encouraging. For all the absurdity and farce of Italian politics, Italo-American relations are apparently quite important to my fellow countrymen. Italy is, after all, a member of NATO and, sticking out as it does smack in the middle of the Mediterranean, it's very strategically placed as a staging post to North Africa and the Middle East and all those other delightful breeding grounds of terrorism and slaughter. So, what Larry reckons is that the Americans may do a deal in order not to rock the boat with Italy. Miriam is a big fish, but Arthur's just a minnow as far as they're concerned. So they'll throw Arthur to the *Carabinieri* wolves in exchange for soft-peddling the Getty thing. And that, I fear, will be tough on Arthur. Very tough indeed."

"What's happened to Arthur?"

"So far nothing. But I saw him last week and he looks like a member of the living dead, walking around Manhattan, just waiting for the axe to fall. Which it surely will."

For a moment we stare at each other in silence. The same thought must be echoing in both our heads: *This, under other circumstances, could equally well be me.*

At that moment the waiter materializes with my eggs and bacon and David's evil-smelling kipper. For once I don't have the heart to tease him and for a while we pick at out food in sombre silence, while I regather my sense of the normal.

"But none of it makes sense," I say at length. "The Americans don't even recognise the export laws of other countries, let alone enforce them. We all know that. Neither do the British, nor the Germans, nor any other northern European country. So there's not a hope in hell that the Italians can get Arthur extradited on a smuggling charge. And besides, what's going on in Italy that this stuff is suddenly so bloody important? They don't have the resources even to take care of the antiquities they already have. Just look at all the ancient monuments that are collapsing, the museums they can't afford to staff. Every major museum in Italy – in Greece and Egypt come to that – has vast store rooms stacked to the rafters with objects they can't even clean, let alone put on display. The Italians know that as well as we do. That's why, export laws or no bloody export laws, they've been turning half a blind eye to our trade for decades." Suddenly I feel like a courtroom advocate for Arthur Seligman. Only it isn't Arthur I'm really defending. It's my own badly-disturbed peace of mind.

"Everything you say is precisely true," responds David evenly. "Or, *was* precisely true. But I fear that our once semi-legal profession has suddenly become very dangerous. The problem is that our Italian friends have started to move the goal posts and it seems there's someone in there behind the scenes doing the moving. A man named Aldo Diamante, an ex-lawyer turned politician. A nasty piece of work by all accounts and as ambitious as they come. He's out to make a name for himself by tub-thumping some nationalistic, high publicity cause. And defending the great Italian cultural patrimony from greedy capitalist tomb robbers like you and me is a perfect platform for him. Never mind that he wouldn't know an ancient Roman marble frieze from a slab of mozzarella."

"David, what the hell are you talking about?"

David abandons the laborious filleting of his kipper and leans back against the banquette. "Listen up, as we so inelegantly say in the States, and I'll tell you the whole of what Larry Darzio divulged to me yesterday. He rated it as 'gossip', but Larry's gossip is as good as another man's gilt-edged inside information – and it's pretty compelling stuff. I don't want to be a Cassandra, but I fear I bring you bad tidings from beyond the pond this day."

He pulls in a deep breath. "Firstly, you're right that America doesn't recognize other country's export laws, and right again that therefore the Italians can't hope to extradite Arthur or Miriam or anyone else for smuggling. That bit of the charge would be swiftly kicked into the long grass by the US courts – as the Italians well know. No, the sting is in the other part of the charge – the dishonestly handling stolen goods bit."

"But it's not *stolen*?" I protest. "Smuggled maybe, but not stolen. Unless, of course, they claim it's been lifted from a museum. But they don't. They say it comes from a building site. So once it's out of the country, it's technically in the clear. So what's the problem?"

"That's where Signor Diamante has gotten crafty. He's a lawyer, remember? And it seems he's unearthed and dusted off some obscure law enacted by Mussolini in a fervour of Fascist nationalism in 1936. Nobody had been aware of it until now, but it appears that it's never been revoked and therefore technically it's still on the statute books. And it says that any archaeological item of whatever age or importance found in the soil of the Italian motherland or within her glorious territorial waters is *de facto* the property of the Italian state. This means, my friend, that anything that has ever been dug up or fished up in Italy since 1936 belongs to the Italian state, and anyone who doesn't hand it over to the authorities – which no Italian in their right mind is going to do – is automatically guilty of theft. *And* – and here's the rub – anyone who subsequently buys or handles it is automatically guilty of dishonestly handling stolen goods." David pauses and stares at me. "And that is not only an internationally extraditable offense, it's also a *criminal* offense, and if you're found guilty of it in an Italian court – which you surely will be, no matter what the evidence – that means an absolute minimum of three years in an Italian slammer. An that's what Arthur is looking at right now."

I can feel the anxiety that has been percolating inside me expand now like an air bubble in my stomach. The thought of what might happen to Arthur, slight, bespectacled, extravagantly gay, in an Italian prison, rubbing shoulders with drug pushers and child molesters hardly bears consideration. Although my mind has no option but to follow David's impeccable logic, another part of me is suddenly desperate for some kind – *any* kind – of reassurance.

"But still it doesn't make any sense." I can hear the tightness in my voice. "The Italians have made these kinds of noises before. You know that. Okay, maybe not as loud and threatening as this, but still, they always fade away in the end. Why shouldn't this be just the same? Another absurd, dramatic storm in an Italian tea-cup. The whole of Italian politics is like a comic opera anyway."

David shrugs. "Maybe. Maybe not. We're in uncharted waters here. But Larry seemed to be clear on one thing: that whatever deal the Getty, with all their money and influence, may manage to do, the Italians are after Arthur's blood and they mean to get him."

At that moment the waiter arrives and clears our plates. He then deposits a silver rack of thinly sliced triangular wedges of toast and an array of jams in cut glass bowls. There seems little more to be said on the topic that won't sink us deeper into the swamp of gloom and anxiety. So, by tacit agreement, we allow the conversation to drift into more comfortable directions – the latest auctions, the scandal of a wealthy German collector who has been duped into paying a reputed million dollars for a fake head of the Emperor Augustus, a spectacular public falling-out between two museum directors – but our thoughts are clearly still circling round Miriam Gorst, Arthur Seligman and what this sudden change in the politics of our world might presage.

It is only after David has called for the bill that I notice him hesitating. He's clearly still ill at ease. At length he clears his throat and leans forward, forearms folded on the white table-cloth. More bad news about Miriam?

"There's something else I wanted to talk to you about."

"Oh?"

"It's Sylvia. She wants to see you."

At the mention of my ex-wife I can feel myself bristle like a feral animal preparing to ward off a sneak attack. David is probably the only person who has managed to stay friends with both of us, following our acrimonious divorce. Sylvia is a divider. If you aren't for her, you are treacherously against her. And if you are against her, you are automatically exiled from her circle, your reputation publicly shredded. How David manages his precarious balancing act without affecting our relationship I have never quite understood, but this is the first time he has ever brought her into the conversation, and I am wondering what trick Sylvia has up her sleeve and how she has finally managed to subvert David's neutrality. I wait for him to continue.

"She's ill."

"How ill?"

"Very ill indeed. I think she's dying."

There's a clichéd expression about one's heart sinking. But suddenly this is precisely it: a heavy contracted downward pull in my chest. And with it an illogical feeling that, in some obscure way, I have always expected – and dreaded – this moment. Childless, I was free of her; but this is the last loop she can throw around me. Or is it just possible that this is yet another of Sylvia's elaborate manipulations?

"Have you seen her?"

"Yes. I went straight to the hospital yesterday evening when I got in. She seemed pretty drugged up, but she made it clear she wanted to see you."

"Are you sure it's really that bad? We both know she's a drama queen. Did you speak to a doctor?"

David gives me a long look. It's impossible to read what is in that expression. Sadness? Disappointment? Or just plain exasperation that he has to deliver this message at all and finds me uncooperative.

At length he says, "This isn't drama, Bronson. This is real. It's a brain tumour and a particularly aggressive one. Apparently she'd been having headaches for some time, but didn't want to go to a doctor and it went undiagnosed until now. And now it's very advanced indeed." He pauses, presumably to let his words sink in. "And yes, I did see the doctor. He was very sympathetic, but quite cagey with me. Not surprisingly. After all, I'm not next of kin."

"She hasn't got a next of kin."

"I know. Except…"

"Except me?" I can feel the claustrophobia in my chest tighten another ratchet.

He shrugs. "I guess".

"I'm *ex*-next of kin, remember?"

David spreads his hands on the white table cloth and gives me an appraising look. "Don't you think you owe her at least that?" he says.

And under that look I relent. "Okay. I'm sorry. I'll go and

see her, if you think that's the right thing." But even as I speak, I'm uncomfortably aware of the lack of generosity in my tone.

Outside the sky has lidded over and bruised-looking clouds are beginning to threaten.
"Nasty storm coming on, sir," says the top-hatted doorman encouragingly. "Taxi?"
I refuse his offer and begin walking in the direction of Park Lane. Like a condemned man, I need more time. The wind is gusting now and sharp points of rain begin to sting my face. On Park Lane the car wheels are hissing across the tarmac, sending up fountains of spray. I raise my arm and a taxi glides to a halt beside me. The driver reaches out and opens the back door and, with a heavy heart, I climb in, sink back in the creaking seat and tell him my destination.
How do you say no to the dying?

TWO

Room 402 of The Princess Grace Hospital is at the end of a long side passage. It's a corner room, of course; even now, nothing but the best for Sylvia. But I can't help noticing that, unlike all the other blonde wood doors that I have passed on my way here, the perspex name pouch is empty. As I stand there hesitating, I can feel the blood thrumming in my head and the sweat gathering on my palms. Then suddenly the door opens and I am face to face with a burly figure in a white hospital coat.

For a long moment we stare at each other in surprise. He is almost a head taller than me, with close-cropped grey hair and intense light blue eyes set into a lined face. The nose is large and hawk-like and a pair of gold-rimmed half-moon spectacles balances precariously towards the curved tip. A thick stack of buff-coloured files is wedged securely under his left arm. After a moment's pause he closes the door behind him. A little too deliberately, I register, as if barring my way. Then he asks, "Did you come to see Mrs Tullis?"

As concisely as I can I give him a resume of the situation. He regards me with renewed interest. "Ah, the ex-husband." He clears his throat. "I'm afraid I have to give you the sad news that Mrs Tullis died an hour ago. She went peacefully," he adds. "She had no pain."

He's doing his best to sound reassuring, even though it's obviously a mantra learnt in medical school. In the long silence that follows he observes me over the top of his glasses with a concerned frown. Probably he is wondering whether he will now have to deal with a minor psychotic breakdown as well as a recent death. And, in fact, I feel winded and faintly giddy. David's bleak prognosis should have alerted me, but still I find I'm barely able to take in the situation.

Luckily there's something reassuring about the doctor's unruffled sturdiness as he stands there waiting for a response. It's obvious that for him this is all in a day's work. He is a professional in death, a modern white-coated shaman helping people to shuffle off their mortal coil and move on. But I? I am a complete novice in this territory, totally lost, standing – as I do now, literally – on the threshold of such mysteries.

As if to emphasise my discomfort, he asks, "Would you like to see her? She's still here."

Instinctively I shake my head, feeling ashamed even as I do so. But still, let's face it, if we couldn't communicate when she was alive, what would be the point of trying to commune with her now she's dead? I half expect to see a look of disapproval on his weathered face, but instead he pulls back the white coat, delves into his jacket pocket with his right hand and fishes out a slightly crumpled white envelope.

"This is for you. Technically, if we follow all the rules, I suppose I should give it to the registrar to forward. But I don't think there's really any reason why you shouldn't have it."

He holds out the envelope and I take it. To my surprise it is thick, clearly containing more than a single sheet of paper. My name is scrawled erratically across the front in black ink. I remember David's description of her as barely conscious.

"But surely she can't have written this?"

"Last night apparently. I gather it took her a long time."

I stare at him. "But how was that...?" My voice trails away.

"Possible?" He gives a small shrug. "Actually it's not that uncommon. Some people seem to rally the day before they die. It's as if their spirit has one last thing to do before they leave. Then the dying can be surprisingly energetic, sometimes even joyful. Or," he inclines his large head towards the envelope, "against all the medical evidence, they seem to find the physical resources to complete one final task they feel has been left undone. I imagine this letter must have been very important to her." He gives a wry, sympathetic smile. "After all, let's face it, your ex-wife didn't lack for will power, did she?"

He gives my arm a reassuring pat before he moves on down the passage, a burly figure lumbering slightly, like a galleon in a heavy sea. But I don't feel reassured. I feel shocked and slightly sick. I suppose there's a limit to how far the imagination can prepare you for such an event. And even though I haven't laid eyes on her for five years, scarcely thought of her for the last three, there's a brutal finality to this situation, which I'm struggling to accommodate. It may be *her* death, but the implications are stealthily leaching their way into me. And the bulky envelope in my left hand isn't helping. It's as if, Odysseus-like, I'm being taken down into the Underworld to converse with the dead. And I don't want to.

*

The roar of the traffic surging down Marylebone Road drums mechanically in my ears – hundreds of people barrelling onwards with their daily lives. In the sharp north breeze the budded daffodils are nodding erratically. I pull my coat closer around me and turn up the collar. I am sitting on a rusting iron bench in Regent's Park, just across the road from the Princess Grace Hospital. On my lap lies a letter written to me by a woman now dead. My ex-wife to be precise, whom I haven't seen since we last parted in rancour and bitterness in the elegantly panelled offices of Carter and Ruck, London's most feared and most expensive – I know, I had to foot the bill – firm of divorce lawyers. Opposite me stands a skeletal oak. A bedraggled crow has settled on one of its stripped branches. The sky is a dirty, bruised grey, and the wind is picking up. Nature feels at her most heartless and implacable. I suspect she may be conspiring in some cosmic joke that is about to break on me. It's one thing to have your ex-wife accuse you to your face, when you have an arsenal of irony and malice, carefully honed over a decade of marital guerilla warfare, conveniently to hand. Quite another to be held accountable by someone with all the weight of death in their words. I know I'm going to have to read this letter all the way to the end. Just as Sylvia must have calculated. And I know I'm not going to like it.

As if hoping to gather apotropaic protection around me, I try to conjure up images of her – benign and positive images that is. But, to my shame, *even now*, all I can dredge from the recesses of my brain are memories of the ferocious anarchy of her emotions boiling up like magma, her snakelike cunning and her skill to turn facts around until you felt trapped in a hall of mirrors and didn't know where the exit was or what your own thoughts were anymore; her uncanny ability to find your wounds and then, with ill-disguised glee, to poke her fingers in and twist them until she could feel you begin to crumble....

Clearly this isn't working. So, with a heavy heart – I can feel the weight of it again in my chest – I pick up the envelope, slit it open with my thumb and extract three sheets of paper.

Incredibly, they are closely written on both sides in an only slightly shaky hand.

> My Darling,
>
> I expect you're wondering why I'm writing to you. We haven't spoken for five years and I suppose we both thought we had shut the other one out of our lives. But the truth is that no one can really shut their past away. If we try, it only comes back to haunt us in ways we can't imagine.
>
> When you left I hated you. I wanted you dead and I poisoned myself with my hatred. That lasted for several years. But it all seems far in the past now. I knew I was dying long before I got the diagnosis. And in these last weeks something inside me has shifted, something that has been straining to shift for a long time and just couldn't. I haven't gone through all those slow stages they write about – denial and bargaining and all the rest. Perhaps deep down I knew I didn't have the time. It has been more like a switch being thrown. And when that happened everything suddenly looked different, as if I was seeing the world as I should have seen it before and just couldn't. And that's what I want to tell you about.
>
> Why? You will be asking. Why is she telling me of all people? Well, the answer's simple – because I still love you and I don't have children and if I leave one thing of value behind on this planet when I go I want it to be this:
>
> Do you remember how we met? How we clicked so immediately, as if somehow we recognized each other. Perhaps it was because we both felt like outsiders pretending to play the insiders' game. We walked out of that boring British Museum party half-way through and

went for dinner and that was when we discovered how much we had in common – or thought we had – and afterwards we went back to your flat and made love like I had never made love before. Of course, I could tell you were a womanizer. That was obvious. But I believed that with me you would change. And, for a while, I think you even believed it too.

Looking back now, I can see how you dazzled me and perhaps that dazzling was what made me so desperate to hold on to you. Back then there was a kind of freshness to you. I remember so well the first time you took me to Greece. You were so alive, so sensitive, so open to things, so moved by the myths and the history, as if you were inhabiting another world. But gradually, somewhere along the way, as you became more successful, all that got buried by your ambition, your need to make your way in the world. But there was one thing above all that I couldn't have named in the beginning, that made you so attractive. It was what I came to think of as your 'x-ray eyes'. It was more than just intuition. I always watched you when someone new came into your gallery. It was as if you could see clean through them and size them up within seconds. You could sense their strengths and weaknesses, their pretensions and ambitions. You could even sniff their guilty secrets. That was the real secret of your success. Not your art knowledge or your daring, as you liked to think, but those incredible x-ray eyes. They're a gift, you know, a real gift. But do you realize that you've only ever used them to gain advantage over others so that you could manipulate them? Or to protect yourself if you felt threatened. But you have never ever used them to see people for who they really are and look at them with any kind of compassion. Never.

And have you ever turned those wonderful x-ray eyes on yourself? I wonder what you might see if you did.......

I realize now that what I hoped for back then – what I longed for more than anything in the whole world – was for you to use that gift of your sensitivity and your x-ray eyes to see into me. See into me and see all the damage and the pain – and love me still, in spite of it. It was the most beautiful, the most desperate – and I see now, the most absurd – hope in all my life. And, of course, you never did. I even tried to manipulate you into it. And I came to resent you and finally to hate you, because you just wouldn't – or couldn't – really see me. And I felt then that you were not just betraying me, but that you were betraying your true self. Well, perhaps you were. But what I also know now is that we were betraying each other.

Oh yes, we looked like a good match in the beginning, you and I. We were a glamorous couple and everyone said how right it was, how well suited we were. And we thought so too, especially because of that odd feeling of recognition that we had, so that we both thought we were 'fated'. Even you, who didn't believe in destiny or God or anything else that you couldn't see or touch believed that. Or, at least, you said you did. It was a word that we used a lot in the beginning – fated. Well, we were right. We were fated. But not in the way we thought. And certainly not fated to be happy. Because what we didn't know as we stood at the altar that fine June day was that somewhere below us, deep in the crypt, another marriage was taking place, a much darker one. A shadow marriage. And that's where our real union took place.

Do you know when I first realised this? We were sitting in a plane and, for some reason, I was feeling light, free, and unusually safe, almost intoxicated with that feeling, and I started to tell you about how it had been for me growing up in post-war Holland with no father and a deranged, manipulative mother. I had never told anybody before; I felt so deeply ashamed of it. And I spilled it all out in front of you.

I told you how absolutely terrifying it was to be cooped up in that mildewed flat alone with this crazy, raging woman and outside the whole country crushed by poverty and covered in a shame that felt so deep it was like slime sticking to everything. I told you too how I cut my leg on some scrap metal on the bomb site next to us and there weren't any drugs or penicillin. Not unless you had money – which we didn't. And how I got gangrene so that my leg smelt like rotting meat. It smelt so bad that whenever I came close to other children they held their noses and ran away. And I actually heard the doctor tell my mother that they would probably have to amputate my leg. They hadn't even bothered to shut the bloody door so that I wouldn't hear! I told you too how I sat all alone, aged seven, at the back of the class thinking about that, and how I just knew I wasn't going to let them cut my fucking leg off. I would rather die first. And in the end they didn't. It healed and no one quite knew how. A miracle they called it. And so I got to keep my legs. The perfect legs, you once called them. And I told you too how that terror could still haunt me, the terror of losing my legs. Insane, irrational, shameful. But still it could come like some ghoul leaping onto the stage of my adult life right there in the middle of a dinner or a conversation, and I would have to choke down the panic of being back in that stinking classroom with my stinking leg. It never fully left me.

I told you all that. It was the most intimate, the most exposing thing I'd ever done in my whole life. And do you know what you did? You turned and looked out of the window. And the next moment the stewardess arrived with drinks. And we never, ever, mentioned it again. It just disappeared like it had never been there and we got on with our lives.

But in that split-second when you turned away, I realized something with a clarity I had never known before – the same clarity that I have now. I realized that I wanted you to look into me with your wonderful x-ray eyes and see my fear and then reach into me as if I were a glass vessel and take my fear away and carry it for me and then I would be bright and free, just like I was born to be. But in that same moment I realized that it was never going to happen, because I saw that you had too much fear of your own. Behind all your charm and bluster you were awash with it. Just like me. That was what we truly recognized in each other. That was the sacred pact that bound us together deep in the crypt of the church that day. Not our love, as we so fervently wanted to believe, but our fear.

And what I know now is that no one can ever carry anyone else's fear for them. Ever. That's something we have to face and go through all on our own. That's what I've been doing in these last weeks and now I'm out the other side. And I'm more light, more free than I've ever been and I'm not afraid any more. I go with a light heart, because in these weeks I've really fallen in love – fallen in love with life. Oh, I know that sounds like a cliché – something you would loathe and pour scorn on. Only it's not a cliché when you live it. When you have only a few

> days and hours left, every second is transformed and the world becomes indescribably beautiful. That's only possible when you turn and face your fear and then you're left with just the pure spaciousness of life.
>
> In the end, you know, there are only these two things: love and fear. Love drives out fear. But fear also drives out love. We were awash with fear, you and I. Only we just didn't know it. And you? I think you will have to decide soon, which side you want to live on. Love or fear? And I wonder where will your fear settle one day when you have to face it?
>
> I say this without rancour. Perhaps only with some sadness. And I wish you well. S.

I put the letter aside and draw in several deep draughts of breath. I feel stripped. Stripped back to a place so elemental that everything around me, the nodding daffodils, the blackened trees, the parched grass, the bruised clouds has become hyperreal. Yet I have no part in it. I am cut adrift like a man in space. In other circumstances I could brush the letter aside as Sylvia's usual malice or sentimental indulgence. But, coming as it does from the other side of death, it brooks no denial. I can argue with it as much as I like, but I know that from here on the words will forever be with me. They have the inexorability of a grave marker.

For the voice that echoes off these pages now – honest, wise, even *compassionate* – seems as far removed from the Sylvia I have known, with her manipulations and her savage inflexibility and her cyclonic rage, as it is possible to be. Or is it? Is it just possible that *this* is the person I had glimpsed all those years ago when we first met, before we embroiled each other in pain and recrimination? The person I had been blindly in search of, but lacked the skill and understanding truly to see? Lacked the ability and the courage to use, as she has said, my x-ray eyes with compassion, chose instead to turn away....

From out of nowhere a Japanese koan floats into my mind: *Show me the face you had before you were born.*

And suddenly I am gripped by an appalling sense of waste. Christ, what a fucking mess we made of things! I slide the letter back into its envelope and stuff it in my coat pocket, pull the collar higher around me.

And then, for the first time in my adult life, I weep.

THREE

The E55 *autostrada* winds its way along Italy's Adriatic coast from wind-torn Trieste in the north down to the grimy ferry port of Brindisi. For the most part it's a flat and rather boring drive. Much of the way the road runs beside the railway tracks. This morning the section between Venice and Prosaro (where I am headed) is choked with traffic. A stolid convoy of trucks packs the two inside lanes, nose to tail like a herd of purposefully migrating elephants. The outside lane – which I occupy when I can – is the preserve of the Italian speedsters. They swish past, lights flashing, a staccato symphony of warning blaring from their two-tone horns.

When I had flown out of London just after dawn, the weather had been grey and windswept. It was the kind of morning that makes you wonder if the sun is ever going to put in an appearance again. But two hours later I arrived at Venice's Marco Polo airport and stepped out gratefully into the opalescent spring light of the lagoon. It was a euphoric sensation, like being let out of school during term. But the further south I go now, despite the playful dazzle of the Adriatic to my left and the cloudless sky above, this feeling of euphoria is beginning to fade, replaced by the sense of anxiety that has been plaguing me for the last few days, ever since my meeting with David and the shock of Sylvia's death.

And, to make things worse, my strange dream of the previous week, the night before Carla Ruspolini came in to the gallery, keeps coming back to me. Perhaps the proximity of the sea is suggestive. Jungians believe that dreams carry deeply encoded messages from the unconscious. All you have to do is crack the code. Simple. But I think even the Jungians would have a hard time with this one. The dream consisted of an indistinct dark shape that heaved itself out of inky black water, then slipped silently back into the depths. Like some obsessive film loop, this scene had repeated itself over and over again. And with each disappearance I felt a strange, aching sense of loss.

Plotless and incoherent though it was, the effect had been powerful enough to wake me, leaving me lying sleepless and disorientated until the dawn light began to filter round the curtains. And now this apparently meaningless image seems to have lodged itself somewhere in my psyche and is proving annoyingly reluctant to leave. But perhaps strangest of all had been the feeling when I woke that night, a feeling that the dream somehow *wanted* something of me. *But exactly what?* I think I'll leave that to the Jungians.

The green and white exit sign for *Prosaro/Urbino, 1 km* comes rushing towards me. I check my watch – a little after 12.30. Despite the traffic, I seem to have made good time. I flick down the indicator switch, force my way through the two lanes of trucks, arousing an elephantine trumpeting of protest, and onto the curving slip-road. Once through the toll gate I pull over and consult my directions. They are written on headed paper in Carla Ruspolini's looping, slightly erratic hand.

The little seaside town of Prosaro seems emptied of life. Its cobbled streets are melancholy and deserted. Despite the beautiful weather, most of the shops are still shuttered against the winter. Eventually I find my way and pick up the signs for Urbino. At first the narrow road is dotted with filling-stations and bakeries and mini-markets; but gradually these give way to the broad, open hills of *Le Marche* with its faded oak woods and precise geometrical vineyards tilted up towards the sky.

After a quarter of an hour – just as I am beginning to wonder if I have missed the turning – I round a sharp left-hand bend and there, directly in front of me, is the unmistakable mausoleum-like entrance to the *Castello Ducale*, exactly as Toby Debenham had described it. Brick built, the size of a small house, with a white stone cornice and two deep alcoves sheltering marble urns, it's the first sign – as Toby had promised – that the place is going to be impressive.

I swing the car under the broad arch and, for a moment, the darkness seems all-encompassing, the light on the other side impossibly far away. Then I am out again in the shimmering Italian sunlight, trying to shrug off the absurd flash of anxiety that has just seized me. Clearly something isn't right with me today. Feeling slightly shaky, I pull over and climb out. Ahead of me the drive extends a full half mile up the hill before arcing to the right. An alley of tall cypresses is throwing striped indigo shadows across the gravel. Between the trees I can see the house outlined against the rise of the hill, mellow brick under an ochre-tiled roof, grey-green shutters thrown open to the morning sun. On both sides vineyards slope up, the young vines carefully espaliered between rough wooden stakes. The drone of bees saws the still air.

I feel faintly off-balance and I need a moment to gather myself before I announce my arrival. And in this quiet space I can hear the ponderous, sledge-hammer tones of Sol Josephowitz in my ear, speaking with his heavy émigrés accent. Old Sol, sadly now deceased, a Polish refugee who had fled Warsaw and set up shop selling works of ancient art in the commercially liberal city of Basle. Sol, who for some reason, had taken me under his wing. Probably he had seen that without a swift infusion of his ghetto wisdom, I was rapidly going to disappear without trace in the shark-infested waters of the art market. And now, as he so often does, he's whispering insistently in my ear.

Always remember, Bronson, to pause *before you enter a deal. Don't rush in. Pause and* check. *Check the object. Check the story. But, above all, check your instincts. Remember, we dealers live or die by our instincts.*

Old Sol is right: this morning my instincts are strangely on edge. But his advice isn't helping much, because I can't make out *why*. So, lacking better options, I decide to check the story.

*

"You've got a visitor."

Zoe is standing in the doorway of my upstairs office smiling. She holds up a small, rectangular white card in her left hand. Tall and slim, with faintly freckled, vellum-coloured skin, washed-out eyes of the palest blue and long auburn hair, she is, I suppose, attractive in that typically anaemic way that some English girls have. In the five years that she has worked for me, there has never been any mention of a man in her life. Perhaps she's a little too knowing, her tongue a little too caustic for the average Englishman to handle. I imagine there is a problem with her sex life; which is presumably why she seems to take such a vicarious interest in mine.

We began working together when I moved my business from the art world Mecca of London's West End to this quiet, leafy street in Chelsea. The house here is grandly broad-fronted and quite spacious enough to allow room for both my home and my gallery. The move has sent out the silent message – and in the art world the message is everything – that I no longer need a convenient, importunate shop-front in the centre of town. Now my clients must make an appointment and cross half of London to see me. In short, I have arrived. This carries two advantages: firstly, Zoe can deflect bores and time-wasters before they reach me. But, more importantly, it enables me to know who is coming before they step through the door. In the shadowy, occasionally dangerous world of antiquities, it pays to know who you are dealing with. So now no one normally makes the long trek to Chelsea unannounced. In any case, last night my sleep has been fitful and splintered by strange dreams and this morning I am definitely not in the mood to receive unexpected visitors.

"Do they have an appointment?" I ask irritably.

"It's a she," says Zoe firmly.

"Okay. Does *she* have an appointment?"

"Nope."

"Do I know her?"

"Nope. But you soon will. She's downstairs waiting."

Undeterred by my lack of enthusiasm, Zoe lays the white card down on my desk. It reads simply: *La Contessa Carla Louisa Ruspolini*.

No address. No telephone number. I pick it up and run my thumb across the typeface. It is beautifully embossed. I lean back, lace my fingers behind my head and let out a resigned sigh.

"Okay, so we have here an Italian countess – or so she claims – arriving unannounced out of nowhere and bearing an old style calling card. Is she for real?"

Zoe shrugs. "That's for you to judge. But I'd say yes."

"What number?"

After so many years together, our discourse is scattered with these odd codes and little in-jokes. Number Ones are the potential buyers. They usually announce their intentions up front. Number Twos are the sellers. They tend to be more wary, sniffing out the territory like neophobic rats before finally coming to the point. These two categories, of course, are common to the whole art market. But Number Threes are quite a different breed. They are confined to the secretive world of antiquities. Number Threes are the clandestine operators. Sometimes they are just relatively innocuous spies sent out by other dealers, sniffing for information. More threateningly, they may be undercover journalists on the prowl for a lurid scoop on buried treasure and smuggled art. And recently – and this is the real worry – there have been rumours that the Italian and Greek governments have been sending out *agents provocateurs*, posing as sellers of illegally excavated goods, in the hope of trapping unwary dealers in a spectacular sting operation, which will then be splashed all across the front pages of the tabloids. And now, on top of that, there's the new problem with the Getty museum. This is certainly not a time to be taking risks with strangers.

Zoe tilts back her head and gazes at the ceiling, lips pursed. "I'd guess she's a Two. But she's not giving much away."

"You're absolutely sure she's not a Three?"

Zoe shrugs. "I'd be very surprised. In any case she's downstairs waiting. And," she adds with a sly smile, "I promise you won't want to miss her."

FOUR

My first sight of Carla Ruspolini is of a slim figure, dressed in a stone-coloured suit, an umber shawl draped casually over her left shoulder. Her long, elegant legs taper into flat-heeled black suede shoes. At this moment she is standing with her back to me, leaning forward to study the marble bust displayed against the oak panelling of the entrance hall. With her hands clasped behind her she has the look of an attentive schoolgirl on a museum outing. Even from this distance she exudes class and elegance. For a while she is clearly unaware of my presence. But, at the sound of my footsteps on the stairs, she turns and comes forward, her right hand confidently outstretched. She walks with all the assurance of a woman who is used to being admired.

Zoe is right: she's a classic Italian beauty. Her oval-face, with its steeply arched eyebrows and flawless olive skin is framed by a fall of lustrous, immaculately cut, shoulder-length, black hair. At least, she's *almost* classic. For, as I get closer, I notice her curious eyes. One is slightly lazy and the pupils are a shade of pale violet, circled by a ring of deep indigo. There's an unnerving quality about them, something almost feral. As we shake hands an odd thing happens: the room seems to go quite still. It's a moment out of time, like a freeze-frame in an old-fashioned movie. It lasts just a fraction of a second and, in the stillness, my strange dream of the previous night surfaces, the dark figure rising from the water. For a moment I feel caught off-balance. But then I gather myself and begin to guide her towards the studio, making small talk as we go. From the corner of my eye I can see Zoe at her desk with a small, self-satisfied smile on her face.

Inside the studio the early sun is bathing everything in a diffused, amber glow. Competition in the upper echelons of the art market is ferocious; but when it comes to impressing new clients, no other gallery in London can boast a room quite as spectacular as this. Added on to the back of the existing house in the 1920's by the painter Augustus John, it is almost the size of a tennis court. The double height ceiling is panelled with pitched windows that allow the light to flood in from above. Even the wealthiest and most sophisticated visitors usually gasp when they first enter. But apparently not Carla Ruspolini. She glances calmly about her, as if rooms like this, filled with several million dollars worth of ancient art, are exactly what one would expect to find in someone's house. Then, without a word, she begins to move confidently around the room, inspecting the sculptures. She walks gracefully, holding her body very erect, her small feet turned out slightly like a ballerina. She takes her time, standing for a while motionless before each object, as if totally unaware of my presence. There's an uncanny intensity to her concentration. For a long while she circles the marble torso in the centre of the room. Its broad shoulders are sharply twisted, the back ridged with muscle, the concave belly ripples with tension. She cocks her head to one side.

"A discus thrower maybe?"

"Right. It's a Roman version of a lost work by the Greek sculptor Myron."

She nods casually and moves on without further comment. I'm surprised – and impressed. The statue lacks arms, legs and head. It would be nearly impossible for a layman to identify the pose. Could she conceivably be an archaeologist? But I've met a lot of archaeologists in my time and they certainly don't come kitted out like this. Hand-me-down anoraks and scuffed trainers, or tweed jackets and baggy corduroys are more their usual style. All the same, she seems surprisingly knowledgeable, for she then correctly identifies the large relief sculpture of a bearded figure, spearing a lion from his horse-drawn chariot as being Assyrian. I try, rather pompously, to assert my authority by telling her that it shows King Ashurbanipal, from the late Seventh Century B.C. and that the cuneiform inscription across the bottom recounts that he killed a hundred and fifty-three lions in a single day, 'with the force of my own hand.'"

"Hmm. Modesty clearly wasn't his strong point."

"Nor animal rights apparently."

She allows herself a brief smile and glides on to the next object. One thing is already obvious – she's surely no clandestine snooper. Her elegance and poise are far too careless not to be authentic, and I'm guessing that her excellent, almost accentless English is the product of some exorbitantly expensive international boarding school. So she's probably a Number Two – a potential seller. And in that case, I will have to play the long game and be patient. Down-on-their-luck aristocrats who come hoping to flog the family treasures are usually nervous and embarrassed. They need to be handled with great care. If you push too hard, they may simply leave without ever stating their business and go elsewhere.

At this moment Zoe arrives with a tray of coffee. I gesture to my visitor to take the sofa on the opposite side of the low marble table. She settles down on the edge of the linen cushions and smooths her skirt, her long legs angled decorously together. I notice that the fingers of her right hand are drumming on the flat leather bag on her lap and, for the first time, I sense nervousness under the composure. So, to relax her, I pour her coffee – black, no sugar – and allow us to drift back to the small talk until the drumming stops. Then I decide to prod.

"How did you manage to find me here in the backwaters of Chelsea? I'm way off the beaten track for the art market."

From over the rim of her coffee cup, she gives me a cool glance to let me know that she has seen my rather obvious change of tack.

"That's not too hard. Apparently you're a well-known dealer in antiquities. Also, by the way, people speak rather highly of you." She gives a quick smile. "Which, at least in my experience of the art world, is something of a rarity."

I can't help laughing. She's clearly shrewd enough – and experienced enough – to have recognized the inner workings of the art world. "Yes, slitting each other's throats is something of an art market sport – in the nicest and most elegant possible way, of course." I pause. "But are these anonymous people who, for some strange reason, seem to speak so highly of me anyone I might actually *know*?"

Her left hand flutters in an elegantly evasive gesture. "Oh, you know, the auction houses and a few others...." She pauses for a moment and frowns. "Does that make it sound as if I've been checking you out?" She hesitates. "'Checking out' – is that the right expression?"

"Checking out is perfect. And, yes, for some reason the thought did cross my mind."

Clearly the irony isn't wasted on her. She tilts her chin in a hint of challenge. "Well, actually you're absolutely right. I have been. And as it happens, you check out rather well. Which is why I'm here." She pauses, and her face becomes serious. "You see, I come on a matter of some, how do you say? *Delicatezza?* And I need to be quite sure who I'm dealing with."

The immaculately manicured fingers begin to drum again and she falls silent. I have the feeling that we are like a pair of sumo wrestlers, cautiously circling each other, waiting for the opponent to make the first move. "In this business," I say helpfully, "one has to be totally discrete. You have my word that nothing that is said here will ever leave this room."

For a moment she sits with a small frown on her face, obviously weighing my statement. It's a lie, of course. Zoe, of necessity, is privy to pretty much all my secrets. But it's a lie that seems to work, for suddenly her face relaxes. She leans back, puts aside the leather bag and crosses her legs. "Good. That is rather important. Let me explain…." And I know we are over the first hurdle.

She tells me in her warm, slightly throaty voice, that she lives with her mother in a large house on Italy's Adriatic coast that has been in the Ruspolini family since the late Fourteenth Century. She says this quite casually, apparently not trying to impress. Her father had died many years before and she is still struggling to bring order to the sprawling estate, which contains numerous farm buildings as well as vineyards, a large lake and an historic Renaissance castle, known as *Il Castello Ducale*.

"About a month ago, I was in one of the old *cavi* – you know, the vaulted wine cellars – that I'd never been into before. It's tucked away around the back of the *Castello*. It obviously hadn't been opened for years. It was full of dust and cobwebs." She pauses, pushes a strand of loose hair back behind her ear. "It contained all the usual stuff – the big barrels and so on, as well as a lot of... How do you say? Clutter? It must have been used as a kind of store room by the family and then shut up." She hesitates. I nod encouragingly. "Well, amongst all the other things, there was something big in the middle of the floor, covered in rough sacks. And when I pulled them away, I found a statue lying there on the ground." She makes a sweeping horizontal gesture with the flat of her left hand.

I can feel my pulse quicken. "What sort of statue?" I ask, taking care to keep my voice casual.

"A marble figure of a man. Classical. You know... naked."

"Nude?"

"Oh, is that how you say it? Forgive me. My English, you know..." She glances down for a moment, colouring, then shoots me a flirtatious look from under her long lashes. "Yes, nude."

"Do you know how it came to be there?"

"Well..." She edges forward on the sofa and puts her elbows on her knees, her ringless fingers steepled under her chin. "I had no idea. But when I asked my mother, it turned out that she did remember it. Apparently it had been in the entrance hall of the main house when she married my father before the war; but when she moved in she had a big clean-out – according to her the whole place was cluttered like a junk shop with all sorts of family relics – and the statue was banished to one of the outbuildings and forgotten about."

"So it sounds as if your mother doesn't greatly care for it?"

"Apparently not."

"And you?"

She lets out a puff of breath and hesitates. "Well, to be honest, I don't find it that attractive either." Then she hesitates, obviously caught in two minds. There's a brief pause, then she adds, "At least… of course, it *is* beautiful,. But it's just not the kind of thing you really want in your hallway these days."

The wailing of a police siren blares along the King's Road. I wait to see if she wants to say more, but she has gone quiet and her glance slides away to circle the room.

"So if neither of you wants it in the house, does that mean there might be a possibility of selling it?"

She fixes my eyes again and nods slowly. "Yes, there *might* be. But there is a problem. You see…" She hesitates. "Of course, you may know all about this, but in my country things aren't quite so easy. We can't just export works of art – especially works of *ancient* art – like…." She makes a vague gesture with her left hand, but shows no signs of continuing.

She looks at me questioningly, her head tilted to one side. She's obviously waiting to see if I will walk through the door that she has just discretely nudged open.

"I have some experience of the problem," I say. "Ways can usually be found."

She purses her lips. Then she says quietly, "Yes, that is, of course, true. In Italy most things can be arranged – one way or another." She holds my gaze and there's an imperceptible easing in the atmosphere as we both silently acknowledge that we have just crossed a small threshold of complicity. From here on we're potentially partners in something illegal – at least as far as the Italian government is concerned. We stare at each other in the silence. There's a curious intimacy in the moment, something faintly erotic.

I lean back and fold my arms. "Well, I suppose it might be of interest. But obviously I couldn't say more without at least seeing a photograph."

This is clearly the moment she has been waiting for. Without speaking, she opens her handbag and extracts two

Polaroid photographs. She pushes them across the table towards me.

They are of poor quality and, at first sight, not encouraging. I take in a curved brick vault, several large barrels and a jumble of packing cases. The statue lies in the centre amongst some sacking, its length hopelessly foreshortened by the camera angle. My immediate impression is that it must be a nineteenth or early twentieth century forgery – and there are plenty of those lying around in grand old country houses. Then I look closer. Is it possible, *just* possible, that the torso is ancient and the limbs and head have been added much later to make the fragmentary statue presentable for an eighteenth century villa, and only these restorations give the figure its grotesque appearance? And, as I mentally begin to excise the newly added parts, placing my fingers over them to help the process visually, I realise that I am looking at an unquestionably ancient torso. Its pose is slightly stiff, but beautifully carved. I focus in closer and suddenly I can feel a flood of adrenalin. For a moment I can scarcely believe my eyes. The torso surely comes from a sculpture of an archaic Greek *kouros*, an iconic series of statues of young athletes from the very birth of Classical art in the Sixth Century B.C. Such figures are extremely rare; only a handful were ever made in antiquity. They hardly ever surface in the art market, and when they do, they are incredibly valuable.

But then, in quick reflex, my dealer's skepticism clicks in. Five hundred years after the Greeks produced these luminous sculptures, the Romans invaded Greece, plundered the art and then started churning out their own mechanical copies for their bourgeois mass market. To the layman the artistic nuances between the two may be slight, but to the expert they open up a seismic gap between a masterpiece and a cheap replica. And to the dealer the difference is quite simple: several million dollars on the price tag. And that makes a big difference when you're buying. So, to think *logically*, how would an ancient *Greek* original come to be lying in the cellar of a north *Italian* villa? It makes no sense. The figure must surely be a run-of-the-mill Roman copy. And yet, despite all my impeccable logic, my instincts are continuing to bristle. I wonder what old Sol would have made of this. I gaze for a while longer at the photographs before laying them down on the table.

"Hmmm. It's hard to tell from these." I say casually. "It looks as if the arms, legs and head were probably broken off and lost in antiquity and have then been restored much later. It was quite a common practice in the Eighteenth and Nineteenth Centuries. They didn't care for fragmentary statues back then. But it does seem possible that the actual torso may be ancient. But," I add pointedly, "of rather poor quality."

I had anticipated her disappointment. Actually, I had intended it. I need to lower her expectations before we begin to negotiate. But what happens next is totally unexpected. Her face suddenly seems to collapse into the silent, abject disappointment of a child. The look is there only for an instant and then gone, but I can feel its impact viscerally. It's as if I have just witnessed something very private I should not have seen. "But still," I add hastily, "it would certainly be of some considerable value."

I know from experience that potential sellers who feel too badly let down are likely to go swiftly in search of other opinions to console them – and to have her rushing off to Christie's or Sotheby's is the last thing I want at this crucial moment. But that's not the only reason I have tried to reassure her. The truth is that there was something so raw in that look that I still feel unsettled by it. "Let's say, it's potentially of some interest," I add encouragingly, "but I would need to see it in reality."

She looks at me quizzically. "Of course." The old self-confidence seems to have returned.

"And then it would depend on the price."

"Obviously." She gives me a faintly amused look. "I'm not a greedy woman, Mr. Tullis. At least not in matters of business."

As I escort her across the hall, I try again, as casually as I can, to discover how she has heard about me. I'm potentially entering a big and possibly dangerous deal here and so far I'm flying blind. A little extra information would be reassuring.

"Oh," she says, her eyes widening innocently in apparent surprise. "Didn't I mention it? From Mr. Debenham at Skerry's. My family has been doing business with him for years." Then she holds out her hand and gives me a small, knowing smile. "Just in case you want to check *me* out."

Outside a black limousine is waiting. The chauffeur in his grey peaked cap leaps out and opens the door and she slides gracefully into the back seat. As her car glides away down the quiet tree-lined street, I am assailed – there is no other word for it – by a bizarre thought: that, in some quite inexplicable way, Carla Ruspolini has just brought the waiting future into the house with her. The idea is so odd – I'm not much given to this kind of metaphysical speculation – that for a long while I stand transfixed, gazing at the sunlight glinting in the puddles

*

"It's a bloody nightmare out there this morning! There's some demo in Trafalgar Square – gays or lesbians or something

– and it's backing up everywhere. Fuck all we can do about it, I'm afraid."

I am on my way to Bond Street. Or I would be, if my taxi wasn't snarled in traffic at the entrance to Park Lane. I lean back in the creaking seat and allow my mind to wander over the past hour. Carla Ruspolini is surely the real thing – a genuine Italian countess. I don't have any doubts about that. But still….. an incredibly valuable archaic Greek statue lying unknown in a mouldering cellar, owned by an Italian family who clearly have no idea of its true value? It seems too good to be true. And I don't need old Sol to tell me where that can lead.

But it feels as if my speculation about Carla Ruspolini – the *story*, as Sol would have called it – is only the top layer. There's something obscure underneath that I can't quite get at. Anyhow, I'm now going to check out her story with Toby Debenham.

Toby is a director of Skerry's, London's oldest and most revered firm of dealers in old master paintings. The place is a mausoleum of threadbare carpets, brown velvet hangings and lingering cigar smoke, like an archaic London club. It's virtually a temple to all that is supposedly best and noblest in the art world. Toby is portly, affable, almost a caricature of the upper class London art dealer. But under his apparently benign and slightly bumbling exterior lies more than a streak of icy ruthlessness. He has been known to cut a swathe through the lesser art-market minions and charmingly sell would-be associates down the river without a backward glance. I am quietly on my guard. But at least this time – for once – it won't pay him to lie to me. What he wants is for me to do the deal as quietly and scandal-free as possible and then reward him with a handsome introductory commission. The commission, of course, also buys his silence about the small matter of smuggling the statue out of Italy. The art market runs on these kinds of invisible checks and balances. To outsiders it's all a mystery; but to us, like the rising of the sun or the migration of the Canada goose, it's just a basic law of nature. We don't even bother thinking about it.

The receptionist behind the mahogany partner's desk is engrossed in the latest copy of Tatler. When I finally get her attention, she regards my jeans and open shirt with obvious suspicion. She doubts – she informs me in a cut-glass accent – that Mr. Debenham is free. But persistence pays off, and thirty seconds later Toby is barrelling towards me down a long, dimly-lit corridor, flapping his arms against his sides like an over-inflated penguin.

"Wonderful to see you, dear man!" He offers me a plump hand. "Absolutely wonderful. It's been simply ages! The West End's been quite bereft since you moved out to the sticks. Come along. Come along."

I follow his broad back down the gloomy passage, where the walls are covered in faded chocolate-brown felt and hung with what appear to be grizzly Goya etchings in gold frames. Toby is wearing a striped – presumably old school or regimental – tie which, like Toby, looks as if it has been the recipient of too many good lunches. His suit is broadly pin-striped and expensively Saville Row cut, with two vents at the back which make his bottom protrude like a waddling duck. Like the striped shirt beneath it, the suit is shiny with use and fraying at the edges. Why people regard this clapped-out English look as a genuine sign of class, I've never been able to understand. It's as if you have to be coming apart at the seams to appear reassuringly aristocratic.

I decide to skip the small talk, knowing that once Toby

starts gossiping he can go on for hours. I say, "I had a visitor this morning who says she knows you."

Toby rubs his plump hands. "Visitor? How very nice. A good-looking Italian lady by any chance?"

"That sounds like her. What do you know about her, Toby?"

"Aaaah. La Contessa Carla Luisamaria Graziella Albani Ruspolini." Toby rolls off the name in an appalling Italian accent. He sounds like a third-rate tenor being slowly garroted in the middle of an aria.

"Is she a real countess?"

"Oh, God, yes! No problem there. The Ruspolinis have been around since before the flood. They're the real thing all right, not some of your jumped-up nouveau Victor Emmanuele aristos. The family tree's littered with Popes and Doges and all that stuff. They can probably trace their lineage all the way back to Charlemagne. Back to Julius Caesar for all I know. The father was an old-style Italian aristocrat and fascist. A one-time crony of Mussolini's and a nasty piece of work from what I hear. Eventually he fell out with *Il Duce* and retired to the country to lick his wounds. He died years ago. Apparently nobody wept too much, not even the old *Contessa*." Then he shifts his bulk in the chair and his eyes sparkle. "But isn't she a corker?"

I decide to ignore the first of what I know will be countless innuendos. Despite his unprepossessing appearance, Toby is a notorious lecher.

"It appears they may have something to sell."

"Well, well," exclaims Toby as if the idea comes as a total surprise. "Isn't that nice."

"If anything comes of it, shall I cut you in on the deal?"

Toby rubs his hands again. I see he is wearing rope-coiled

cuff-links that look like miniature golden cowpats. "That would be frightfully generous." He beams benignly. I'm aware, of course, that if I don't cut him in, he'll probably find a couple of unemployed Irish labourers to break my knee-caps on a dark night. Toby may come across as an overweight, intellectually challenged buffoon, but there are more than enough people around who have learnt better than to mess with him, and I'm not about to try to prove them wrong.

"Do you know the house?" I ask.

Toby nods. "Went there once with Craig Hemmings. You know, the Renaissance scholar from Harvard. He wanted to look at the frescoes. Queer as a coot, old Craig. Anyhow, it's a massive pile close to the Adriatic. There's an amazing fifteenth century *castello* in mint condition, with a huge sixteenth century addition with frescoes by Julio Romano."

"You mean they *live* in it?"

"Used to," says Toby. Like most members of the English upper class, he seems to have abandoned the personal pronoun years ago, so that he speaks in this odd truncated dialect. "But after the war must have decided to cut the heating bills and move along the hill to a charming eighteenth century villa. Only about twelve bedrooms there. Much cosier."

"And what about her? Is she married?"

"Hah!" Toby pounces triumphantly. "Thought you might ask that! Can't imagine why. *Was* married. Once. A big society do. All over Hello magazine, I expect. Didn't last long though. Only about six months. Very odd."

"What happened?"

"Don't know, old boy. Wasn't there." Toby chortles at his own joke, dewlaps flapping.

"No, Toby. *Really*. What happened?"

He rubs the side of his cheek thoughtfully. "Well, there

were quite a lot of rumours at the time. Usual stuff." He pauses. "Actually, come to think of it, it wasn't *that* usual... She's a corker of course, absolute corker, but..."

"But what?"

"Oh, you know," says Toby, shifting a silver paperweight in the form of a horse's head uneasily from side to side across the leather top of his desk. "Still waters and all that...."

His voice trails off. I wait. But Toby has lapsed into a stubborn silence and I know I'll get nothing more out of him.

As we pass the reception desk on our way out, where the secretary is now filing her nails with sublime unconcern, Toby takes my arm conspiratorially.

"Try to get yourself invited for lunch if you can, old boy. Great food, terrific wines."

We have reached the doorway onto Bond Street. Outside it is beginning to rain.

"Actually," I say casually, "I'm invited to stay the night."

Toby's eyes bulge in their sockets. "Well, well, well! Are you indeed! Oh, ho, ho, ho!"

His braying follows me down the street as I turn left and start my search for a taxi. The last part isn't strictly true – I'm only invited for lunch – but sometimes I can't resist twisting Toby's tail.

So that, plus two grainy photographs of the statue, is the sum total of my knowledge of Carla Ruspolini. Since her departure I have turned our meeting over and over in my head. But there's nothing there – at least nothing logical – to explain this faint undertow of disquiet that keeps grabbing at me. And now – just when I need him most – old Sol seems to have gone silent.

FIVE

Thunderous barking erupts as I pull up on the wide circle of freshly raked gravel in front of the house. Ahead of me a wall of russet brick is almost entirely engulfed in a cascade of peach-coloured bougainvillea. A pair of dove grey doors is set into this riot of foliage. As I step out, one of the doors swings open and two enormous Alsatians bound out.

"Hannibale! Scipio! Giu!"

The two dogs stop and crouch obediently, their rough pink tongues lolling hungrily from their massive, salivating jaws. I stand quite still. Right now they may look friendly enough as they sit there, their feathery tails dusting the gravel, but I'm very well aware that Italians don't usually keep huge carnivorous dogs purely for decoration. A moment later a tall, slightly stooping figure emerges from the doorway. He is dressed in black trousers and a starched white jacket. I can't help staring in astonishment. Even Carla Ruspolini's easy patrician style hasn't prepared me for quite this degree of old-world luxury. His long, narrow head is topped by a sparse covering of grey stubble. As he comes towards me I notice a limp, and one side of his face seems slightly askew, as if there has been some slippage in his features. He must be in his seventies, but clearly in the Ruspolini household ancient family retainers aren't put out to grass just because of a minor stroke.

"*Ben arrivato, Dottore. Io sono Ricardo*".

He greets me gravely with a faint incline of his head and the usual gracious Italian courtesy title. He escorts me to the door and stands aside to let me pass in front of him. He informs me that '*La Contessa Carla*' is awaiting my arrival and will be down shortly. The two Alsatians trot expectantly at our heels.

Inside it is cool and shady, the glare of the sun reduced to a mere ripple of light filtering through the thick tangle of wisteria that floats above me, supported on a pergola of beautiful old wrought iron. Ahead a long flight of worn brick steps leads up to what appears to be a garden. On every third step a large terracotta tub overflows with scarlet hydrangeas. In this muted light they seem to glow as if lit from within. A gardener has obviously been at work, for the bricks are damp and the lush convex leaves glitter with small diamonds of water. The place has a fragrant feel. As if on cue, somewhere high above me a woodpigeon begins a throaty cooing. It feels quiet here, safe, spacious; and, for a moment, I sense that this is how it must have been in Europe before everything was torn apart by the First World War. How it must have been that is for those with large aristocratic houses and vast incomes to run them.

"*Buon giorno. Ben arrivato!*"

Carla is standing on the top step smiling down at me. She is dressed in light blue slacks and a blue and white striped shirt, which she wears loose outside the trousers, the white collar turned up under her dark hair. Despite the informal attire, she still looks immaculate and stylish. Quite obviously she didn't pick these clothes up at some local shopping mall. As she descends, my gaze is almost level with her feet and, for some reason, I am struck by her carefully painted carmine toe nails in the open leather sandals. For a moment I have a vision of her dark head bowed in concentration, one leg raised with small balls of cotton wool between her splayed, bare toes, delicately at work. It's a strangely vulnerable and intimate scene that my unpredictable imagination has conjured up and I feel a sudden rush of warmth for her.

"*Tante grazie. E un gran piacere di essere qui.*"

"Aha! So you speak Italian after all! You didn't let on about that in London."

"Maybe just a little."

"Certainly a lot more than just a little. I can tell from the accent alone that you didn't pick that up out of a phrase book. You found us all right?"

"The entrance would be pretty hard to miss."

She laughs. "Oh dear. It is rather bombastic, isn't it? My great-grandfather obviously felt that a normal set of iron gates wasn't good enough. Mama thinks it makes us look like a crematorium. She would love to pull it down."

By now she is on the step above me, so that we are almost at the same height. To my surprise she kisses me lightly on both cheeks – perhaps all guests to the *Casa Ruspolini* are greeted in this way – then takes my arm and steers me up the steps. The pleasant feeling of warmth is still percolating in me and I'm conscious of the soft press of her body against my captive arm. At the same time I can hear Sol's insistent voice in my ear: "This is a deal, Bronson. Remember? *A deal! Beautiful women are dangerous in a deal.*" Sol knows – and I know – that this is potentially my Achilles heel. Or at least one of them. I do have a few. But he needn't worry; this time I'm on my guard.

"Mama has had to go into town," she says, "but she'll be back in about half an hour, then we can have a drink before lunch. In the meantime let me show you around."

I assent, noticing that she has made no mention of the statue. Presumably that will come later – after I have been wined and dined. At least it's a switch on the usual seduction theme. She's setting the pace. And why not? After all, it's her territory.

Despite Sol's admonition I fall easily into her company as we explore. She feels younger here than in London. Shorn of the Armani clothes and city image, the edge of brittleness I had sensed there, is gone. She is almost naively enthusiastic about the place and I wonder how it must have been for her growing up here in such surroundings, her own small shoot automatically grafted onto the sturdy trunk of countless generations of Ruspolinis.

The house turns out to be curiously constructed as a result of its position on the flank of the hill. It seems that the level on which I arrived is given over only to storage and wine cellars, the kitchen and scullery, since most of it is dug out from the limestone of the hill. Above lies the main living area – the *piano nobile* – and the garden where we are now walking. Above that are the bedrooms. I catch sight of a long loggia fronting on to the garden with massive lanterns suspended from a vaulted ceiling and a knot of pale green wicker furniture such as my grandmother used to sport, and in which I had to sit quietly and uncomfortably devouring insipid cucumber sandwiches.

The huge garden is a Mediterranean mix of order and wilderness. Banks of sprawling lavender and rosemary border neat beds of roses and hydrangeas. The perimeter – and it's a long way off – fades into shady thickets of pine and cypress. There's a rose garden with a sundial, a small orchard of carefully pruned and espaliered fruit trees and an ornamental pond where lugubrious carp seem unconcerned as our shadows fall across them. At the very far end a bower has been cut into a tall hedge of cypress. It shelters a bench of rough slatted wood and we settle down here for a while in its fragrant shade and chat about relatively inconsequential things, but definitely not about the statue. At length Carla rises and we begin to make our way back towards the house. To our right is a towering – it must be almost ten feet tall at this point – cypress hedge, which borders this edge of the garden. Somewhere beyond lie the barbarian hinterlands of shopping malls and petrol stations, tourist hotels and fast food outlets, but from this vantage point they might be a million miles away. Suddenly Carla stops. Just ahead of us I can see a gap in the hedge.

"Close your eyes."

It's obviously going to be some kind of party trick. I normally find this sort of performance irritating, but I know it would be rude not to acquiesce. So I allow her to put her hands on my shoulders and guide me forward several paces. Then she gently revolves me to my right. I can feel the palms of her hands being placed over my eyes and the disturbing pressure of her body tight against my back. Several seconds pass like this. Then suddenly,

"Open your eyes!"

For a moment darkness. Then she whips her hands away. The view is breath-taking. It must have looked like this for hundreds, perhaps thousands of years. There are small copses of pines, olive groves, tiny vineyards and here and there the dark spikes of cypresses as the land falls away to the distant, smoky blue of the Adriatic, where a tanker is making its way up towards the port of Mestre. The boat looks like a toy suspended in the haze. It is a scene of such utter unbroken calm that I find myself deeply moved and vividly reminded of my first sight of Greece, of that early explosion of the Mediterranean into my psyche. I turn to her.

"It's absolutely beautiful!"

Something in my tone clearly touches her. Her whole expression softens and, for a moment, the habitual guardedness falls away from her eyes as we stand and stare at each other. It's like a sudden flash of nakedness. Then she drops her gaze, wheels quickly round and begins walking towards the house.

"It's a very Italian form of ha-ha," she calls over her shoulder. "We reserve it for our guests, especially the snobbish Tuscan ones, who think they've got all the best landscape. That puts them in their place."

Although her tone is bright, it's also brittle now. Clearly she's warding off any further intimacy. I sense that what has just happened has frightened her in some way.

"I'm going to check on the kitchen," she says without turning round. "Why don't you go inside and pour yourself a drink. Make yourself at home. Mama will be back any minute."

The lunch table has been laid in the shade of the loggia and Ricardo is busy straightening knives and polishing glasses. So I decide to wander into the sitting room. Despite its grand dimensions it has a surprisingly homely feel. It is carelessly scattered with books and magazines. A pile of letters is stacked on a brocaded stool. On the wall to my right hangs a beautiful painting where nymphs and shepherds are feasting amongst a tumble of ancient ruins in the shade of an enormous umbrella pine. Below it sits a long linen sofa plumped with brightly coloured cushions. On the opposite wall, a handsome marble-topped commode carries a spread of photographs and silver ornaments, as well as a silver cooler containing an opened bottle of wine. Above it the light scintillates off rectangles of coloured glass that frame a huge Venetian mirror, blackened by age. At the far end of the room, double doors are open on to a broad terrace, where the sun is beating fiercely off the flagstones.

Curious, I cross to the commode and begin to inspect the photographs. There's the usual display of family portraits, apparently spanning several generations of the Ruspolini family. In almost every one the backdrop is of elegant colonnaded *palazzi*, perfectly groomed horses or exotic open-topped cars. Carla features in one or two. She's a surprisingly gangly child, her hair cropped short, her enormous dark eyes looking – at least to my mind – strangely troubled. Right in the centre of the display stands a large black and white photograph in an ornate silver frame. I pick it up. A swarthy man, probably in his thirties, glossy haired and moustachioed, is pictured wearing a military uniform so heavily smothered in gold braid that it looks as if it might be a cast-off from a comic opera. This presumably is the infamous Count Ruspolini, the one-time crony of Mussolini's. He certainly looks the part. Holding a thin swagger stick with a silver pommel between his hands, he gazes out arrogantly, as if issuing some kind of challenge to the viewer. The face, handsome and narrow-jawed, with fierce dark eyes, looks vain and sensual. And there's a kind of cruelty in those eyes and the set of the mouth that I find chilling. I recall Toby Debenham's comment that not even the old Countess had mourned him.

Feeling uneasy, I replace the photograph and pick up what appears to be a pack of outsized playing cards. But when I turn them over I'm surprised to find a series of brightly coloured, dreamlike figures that look as if they have sprung from the pages of an illuminated manuscript. Each one carries a subtitle – *The Magus, The Hanged Man, The Tower*….. Thanks to T.S. Eliot, I know enough to recognise a set of the Tarot when I see one. I am shuffling through, curious as to what they are doing here, when I hear soft footsteps coming in from the garden.

"Hi, you must be Bronson Tullis."

I turn to find a woman dressed in a loose silk shirt of pale lavender over ivory linen trousers. Sunglasses are pushed back into her ash-blonde hair and she's smiling at me.

"I'm Elizabeth – or Elizabetta if you want to go native."

Without much thought, I had pictured Carla's mother as elderly – perhaps it was just Toby Debenham's reference to her as 'The old *Contessa*' – but this woman is anything but archaic. It's hard to gauge her age precisely. No attempt has been made to disguise the lines that web out from the corners of her eyes, but she moves with the athletic ease of a tennis player as she come towards me with her hand outstretched. I check to see if she has Carla's strange, disturbing eyes, but hers are very different: an unusual pale blue-grey. They seem candid, amused and potentially flirtatious.

She's a full generation older than me, of course, and clearly from a very noble family, but there's no hint of condescension as she greets me. Her eyes are widely spaced, her cheek bones high, almost Slavic, her mouth broad. It's a generous face, but not a simple one. There's definitely more here than meets the eye. And I'm aware that, even as she is smiling warmly at me, she's also shrewdly sizing me up. Her voice, like Carla's, is slightly throaty and, as we begin to make small talk, I think I can detect a faint trans-Atlantic burr.

"Oh dear, you must have a very good ear for accents! Yes, I was born and raised in Athens, Georgia." She lets the southern drawl roll for a moment by way of demonstration. "But I've lived here for nearly forty years, so I thought the accent had worn away by now. The locals aren't fooled, of course. They never are. They still refer to me as '*La Contessa Americana*'."

"Even after forty years?"

She smiles. "Things change slowly in rural Italy. It's part of the charm. I'm just hoping that pretty soon I'll be so ancient that there won't be anyone left alive to remember my alien origins and then I'll just simply be *La Vecchia Contessa*."

"I would have thought that was rather a long way off."

She gives me a cool but not unfriendly look. "Ah yes, Carla warned me to be wary of your charm", she says, then reaches out a long sun-tanned arm and pulls the bottle of white wine from the silver cooler beside her. "Would you like a glass before lunch? It's from our own vineyards. A Pinot Grigio. It's very light. Only eleven percent, so you don't have to worry about going to sleep in the afternoon."

She pours two glasses, then hands me one and leads the way out to the shade of the loggia. Her provenance explains her accent, of course, but it also explains something about her long-limbed, easy-going body language, which feels somehow non-European and certainly quite different from Carla's compact intensity. As I follow her slim figure I can't help thinking that, for a daughter, this was always going to be a hard act to follow. We settle into the green wicker chairs. Unlike my grandmother's, they are mercifully plumped with soft down cushions. Somewhere in the background I can hear the plashing of a fountain. She puts down her glass and turns her grey eyes on me.

"Bronson? Is that a common English name?"

"Sadly not. It was a terrible idea of my parents, who wanted to honour some long dead ancestor – and I've been paying for it ever since."

She laughs, but then her face grows serious again. "I'm afraid I'm terribly curious, but Carla told me of your beautiful gallery. I would love to know more about your work. It's such an unusual area of the art world. What drew you to it in the first place?"

I have been asked this question countless times before – although, I sense, not usually with such genuine interest – and over the years, I have refined a series of responses, depending on whether I want to impress, deter, silence or seduce the questioner. So I'm surprised to hear myself telling her quite openly about my first visit to Greece, about the light and the landscape and the sudden shock of Greek art: my fascination with its easy balance between body and spirit, its luminosity and uncanny ability to make marble glow like flesh. Nothing was ever quite the same afterwards, I say.

I'm aware of her leaning forward, studying me intensely as I go on to tell her of the year I then spent wandering in Greece after I had dropped out of Cambridge, followed by another year in Sicily, ostensibly teaching English to bored, half-illiterate students, but actually spending every possible moment in the museums and ancient sites of Syracuse and Agrigento, Palermo and Selinunte, reading every archaeological book I could lay hands on, intoxicated as much by the exuberance of the Mediterranean way of life as by the art of the ancient Greek world. And then my return to the cramped, shuttered world of England and my despair at the prospect of joining my father's investment business and spending the next forty years accumulating money amongst the social minutiae of English upper-class life and its narrow-minded expectations. But even as I'm speaking, I become aware how distant that early passion that had flared in Greece now seems, as if somewhere in the interim some vital flame has quietly burnt itself out.

Elizabetta is nodding slowly. "I think I understand very well", she says. "I remember how it was when I first arrived in Italy from Georgia after I had married Sandro. It was my first experience of the Mediterranean and it was a total revelation. Everything that had gone before suddenly felt stuffy and claustrophobic. That first year I just wandered around in a kind of daze. I couldn't quite believe how free and magical it all was". She pauses. "So you just dropped everything in favour of your grand passion? That's very courageous. How did you get started?"

"Slowly."

She laughs. "No, really. Tell me. It interests me."

And I can tell that it does. There's a level of concentrated attention in her that seems to demand honesty.

"Well, the boring truth is that it really was very slow in the beginning. You can be as passionate as you like about the objects, but you don't get far in the art world without money. Preferably lots of it. I even swallowed my pride sufficiently to ask my father for a loan. I remember stressing that it was an 'investment opportunity' – I thought the language would appeal to him. But he wasn't about to put his money into something as risky and useless as antiquities. He thought I was totally off my head. 'A good brain gone to waste', was how he put it. I was obviously a grave disappointment to him. In his eyes he had paid for my expensive education and he was in no mood to throw good money after bad. Who knows? Maybe he was right."

She smiles while I pause to sip my wine. "So what happened then?"

"Well, in those days the antiquities market was very different from how it is now. It was a tiny, insignificant backwater of the art world. It was regarded more like ethnography – vaguely interesting if you were cranky and eccentric enough, but the objects were seen as being grubby and broken and pretty much valueless as far as most people were concerned. And, in a way, that was my luck, because it was still possible to go to country auctions, or flee markets, or junk shops and discover things in battered cardboard boxes stuffed under tables that no one else had even bothered to look at. And so slowly I worked my way up. But that's all over now," I conclude. "The market has become too professional and the objects far too expensive for that kind of amateurism to be possible any more."

I hesitate, wondering whether to tell her how I had finally broken into the big time. Her warmth and concentration certainly invite confidences. But I'm aware too that I still have a delicate business to transact here, and the story of my sudden, meteoric rise in the art world shows far too much ruthlessness for comfort. I'm here as the honourable, trustworthy gentleman-dealer, well recommended by the aristocratic Toby Debenham. This isn't the right moment to regale her with tales on my part of the cut-throat dealings of the antiquities market.

If she notices my sudden reticence she shows no sign of it. Instead she says, "I've heard it said that art dealers are addicted to buying. Is that right?"

I laugh. "I don't know about *all* art dealers, but for the antiquities market it's certainly true."

"You make it sound as if you're a different breed."

She leans forward, hands clasped under her chin, her grey eyes firmly fixed on me.

"Well, I think we probably are."

"Why? What sets you apart?"

For a moment I am silent. It's almost impossible to describe the strange lure of the antiquities world to an outsider.

"Well," I begin, "let's say you're a normal art dealer and you discover a Rembrandt or a Titian in the attic of an old house that no one knew about. Of course, it must be incredibly exciting. But all the same, for me there's still something missing. It has always been part of *our* world..." I'm struggling to find the right words. "Part of our continuum of time, if you like. But if you're called to some field in the countryside outside Rome, and suddenly you're confronted with an object that's been buried for the last two thousand years and you are pretty much the first person to have seen it in all that time, it's like discovering a lost world. And you suddenly step right into it. The scale of the time span is..." I spread my hands in frustration, "...somehow vertiginous. The first touch of it, the peculiar clayey smell it always has, the glint of the white marble just hidden under the dirt... It's an indescribable sensation. It's like stepping free for a moment from the bonds of time, touching other unseen worlds... I don't know..." I shake my head. "It's such an intense feeling, it's almost..." I hesitate, uncertain how to go on.

"Erotic?" She fills the vacuum helpfully with a slight lift of her eyebrows and, for a moment, our eyes lock.

I nod. "Yes, something like that".

"I think I can understand that," she says. "It must be like..."

But at that moment, from the corner of my eye, I see Carla emerge from the sitting room and start walking along the loggia towards us. Suddenly she stops and her eyes widen as she takes in her mother's position, leaning closely towards me on the edge of her chair.

"I see my mother has managed to charm you," she says. "As she does with everyone."

Her tone is casually ironic. But there's no mistaking the sting in that last phrase. *Don't flatter yourself that you're special,* she's saying. *You're just getting the standard treatment.*

I rise. "I'm afraid so. She's managed to get half my life-story out of me in less than twenty minutes".

Carla clicks her tongue in mock reproach. "And I thought

you told me antiquity dealers are supposed to be so secretive and discrete".

"Apparently some people are able to slip past my guard," I respond as lightly as I can.

Carla tilts her head and gives her mother an unreadable look but, before she can say more, Ricardo emerges from the dining room to announce lunch.

*

For all the weighty silver and crystal glasses and the attentions of Ricardo, who glides silently in and out, the meal is an easy-going affair – *vitello tonnato*, crisp green salad, fruit and an expansive choice of cheeses. Elizabetta is a practiced hostess and we talk easily about the art world, the history of the villa and even a little of her childhood in Georgia. I'm surprised how much Carla allows herself to fade into the background, adding occasionally to the conversation, but initiating little. She's clearly the obedient daughter here. It seems strangely at odds with the confident, slightly combative young woman who had visited me in London. I'm wondering if my unexpected rapport with her mother has caused some kind of resentment. Only at one moment does she thrust herself forward. During a brief lull in the conversation Elizabetta turns to her.

"I found Mr Tullis…"

"Please, Bronson."

She inclines her head and smiles. "Thank you. I found Bronson studying your deck of Tarot cards when I arrived. I think he may be a secret *aficionado*." She folds her hands under her chin and leans forward with a slightly mischievous smile on her lips, as if she has just casually tipped two fighting cocks into a pit.

Carla turns to me in surprise, "Are you interested in the Tarot?"

My knowledge of the subject is limited to Eliot's oblique reference in *The Waste Land* – which I've never really understood anyway – and in general, I tend to think of all such New Age activities – palmistry, psychics, astrology, table turning, Tarot, weegie boards and numerology and, for that matter, most of psychotherapy – as little more than delusion. But I can sense Carla's enthusiasm and I'm not about to speak my mind with her mood uncertain and the delicate business of the statue still awaiting us. So I decide to prevaricate.

"It's not really my field."

"But it should be!" exclaims Carla vehemently.

"Why?"

"Because the ancient world is your passion. I can tell that. You wouldn't be dealing in it if it wasn't. So I just don't understand how you can feel passionate about it and at the same time have no interest in something like the Tarot? Or, I imagine, in astrology or geomancy or oracles either, for that matter?"

Her tone has become heated and I hold up my hands in mock self-defense. "I plead guilty to all of the above," I say. But I'm also genuinely puzzled. "But I don't get the connection."

Carla lays down her knife and fork, barely able to disguise her frustration. "Surely those were precisely the beliefs that underlay all ancient cultures. The Greeks, the Egyptians, the Assyrians – do you *really* think they could have produced those extraordinary works of art if they had lived in a soulless, secular culture like ours?" She lets out an exasperated puff of breath. "Those were spiritually rich, polytheistic societies. They *knew* there was another world from which they could draw inspiration and wisdom, and they were steeped in the means of accessing it – ritual, astrology, augury, shamanism. It just doesn't really make any sense to admire their art as the most beautiful and inspired that man has ever created and then reject their beliefs as mere superstition. They wouldn't take any kind of vital decision, not even go into battle, without consulting the oracle or the haruspex."

I smile, trying to defuse the situation. "I don't think inspecting the entrails of a dead sheep is a particularly good pretext for starting a war." I turn to Elizabetta, but she has her glass to her lips and is observing the two of us quizzically over its rim. Clearly I'm not going to get any help there. I seem to have wandered into some kind of minefield and I need a way to extricate myself before any serious damage is done. If they want to believe in all this weird stuff, it's up to them. But I'm here to do business, not to convert Carla, or even her mother, to scientific rationalism.

"But look," I say quietly, turning back to Carla. "You don't necessarily have to identify with the actual beliefs of a culture in order to appreciate its art. You don't have to be a fully paid-up Christian to enjoy the paintings of Leonardo or Piero della Francesca."

"That's different."

"Why?"

"Because although you may not actually share those religious beliefs, you also probably don't mock them in the same way that I'm sure you mock all forms of augury and divination. Right?"

"Who says I mock them?"

"Well, don't you?"

"Let's say I don't necessarily share them. So how would you describe my appreciation of the art of a culture such as Greece or Egypt when I don't share its superstitions?"

"Beliefs," she corrects me.

"Alright, beliefs."

She ponders for a moment, brow furrowed. In the silence I can hear the fountain playing in the garden. Then, as if trying out the word for its fit, she says, "Perhaps… pedantry?"

I hear Elizabetta stir to my left and murmur, "Carla!"

"I have been accused of many things," I say slowly. "But never that." Then I smile at her, as much to defuse the situation as to cover my own undeniable irritation.

Then Carla seems to relent. "No, I'm sorry, that wasn't fair. But still… If you stand in front of a statue of Zeus or Poseidon or Aphrodite, is it for you really just a lump of carved marble or bronze with a potential price tag attached? Even if you can't give rational agreement to the ancient Greeks' belief in their gods, can't you at least *feel* the power of them in their art? Surely the two are inseparable!"

Something in the urgency of her words strikes home; and for a moment I'm back in Greece, standing for the first time between the weathered columns of Poseidon's temple at Cape Sounion, a ferocious *meltemi* blowing at my back, whipping away the spray from the white-capped breakers below me, causing the sea to surge and dip all the way to the horizon and the black mountains of the island of Kea. To *believe* in the gods – to give rational assent – is clearly absurd. But to *feel* the force of the god – to feel, at that moment, the power of the great sea god, Poseidon? That might be another thing…

"You know Iamblichus?" Carla breaks into my thoughts.

I look at her in surprise. To be honest, the name of this obscure Greek philosopher is only vaguely familiar to me, but I'm certainly not about to be upstaged.

"Of course."

"Well, he wrote: '*You cannot talk rightly about the gods without the gods being present.*' Maybe you should remember that the next time you admire a Greek sculpture. If the statue of the god moves you – whether it's Zeus or Aphrodite or Hermes – then the god must be present."

"I see I'm clearly in the presence of a pagan animist, who…"

The irritation in my voice must have been obvious, because Elizabetta cuts deftly across me.

"Perhaps," she says quietly, with a faint lift of her eyebrows, "there are more things between Heaven and Earth…"

"Than are dreamed of in my philosophy?"

"Could just be," she says with a wry smile, allowing the Southern drawl to come through. "Could just be… And I have a sneaky feeling Carla is going to try to convert you."

"And why not?" Carla tilts her chin at me. "Besides, what's wrong with being a pagan animist anyway? Better than being some kind of dried out rationalist."

But then she smiles, and I'm only too happy to let the whole matter drop before the atmosphere becomes hopelessly disrupted. And with it any chance of a deal.

*

After coffee, Carla and Elizabetta retire for a while and I go out onto the stone terrace. The sun has shifted and a wedge of shadow brings relief from the building heat. The view on this side of the house is less pristine than towards the Adriatic. The valley is bisected by the main road and spotted with occasional clumps of development. The air is fretted with the drone of distant trucks making their way towards the coast. But beyond that the land rises again in undulating hills. Between a double line of cypresses a chalk white track winds its way up towards an old farm house, half hidden by the trees. The scene is so timeless that I wouldn't be surprised at this moment to see a pair of slumberous white oxen pulling a painted cart up the meandering pathway.

At a soft noise behind me I turn to find Carla standing there. She has changed into a faded man's striped shirt that is far too big for her. She looks cool and somehow innocent. To my relief, all trace of her earlier combativeness seems to have evaporated. She comes and stands beside me.

"Like it?"

"I was just thinking that you were right about the landscape here. Compared with this, Tuscany feels overgroomed, almost pretentious. But this," I gesture towards the far hills, "has a kind of earthy, peasant quality to it. It's as if it has just materialised out of a Renaissance painting."

"That's why it produces earthy peasant girls like me."

I laugh. "I think I won't comment on that. Though I see the peasant girl has changed."

She smiles. "I was wondering if I could show you round the *Castello* now. But before that, of course, we need to look at the statue. And that," she holds out the baggy shirt on both sides and does a small pirouette, "is probably going to be dusty work."

SIX

The *Castello* lies at the end of a long curving alley of tall cypresses. At first it is hidden by the flank of the hill, but eventually the panorama opens up and it comes into view. It looks so squat and rooted it feels as if it might have pushed its way up through the earth overnight like some huge fungus. The walls are massive and rusticated, the windows thickly barred and surrounded by heavy stonework. Carved escutcheons bearing coats of arms surround the doorway. High above us, the castellated battlements are being softly brushed by a canopy of towering umbrella pines.

Carla leads me along one side of the building and round to the back. The path here is ragged, trodden out through tall grass and brambles. The vegetation grows unchecked and the undergrowth to our left slopes up into a thicket of pines. About half way along this secluded flank, a flight of stone steps drops to a pair of arched double doors. The paint is blistered and peeling. Broad vertical splits have appeared in the woodwork. As I follow Carla down, I can feel the adrenalin begin to pulse. At the bottom, without turning, she digs into her pocket and pulls out a heavy iron key and a small torch. And moments later one of the doors is creaking open on unoiled hinges. I step in behind her.

Inside it is cool and damp. A faint smell of mould and

potatoes hangs in the air. For a moment I stumble in the half darkness. Then, as my eyes become accustomed to the bobbing of the flashlight, I begin to take in the details. I am standing in a long vaulted cellar of blackened, crumbling brickwork. Down one side, wooden barrels have been raised on sleepers. Heavy spigots protrude from their ends. A huge cartwheel, laced with cobwebs, is propped against the opposite wall. Beside it a barrel has burst its iron bands and collapsed outwards, casting grotesque arachnid shadows on to the brickwork behind.

Carla sets down the torch and lights four squat candles that have been arranged on a packing case. Their yellow flames waver, then flare and settle and, as the light spreads around the vault, I become aware of more details – an ancient bicycle, a tall whicker birdcage, a pair of moth-eaten arm chairs – presumably the cast-offs of generations of the Ruspolini family. Just in front of us lies a long rectangular shape covered in rough hemp sacks. Without speaking, Carla takes hold of the sacks and begins to throw them aside. A cloud of dust swirls, then settles. The candle light recomposes itself.

At first, disappointment. In the flickering light the figure looks even more grotesque than in the grainy photographs. The legs are willowy and effeminate, the head an absurd restoration of an androgynous Hermes with his brimmed bowler hat and tiny feathered wings. Then I step closer and my brain tries to excise these additions. And gradually, like some art-house movie, the grotesque limbs seem to dissolve and my vision is filled only by the ancient torso, its powerful chest, its flat, muscled belly and massive potent thighs. And suddenly, as if my brain is playing tricks again, I am tumbling back through time.

Sunlight and cicadas, the heat beating off the rocky soil. The air rinsed clean by the Aegean wind. A small, squat, stone-built museum on the sacred island of Delos, ten miles across the wind-churned sea from Mykonos. And there, aged eighteen, without warning, my first sight of a *kouros* statue. Body tensed, a small, secretive smile on the lips, he seemed to carry some kind of message from a world quite beyond my experience. *We know not what we may be…*

I blink to blank out the memory. This kind of dreaming is dangerous stuff in these circumstances. We dealers can too easily be led way off track by our emotions and our optimism when we're buying. Above all optimism, *over*-optimism, is the greatest danger of all. What I need now are some hard facts to rein in my fertile imagination. I turn to Carla. "Do you know anything about its history?"

She sits down on one of the packing cases and pushes a slim hand through her hair. "I asked Mama again yesterday and she wasn't sure, but she thought my father had told her that it came from his great uncle Ludovico Sanudo. Apparently old uncle Ludovico was… how do you say? An indulger? A womaniser, certainly."

"A reprobate?"

"Yes, a reprobate. He lived in a crumbling *palazzo* in Venice on the *Canale Grande* with a Frankenstein-like butler, who procured girls for him. When he died he had no children." A small smile. "I mean, of course, no legally recognised children. So everything passed to my father. Actually, there wasn't much because, by the time old Uncle Ludovico's gambling debts had been paid off, the *palazzo* and the silver and the paintings were all gone and my father just got the left-overs. And presumably this," she inclines her head in the direction of the statue, "was amongst them. After all, to be honest, it doesn't look like much." She pauses frowning. "It's a strange story really. Sad too."

I nod. But my brain is starting to click through the gears. Perhaps it isn't so strange after all. Carla has thrown off the name Sanudo casually, as one might with any distant relative; but the Sanudos were one of the great noble families of Venice, chronicled through centuries in the historical records of the city. In the Fifteenth Century, when the Byzantine Empire was beginning to crumble in the face of Turkish incursions, a group of buccaneering aristocratic crusaders had moved into the vacuum and carved up the territory for themselves. Much of Greece fell to Venice and the Doge Constantino Sanudo gifted the scattered Aegean archipelago to his nephew Marco, who then set up a court on the fertile island of Naxos, and – not a man for understatement – styled himself Grand Duke of Naxos. The island, renowned for its quarries of glittering white marble, had been one of the great artistic centres of the ancient Greek world. When the Venetians arrived two thousand years later, the place would certainly still have been littered with fragments of fallen statues and masonry.

So then? It isn't hard to imagine the vain and ambitious Duke Marco carrying off this strange marble trophy to astonish his aristocratic chums back in Venice. And it isn't hard either to imagine the torso propped casually against the wall of an arcade in his palazzo until a descendant, inspired by the growing vogue of eighteenth century classicism, had called in a local sculptor to complete the missing limbs in line with contemporary taste. After all, most of the grand country houses in England are stuffed with such hybrid monsters, done-up relics of the Grand Tour.

It all seems to fit seamlessly together. Or does it? I wonder what old Sol would say. But for the moment he seems to have gone missing. I glance at Carla. She is sitting with her head bowed, staring at the statue, apparently lost in her own thoughts. Casually I crouch down, careful to keep my body blocking her line of sight. I spit on my fingers and rub gently at a section of the left thigh, at the line of the break, just where the restoration begins. There's no heavy incrustation here. The surface is just grimy, and quickly the dirt comes away under my touch. The marble of the restored lower leg is a dull, heavily veined grey. I know this marble; it's from the quarries at Luna, near Rome, the home of all second-rate later Italian sculpture. But above the break there's something entirely different: a perfectly smooth, luminous white sheen, compact, with large crystalline grains. It feels like silk under my touch. This, without a doubt, is Naxos marble. It was one of the most prized carving stones of the ancient world. And it's beautifully worked; the dense, smooth patina is something that the Roman artisans, with their crude mass-production techniques, could never match. Surely there can't be any doubt. This is the torso of an archaic Greek *kouros* from the island of Naxos, the most beautiful, the rarest and most desired – and by far the most valuable – of all forms of ancient art.

"So what do you make of it?" Carla's voice cuts across my reverie. Carefully I smear dirt back across the marble and straighten. I pause before replying, careful to keep my voice steady.

"Well, it's pretty much as I thought. The head and limbs have been added later, probably in the Nineteenth Century, but the torso is definitely ancient. It's based on a Greek prototype, as most Roman sculptures are."

"So it's Roman and not Greek?"

I'm surprised she is even aware of the significance of the difference – just as I had been surprised by her knowledge of the objects in my gallery. If I'm dealing with a novice here, it's clearly a very well-informed one who has done her homework.

So I will need to be careful. I shrug. "Well, since it's here in Italy one must presume it's Roman."

"And that means it's much less valuable than Greek?"

I spread my hands apologetically. "I'm afraid so." Then to support my case, I take her through a brief tour of classical history: how the uncouth Roman conquerors had crushed Greece militarily and then acquired an insatiable appetite for her sophisticated works of art. And, in good commercial Roman fashion, they had devised a method of measuring and precisely copying Greek statues. It was an early form of mass-production, called 'pointing'. The replicas resembled the original in all respects, except that they were completely lifeless, like a waxwork compared to living flesh, or a Victorian copy compared to an original masterpiece by Leonardo. I spread my hands in apology. "For every Greek original, there are hundreds, perhaps thousands of Roman copies. So, in hard commercial terms, that obviously makes a huge difference."

She looks crestfallen. "But it does have *some* value?" Her voice is almost pleading. I remember that strange look of desolation that had frozen her face in the studio ten days before when I had disappointed her.

"Oh yes, of course," I say hurriedly. "A considerable value. But there are problems. The surface has suffered quite a lot. It's very encrusted."

"You couldn't clean it?"

"Hard. Sometimes it just doesn't work and the whole patina begins to break up."

She stands, frowning, absorbing this information, clearly uncertain. There is a long silence, broken only by the shifting of her feet on the earth floor. Then she looks at me, her head slanted to one side. "Well...?"

"Well, as I said in London, it's potentially of interest, more decorative than anything else. And it would be a difficult object to sell because of the condition and the restorations. And I haven't even seen the back yet. It's too heavy to lift. So it very much depends on the price."

To my total surprise Carla lifts her shoulders and raises her palms in a gesture of helplessness. "That's where I thought you could help me," she says. "That's why I asked Toby Debenham for someone I could trust."

I'm momentarily taken aback. Sellers with no genuine knowledge of the market usually have absurdly optimistic expectations; it's what we call 'the Rembrandt in the attic syndrome', every humble object suddenly inflating itself into millions of dollars. And from Carla of all people I hadn't expected this total lack of guile.

"Well…." I walk slowly round the statue, trying to assess my next move. "I reckon I could possibly pay an absolute maximum of *ottanta millioni di lire*."

I love the sonorous Italian currency. It makes even a cup of coffee sound valuable. I see a flash of surprise in her face, then quickly she shoots back, "*Cento millioni!*" And I know the hook has been taken. Once you get an Italian to start bargaining, you're more than half-way there.

I allow a long silence. "How about we settle on *novanta?*"

A challenging stare. "*Novanta-cinque!*"

For a long time I stand frowning at the statue, feigning indecision. Then reluctantly I say, "Alright then. *Novanta-cinque*. But not a penny more."

She comes and stands in front of me, clearly uncertain, perhaps disbelieving. How much had she really expected me to offer? Probably I could have got it for less than half the price, this cast-off Ruspolini relic that no one wants.

"So – ninety-five million lire, right?"

"Right."

She holds out her hand and, as we formally shake on the deal, I can feel the adrenalin surge inside me like an explosion. Then, to my total amazement, she claps her hands and whoops with delight. "*Novanta-cinque millione!* That's… what? About eighty thousand dollars?"

"Closer to ninety."

Her eyes are shining. "Mama will be *so* happy and relieved! We'll be able to redo the roof of the house now."

I stare at her blankly. "The roof?"

"Yes, it's in terrible shape. It leaks everywhere. The Villa is supposed to be an item of Italian cultural patrimony, but the government keeps refusing to give us a grant, and the upkeep is absolutely overwhelming. Mama will be so relieved!" A broad smile splits open her face. "It's been worrying us to death. We've even been thinking of trying to sell the house."

And suddenly I have a rank taste in my mouth. But before I can think further she takes my arm. "And now," she says, "we must celebrate! Let me show you the *Castello Ducale!*"

Suddenly jolted back into reality, I glance anxiously at my watch. Tomorrow morning I have an appointment with Antonio Galbani in Rome and then, the following day, Sam Schwartz and all his mega-millions will be waiting for me at the gallery in London.

She sees my hesitation. "Please," she says, taking my hand and pulling at it. "*Please.* You mustn't miss it. Not now you're here. We'll be quick, I promise."

SEVEN

Only we aren't quick at all.

As soon as the huge iron-studded door swings open and we step over the worn stone threshold, we enter a different world. Inside a small, austere courtyard lies open to the sky. There is something touching about its simplicity and quiet lack of pretension. This, you sense, is a private place built for work and pleasure, not for ostentation; a place for crusaders and soldiers and hunting parties to gather. The ground is paved with plain russet bricks laid in a symmetrical herringbone pattern, which gathers to a sturdy stone well-head at its centre. Around the sides runs an arcade of pale grey stone columns supporting simple brick arches. On the floor above, the open arcading is repeated on three sides and on the fourth rises a wall of heavily leaded windows.

High above us we can hear the breeze susurrating gently in the tops of the pines with a sound like silk being drawn across a table. But down here there is an almost subaqueous silence. The place has an enchanted feel, as if we have travelled back in time and the Renaissance inhabitants have merely gone out and left it to us for the afternoon. For a long while, we stand side by side in silence.

At length Carla takes my arm and begins to guide me through the frescoed passages and airy whitewashed halls.

Everywhere the floor is laid with terracotta tiles so burnished by centuries of passing feet that they glow like polished leather. The air smells of beeswax and dust. As we move through the rooms, she points out the Ruspolini crest – a haughty falcon with a sprig of oak leaves in his curved beak – which presides over all the massive stone fireplaces and adorns the bosses at the centre of each high ceiling.

From time to time she recounts some of the history of the place and indicates her more illustrious ancestors amongst the numerous portraits. I count three popes; cardinals are ten a penny. I'm surprised by her knowledge and the seriousness with which she takes her role as custodian of this long, distinguished family history. This is another Carla altogether – grave, erudite, restrained. We pause under a luminous and beautiful portrait of Isabella Ruspolini-Albani, who is reputed to have taken numerous lovers while her husband was away fighting the last Crusade. With her half-hooded gaze and plunging neckline and extravagant peacock's feathers in her braided hair, the story isn't hard to believe. But mostly we are quiet, absorbing the dreaming silence of the place. And slowly this quietness binds us together like sharers in a secret. Only vaguely am I aware that I'm beginning to lose track of time.

At length we pass through a high doorway, where the broad marble surround is richly decorated with reliefs of elaborate candelabras and birds perched in stylized foliage, and emerge into a spacious courtyard where everything – the windows, the arches, the carvings – is less austere, more playful. High up, around all four sides runs a stone entablature, engraved with a Latin inscription. *Hic fecit Isabella…*

"This is the Sixteenth Century addition," says Carla. There's a slight breathlessness to her voice. For all her seriousness and knowledge, I'm picking up too something of an excited schoolgirl as she shows me these treasures. It's a beguiling combination. "Gonzago Ruspolini was a renowned warrior and *condottieri*, 'Un uomo corragioso e feroce,' as the chroniclers say – a brave and fierce man. When he went off to the Holy Land to fight the Turks, he was gone for four whole years and left his notorious wife Isabella in charge here. You remember her portrait in the great hall, the beautiful one with the elaborate ringlets and the daring low-cut gown? Well, in the space of those four years, quite apart from taking a whole series of lovers, Isabella added this entire wing. It more than doubled the size of the original *Castello*. Not bad for a lady alone in sixteenth century Italy. And a bit of a surprise for old Gonzago when he got back!" We laugh as she mimes the weary knight's return on his charger, his visor clanking shut with horror as he gazes at the gigantic, fashionable extension to the rustic soldier's castle he had left behind.

Then, as our laughter dies away, she grabs my hand. "Come on!" And she's off, running like a young girl, her dark hair swinging. She pulls me behind her down a long passageway and up a narrow flight of worn stone steps until we burst laughing and breathless onto the upper floor of yet another arcaded court, smaller and more intimate, and we are staring down onto a formal garden of gravel paths and low hedges, a lion-headed fountain splashing at its centre. The air is filled with the dusty scent of box. We turn and face each other. It's another still moment, just as we had experienced in the garden, but this time curiously innocent and asexual. And for an instant I feel myself caught up in Carla's unstoppable delight, the delight of a child before anything outside of this present matters. Later this memory will return to haunt me.

Carla turns away and leans her elbows on the stone balustrade, cupping her chin in her hands. She gazes down into the courtyard. "This is my favourite place in the *Castello*," she says quietly. "Actually my favourite place in the whole world. Usually I never bring other people here. It used to be my secret hiding place when I was a child. I could spend hours here just listening to the fountain and the cicadas and the pines and smelling the rosemary and the box. It always felt so peaceful. So...." Her voice trails away.

"So?"

"So incredibly *safe*."

She lets out a wistful sigh and I can't help registering the force of that last word.

"How old were you?"

"Oh, I came here until I was ten, eleven maybe."

"And then?"

There's a long silence. Then she sucks in a deep breath and lifts her shoulders in a dismissive shrug. "Then? Well, I guess we all grow up and life isn't quite so safe any more, is it?" She straightens and looks up at me. There's a sudden defiant toughness in her face. But before I can respond she changes tack entirely. "I suppose you thought I was being incredibly arrogant at lunch when I called you pedantic?"

I can't help smiling. "The thought did cross my mind."

"You're right, of course. I was being a real pain in the arse. Is that the right expression? I can do that when I feel upset. Sometimes I feel I live in a completely different world from most other people." She must have caught my frown of surprise. *A different world?* Is she talking about her belief in the Tarot and prophecy and augury? She shrugs. "Oh, I know, I've learnt to act my part pretty well. Maybe too well for my own good, pretending that what you see is all there is. But then I can get so disappointed, so desperate if I meet someone... Oh, I don't know..."

"What don't you know?"

She turns away. "I suppose sometimes one misjudges people."

We lapse into an uneasy silence. Am *I* the disappointment? Is she hinting that she's attracted to me, but disappointed I don't share her New Age beliefs? At least that's how I'm reading it. And that leaves me with a conundrum. I don't want to rebuff her or – worse still – humiliate her. In every sense there's far too much at stake. I'm even somewhat flattered by the implication; after all, she's a very attractive woman. But still, I can't bring myself to play along as a fellow New Ager. Apart from anything else, I lack the necessary vocabulary. And something in the whole situation feels too complicated, somehow too far outside my usual territory. But, while I'm trying to muster a response, something seems to shift in her yet again. She gives me a very direct, searching look.

"Perhaps we can rerun our lunchtime conversation in another way and see if it wants to turn out differently?"

"That sounds suspiciously like a challenge. What kind of way?"

"One that brings in more things than were present at the lunch table." She obviously sees my puzzlement. "Let's say a way that allows space for the Other World." The phrase is cast off casually, but there's no mistaking those silent capitals this time. Whatever 'The Other World' means to her, she's clearly naming it as a place as real – at least in her cosmology – as Venice or London or New York. Then she adds, "Perhaps it will offer you an opportunity. If you care to take it."

Her tone has shifted from the playful into something more serious now. Somehow – almost without my noticing – she has moved the whole register of our conversation down an octave. Whatever she has in mind, I'm not at all sure I want to be a part of it. With our business concluded, I might be far better off just leaving for Venice. The late evening flight and dinner in Rome with Antonio beckon.

"And if I don't choose to take this opportunity?"

She gives a small shrug. "Then you don't." She pauses, considering. "But I think that would be a pity, because I believe you owe it to yourself. You owe it to those parts of yourself that you aren't yet very familiar with." Here are more riddles, and pretty presumptuous ones at that! But the seriousness of her tone is too compelling to dismiss completely. Seeing my uncertainty, she adds with a tilt of her head and a wry, teasing smile, "Won't you at least humour me?"

The arcing water patters rhythmically in the fountain. The air is filled with the scent of rosemary and box. A great drowsiness hangs over everything. I have no idea what she has in mind, but there is a look in her eyes that I obscurely register as being somehow beyond my orbit of experience. And, more mundanely, I'm curious. After all, what do I have to lose?

So, on a whim – or so it seemed then – I decide to 'humour' her.

The room into which we emerge is lofty and spacious, the walls lined with heavy oak bookcases, each crowned at its apex by a Roman numeral embossed in gold within a beautifully carved scroll. Overhead the sturdy cross-beams are painted a deep Renaissance blue decorated with golden stars. The late afternoon light slants in through leaded windows set high up above the cases. I guess we must be in some sort of tower, rising clear of the battlements of the *Castello*, designed as a private library. It has the feel of a monastic retreat from the world. Through the windows I can see the slowly moving tops of the pines almost level with us.

Carla has led me here, silent, not once looking back, by way of a long passage. Towards its end she had pushed open a low wooden door and we stepped through into a cramped vestibule. Above us a narrow stone staircase spiraled out of sight. For a moment my mind flickered on my flight to Rome. I was already late and facing the likelihood of a long drive in the dark and an unscheduled night in Venice. As if sensing my hesitation, she turned.

"Don't worry," she said teasingly. "I shan't turn you into a toad. And, if I do, I shall turn you back again afterwards. That much I promise."

As I look around now, I notice that the ancient books are heavily bound in rich, dark leather or dumpy, ivory coloured vellum. The gilded titles proclaim their seriousness: *La Divina Commedia, Le Vitae di Plutarcho, Ovid – Le Metamorphose…* The place has an air of intimacy, scholarship and a quiet so intense as to feel otherworldly.

The centre of the room is dominated by a large oak table carrying a scatter of books and a white laptop, which looks strangely out of place in this Renaissance setting. On the wall beside the door hangs a faded tapestry depicting two unicorns facing each other heraldically; at their feet tiny rabbits nibble contentedly on some chamomiles. On the far side of the table stands a high-backed brocaded chair. Opposite are two smaller wooden armchairs with curved, slatted sides, placed close together. At Carla's invitation I settle into one of these and face her. For a long moment she sits looking at me with a stare that is unnervingly detached. And here, I suddenly realise, is another Carla altogether. Not playful or flirtatious or brittle or adolescent or uncertain, but confident and quietly authoritative. Whatever is about to happen, this is clearly her realm.

"Despite your obvious reservations you have agreed to come," her voice has become strangely formal, "and I thank you for that. I think it may be important to you. This is my private room. I allow very few people to come here. You may say later that what we create in this room is not 'real', in the sense that we usually use that word. So let us just agree that what we are making together here is a *mythos* in the classical sense of the word, something not of this world as we normally know it, but with far deeper roots." She pauses. "And, as Plato says at the end of the *Timaeus*, 'You may profit from this myth.'"

"Meaning me?"

"In this case, yes, of course, you. If you will allow it."

"And you?"

"I am, for this purpose, of no consequence."

"A bystander?"

"No, not a bystander. Shall we say, in modern parlance, a facilitator? A conduit, if you like."

"You mean a medium?"

"No, not a medium. For that would be to give it a precise esoteric meaning that is not appropriate in this case."

I have the sense of everything being slowed down. She is making it quietly clear to me that no play of words is going to distract her from her purpose – whatever that might be.

I shrug. "Well then… How can I humour you?"

"Firstly by listening to the silence. Just close your eyes for a moment."

If she sees my look of disquiet, she gives no sign of it. So, lacking good alternatives, I decide to cooperate. At first it isn't silent, not quite. I'm aware of the faint swish of the pines, the distant anarchic crowing of a cockerel. Then these begin to fade, slowly the room slips away, and I am enclosed in a deep, velvet blackness, dreamless, thoughtless, narcotically perfect.

Time seems to lapse, until I become aware of Carla's voice calling me back to reality. But by now that word is beginning to lose some of its hard-edged clarity. I am not asleep. I am not in a trance. And yet not quite fully awake. Somehow not quite fully *myself*. It's as if something in the austere silence of the room has shut down my normal senses. I emerge from the darkness to find Carla looking at me, her face impassive.

"Good. Now I will ask you to humour me a little more. Would you please give me your date, time and place of birth."

So it's going to be some kind of astrological séance! I should have guessed from the Tarot pack that it would be something like that. After the strange, relaxing sensation of drifting in the darkness I feel disappointed by the banality. I've half a mind to refuse. For a moment I hesitate. Then I decide to give her the information. After all, what does it matter? She pulls the white laptop towards her and flips open the lid. Then she begins to type.

For a long while she says nothing. Distantly I can hear a wood pigeon calling, but here in the study the silence feels claustrophobic. It's as if all inessentials are being incinerated by the intensity of her concentration as she sits, lips pursed, hands clasped under her chin, staring at the screen. At length she says, "It's very much as I had guessed. As I'm sure you know, you have your sun in Leo. And, from my observation, you have most of the usual, obvious Leo qualities: self-confidence, humour, charm, a certain magnetism. That kind of thing."

This time there's no attempt to flirt. In fact, from the tone of her voice it sounds as if she doesn't rate these qualities very highly at all. She's simply a physician delivering a diagnosis. A diagnosis, I can already sense, that is likely to have a sting in the tail. Totally absorbed in her own concentration, she brushes her hair back behind her ears, then leans forward and revolves the computer so that I am presented with what looks like an elaborate spider's web transected by lines and dotted here and there with arcane symbols.

"This is your natal chart. It shows the placement of the planets at the moment of your birth. It's what I would call Fate's thumbprint on your life. You can't change it. You can only try to navigate it as gracefully as possible." Her index finger taps on one of three symbols wedged tightly together in the top left quadrant. "Here you see your Leo sun in the Ninth House. That part is simple. But right up beside it," her finger drifts sideways, "are two other planets – 'conjunct' as we say in astrology – Saturn and Pluto. So this is by no means a straightforward Leo situation. Not at all." She pauses and gazes up at the ceiling for a moment. Perhaps she's wondering how to convey her esoteric message to someone as ignorant as myself. Then she goes on, "Your knowledge of Greek mythology is possibly already telling you something of the significance of this conjunction for your life."

It's hard not to hear a certain irony in her tone. I know all too well that Pluto – called Hades by the Greeks – is the sinister, brooding god of the Underworld, the dispenser of death, the brutal abductor of Persephone. And Saturn? A dark, malevolent deity, the implacable god of time, who ruled over all forms of imprisonment and punishment and who, in fits of paranoia devoured his own children. Amongst the whole classical pantheon, Saturn and Pluto are definitely the ones you don't want at your party. They're the guys in black capes. And apparently – at least according to Carla's reckoning – they are right beside my sun, which my untutored brain presumes is an image of myself. This isn't good news. Despite my skepticism, I'm aware of a faint thud of anxiety in my chest.

It's like sitting with the doctor while he studies your x-rays. *Of course* you know there's nothing wrong with you, but still…

"Not nice company," I say in an attempt to keep the unease at bay.

Carla doesn't smile. She stays silent for a moment, thinking. At length she says, "You will also know from your mythology, I'm sure, that these two particular planets can be dark, quite implacable, even brutally vengeful."

"But presumably everyone has Saturn and Pluto somewhere in their charts," I counter. "So it doesn't really…"

"Of course." She cuts across me with surprising authority. "But usually they are in what we call 'weak' aspects to each other, so they have only a peripheral influence. But your chart is quite different. It's rare to find them grouped together like this, but when you do, it means that their effect on your life is going to be very powerful indeed." She gives me a strange, unremitting stare, as if willing me to focus on her words. "You can't just ignore them, you know. Least of all if they fall right beside your Leo sun, as they do here. If you try, the eventual consequences are likely to be disastrous."

I can feel another swirl of anxiety. I would like to banter with her, to lighten the unwelcome intensity that's gathering in the room now. But it's as if those two malevolent gods are suddenly freighting the air with their darker tones, making my irony feel trivial and self-indulgent. And there's an unexpected weight and authority about Carla now which I can't ignore.

She has stopped talking and, in the silence, I become aware of those uncomfortable violet eyes studying me. Then she says, "You see, what the planets in our charts – or the gods, if you prefer that way of looking at it – require from us is our attention. We must recognize their presence, honour them and worship at their altars."

"*Worship at their altars?*"

She brushes aside my attempted irony. "Not literally, of course. At least, not in this century. But the symbolism is still valid. The planets and their placement in our charts represent different aspects of our characters, and the challenge is to recognize and ultimately include *all* these aspects in our lives, particularly the ones we do not like. For without those rejected aspects we remain only half a person. I think that is something you have yet to understand." Her tone is authoritative, even didactic, and I'm not at all sure I like it. But if she senses my irritation she shows no sign of it. Instead she pauses for a moment, frowning. Then she goes on, "Saturn and Pluto represent the darker sides of life – suffering, depression, loss, grief, monastic silence and withdrawal. These aren't attractive options for a Leo, who prefers to live his life in the sunlight. But what I sense here," she gestures to the chart, "is that you have indeed failed to acknowledge the depth and darkness of these two planets in your horoscope. That you have, in fact, willfully turned your back on them, and somewhere along the line made an inner choice to enjoy a life dedicated to quite other things – money, pleasure and, yes, probably sex. So you have actually been running directly in the face of your fate, running away from what your astrological chart requires of you. It seems you have a great facility for turning away." And suddenly the memory of Sylvia's letter – me turning to look out of the aeroplane window, ignoring her vulnerability and pain – bores into me, leaving me breathless.

For a while Carla seems to allow me space to reflect. Then she says, "Of course, for someone who doesn't have this particular Sun-Saturn-Pluto conjunction, that might be a possible way to lead one's life, but…" she pauses, clearly weighing her next words carefully, "…but I need to tell you that for you this is not an option. Not with *this* conjunction. And one day this darkness must rise to the surface, probably in some quite unexpected way. If you continue to ignore these dark companions, you will make enemies of them. And these are very, very dangerous enemies to have. They are like emissaries from the Other World. They won't let you turn away from them for ever."

My brain may be cynically discarding all this, but at the same time I'm uncomfortably aware of my heart thudding treacherously in my chest. As if from a distance, I hear myself say, "Go on." Despite the threatening tone of what she is saying, it seems I need to hear her out.

She reaches over and taps at the computer again. "Let's take a look at your progressed chart for a moment. That will show what is going on for you right now and in the very near future."

The screen goes through a series of shifts, then settles again. For a long while she doesn't speak "Ah, yes," she says at length. "A lot of very important things are going to happen very soon. They may already be happening. Firstly Venus – Aphrodite to the Greeks – is now directly opposing your sun. That means that she too is struggling to gain attention in your life. The modern world makes the mistake of identifying Venus-Aphrodite only with sex. But, in reality, she is connected with all things inherently feminine – warmth, love, compassion, intuition." She looks up and raises her eyebrows enquiringly. "Perhaps qualities that you need more of in your life? Also you are beginning an important Uranus transit. Uranus activates whatever is dormant in your chart when it passes over a particular conjunction. This means that, right now and in the coming months, Saturn and Pluto and also possibly Venus, will begin to make their presence strongly felt in your life. Whether you like it or not." There's no mistaking the veiled threat in these last words.

"How?"

She gives a small shrug. "Well, it could be in many different ways. That is not mine to say. And it may well depend on how you choose to react. At first you may notice strange, apparently illogical things happening to you: small shocks, unexpected meetings, disturbing dreams, odd dark moods that you can't quite explain, apparently impossible coincidences. At first you will probably choose to see these as unrelated, simply a run of bad luck. But they aren't. They are all part of this powerful astrological pattern in which you now find yourself." There's a pause as she stares at the screen, screwing up her eyes in concentration. Then she says, "One thing I do know is that trying to turn your back on this situation won't work this time. If you have ignored Saturn and Pluto in the past – as I believe you have – and you choose to try to ignore them again now, they will almost certainly seek retribution."

I try to keep my face impassive but that last phrase has released a flood of adrenalin into my system. "Meaning?"

At first she doesn't answer. Then she says quietly, "Meaning that, like Persephone, they may finally require you to visit their domain of the Underworld. In other words, you may be *forced* to worship at their altars. And that, I fear, could be a very uncomfortable experience indeed."

The silence in the room is claustrophobic. My brain may still be trying to treat all this as mere astro-nonsense, but something inside me is jerking around now like a boat about to come loose from its moorings. And suddenly, despite my powers of reason and logic, I am a non-believer trapped in all the raw power of belief. I want to brush her words aside, to walk out, to leave all this behind. But I feel skewered by the realization that she has somehow seen clean into me, seen things that I hadn't even known myself. At least, not with my conscious mind. For a long while we stare at each other.

"So," I say at last, trying to keep my voice casual, "If all this is true, what am I supposed to do about it?"

She draws in a deep breath, then lets it out slowly and begins to tap into the computer. "I am going back to your natal chart." For a long time she sits staring at the screen in silence, her brow furrowed in concentration. Then she says, "It's a challenging horoscope. I can't hide that from you. And it looks as if there is about to be a huge upheaval in your life. But that may not be all negative. If you like, it's an opportunity to rebalance your life in a more positive way. Saturn, for example, is not just the god of imprisonment. He is also the great teacher and, if one is prepared to learn from him while you are struggling in his chains, he can bring deep wisdom and maturity. Pluto too is a very ambivalent figure. As well as being the god of the dark Underworld he's also the god of wealth, of the unexpected riches that can come if you are prepared to submit to the destruction of your existing life and just trust in what will follow."

She allows a brief pause, possibly to let me digest all this. Then she goes on, "You also have in your natal chart Venus and Mars conjunct. This too is highly ambivalent and the ambivalence gives you a choice. If you choose to live your life only on a superficial plane, then this is a constellation that can result in endless, repetitive sexual exploitation. Ultimately that will mean the death of love in your life – a very sad prospect." For a moment her eyes flick up, then down again. "But if you are prepared to learn from these events that you are about to undergo, this is a conjunction that can bring out your natural sensitivity and your capacity to love and nurture both yourself and those around you. A gift which, I suspect, you have squandered or abused until now." There is another long pause. The light is almost gone now from the room and we are in semi-darkness. Sylvia's letter is flickering at the edges of my mind. "You asked me what you should do…" She sits back and closes her eyes. I feel faintly giddy and disorientated, as if she has applied solvent to my brain. "What you need now," she says at length, "is a bridge."

"A *bridge*? What kind of bridge?"

"Something that will help to carry you from where you now find yourself, which is a place of great challenge and possible danger, to where your fate demands that you go. Otherwise the crossing may simply be too perilous." She lapses into silence, as if she has forgotten my presence, and when she speaks again her voice has taken on a strange, distant quality, like a mantra. "Love is the bridge," she says quietly. "Yes, *love is the bridge*."

For a long while she sits quite still. Her face is blank now, abstracted, like the faces of those saints you see in mediaeval paintings. The silence becomes dense. The air between us seems to thicken and the edges of my vision darken, until I am viewing her down a long, narrow tunnel of light. For a fearful moment I feel I may faint. Then something happens so extraordinary, so utterly beyond the bounds of normal comprehension, that I can only sit and observe it like a watcher from another galaxy.

Carla's face seems to detach itself from my vision, as if it assumes total autonomy. And then slowly, almost mechanically, her head swivels through a right-angle and I am looking at the same face, but dramatically aged, the face of a crone, white haired, wrinkled like a discarded fruit. Then the head revolves again on its unseen ratchet and there is the face of a child, dark eyed, impassive, staring through me. Then another shift and

I am gazing at a gold mask, neither male nor female, hieratic, implacable, god-like.

For perhaps two minutes this procession of images revolves before me, always the same. Strangely, I observe this phenomenon with detached curiosity, as if it is within the normal orbit of my experience. I am not anxious. I am not afraid. Not even startled. And I know it is quite within my power, by a simple act of will, to bring this shape-shifting procession to an end. But most powerful of all is the total certainty that this is not a mirage, not an illusion, not an 'as-if' experience at all. What I am witnessing is as real – and as normal – as the chair on which I now sit or the terracotta tiled floor beneath my feet.

Then the pressure in the room changes. The darkness draws back from the edges of my vision. The light filters in from the high clerestories above and the wood pigeon – as if commanded by an electric switch – is calling full-throated from beyond the pines.

Carla smiles at me.

By the time we return to the house, dusk is gathering and bats are scudding through the twilight. Overhead the air is filled with the chatter of roosting birds. We find Elizabetta in the *salotto*. She stares at us in surprise. "Oh Carla!" she says sharply. "How could you have kept Bronson so long? He'll never make his flight now. It's a two hour drive to Venice and you know what a foul road that is in the dark!"

Carla looks down and a guilty flush spreads across her face. The sudden change is startling.

"Really," I put in quickly, "it's entirely my fault. I wanted Carla to show me the *Castello*, and then we sat and talked in her library. I'm afraid I totally lost track of time."

She shoots Carla an enquiring look and something unspoken seems to pass between them. But when she turns back to me her tone has softened. "But still, it *is* a horrible drive in the dark. Why don't you stay the night and leave in good time in the morning?" She must have seen my hesitation. "It's really no problem for us," she insists. "It would genuinely be a pleasure."

I slide a quick glance at Carla. Her guilt seems to have evaporated and her eyes are suddenly bright with interest. "That's extremely kind," I say. "If you're sure it wouldn't be a problem."

"That's settled then. I'll tell Ricardo to make up your room." Smiling, Elizabetta disappears out to the loggia, where the lanterns have now been turned on, cloaking the stone columns with amber light. I turn to Carla. Her shoulders lift in a faint shrug as if disclaiming responsibility. But a wry tilt of her head suggests triumph.

EIGHT

My bedroom faces out over the valley. It is white and high ceilinged, the furniture painted a pale dove grey, flecked with traces of ancient gilding. The broad bed is draped with an elaborately embroidered linen coverlet and plumped with a snowdrift of pillows. A quick tour of the bathroom has revealed a stack of thick white towels, a bathrobe, as well as a toothbrush, toothpaste, comb, razor and shaving cream. In short, everything one might need for an impromptu overnight stay. Apparently the Ruspolinis are used to unexpected guests.

I lie for a long time soaking in the massive, claw-footed bathtub. I'm uncomfortably aware that this escapade with Carla is going to cost me an entire day. I will have to call Zoe in the morning and get her to rearrange my schedule as best she can and persuade Antonio Strozzi to wait with whatever it is that's exciting him so much down there in Rome. Worse still, Sam Strauss, a new, hugely wealthy New York collector, is due to visit the gallery for the first time at ten o'clock the following day. Sam is notoriously difficult and egotistical and needs to be treated with appropriate deference; so I suspect I'm going to pay heavily for my missed flight.

As I lie there my mind is lurching erratically like a learner on a skateboard. When I think of the *kouros* statue displayed in the studio, cleaned and freed of its grotesque restorations,

I feel a surge of adrenalin that leaves me light-headed with euphoria. But when I turn my mind to what has happened in the library of the *Castello*, the euphoria vanishes, leaving in its wake a strange emptiness, as if my vital juices have been leached out. The astrology – all those elaborate trines and sextiles, oppositions and conjunctions – is obviously just New Age superstition. And yet – and this is the troubling part – there's a disturbing familiarity in some of the things Carla has said, especially those with the uncanny echo of Sylvia's letter. It's as if she has somehow managed to poke her fingers clean through the fabric of who I have always taken myself to be and touched another part of me, lurking just out of sight. And this has left a shadow of anxiety over me that I'm finding hard to shed. But still, if there really is, as Carla seemed to be suggesting, some kind of profound message hidden in all this astrospeak, it's apparently written in an arcane script I can't decipher.

And what of that bizarre, inexplicable head-turning episode? Had I imagined it? Was it some kind of hypnosis, which Carla, like a modern-day Circe, enjoys practising on unsuspecting, cynical males like myself? Whatever the rational explanation, I have to admit I feel embarrassingly rattled by the whole performance. It's as if everything that has happened in that lofty room has taken place in some other, parallel reality, somewhere quite beyond my normal orbit. Perhaps I should just think of it as a spectacularly staged piece of theatre. And now, as far as I'm concerned, the curtain is coming down and I'm going to reinstall myself firmly in the real world.

But there's still the uncomfortable matter of reroofing the villa. It had never occurred to me that a family like the Ruspolinis might actually *need* the money. I had always assumed I would merely be adding to vast piles of ancient wealth stashed in a

Swiss bank account – which is fine by me. There's room here, of course, for self-flagellation. But the fact is that we dealers are obliged to live – or die – by our wits. If I had offered Carla a realistic price for the *kouros* – probably in the region of five million dollars – and my intuition later proved wrong and the statue turned out to be a Roman replica after all – or, worse still, a nineteenth century forgery – I know perfectly well that I can't go back to the Ruspolinis for a refund. I will be left washed up, honourable but bankrupt. In the jungle world of dealing the law of *caveat emptor* rules implacably. And besides, how many generations of connoisseurs and art historians, archaeologists, even other art dealers for all I know, must have passed that sculpture in the halls of its Venetian *palazzo* without even giving it a second glance? Let's face it, *I* was the one who had discerned the ancient torso hidden amongst all the grotesque restorations. It had taken *my* hard-earned knowledge and practised eye. And I alone am now taking the risk. To the victor the spoils.

And so, as the bath slowly cools around me, I talk myself back to normality. And those questions that are too difficult to answer, I leave unasked.

*

I find Elizabetta in the *salotto*, talking quietly on the telephone. She smiles and gestures with her free hand for me to make myself at home. Ricardo, now white jacketed and white gloved, hands me a glass of *prosecco*, then disappears out to the loggia to put the final touches to the dinner table. Elizabetta finishes her conversation and sets down the telephone. She picks up her glass and turns to me.

"I'm sorry I snapped at Carla earlier," she says. "I was just upset that we had disrupted your plans so much. At the same time, I have to admit I'm delighted to have you here for dinner."

"It honestly was my fault as much as hers. There's something magical about the *Castello* that just makes you forget about time." I hesitate. "And I also wanted to say that *I'm* sorry I ran off at the mouth so much this morning when you asked me how I became a dealer. It was rather 'un-English' of me. I felt embarrassed afterwards."

" But no!" she exclaims. "It was lovely. Very nice to see an Englishman become so animated." She gives me a teasing smile. Then her face grows serious. "I think people who are actually born here in the Mediterranean, like Carla, never quite understand. They just relax into it quite naturally. It's only some of we deprived northerners who are condemned to come here and fall truly and hopelessly in love with it. And when that happens it's a bit like rediscovering a chromosome that got mislaid somewhere along the way. So it's always nice to meet someone who so obviously feels the same." She stops and gestures towards the sofa. "Why don't we sit down? Carla seems to be taking her time."

I watch as she crosses the room. She is slim and easy in her movements as she sits and crosses her long legs. It's not hard to see where Carla got her physical assurance from. If she's aware of my eyes following her, she gives no sign of it.

"I was wondering," she goes on, "when you talked about the *Castello*, whether you're also interested in Italian art?"

"If I hadn't been so overwhelmed by Greece when I first went there, I think I would have become a dealer in Italian paintings instead."

"Well, if you have time tomorrow morning, there are a couple of things in Prosaro, which aren't in any of the guidebooks, that may interest you. Apart from the long sandy beach and a lot of very pretty girls in the summer, the town doesn't have too much to recommend it. But it does have two hidden gems. One is the Town Hall itself, which is a beautiful fifteenth century brick building. It's buried in a small square in the old part of town, which is well back from the sea and not much visited. And inside it – placed right above the desk of the local mayor, if you can believe it – is a virtually unknown fresco by Giovanni Bellini of a Virgin and Child. It's wonderfully tender. Of course, it's not normally accessible to the public, but if you were interested I could call tomorrow morning and persuade them to let you in." She smiles. "The mayor owes me a few favours. That's how things work here in Italy."

I am about to thank her and say I will have to establish my new flight times first, when Carla arrives. She comes in quietly, but with all the assurance of the lead actress making her entrance from the wings. She looks cool and immaculate in a petrol blue silk dress. Her black hair glistens in the lamplight, a pair of small diamond studs sparkle in her ears. Despite the loose dress, the free movement of her body makes it clear that she's wearing very little underneath. I guess that the undeniably erotic effect is quite deliberate. As she takes the glass of *prosecco* I offer her, she looks down for a moment and smiles flirtatiously up at me from under her eyelashes. I feel completely wrong-footed. Gone apparently is the impersonal, authoritative Carla who had sat with me in the *Castello* library less than an hour ago, holding sway over events like an empress while she implacably pointed out my failings. I've always been attracted to mercurial women – Sylvia, my ex-wife, was a slightly unhinged variant of the type – but, to tell the truth, there's something unnerving about the way Carla seems to be able to transmute into a completely different personality without warning.

Dinner is a more sumptuous affair than lunch. An air of formality has been added by the presence of two elaborate Venetian glass candelabra. The food is delicious and the wines – as Toby Debenham had promised – are excellent. From time to time moths flutter down from the creeper-clad columns to investigate the flames, but Ricardo materializes magically from the shadows to remove them before they become fastened to the wax and incinerated.

Once again Elizabetta and I share most of the conversation. She relates with a dry southern wit stories of the monumental corruption and absurdity of Italian politics. She talks too – with obvious knowledge – of the art of Umbria and Le Marche. It turns out that she had been studying History of Art at the Corcoran when she met her husband in Washington. As at lunch, Carla is largely quiet, responding only when a question is directed at her. But it's clear that she has seen my admiring look as she entered the room, and whenever our eyes meet she gives a small, secretive smile. The electric charge between us feels so palpable that I wonder if Elizabetta is aware of it. Shortly after Ricardo has served coffee and made his exit, Elizabetta withdraws too, wishing me a good night's sleep and recommending that I try the grappa that they have distilled from their own grapes.

Left alone, for a moment there is an uneasy silence. Then, at Carla's suggestion, we go out on to the large stone-flagged terrace on the south side of the house to admire the view of the valley. For a while we stand at the balustrade side by side. The night is warm and a smell of jasmine drifts up from the pergola. To our left Prosaro, hidden by the flank of the hill, is an orange glow against the sky. I can feel the heat stored in the stone parapet under my hands.

At thirty-five, I have slept with more women that I can

count or remember. Yet there still seems to be a hyper-excitable adolescent lurking somewhere in my psyche. Even now the first touch of a woman can become magically transformed into the very first teenage touch, the anguished desire apparently undimmed by the years of experience, which should by rights by now have left me jaded and blasé. Perhaps it has something to do with the intense separateness I always feel in women, a strange transgressive desire to break through their poise and social personas and penetrate not just their bodies, but also the sheer unknownness and unreachability of them. I am sure Freud would have something devastating to say about the infantile nature of this. And with Carla, this adolescent hunger seems achingly intensified. I suspect it is connected with the shifting multiplicity of her personalities. It's as if there's a primitive desire in me to nail her down to being just one thing, so that I can finally really possess her. And then there's something else that feels even more crudely male – a wish to regain my power after the disorienting experience of the afternoon.

So when her hip, apparently casually, makes contact with mine and I feel the heat and softness of her through the thin silk, it's like setting off an erotic chain reaction in my body. We stand like that, neither of us speaking, as we ostensibly marvel at the spread of stars above us. Imperceptibly she leans closer until I can feel the whole length of her warm thigh against mine. Then she turns slightly in a movement that presses her soft, unfettered breast against my upper arm.

"Would you care for that grappa that Mama mentioned?"

I nod and follow her along the terrace and through the open doors into the sitting room. As I watch the swell and roll of her bottom under the thin silk, I'm achingly aware of the insistent gathering of excitement at my groin. Obscurely aware too that we are now on some kind of autopilot that is taking us further out of depths than either of us really understands.

I sit on the sofa and watch as she fills the two fluted glasses from the tall bottle with its hand-written label. Then she replaces the bottle, turns and walks slowly towards me. She extends her right hand with the glass, silently, in an almost ritual gesture. An offering. She sits down beside me. I sip the grappa, holding it in my mouth for a moment, then swallow it down and feel the immediate hit of the alcohol. Then I put the glass aside, turn and remove Carla's from her hand. She opens her fingers slowly and drops her gaze. For a moment everything seems to be happening in slow motion. Then she is in my arms, her mouth opens under mine. Her whole body seems overcome with a strange sensual passivity, offering itself without reserve. She slithers easily out of her dress. Underneath she is, as I had guessed, naked and beautiful. I too swiftly undress. But as I rise above her, urgent in my need, she presses the flat of her hand to my chest and shakes her head. I hesitate. Is this yet another Carla with another kind of game? Or does she want me to force her? She murmurs something I don't understand. Her eyes have gone opaque and she wears a strange glazed expression. She turns her head to the side and gazes across the room. "The commode," she whispers. "The top drawer."

Puzzled, naked and aroused I cross the room. I feel mildly ridiculous as I catch sight of my oscillating erection in the stately Venetian mirror. As I slide open the top drawer it yields a musty smell of dust and leather and wood polish. At first I can see only stacks of old-fashioned photograph albums. But just as I am about to turn, wondering what to do next, I become aware of something pressed up against the front edge of the drawer. And then I understand.

I take the slim cane in my hands. It is about eighteen inches long, maroon-lacquered, with a round, silver pommel at one end, the kind of thing a nineteenth century gentleman might use to keep small dogs in order. From behind me comes a faint rustling sound. For a moment my eye falls on the portrait of Count Ruspolini. Only for an instant I hesitate. Then I turn. Carla is lying on her front, her head angled away, the fall of her dark hair covering her face. The glow of the lamp gives a sheen to her long back, picks out a tiny cluster of hairs at the base of her spine, shadows the cleft of her bottom. Aware of an almost too intense pulsing of desire, I cross the room, raise the cane and bring it down sharply on her buttocks. She groans and arches her hips.

"*Forza!*" Her voice is muffled. "*Forza!*"

I bring it down harder, then harder again as she presses her face into the cushions to stifle her cries. Twelve times I bring the cane down, striping her flesh. Then suddenly her hands shoot back, covering herself protectively. And, as I watch, the slim fingers holding her buttocks pull slowly apart, revealing herself in a totally unambiguous gesture of invitation.

NINE

"Good morning."

Elizabetta smiles at me as I settle down next to her at the breakfast table in the shade of the loggia. The morning has dawned bright and cloudless. The previous night's events feel as if they have taken place in some kind of parallel dream world. Elizabetta seems her usual relaxed self and we chat easily until Carla appears. She is wearing a simple cornflower blue dress, her hair drawn back severely in a knot. There are dark rings under her eyes and she looks tired and strained. She addresses a general 'Good morning' to the room, kisses her mother on the cheek and sits down opposite me, ostentatiously avoiding my glance. The atmosphere instantly freezes and I'm aware of Elizabetta's gaze flickering between us as Carla sits stony-faced, while Elizabetta and I try to carry on a stilted conversation as best we can. Having downed a single cup of black coffee, Carla rises and leaves the table without a word. I put down my napkin and make to follow her, but Elizabetta places a warning hand on my arm.

"Please try not to be upset," she says quietly. "She can be like this sometimes, I'm afraid. It has nothing to do with you."

Her tone is gentle but guarded, as if she is holding something back. And, for a stomach-churning moment I wonder if she knows what has happened the previous evening.

Although I'm sure that the *Contessa* Elizabetta is broad-minded – she hardly comes across as a prude, and I'm guessing that she may have something of a past herself – I imagine that even she would draw the line at entering her grand *salotto* to find her unscripted guest sodomising her daughter on the damask sofa.

But then she goes on, "I was going to ask you to stay for lunch. I would have liked that. But, given the situation, it's probably not a good idea."

I can't help raising an ironic eyebrow. "I think I'd have to agree with you there."

"Still," she says, "I hope you will return one day. You have an open invitation. I think you and I may have a touch of the kindred spirits about us."

Surprised by her openness I glance across at her, wondering for a moment if she is making a pass at me. After all, she's still a very attractive woman. But all I see is a perfectly straightforward honesty.

"Yes, I would like that too. But I can't quite see…"

"You mean how? Under the circumstances?"

I nod.

"In my experience," she says, "given time, these things can usually heal themselves." She pauses. "If there is willingness enough."

Twenty minutes later I am standing on the circle of gravel. My car has been freshly washed. Clearly five-star service comes as standard in the Ruspolini household. Carla has not reappeared since her brusque departure from the breakfast table. For all my attempts to shrug off her behaviour as infantile, I feel exasperated and upset and strangely desolate. Just as I am preparing to get into the car, I hear the squeak of the doors behind me and Carla emerges. For a tense moment we stand facing each other. She stares stubbornly over my left shoulder, her face fixed in a kind of rictus.

I say, "When I get back to London the day after tomorrow, I'll have the money wired to the account in Switzerland you gave me. As soon as that's done a man called Enzo will contact you to arrange transport. He's completely reliable and discrete. You won't have any problems with him."

I keep my voice neutral; two can play at this game. But as I look at Carla, I'm aware of a pain tightening my chest. I move towards her and hold out my hand. She takes it and finally our eyes meet; and for a moment her face seems to implode as if all the muscles that hold it in place have suddenly been unfastened. She starts to say something. "I'm so…"

Then she stops and the mask reappears. She lets go of my hand.

"So… what?"

She shakes her head. "Go now," she says in a voice entirely devoid of emotion.

"But surely…"

"Just go."

She turns and starts towards the door. But now she walks with a strange adolescent awkwardness, her arms clasped defensively around her chest, her shoulders hunched. Something about her at that moment gives me a strange stab of dread. But her total implacability leaves me no choice. I climb into the car and start the engine. Within seconds the view of the Villa is unspooling behind me in the rear-view mirror. Carla has disappeared and closed the doors without once looking back.

I allow the car to coast down the gravel drive between the long alley of cypresses until I am out of sight. Then I pull over and step out. The sun is beginning to bake the surrounding vineyards and even here in the shade the heat is building. I can well understand that Carla might feel embarrassed or regretful after the previous night's encounter. But there's something deeply disturbing about her sense of disconnection this morning. It's as if she's a being from another planet, totally unavailable to human contact. And that has left me feeling jarred and drained. I'm certainly in no mood for the stress and relentless speed of the *autostrada*. So I duck into the car and pull out the map.

The road I eventually choose dips under the roar of the main highway, then narrows and winds up amongst fields of trailing vines until I emerge onto a ridge with the glitter of the Adriatic to my right and, on the other side, the gentle, wooded hills of *Le Marche*. As I drive, I become aware of a swell of unwanted feelings washing inside me – Resentment? Regret? I'm not good at categorizing these things. But uppermost and unmistakable is a bleak sense of desolation. I've certainly had my share of post-coital downers and disappointments, particularly after one-night stands. It comes with the territory, I suppose. But I've never had any problem brushing these off. So how come these feelings seem to stick to me like tar this morning?

There's something unnerving about Carla's endless, unpredictable multi-facetedness. She's like a human gyroscope, by turns fragile, tough, sensual, vulnerable, charming, seductive, naïve… The list goes on and on. And, most disturbingly, a child. And, added to all that, the previous afternoon in the tower has revealed something totally unexpected. No matter how much I may want to dismiss it, it's clear that she is genuinely receptive to frequencies that are simply beyond my range, like a dog whistle inaudible to the deadened human ear. And yet, despite that sudden authority and apparent wisdom, I can't shake the feeling that all these personas are somehow just evasions, desperate offerings to propitiate something terrible at the heart of her secret labyrinth. And with this realization comes a creeping sense of guilt.

But what else was I supposed to do, for God's sake? She is, after all, an adult and a beautiful woman. And – let's face it – as sexy as hell. And all her protean shifts of character – her faux innocence and schoolgirl coquetry – make her even more desirable. The uncertainty is a constant titillation. To put it crudely – which Carla will you actually be fucking when it finally comes to it?

But my macho attempts to exonerate myself aren't working too well. My thoughts keep returning obstinately to that moment in the *Castello*, when she had turned to me, with those strange, beseeching eyes.

"It felt so incredibly *safe*."

So much aching loneliness and vulnerability had been packed into that single word.

I hate this kind of morbid introspection. So instead I try to comfort myself by conjuring up again the erotic image of Carla's long body stretched naked, face down on the sofa. I hear again her barely muffled scream as I force her head into the cushions and she climaxes with almost frightening intensity. But then, as if led along some infernal path, my mind moves to the photograph of Count Ruspolini, the blank cruel stare and the thin swagger stick with the silver pommel between his hands. And now, unbidden, I picture the scene again in quite another way: Carla stretched full length on the sofa, slim, fragile, with all the innocence and vulnerability of adolescent nakedness. And I, poised above her, hirsute, satyr-like, lecherous, ready to pin her in an act packed with potential violence. No good trying to hide behind my mask of hurt and disappointment. No good trying to anaesthetise myself with eroticism. I know in my depths that I have taken part in an act of abuse.

I have descended from the ridge and the landscape has flattened out into the fertile plain of the Veneto. Far to my left the Eugenian hills are wreathed in mist as the first hot sun of the year pulls moisture from the earth. The feelings are coming thick and fast now, as if someone has lifted the lid on a boiling pot. A sudden hot wave of anger washes over me as I remember how Carla has treated me this morning, arrogantly discarding me like an unwanted flunkey, an expendable tarnast, my purpose apparently served. It's obvious that I have been trapped in some kind of perverse private ritual, where I have simply served an ugly purpose.

But, asks an ironic voice in my head, *what right have you to feel angry? Isn't that precisely what you've been doing all your life – trapping others in your own private rituals?*

And, as if that enquiring voice has thrown a switch, something opens up inside me like a dam bursting. The boundary between Carla and myself seems to give way and, for a giddying instant, I can feel, *as clearly as if it is my own*, the pain and humiliation behind those blank eyes, the hopelessness of that dark ritual that can yield no release, only an endless longing and repetition.

It's a bottomless feeling, terrifying. I'm shocked by what I have just glimpsed. Then, by a sheer effort of will, I wrench myself back, grip the steering wheel hard and concentrate on the road ahead.

TEN

"*Signor Bronson, che bella sorpresa!*"

I am gazing out across the water with the Doge's Palace at my back. A breeze has got up and small waves are beginning to slap against the stone key below me, making the tethered black gondolas buck frantically on the swell. When Canaletto painted this view in 1764, it looked pretty much the same as it does today. The water of the *Bacino* is still green and corrugated. Beyond it the spire of the church of *San Giorgio* is still dissolving in the smoky light. Off to the right, the sun glitters off the huge golden globe that tops the *Dogana*. The only differences are the occasional passing *vaporetti* and the whiff of sulphur drifting from the toxic wasteland upwind at Marghera. And now, of course, the unwelcome voice rasping in my ear.

Reluctantly I turn. And sure enough, there stands the familiar sturdy figure, dressed in an open-necked white shirt and a dark suit that glistens in the sunlight as if it has recently been sprayed with lacquer. I'm still fragile from the emotional rollercoaster of my drive from Prosaro, and company is the last thing I want at this moment. Least of all the company of Giacomino di Simone. Predictably Giacomino fails to register my reluctance. He comes barreling towards me, arms outstretched, a broad smile on his face. As he lunges to embrace me, I manage to side-step him so that he has to settle for a handshake. But he takes his revenge by digging a colossal gold ring into the side of my hand as he crushes it in an ostentatious gorilla grip.

"Only this morning I think to telephone you," he says. His voice has a gravel tone, rasping from a lifetime of unfiltered Italian cigarettes. "We must talk. Something very important. You, me, we have history, remember? We take a coffee. I know a café which serves the best espresso in all of Venezia. Come."

And, smiling, he links his arm through mine. It feels like a steel brace. But there are no two ways about it: I'm trapped. At least for the next hour. Giacomino is not a man you brush aside easily. And I sense he has something up his sleeve.

*

We have history. We sure do. For Giacomino had been at the heart of the story about my rise in the art market that I had related to Elizabetta the previous day. Only I had carefully excised the episode concerning Giacomino. I had told her, as if it were a mildly amusing anecdote, of my early years as a humble 'runner' moving between wealthy dealers, knocking on the doors of big-time collectors. But what I had failed to mention was the humiliating off-hand snubs and the casual, arrogant rejections, as I was treated like a lower form of pond life. The art market does a good line in humiliation for those at the bottom of the pile. And, of all people, it was Giacomino, who – unwittingly – had sprung me loose from that trap.

It had been early April ten years before and the antiquities world was abuzz with excitement. There were rumours that a superb Greek vase had been discovered in a tomb near Cerveteri, just north of Rome. But there were problems. The tomb fell exactly on the border between the territories of two rival bands of *tomboroli* – Italy's notorious tomb robbers. These are men with their own codes of honour and their own means of vengeance for transgressors. The arguments had raged, and then one morning the small town of Cerveteri woke to find a body propped against a wall in the main square, the throat slit from ear to ear and the word *'Porco'* smeared across the forehead in blood. Even by the macho standards of Cerveteri this was considered excessive. The vase was rumoured to be extraordinary, a superb red-figured krater, a large vessel used in antiquity for mixing wine, decorated all around with mythological scenes. But with the elite *carabinieri* from Rome beginning to close in, no one – *no one*, it was said, *in their right fucking mind* – was going to be crazy enough to go down there into that mess.

It had been six o'clock when the telephone jarred me awake in my cramped one-bedroom flat in Bayswater.

"Signor Bronson," Giacomino's voice purred silkily, "perhaps we do some business at last."

The truth was that I had met Giacomino only once, at an auction in Geneva. He was slimmer then, smoother, dressed all in Armani black. He had eyed me up like some piece of meat on a butcher's hook and clearly found me unsatisfactory. There was no way he was going to do business with someone as impoverished and lowly as myself. At least, until now.

Only half aware of what I was doing, I took the first plane to Rome and there, in a lock-up garage on the outskirts of Cerveteri, within half an hour, we concluded the business. The vase was mine for the paltry sum of twenty thousand dollars. At any other time the price would have been many multiples of that, way beyond my meagre means. But for Giacomino it was just damage limitation. He needed to get rid of the goods any way he could before the Carabinieri got too close.

I didn't have the money, of course. And even though I knew Giacomino would blow my knee-caps off if I didn't pay him, I didn't hesitate. I went back to London, sold everything I possessed, borrowed the rest from friends and dubious financiers at exorbitant rates and ten days later a truck, routed via Geneva, arrived outside my flat. Within a month I had sold the vase to a well-known New York collector for a million dollars. The established dealers were incandescent with rage. What right had I, a mere lowly 'runner', to muscle in on their high-priced territory? They told the collector – for his own good, of course – that the goods were hot and dangerous and shouldn't be touched at any price. Someone even tipped off Interpol. But, in the end, the collector stayed firm and Interpol showed little interest in the chaotic goings-on in Cerveteri. The deal held. And, at last, I was through the hoop into the big time.

But in all this slice of my history, there was one brief episode that stayed like a splinter lodged forever in my memory. Giacomino had been driving me back to the airport in Rome. He always drove a stretched black Mercedes with tinted windows, as if he were advertising himself as a gangster. We stopped at traffic lights and, for some unknown reason, I had the urge finally to ask the obvious question:

"*Why me?*"

Giacomino removed the wrap-around shades that were part of his uniform and turned his sardonic gaze on me. "I call *you*," he said with exaggerated slowness, "because *you* are hungry".

Giacomino steers me to one of the shaded cafes under the arches of the *Libreria Vechia*. He sinks into a wicker chair and claps his hands like a pasha. Instantly a white-jacketed waiter scuttles out from the gloom of the interior. Without consulting me, he orders two *café correttos*, as if there's no other drink possible for men of the world at this time of day. Then he leans forward conspiratorially, one elbow on the zinc table-top.

"Something has, how you say...come through?"

"Come up?"

"*Si*. Come up. I wanted you to be the first to know. Something *very* special. Long time we haven't done business, you and me, my friend. I wanted you to be the one." He gives me an easy smile and for a brief moment I see a flash of the charm that had originally helped to ease him into the upper echelons of the antiquities world, long before he discovered that brute force alone could do the job.

Throughout the antiquities market, and most particularly in the reaches of its dark underbelly, he is known as 'Giacomino'. The diminutive form – Little Giacomo – suits his spreading girth badly these days. Perhaps it's intended rather to propitiate something in the shadow of his character that you hope never to see let loose. Shortly after the event in Cerveteri – and probably trying to recoup his losses – Giacomino had tried to sell me a group of Roman sculptures carelessly strewn across the concrete floor of his warehouse in Geneva's infamous 'Freeport', the mecca of all European art smuggling. Back then I had been naïve enough to tell him the truth – that they were all forgeries and not even very good forgeries at that. He was crouching down, lovingly caressing one of the grotesque marbles. I saw his back stiffen like some feral animal suddenly on watch. Then he rose and shrugged. "If that is what you think..." he said, showing good-natured contempt for my callow judgement. But, just as he was turning away, I caught a look in his eyes of fierce, calculated malice.

For years after, remembering that look, I tried to avoid him. I feigned lack of time, lack of money, lack of clients.

But, in the end, Giacomino had his revenge. I have never understood why, on that particular January day, against all my better judgements, I responded to his telephone call. The next morning I was on the first flight to Geneva. Inside the dingy, echoing, padlocked room of the Freeport, he cleared the wrapping materials from the top of a wooden crate and flourished a magnificent Greek cup into the morbid neon light. The shallow vessel was decorated with scenes of Greek banqueters reclining on couches. A naked girl was seated cross-legged playing on the double pipes. It had been irresistible.

Then, one morning several weeks later, I came down into the studio early. The cup was sitting on the long oak table. As the light played across it, something about its shape disturbed me. It seemed to lack the easy grace of true Greek potting. I picked it up and turned it over in my hands, examining each detail with fresh eyes: the faces were all too similar, the smiles too smug and knowing, the torsos twisted in a way impossible for an eye that hadn't seen Renaissance perspective. And then the truth hit me like a rock.

Of course, there was no way to recoup my money. Giacomino operated far outside such petty legal restrictions. But it wasn't so much the financial loss that shocked me – though that had certainly hurt. There was something else less definitive, an obscure sense of inner betrayal. I had allowed Giacomino, like a master magician, to hook my dealer's greed and ambition, blinding me to every true instinct my heart had ever felt about the beauty of Greek art. An accident waiting to happen perhaps? And Giacomino? He was probably laughing all the way to the bank. But for me it had been like falling into the web of a patiently waiting spider. It was then that I began to understand the ancient Mediterranean fear of the man with the evil eye.

The coffee arrives. I sip mine carefully. The added grappa makes me feel faintly nauseous. Giacomino leans back in his chair and ostentatiously scratches his crutch. It's a favourite gesture of his, like a tomcat marking its territory. In spite of his spreading girth, he still wears his clothes excessively tailored, as if he's a youthful matador. The midnight blue trousers cling to his hips, the creaseless shirt is trapped in under a snake-skin belt. The profile of his chest extends in a smooth unbroken arc from neck to navel, giving him the strange hardened appearance of a stout pouter-pigeon. I have occasionally wondered if this sleek outline might conceal a bullet-proof vest. But today the marsh-like tufts of black hair sprouting from between the straining shirt buttons belie my exotic fantasy. I feel mildly disappointed.

"What you do in Venice?" asks Giacomino, fixing me with his black eyes.

"I'm on my way back from visiting friends in *Le Marche*…"

"And you stop and see *Venezia* on the way? Of course! *Bella citta!*" Giacomino widens his eyes in mock surprise. Antiquity dealers lie all the time, of course – it's part of the skill-set – particularly to cover their tracks if they accidentally meet abroad. And it's clear from Giacomino's ironic response that he assumes he has just been presented with a colossal red herring.

"And what are *you* doing here?" I counter.

"I told you. Something has come through."

"Come up." He scowls at me. "Where? Not here in Venice surely?"

"No, no. On the *terra firma*. Inland." He gestures vaguely over his shoulder.

"I thought you only operated in Etruria."

Giacomino guffaws at such naivety. "Giacomino di Simone operates *everywhere!*" He spreads his short arms in a dramatic gesture. And, as he does so, the sun glints off an enormous gold bracelet on his left wrist. Doesn't he know, for God's sake, that wearing ostentatious jewellery in Italy is an open invitation to get mugged? There are many myths that cluster around Giacomino: that he drives a red Ferrari; that his sexual organs are so small that they have to be coaxed into the light of day, or so huge that women faint at the sight of them; that he had once had an unreliable supplier of antiquities, Julio Carozza, murdered, shot in the head, then run over by a truck for good measure – just so that no one would miss the point. But one of the most persistent is that he has powerful Mafia connections. Is there some way that the average Italian street mugger can actually recognise a member of the Mafia on sight and allow him safe passage…?

"Is something fantastic! Really fantastic!" Giacomino breaks into my unruly thoughts.

"What is it?"

Before replying, Giacomino takes a gold cigarette case from his hip pocket and extracts a small cigar. He lights it and blows the smoke directly across the table in my direction, then snaps the case shut and leans forward.

"Last week a farmer inland in the Eugenian hills was crossing a field on his tractor when suddenly – Paff!" He slaps the flat of his hand on the zinc table. Coffee slops into my saucer. "One wheel goes down. Of course the farmer called *me.*" He pats himself on the chest. "Is fantastic!"

"What is it?" I repeat. "Vases?"

"No! No! Nothing like that. Is a tomb. A complete underground room sculpted from the… how you say?"

"From the rock?"

"Yes, yes. From the rock! And painted as you won't believe. Like done yesterday! Like a beautiful woman who just did her *maquillage*." He leers at me and rubs his hands.

I lean back and run my hands through my hair. A painted rock tomb in *this* part of Italy? Surely that's impossible; we're far beyond the territory of the Etruscans. Perhaps Giacomino is setting me up for another forgery. This time a spectacular one by the sound of it. Such things have certainly happened before – entire Etruscan tombs fabricated to ensnare wealthy buyers. And somehow I have the feeling that he has never quite forgiven me for all the money I made from his cut-price vase in Cerveteri.

"But I don't get it," I say. "The painted figures – aren't they carved in relief? Surely they must be joined to the walls?"

Giacomino shoots me a perplexed glance from under his dark eyebrows, as if to suggest my stupidity. "Yes, yes, of course. Figures, busts, whole bodies lying down. All fixed to the wall. So they can't run away!" He guffaws.

I frown. "So what can you do with them?"

He treats me to another uncomprehending stare. "Do? Why do? *Facile*. Zzzz…" The flat of his outstretched hand circles through the air to the accompaniment of the imitation buzz of a chain saw. "We are organised. Well organised. We free them from the rock. After so many centuries, it is an act of liberation." He smiles.

I manage to keep my face impassive, but my stomach is turning itself inside out at the thought of Giacomino and his henchmen cutting an ancient tomb to shreds. But it's no good arguing morality here. And besides, whispers an ironic voice in my ear, if you mix with the likes of Giacomino, isn't *this* what it comes to in the end?

"With that number of statues," I say, hoping to deflect him, "it sounds like it's going to be expensive. I'm not sure I have that kind of money at the moment."

But Giacomino is equal to the move and not about to be denied. For some reason he has me in his sights. He leans across the table and stabs a finger at me like a pistol barrel, as if he's trying to perforate the air.

"Look," he says, managing to make the word sound like an unspecified threat, "no worry about the money. Is no problem. You come look first, then we talk money." He must have seen my continued hesitation. "If you no come, you make a mistake. A very big mistake." He grinds out his cigar in the metal ashtray. "I tell you the first because I like you." Then, to my horror, he stretches out his hand and takes mine in a vice-like grip. "You, me," he says with undisguised menace, "we brothers. We have history. We do this thing together."

Then he rises and walks stiffly away across the piazza, leaving me to pay the bill.

ELEVEN

Somewhere between Venice and Rome everything changes. It's as if someone has turned up all the dials, particularly the volume. Emerging into the arrivals hall at Rome's Fiumicino airport is like stepping into a soccer crowd at full throttle. Antonio is standing off to one side with his arms folded. When he sees me, he raises a hand in greeting and begins to elbow his way through the crush. He embraces me warmly, then takes my arm and steers me towards the exit like a protective bodyguard.

"God, it's noisy!"

"You think this is noisy?" He chuckles ironically. "You've just been away from Rome too long, my friend. Compared with Naples or Sicily, this is as silent as a monastery. You'll get used to it again. You know what we Italians say? South of Rome is Africa. Welcome back to Africa!" He claps me jovially on the back.

Outside, amongst the chaos of hooting cars and hostile, whistle-blowing policemen, Antonio's Mercedes stands unmolested at the kerb. As we approach, an officer steps forward and holds up the traffic for us with an officious white-gloved hand. Then, with a smart salute, he bids us *buon viaggio* and sets us on our way. Down here in the south, if you know what's what, you don't stand in queues or pay your fines. Here the system is more flexible and Antonio has always known how to navigate these invisible tides of power and influence. In this society everyone needs a local protector. As an outsider you wouldn't stand a chance. And Antonio is mine – of a sort.

I settle into the leather upholstery as he eases us into the traffic. As usual, he's dressed with that off-hand elegance that only Italian men seem to be able to master: dark blue shirt open under a discretely checked cashmere sports jacket, rumpled khaki chinos and a pair of immaculately polished brown brogues; not the massive English variety, designed for clonking across sodden London pavements on bleak afternoons, but a lightweight, stylish Italian version. Although slightly older than me, Antonio has somehow managed to retain his boyish good looks. Whatever the season, the suntan appears indelible. The soft chestnut eyes and long, curved eyelashes make him look like a soulful kangaroo. And women – to the despair of his long-suffering wife, Gabriella – apparently find him irresistible.

Antonio had inherited the clandestine dealing business from his father. Old Giuseppe Strozzi, had operated from a respectable-looking antique shop on the Via del Babuino, where he sold boring mahogany furniture to the Italian bourgeoisie. But behind this innocuous facade lay a back room. And beneath the back room a cellar. The rear of the building gave onto the narrow, secluded alley of the Via Margutta and here at night, trucks ostensibly laden with fruit and vegetables would draw up and unload their secret merchandise. Over the years, Giuseppe Strozzi had achieved a near-stranglehold on the market for ancient art, so that nowadays, whenever an important antiquity is discovered, whether by a builder digging foundations, a farmer ploughing his fields, or a workman relaying drains in a small Roman back garden, it will invariably find its way to the Strozzi stronghold. It's a tough business, with the ruthless, grave-robbing bands of *tomboroli* from the south constantly trying to muscle their way in. But, despite this, Antonio has somehow retained a kind of integrity of the honour-amongst-thieves variety. At any rate, as far as I'm concerned, compared to a sinister operator like Giacomino, he's a 'gentleman-dealer'.

Gaining access to his inner circle – which meant being the first to be called when a new discovery arrived at one of his secret storerooms – wasn't easy. In those days there was a phalanx of important dealers ahead of me who had established a ruthless pecking order. But, in the end, what had catapulted me clean through those ferociously guarded ranks had been extraordinarily simple. I was in New York when Zoe called to tell me that old Giuseppe Strozzi had died. I liked Antonio and I liked old Giuseppe and, almost without thinking, I immediately booked myself on the next flight to Rome. At the time it just seemed the natural thing to do. The next morning I got off the red-eye in Fiumicino and took a taxi straight to the church, a gigantic baroque mausoleum on the outskirts of Rome. Antonio emerged from the black crush of mourners, tears in his eyes, and came forward to embrace me. It was only later I came to realize that that one single act had carried more weight with him than a thousand lucrative business deals ever could. After that I was *persona grata*, almost an honorary member of the closely guarded Strozzi clan.

"This time I have something that will knock your shoes off." Antonio's voice breaks into my thoughts.

"Socks." Antonio's English is fluent but erratic and I occasionally enjoy correcting him.

"Okay, socks," he says irritably, then hits the horn and

sweeps past a small Fiat that has been dithering in front of us. "Anyhow," he retaliates, "it's lucky you come so quickly."

I recognise the implicit threat – others are just waiting to knock me off my perch – but decide to ignore it.

"A sculpture?"

"Hmm. Sort of." He smiles. The incipient crows' feet at the corners of his eyes crinkle. Then for a while he stares silently at the road ahead. Finally he concedes, "You will see. As I told you on the phone, it's very beautiful. *Bellissimo!*".

"But you didn't tell me *anything* on the phone!"

Antonio laughs. It's an old joke between us. Actually I've never quite been able to decide whether he genuinely thinks his phone may be tapped by the *Carabinieri*, or whether he simply gets a massive buzz from the risk and potential danger of our business. Probably he's just an adrenalin junkie. Most of us in this business are. Either way, his telephone calls are always anonymous, made from public phones and cloaked in absurdly transparent codes telling me that the weather has suddenly become *very* beautiful in Rome, or that a new *beautiful* baby has been born – and I must come to Rome as quickly as possible to see it. *Il piu presto possibile!* Frankly, it's hard to believe that even the most brain-dead *Carabinieri* eavesdropper would be fooled by that one.

We have turned off the *autostrada* and are weaving our way through some run-down outpost of the city. We pass through a cobbled square where a fish and vegetable market is packing up. The stalls are being shuttered and men in green overalls and rubber boots are throwing wooden crates into a skip and hosing down the cobbles. A residual stench of fish drifts in the air. We pass two girls in tank tops and skin-tight jeans.

"*Belle cule,*" he murmurs.

I nod, but I don't want to get sidetracked into a conversation about women – a perennial topic with Antonio – just yet. I need to settle something with him before we reach our destination and the dealing process inevitably takes over.

"I've got a favour to ask".

He nods. "Try me."

"I did some business while I was up north."

The eyebrows lift in surprise. "In Venice? Not a lot of digging up there, is there?"

"No. In *Le Marche*. Something from an old collection. The daughter wants to sell it. It comes from a small private *castello*."

"Okay. How can I help?"

"Transport. I need to get it into the Freeport in Geneva."

"Quickly?"

"Right. Before the seller changes her mind."

"Women, huh?" He shrugs. "How big?"

As concisely as I can, I fill him in on the details, mentioning only that it's a heavily restored Roman work of purely decorative value.

"Do you think we could send Enzo Garofano up there alone with some lifting gear?" I ask. "I don't want to involve people I don't know. And I certainly don't want some gorilla of a tattooed truck driver suddenly pitching up at the *castello* unannounced."

Antonio considers this for a minute. "It should be possible. Enzo's good at handling big marbles by himself. With the right equipment he could probably crate it and leave it at a local depot for collection. Then it could go out through the airport in Venice. I've got connections there. That way we won't have to bring it down to Rome. Things are getting more difficult around here, you know. They've begun stopping trucks at random and searching them. They're really after drugs, black money, illegal immigrants, that sort of thing. But if they happen to find you with an antiquity, you're fucked anyway." For a while he's silent, nodding to himself. "Okay," he says finally, "That should be fine, but it's going to be expensive. All the bribes and everything."

"How much?"

"Oh, well..." He shrugs and lets out a sigh, as if the subject is too boring to be worth discussing. "We can talk about that when you've seen the other thing I've got waiting for you."

Ten minutes later, in an anonymous suburb where broken-down peasant cottages rub shoulders with factories and brutal high-rise apartment blocks, Antonio bumps the car up on to the shattered pavement and cuts the engine. Ahead of us a Roman aqueduct strides through these dystopian surroundings like some giant planting his feet contemptuously amongst the squalor of an inferior civilization. Mountains of garbage are piled under the towering brick arches. Just beside us a high clap-board fence is almost buried under a riot of blue volubilis and purple bougainvillea. Traces of razor wire peep out from amongst the foliage. A lurid picture of a slathering, open-jawed Alsatian is nailed to the stout wooden gate, accompanied by the words, *Cave canem!*

"*Siamo arrivati*," says Antonio as he climbs out and slams the door. "You're in for a surprise."

He takes a ring of keys from his pocket and unfastens two heavy padlocks that clamp together a massive swag of chains. Instantly thunderous barking erupts from within. He pushes open the creaking gate and beckons me inside.

I follow him through. What greets me is some kind of sculptural madhouse. The whole place is littered with fragments of ancient marble – columns and capitals, toes and fingers, arms, legs and genitals are strewn everywhere. The floor of the courtyard is paved with a random mosaic of coloured stones. In the centre of this psychedelic explosion stands a small peasant cottage, roughly whitewashed and capped by a sagging ochre-tiled roof. On one side a vine-covered trellis extends from the level of the guttering to the top of the high fence. The sun filters through the tangle of vines onto the multi-coloured floor beneath, setting up a giddying pattern as the foliage shifts in the light breeze. The walls of the cottage are inset with more marble fragments, half a hand here, a protruding nose there, a set of toes seemingly forcing their way through the rough plaster. On one side of the open door stands a waist-high terracotta vase overflowing with herbs. On the other, three rush-seated green chairs flank a wooden table, which bears a large, unlabelled bottle of red wine and some plastic cups.

Above the lintel of the door a marble portrait bust is perched on a ledge, leaning precariously forwards to inspect new arrivals. It's a fine sculpture, beautifully carved. The benign features and the thick wavy hair make the portrait instantly recognizable – the Emperor Hadrian. But the right eye is closed in an absurd, knowing wink. And then I realise where we are.

A moment later, as if in confirmation, Enzo Garofano emerges from the darkness of the house, rubbing his hands on a piece of paint-stained rag. He is closely followed by a hugely overweight basset hound, its flaccid ears and giant belly almost dragging on the ground. For a moment the dog surveys us through its bloodshot eyes with an expression of utmost boredom, then waddles lugubriously across the yard, raises one hind leg and urinates copiously against a marble column, before waddling back to Enzo's side.

Enzo Garofano looks as if he might have just stepped out of a tabloid cartoon. Everything about him is exaggerated. He is comically short, barely five feet tall. His squat artisan's body is surmounted by an almost spherical head. Heavy brows overhang his darting black eyes. A thick moustache bristles on his short upper lip. The two wings of black hair that sweep round the polished dome of his otherwise bald cranium make him look as if his head might suddenly take flight. Today, as every day, he is dressed in a long, brown stonemason's coat, with black baggy trousers and heavy boots protruding from beneath. A small round workman's cap perches on the back of his head.

Throughout Rome Enzo is renowned as the city's most talented stonemason. A humble man of humble origins, he moves now in exalted circles. Bishops, famous architects and renowned master builders all flock to him when a church or a monument begins to crumble. Although nearly illiterate – I once watched him take almost five minutes to copy a four line address – he can size up a restoration project in seconds. Something in his Roman DNA seems to have endowed him with an uncanny symbiosis with marble, so that it's often impossible to discern just where the ancient work ends and Enzo's twentieth century restoration takes over.

And that's part of the problem, because less well known is the fact that he is also Italy's greatest *falsario*. Some of the world's most famous museums unwittingly display 'ancient masterpieces' that have emerged stealthily from Enzo's tiny, cluttered workshop. Oddly it doesn't seem to be the money that drives him. He has simple tastes and lets these forgeries go for meager prices, knowing that they may fetch millions on the open market. The sport seems to lie in the deception.

For a long while we sit in the dappled shade of the trellis. We drink several cups of Enzo's pungent home-made wine and chat as if we have nothing else on our minds. This is standard art market foreplay and doubtless they are hoping that the wine is going to soften me up. Enzo and Antonio are an odd pairing, a kind of Italian Laurel and Hardy double act, only a lot more savvy. Enzo is apparently the Stan Laurel of the duo – the simple one. He has lived in Rome all his life. Like some neophobic creature, he never leaves the city, and has his own extensive underground local network of builders, farmers and clandestine middlemen, who bring him a constant stream of objects randomly dug up in and around Rome. Usually it's fairly minor stuff, but occasionally some unexpected masterpiece falls into his hands. But he lacks Antonio's sophisticated outside connections and foreign languages and without these he would be permanently confined to the local market. So the two of them have mutually swallowed their pride just enough to form an unpredictable partnership.

From time to time Enzo shoots me a sidelong glance from the corners of his sardonic eyes. He's playing with me and I do my best to deny him the satisfaction of showing my growing impatience. At last, apparently satisfied with the formalities of wine and conversation and tired of the game of teasing me, he rises and, without a word, crosses to a small brick outhouse with double doors at the far end of the courtyard. He takes a key from the pocket of his overalls, unfastens a padlock and slides back the heavy bolt. Then he pushes both doors open and disappears into the gloom of the interior. A moment later he reemerges, pushing a tall object swathed in a white sheet. It balances precariously on a thick wooden platform. The heavy castors underneath swivel and clatter on the uneven paving. Enzo steadies the trolley, flips down the metal brakes and wedges in a block of wood for stability.

There's a long theatrical pause. He looks like a comic magician about to perform his *tour de force* as he stands there, dressed in his long brown coat, dwarfed by the massive shape beside him. Then, with one quick movement, he shoots out his right hand, grips the sheet and pulls it away. And for a vivid instant my brain freezes and my heart literally seems to stop.

In front of me stands an over-life-sized, nude figure of Aphrodite, caught in the act of laying aside her robe. The head and most of the arms are missing, but enough remains to make the pose certain. The lower legs and the circular base are whitely encrusted with barnacles. Even in this eccentric setting, with the dappled light seeping through the vine-clad pergola, and incomplete as she is, the figure is breathtakingly beautiful. But, most extraordinary of all, the statue is completely black.

And that blackness is setting off a detonation in my brain that is making me light-headed with disbelief. I put my hand against the table to steady myself. *I have seen this figure before!* Not *seen* in the sense that I am now seeing the vine covered trellis, the shifting sunlight, the two figures standing off to my right, arms folded like Tweedledum and Tweedledee. But *seen* it nonetheless. For deep in the recesses of my mind some hidden memory capsule has broken open. This, *beyond any doubt*, is the dark shape that had breached the surface of the water in my dream ten days ago, then slid back into the depths. Headless, armless, glistening black like oil, this is precisely the form that has, until now, been hidden from my waking mind. The dream, the object, suddenly fitting perfectly together.

For a moment the world around me seems to sway. Is it possible, *just possible*, that two events, so utterly separated in space and time, from such totally different levels of reality, could somehow be joined? And something Carla has said to me is ringing in my head: "*You may begin to notice apparently impossible coincidences…*"

Slowly I become aware of Antonio and Enzo staring at me with concern.

"*Non e un falso*," says Enzo defensively, clearly misreading my silence. "Is no forgery."

I ignore him and turn to Antonio. "When did they find it?"

Antonio gives me a frown of baffled irritation "What do you mean, *when*? What do you want to know that for?"

"*When?*"

Clearly disconcerted, Antonio turns and the two of them begin to confer. But I already know the answer.

"A week ago last Tuesday," Antonio is saying. "Two fishermen pulled it up after a storm off the Amalfi coast. We had to delay the transport for a few days because there was a big fiesta going on and the place was crawling with *carabinieri*. That's why I didn't call you..."

But I am no longer listening. My mind is elsewhere, slipping into free-fall. After two thousand years, lying undiscovered on the Mediterranean sea bed, this statue has been dredged up *on the same night* – and, for all I know, at precisely the same moment – as it had also risen blackly in my dream. And, a voice slyly reminds me, just hours before Carla's unexpected arrival at the gallery. I'm grappling for a hold on reality. *Surely it's just a coincidence?* Whatever that may mean.

But my reason seems to be fighting a losing battle. And dimly I can again hear Carla's echoing words:

One day the darkness will need to rise to the surface...

*

The drone of the engines shifts note as the Alitalia plane breaks through the dense layer of cloud that has blanketed Rome in the late afternoon, turning the city into a claustrophobic sauna. As we emerge into the evening sun, I tilt back my seat and let my mind drift over the events of the last hours.

Antonio had suggested we adjourn to a nearby restaurant for an late lunch. He was clearly unnerved by my reaction to the statue and desperate to get the deal back on track. At first the tactic seemed to work as we relaxed over the antipasti and an excellent bottle of Pinot Grigio. And soon the two of them were warming to their subject. The statue, I readily agreed, was no forgery. Not even Enzo's sculptural ingenuity could come up with a work as fine as this. The issue of authenticity settled, they begin to make much of the figure's rarity, working the conversation like a smooth double act, moving stealthily towards their quarry. They try to convince me that they have just unearthed the new Venus de Milo. Only *rarer*, they insist. *Much rarer, because it's black.* But I'm quick to counter that although rarity might appear to add a premium, it also narrows the market. The greater the rarity and the more esoteric the object, the fewer the potential clients. Reluctantly they agree, nodding their heads slowly. But still…

And so, as we eat our way through the *spaghetti alle vongole*, we continue to fence until the main course arrives and Antonio finally feels sufficiently emboldened to name their price – a cool half a million dollars. *Cinque cento mille dollari! Siete pazzi! Completamente pazzi!* I became theatrically outraged and there follows a heated argument between Antonio and myself whilst Enzo, who presumably understands almost none of it, keeps bobbing up and down on his chair, interjecting, "*Raro, raro! Nero! Bellisimo, bellissimo!*" like a ventriloquist's dummy.

By the time the *panna cotta* and strawberries appear and a bottle of *vin santo* has been uncorked, we have all mellowed. After all, this kind of theatre is almost *de rigeur* in the art market, especially here in Italy. And finally we shake hands on a figure of two hundred and fifty thousand dollars, to include the transport of Carla's sculpture to Geneva. I may have cut their price in half, but it's still a huge sum to pay for a headless statue. Antonio and Enzo give each other meaningful glances. They can barely contain their jubilation. It's clear that they must have made a killing. Probably, if I had gone on bargaining, I could have got the sculpture for half the price. But some obscure instinct seems to be compelling me to do this deal at whatever cost. Which now leaves me with the intractable problem of how to turn a profit on such a fragmentary, eccentric object.

Outside the window the clouds are evaporating and the snow-capped peaks of the Alps begin to stretch out below me. A strange thing happens to me in aeroplanes – my brain expands. It's as if, with its earth-bound shackles released, it suddenly floats free. Most of my more creative ideas are born up here above the clouds. To be honest, this normally involves inventive new ways of making money. But, right now, I can sense something quite different coming across the wires. The inexplicable coincidence with my dream has badly unnerved me. There is no obvious explanation. Such things just don't happen, for God's sake! At least, not in my reality. And there had been something deeply disturbing about the simple fact that the Aphrodite was black. As the Greek goddess of love and desire she was born from the white foam of the Aegean sea into the dazzling Mediterranean light. So surely the *light* must be her element. There are just too many mysteries here.

Searching for answers, I lean back and close my eyes. But, in the darkness, comes not logic but an unexpected ragbag of sinister images, as if someone has just opened up a secret corner of my mind: gaping graves in desolate churchyards, crepe-shrouded coffins and top-hatted mourners, black-plumed horses and solstice sacrifices, fantasies of death and decay, blackness as sinister and purely evil. *But was this really what blackness had meant to the ancients?* Surely in their wisdom there was something more, some deeper roots now lost to our more trivial, light-seeking minds; some profound belief that might have given birth to a black Aphrodite? Many ancient cultures had actually worshipped darkness. They had seen it as a place of healing and regeneration, packed with potential, like the germinating blackness of the winter soil, or the fruitful darkness of the womb. They had lacked entirely the Christian dogma of the light being separated from the dark. Not for them all those mediaeval paintings of an implacable, bearded God the Father leaning down, one long arm outstretched to divide the righteous from the damned with unwavering certainty. As the righteous spiral upwards, arms joyfully outstretched, into the radiant light of Heaven, the sinners creep hunched and naked into the darkness of eternal torment, where wolf-fanged demons wait with pitchforks and branding irons. Certainly no room for grey areas there. No room for divine Aphrodite, fertile and desirable, yet amorally lustful and adulterous. No room for slippery, duplicitous winged-footed Hermes, god of thieves and pick-pockets…

"Drink from the bar, sir?"

The stewardess is smiling at me from behind her chrome trolley. For a moment I am totally disorientated. I feel shaky, the way one does after a minor accident. I order a double scotch and with the first hit of the alcohol, I can feel myself begin to settle again. All the same, this is the second time in the last two days that my mind has gone into this kind of freefall in broad daylight, as if the division between the dream world and the real world has suddenly become unsettlingly porous. So, to restore normality, I decide to revert to a strategy I often use when I'm feeling overstressed. I begin to tick mental boxes. It usually works.

So, let's run through it all again *logically*. In the space of the last forty-eight hours I have:

One – Completed two deals which will, in all probability, earn me a small fortune.
Two – Dined sumptuously and slept well between linen sheets in a grand Italian villa and,
Three – Ended by scoring (the crude Americanism feels suitably comforting) with the lady of the house, a beautiful young Italian aristocrat. And scoring, I remind myself, in an exotic and unusual fashion.

And here I am now returning home triumphant.

On the surface, I have to admit, it all looks pretty good. But, at the same time, I'm treacherously aware of Carla's indictment that I'm adept at turning away; and Sylvia's letter isn't helping. For I can sense something moving unseen beneath my triumphant narrative, like two tectonic plates slowly beginning to grind together.

*

"*Kalispera. Ti kaneis?*"

A heavy hand claps me on the shoulder just as I am making my way out of the crowded baggage hall at Heathrow. Startled, I turn and there, right in front of me, is the suntanned face and sharp blue eyes of Alexis Koromilas.

"Alexis! Hi. Where have you been?"

"Zurich. Most boring fucking city on the planet. The Swiss idea of excitement is sitting up at night counting their money." He stoops and hitches his flight bag higher onto his shoulder. "I've got a car waiting for me. Why don't we share the ride into town?"

As the huge black limousine pulls away into the windswept evening, Alexis presses a button in the armrest and a glass partition slides silently up into place. Then he thuds back in the leather seat and stares at me with his usual unvarnished Greek curiosity.

"You know what?" he says amiably, "You look like shit. What the hell have you been up to?"

"Thanks. That's really encouraging. Actually I'm just back from a business trip." But the truth is that I'm unnerved that even someone as emotionally obtuse as Alexis can see the strain of the last few days in my face.

"Okay. It's just that you look kind of sick, like someone might have ripped you off."

"Quite the contrary. I just did two extremely successful deals." Even to myself my tone sounds prim and irritating.

"Anything for me?"

"I doubt it," I say, trying to put him in his place as a collector of minor significance. But the implicit snub bounces off Alexis's well-hardened skin.

"Pity."

He settles back comfortably into his leather seat. The top button of his crisp white shirt is open as if it has just been popped by his rock-hard Adam's apple. The Hermes tie is casually adrift. His long boxer's jaw is heavily stained by a piratical blue shadow. No matter how much money Alexis amasses, or how expensive his clothes become, he will never be able to shake the appearance of a rough sailor who has been scrubbed up and stuffed into a suit for some kind of festive occasion.

Alexis had come into my gallery five years before with the single-minded intention of becoming a collector of Greek antiquities. He openly despises the failings of his fellow countrymen, their laziness and dishonesty, their exaggerations and lack of order. And yet, like most expatriate Greeks, he harbours a deep nostalgic attachment to his homeland; although it's an attachment that doesn't stretch quite as far as actually wanting to live amongst its chaos and corruption. For Alexis this has resulted in a peripatetic existence between London, New York, Los Angeles and occasional visits to his sixty-foot sailing yacht moored in the marina at Piraeus. And all the time he is busy accumulating a small fortune as a commodities trader. In the early days his knowledge of Greek art and history had been – to say the least – rudimentary. But his enthusiasm was infectious and before long I was helping him to assemble a small but respectable collection.

Alexis stretches out his long legs and pushes at the partition in front of us as if he's trying to annihilate it. He tilts back his head and frowns, apparently lost in thought. The sinews in his neck strain like steel cords. For Alexis, even thinking is a physical activity. Then suddenly he sits forward, as if jolted by an electric shock. "I've got an idea," he says. "You look knackered. You should take a rest." He thrusts his hand inside his jacket and pulls out a brown leather wallet. "Remember my house in Greece, the one on the island?"

"Sure."

He had mentioned it a number of times over the years, along with a potted history of his family. They had originated as humble fishermen from a place called Katakalos, a tiny island of sailors just off the southern tip of the Peloponnese. During the long Turkish occupation they had prospered by using their boats to trade contraband throughout the eastern

Mediterranean. When the Turks were finally driven out in 1832, his newly rich ancestors moved to Athens and began to turn themselves into more respectable sailors, gradually developing into a distinguished line of naval captains and admirals.

Alexis's grandfather, Konstantinos had returned to the island around the turn of the century, took possession of the family land that had fallen into disuse and built there a small hunting lodge on a wooded peninsula. It was intended to provide a primitive overnight shelter for him and his newly rich friends from Athens when they came for two weeks each autumn to shoot the migrating flocks of quail. Thirty year later Alexis's father had 'modernised' it to make it suitable for longer stays. But the modernization still didn't boast electricity and relied on a rain water tank for sanitation.

"I found an old photograph of it last week," Alexis is saying, "tucked inside one of my father's books. Look."

He extracts a small black and white print from the wallet and hands it across. It is square, badly faded and slightly crinkled. It shows a man in his fifties, fierce-eyed and moustachioed, dressed in heavy tweed plus-fours and a belted Norfolk jacket, with a flint-lock shotgun sloped over his left arm. On his head sits an eccentric Tyrolean feathered hat and at his feet lies a small mound of birds and two recumbent rabbits, their back legs stretched out as if in traction. Off to the left a brown and white spaniel gazes up at him expectantly. Just visible in the background is a wooden door, framed by a heavy stone surround. If it wasn't for a clump of asphodels sprouting from the dry earth and a large incongruous watermelon balanced on the top step, I might have taken it for Scotland or Cumbria. But this, Alexis informs me, is his grandfather, Konstantinos Coromilas, circa 1900 in the southern Aegean.

As I gaze at the odd little photograph I feel drawn into a kind of time-warp. Perhaps it's just the seeming innocence that old photographs exude, the allure of a life less complicated. Perhaps it's the strain and oddity of the last few days. Perhaps just a nostalgic longing for the simplicity of my own early visits to Greece. And suddenly I am seized by a great inarticulate longing.

"Go there any time you like," says Alexis. "It looks like you could do with a break."

TWELVE

I take a sleeping pill and sleep late. By the time I pad downstairs, rumpled and heavy-lidded, still wearing my toweling bathrobe, Zoe is already at her desk, opening the post.

"Nice to see you back *at last*," she says, scarcely looking up, except to cast a disparaging glance at my bare feet.

"Anything special happen while I was away?"

"Well," she picks up her note pad and begins relating events in reverse order of importance. Clearly she hasn't taken kindly to my extended absence. "A Mrs Ballantyne telephoned. It seems she met you at Sotheby's recently. She was *frightfully* chatty. We're now new best friends. And she did manage to drop into the conversation oh-so casually that her husband's away on business *all* this week. She also left her number. Funny that," she adds with a puzzled frown. "Do you want it?"

"I don't think so."

"Hmm. There's also…" She fills me in on two other items of trivia before getting to the only event of importance. "Sam Schwartz arrived yesterday and, *as you know*, I had to deal with him alone." She glances up, but getting no response, goes on, "Just for the record, he's a nasty, pompous little pig of a man."

"It sounds like you weren't best pleased."

"No, I certainly wasn't and nor was he. He was pretty

pissed off you weren't here to see him as arranged. I think he's not used to being stood up by lesser forms of pond life like yourself. I reckon it will take a serious amount of grovelling to get him to come back, dragging his mega millions with him."

I shrug. "It probably did him good. The super-rich like to be treated badly from time to time. It gives them the illusion that they're real."

Zoe lays down her note pad and gives me an appraising look. "Well, I trust that whatever it was that kept you so extraordinarily long in Italy was worthwhile."

"It was." I remove the envelope Carla had given me from the pocket of my bathrobe and lay it on the desk. "Could you transfer the Swiss Francs equivalent of eighty million Lire to this numbered account at Credit Suisse in Zurich?"

Zoe slits open the envelope and studies the piece of paper. Then she treats me to one of her frozen stares. "We haven't been notified that anything has arrived at the Freeport in Geneva yet, you know."

"I'm aware of that."

She leans back in her chair and folds her arms. "So how do we know that the glamorous countess, who appears to have addled your brains, won't just double-cross you?"

She has a point. In the darker dealings of the antiquities world, payment and exchange of goods is always a delicate balance. It's a bit like a kidnapping hand-over, a question of who blinks first. My normal rule – as Zoe knows – is simple: no goods in the safety of the Freeport, no money. But nothing is quite normal about this transaction.

"She won't for two reasons. First, because I have the details of her Swiss bank account, and if the statue doesn't arrive as agreed she'll have the *Guardia di Finanza* on her doorstep pretty quickly. Which, to someone of her social standing, would be more than a little embarrassing. And secondly, just because she's a nice lady."

There's a little pause. "Well, I trust she was nice and ladylike with you?" she says with the faintest lift of her eyebrows.

"We did the deal," I reply drily and tap the paper in front of her. "As you can see."

Zoe lets out a puff of breath and gets up from her desk. "I think I'd better get you some coffee," she says in a tone that suggests it might improve my mood. Then, over her shoulder, "And you're meeting David Anselm at twelve at the café in Hyde Park – although God knows why you would want to meet there. I imagine you've forgotten all about it. I wouldn't want you to be two days late for that as well."

*

David and I decide to skip the coffee and begin walking along the north edge of the Serpentine. A few disconsolate ducks waddle around at our feet, waggling their heads from side to side like senseless mechanical toys. Occasionally they turn up their round eyes and amber beaks in an attempt to shame us into producing some bread. It's a bleak, milky-grey morning. It's the kind of quietly malevolent London day that I hate. For some reason it carries intimations of mortality.

Like Zoe, David is probably wondering why I have asked to meet him in Hyde Park. Bars, restaurants and art galleries are our normal habitat. He will also be wondering what I want to talk to him about (I've made it explicit that I need his advice) but he's far too polite to ask. Probably he thinks I need to unburden myself about Sylvia's death and our disastrous relationship. But, frankly, what is there to say? That I fucked it up? That *she* fucked it up? *We* fucked it up? It has been fucked up. It was a fuck-up… It starts to sound like a Latin grammar class. But look at it any way you like, we were a bad match, pure and simple. No, it's not really about Sylvia – at any rate, not only about her – that I'm feeling this uncharacteristic urge to talk. To 'share', using the current irritating jargon. It's just that there seems to have been one jarring event after another recently, so that I'm starting to feel like a boxer pinned against the ropes, going down under too many blows.

My peculiar dream, for example, won't leave me. Even in broad daylight, the image of that half-submerged dark figure can resurface at any time, as if it were Banquo's ghost come to remind me of… of just what exactly? And then there's the inexplicable appearance of the black Aphrodite in Enzo's yard; Carla's unexpected arrival, her theatrical – but admittedly unnerving – astrological performance; Sylvia's sudden death and her excoriating letter.… Even buying the *kouros* – which should, by any normal standards, have left me euphoric with excitement – has begun to assume a malign penumbra. I am haunted by a vague, uncomfortable feeling that there might, after all, be some kind of hidden meaning that binds these disparate events together.

Of course, it's Carla with her talk of Saturn and Pluto who has kicked off this whole idea that there is a meaningful pattern, a kind of fated inevitability at work here that is slowly closing in on me. Normally I don't believe in patterns. Or even meaning, come to that. As far as I'm concerned things happen at random (isn't that what Heisenberg was on about?) and then I react. It may not amount to much of a grand philosophical scheme, but it has worked pretty well for me. At least until now. And that's where Carla has slid her stiletto of doubt into me, with the thought that it may not be working quite so well any more. That the crackling flame (as she has so kindly suggested) may be nearing the gunpowder. At any rate, the fact is that I'm unnerved and edgy and clouded with a vague sense of foreboding.

We have reached the end of the Serpentine and so far I haven't said a word. David isn't used to me being brooding and introspective. We're close, but we don't do intimate conversations. If anything, we're like two Edwardian gentlemen lounging in their leather armchairs at their club. We've tacitly agreed the limits of good taste. Deep explorations of the psyche and displays of emotion make us uncomfortable. Actually, if I'm really honest, it's probably only me that feels uncomfortable. I'm the one who silently sets the boundaries. David, I know from random hints, has other sides to him that I have never explored. There's a persistent rumor in the antiquities world that he's been seeing a shrink for years. Most art market gossip is pure fantasy (mostly toxic), but this one has the ring of truth. Of course, I've never asked him, but I'm not altogether surprised. Clearly he has what might be called 'hidden depths' – something that I apparently (at least according to Carla) so significantly lack. And that's precisely why I want to talk to him now. Anyhow, who else is there in my life who would listen to this kind of stuff?

"I guess Sylvia's death must have been hard for you?" he ventures helpfully at last, presumably trying to break the logjam.

I shrug. "It wasn't much fun, that's for sure." I hesitate. "But that's not really what I wanted to talk about. Or at least not just that…"

I realize that I have absolutely no idea how to begin. My normally well-ordered brain feels like the inside of a garbage bag. Anything I take out will be purely random. In fact, I'm not sure what I want to say at all. But I have to start somewhere.

"The whole thing is very weird."

"Try me," says David. "I do weird. Start anywhere you like."

I suck in a deep breath. "Okay. Well, it all started about two weeks ago when a rather beautiful young Italian woman came into the gallery. She wanted to sell a statue that had been hidden away in the cellar of their family home and… ." I stop in mid-sentence, aware that I'm omitting something that suddenly feels crucial. I begin again, "Actually – this is going to sound very odd – I think it really all started the night before she came. I had a very peculiar dream…"

I glance across at David to gauge his reaction, but he's staring straight ahead, his brow furrowed in concentration. "Go on," he encourages. "Remember, nothing's too odd for me. Anyhow, I like dreams."

And so I begin to tell him about the dream, about Carla's arrival at the gallery, my sense of unease, the photographs, the *Castello*, the *kouros* statue, the deal, the astrological reading and an expurgated version of our encounter later that evening. I then go on to relate the shock of being confronted with the black statue the following day in Rome. David listens in silence, nodding occasionally. I guess he's thinking that I've either lost my mind or I'm looking for advice on some complication with the deal or possibly even an emotional entanglement with Carla. But when I begin to tell him in detail what happened in the tower room with Carla, he stops and looks at me in surprise.

"Do you believe in astrology?"

"No," I say, with less conviction than I might have expected. "Of course not."

"I do," says David and begins walking again, his hands thrust deep into his trouser pockets, staring at the ground. I'm not entirely surprised. I suppose this is part of his 'hidden depths'. And after my experience with Carla, I realize I'm less inclined to sneer. All the same, I can't let his credulity go totally unchallenged.

"So you think you can read your horoscope in the tabloids and then know what's going to happen to you for the rest of the day?"

"No, of course not. That's just astro-fodder for the masses. But I've seen and experienced far too much with astrology over the years *not* to believe in it. Even on a purely practical level, if the moon can shift the ocean tides around, it's absurd to think that it won't have any effect on us, given that we're ninety-five percent liquid. And the same must be true in varying degrees with the other planets. It's just a question of knowing how to interpret the data."

"But that's still a hell of a long way from thinking that you can look at the position of the planets at the time of someone's birth and tell them all about their deep inner character traits – as Carla claimed to do – and what's likely to happen to them in the near future."

"Agreed," says David calmly. "And yet I know it to be true and nothing is going to shake that belief." He pauses. "Okay, scientific rationalism holds sway in our culture right now. If you can't prove something in a controlled double-blind experiment in the confines of a laboratory, then it simply doesn't exist. Right? So out go astrology and geomancy and prophecy and even alchemy, come to that." He's starting to sound uncomfortably like Carla. "But you know what? That's an attitude that would have baffled our beloved ancient Greeks and Egyptians, even our Elizabethan ancestors. And it would have seemed quite irrational to Isaac Newton. He was an alchemist, don't forget."

I'm caught off balance by the unexpected passion in his

voice. The conversation has obviously uncovered a whole area of him that I've never glimpsed before. But before I can say anything, he goes on more quietly, "But let's not get sidetracked by that for the moment. Why don't you tell me more about what happened with your dark lady in the tower? It sounds like something out of one of Grimm's Fairy Tales."

"That's pretty much how it felt. And just about as believable."

David laughs and the atmosphere eases. So I begin to relate, in layman's language, the details of Carla's astrological reading. I omit only her bizarre head-spinning trick at the end. Even to think about that now feels deeply embarrassing and unsettling, and I'm certainly not going to expose it to anyone. Not even to David.

For a long while after I've finished, we walk in silence. We have reached the western limit of the park and are making our way slowly back towards the Serpentine. Despite the grey day, young mothers and dutiful nannies are out pushing buggies, while the children chase each other or kick stiff-legged and ineffectually at rubber balls. In the background the traffic hums along Bayswater Road.

At length David says, "I'm not an astrologer, of course; but when I think of you as I know you, then I must say that the symbolism of it all makes perfect sense to me. You have to admit that what you've been experiencing in the last couple of weeks is an extraordinary cluster of psychic events. Genuine synchronicities."

"*Psychic?* They were *real*, David! And bloody uncomfortable."

"Real *and* psychic. That's exactly what synchronicities are."

"You mean coincidences."

"No. That's just a convenient word that modern scientific rationalism has dreamed up to cover up anything it can't explain. Look, you dream of a statue of Aphrodite and then ten days later it actually appears *in your life*. The very same figure! You really want to tell me that's just a coincidence? Of course it isn't. But you can't find a scientific explanation for it either, can you?" When I fail to answer, David goes on, "It sounds to me like your lady in the tower was talking a lot of sense. Even without her astrological knowledge, from where I'm standing it looks as if some big shift is starting to take place in your life. I can certainly agree with her on that."

"David, she was nuts," I say defensively. I have told David that I want his advice. But only now do I realize that I have actually come here in search of his support *against* Carla and all that she had been suggesting. Come here in fact, in search of a sane, rational view that would dispel my nagging anxieties and make the world *normal* again, for God's sake. And here he is apparently throwing in his lot with her!

"Of course she was," says David with irritating calmness. "That's how all clairvoyants and psychics and shamans would appear to you. If you met the Delphic priestess herself in the street, you would probably have her sectioned. But perhaps that may say more about you than it does about her."

I'm about to make a harsh riposte, then bite it back. I'm not here to argue with him. So instead I say, "I don't know what it all means – if it 'means' anything at all. But what I do know is that there have been some moments in these last two weeks, like when I saw that black statue, or on the flight back from Rome that I told you about, when I've felt completely spaced out. It's almost as if I'm dreaming in broad daylight. It's bloody disorientating. It's as if I've lost my anchors and I'm floating backwards and forwards between two separate realities. Now you see me, now you don't."

"Just like the black Aphrodite in your dream."

"Oh, *please!*"

"Well, perhaps for the first time in your life you're allowing yourself to see flashes of what your Carla called 'The Other World', instead of just being imprisoned in the literalism of the here and now. Perhaps it's true that Aphrodite is quite deliberately beginning to make her presence known in your life – just like Carla suggested. You dream of her, and then a week later she pops up in a courtyard in Rome. How much evidence do you really need?"

"If what I've experienced in the last couple of weeks is a fair taste of what you call 'The Other World' – or Aphrodite for that matter – then I think I can manage quite well without them. Anyhow," I add, trying to steer the conversation back towards more manageable ground, "Why black? I've never heard of any other ancient black Aphrodite, have you? If you want to interpret the whole thing symbolically, perhaps you can explain that to me."

For a while David is silent, his brow bent in concentration. At length he says, "Black can mean many things, I suppose. Certainly different things for the ancients than for us. But the fact that a black Aphrodite comes out of the sea, both in reality and in your dream, would suggest to me that there's something that's hidden, occluded, not currently available to your consciousness. And now it's pressing to become visible. Something, I suppose, that's profoundly part of who you really are, but not currently included in your life. It's what Jung would call part of your shadow – something you have chosen to turn away from."

Again the precise echo of Carla is unnerving.

"What does that mean?"

"Shadow? It's everything that, for one reason or another, we have repressed, banished from our lives."

"But if it's banished and not included in my life, why the hell would I dream of it?"

David gives a wry chuckle. "That's precisely why. Dreams are purposive, you know. They may be disturbing, but they come to bring us intimations of what's wrong or missing in our lives. Ultimately they mean well by us. They come to bring us greater wholeness. They use their own language, of course, but they can unquestionably open up a whole new world of possibilities for us, instead of leaving us imprisoned in our own mundane, narrow prejudices. They come because they know better than our conscious minds what we really need. And sometimes, if the psyche feels that the situation is getting out of control, they can have a sense of urgency."

I remember that intense feeling when I woke that night that my dream had actually *wanted* something of me. And suddenly I can feel the hairs on the back of my neck begin to rise.

"Like what?"

"Well, put simply, it sounds like that statue – or, at least, what the statue represents symbolically – is crying out to be included in your life. It clearly wants to break through and finally be noticed. That's why it suddenly appears almost simultaneously on two different levels of your psyche."

"You mean Aphrodite?"

David nods. "Yes, primarily. But perhaps, in different ways, as Carla seems to have suggested, Saturn and Pluto too."

"I think this is getting a bit beyond me." I hesitate. "But even if – just for the sake of argument – I were to accept what you say, what does Aphrodite actually mean in your so-called symbolic terms?"

David shrugs. "Well, you know the mythology as well as I do."

I keep silent. I've asked the question, but now I suddenly feel reluctant to hear the answer. After a while, when I don't respond, David goes on, "Well, she means beauty, of course. Sex too, obviously. The joy and pain of love in all its forms. But she also represents all things feminine, gentle, compassionate, imaginative, intuitive, beyond the reach of reason, outside the rational mind… Ring any bells?"

"Meaning?" I can hear the stubborn defensiveness in my own voice.

He stops and looks at me, and there's both warmth and exasperation in that look. "Bronson," he says quietly. "How much real love do you have in your life right now?"

I feel as if I've been winded by a low blow. For a while I can't speak. Quite irrationally I can feel tears welling, but I force them back. How am I supposed to answer such a question? David obviously sees my confusion.

"I'm not criticising you, you know," he says gently. "You're one of my oldest and dearest friends. We've been through a lot together. We could make a joke of this whole thing, of course, and just dismiss it. But I know that if I did that, if I colluded with you in trivialising it, I wouldn't serve you. And I would never forgive myself."

There's a level of seriousness here that we've never touched before.

"Forgive yourself for what?"

"For not being honest about what I feel is going on for you right now."

"Well, what *is* going on for me? That's why I wanted to talk to you, for Christ's sake. And now I'm more confused than ever."

David looks down for a moment, then up again and fixes me with his very blue eyes. We've been friends for a long time, but now we're suddenly in uncharted waters.

"You may not want to hear this, but my instincts are screaming at me that everything Carla said to you is precisely right."

"Meaning?"

"Meaning that you are at a crucial point in your life. Whether Carla saw it intuitively or astrologically doesn't really matter. But what she obviously did see was that your life is out of balance. That there are those deities that you have exiled and pushed into your shadow who are now demanding entry. And with them they will bring their own particular qualities into your life."

"Which are?"

"Put very simply: Pluto – darkness. Saturn – depth. And Aphrodite – love. So the real questions here are – Why have you excluded them? And what might happen if you let them into your life? What's the fear around that?"

The word fear springs loose memories of Sylvia's letter. *Where will your fear settle, I wonder...*

When I don't respond, David says, "Bronson, you're my dearest friend, but I'm terribly afraid that, if you don't take all this seriously, you may be heading for a fall."

I can hear the concern in his voice and I know he's trying to help. But I don't feel helped.

We are back at the Serpentine and the busy ducks. Only now their impassive, round-eyed stares seem to carry a trace of irony. I think I'm trapped in a situation where everyone seems to get the joke, except me.

*

Back at my desk I feel restless and ill at ease. If I had hoped for some tacit support from David for the world as I know it, I certainly haven't got it. Instead I feel like a man trying to balance between two rowing boats in a heavy sea. And right now they are moving further and further apart. My fractious mood seems to infect Zoe, who is at her most waspish and irritable. David's unwillingness to share my views has certainly set me thinking. Is it just conceivable, as he and Carla both seem to be indicating, that there really is some kind of parallel world to the one I inhabit, at least in some symbolic sense? A world with different laws and different lattices of connection? Might there really be a hidden undersong to life that I have so far entirely missed? It all seems quite beyond me. We had touched too, before we parted, on Sylvia's letter, but only lightly. If I'm really honest, there's far too much rawness there for me to want to go deeper. Carla's ironic comment keeps echoing in my head – *Adept at turning away*. Away from what exactly? From things that are unpleasant? Well, why the hell not? Who wouldn't?

I sit upstairs in my office brooding. I toss letters aside, shuffle paper, refuse – to Zoe's growing frustration – to take phone calls. Downstairs the door bell rings, followed by a hum of voices from the hall. Then my telephone buzzes. Irritably, I pick it up.

"It's Alexis Koromilas."

I feel disorientated. "On the phone?"

"No, not on the phone," she says impatiently. "He's *here*. He's going to lunch nearby and just thought he would drop in. Shall I let him come up?"

But her question is forestalled by the heavy thud of the stairs being taken two at a time and the boom of Alexis's voice.

"*Kalimera! Kalimera*, Bronson *mou*."

An unlikely angel he may be with his bulky frame and boxer's jaw, but at that moment, as he stands in the doorway, the light falling from behind him, he holds all the brief magic of an apparition. Without saying a word, he extracts an envelope from his jacket pocket and tips its contents onto my desk – a heavy iron key, slightly rusted, its finial decorated with a rosette pattern. I stare at it dumbly.

"Just go, Bronson," he says at last. "Just go, for fuck's sake."

THIRTEEN

The car wheels clatter on the metal bridge.

The Corinth Canal was completed by the French in 1872. Using picks and shovels, donkeys and a few primitive steam engines they cut through the isthmus and removed over a million tons of rock and earth in order to link the Ionian Sea to the Aegean. The megalomaniac emperor Nero had tried his hand at it two thousand years ago. Not surprisingly, he didn't get far.

The bridge that now spans this engineering miracle is a rickety iron affair that looks as if it might have been hastily thrown across by British sappers as part of an impromptu invasion. As I gaze down through the rusted iron latticework at the thin pencil of water a hundred feet below it looks absurdly narrow, barely wide enough to take a large fishing boat; though at its western end I can see a small steamer disgorging into the Ionian Sea. At this moment the entire length of the canal is flamed scarlet by the setting sun.

Alexis had advised me not to risk the unpredictable boat trip from Piraeus along the coast of the Peloponnese. "The island's small and less than a mile off the mainland," he explained, "so the boat often doesn't bother going down that far if there aren't enough passengers. It's much safer to rent a car at the airport and drive. It's a bit of a long haul, but it's a whole lot better than waiting days for a boat that never shows up."

I hope he's right. It's already seven thirty. My flight from London was delayed by three hours and now I am facing a gruelling drive in the dark, mostly on unpaved roads.

Shortly after the bridge the road divides. The right fork is the main highway from Athens across the northern Peloponnese to the busy port of Patras on the west coast. I swing over and take the small turning to the left. Instantly I am in another world. The roar of the traffic ceases. The road here is little more than a single track, snaking down towards the sea. Vegetation encroaches energetically from both sides. To my right rises a dense forest of pines. As soon as I reach the first shingled cove, I pull the car over and step out. Dusk is falling. From above comes the sweet resinous scent of pines. In the gulf ahead of me four small islands, smooth as turtle backs, hump blackly out of the water. The silence throbs in my ears. And suddenly something that David had said as we parted that morning at the Connaught comes back to me:

"Law suits, police, prison! Christ, Bronson, how the hell did we get *here*? Tell me that! Okay, you're rich now and I'm a respected scholar, but don't you think we both lost something important somewhere along the way?" Then he had given me a desperate-eyed look. "Remember Greece, Bronson? *Remember Greece?* What the hell happened to it all?" And, without another word, he had turned and disappeared into the hotel. And with those words ringing in my head, a trapdoor of memory swings open.

We had been eighteen and come with rucksacks and a copy of *The Colossus of Maroussi*, Henry Miller's ecstatic (and probably drug-fuelled) account of his pre-war visit to Greece. We had hitched and trained our way across France, down through Italy, taking in the obligatory sights – Florence, Venice, Sienna, Rome, Naples. Then across to the harsh, barren heel of Apulia and the grimy ferry port of Brindisi.

As we boarded the boat that night under the glare of arc lights, amongst the growl and shuffle of trucks, I felt I was leaving behind not just a country, but a whole continent. The sense of separation was total. Ahead lay only the unknown. We unrolled our mattresses on the top deck, uncorked a bottle of wine and eventually fell into a deep sleep under the spread of stars, as the ferry pushed out into the Adriatic.

The next morning I woke to the shudder of the steel deck under me as the engine changed note. The dawn sky was metal-grey and bleached. Half drugged with sleep and the after-effects of the wine, I threw aside my thin covering and staggered to the rail. And stared in shock at the little town of Corfu. It was as if my eyes had been washed clean in sleep. Narrow-fronted houses, pastel-coloured and ochre-tiled, tumbled down to the sea. Above them rose a church tower with an umber Turk's-cap dome and, arcing behind it all, an amphitheatre of hills furred green with olive and ilex. In the bay lay three small islands, spiked with cypresses, and between them the sea stretched black like a skin. Somewhere in the distance a donkey was braying. Nothing moved as the ferry nosed its way in.

I had marvelled at Italy, at the folded hills and ordered vines of Tuscany, at the martial planes and towering umbrella pines of Campania, at the pearl-white light of Venice. But nothing had prepared me for the shock of this first sight of Greece. Nothing had forewarned me of a light so pure, so crystalline that it washed clean my mind. It was as if I had lived my entire life under water and only now was I finally coming up to breathe the air. Yet, despite the newness, despite the shock and sense of wonder, there was a strange feeling of familiarity, a haunting sense of arriving for the first time at a destination I had always known. And a voice, insistently and illogically, repeating in my head, "*I am home… I am home…*" In a country on which I was yet to set foot.

All day, as we headed south, threading our way between the scattered islands – Meganisi, Lefkada, Kefalonia, Homeric Ithaca – the names reverberated like music – and the wild north-west coast of mainland Greece, towards our destination of the port of Patras, I stood at the rail, transfixed, not eating, scarcely drinking, drunk with the light and the newness of the vision.

For the light was everywhere. It sculpted every rocky cove and headland, illuminated every tree and slow-moving figure. It drew the darkness from the sea and bleached the sky. I gazed at the landscape – at the barren flanks of the mountains, the scrub covered hills, the tiny white villages bedded on the shingle, shaded by planes and eucalyptus – and the landscape seemed to gaze back and see me. And, strangest of all, what I felt in this harsh, unforgiving place, raked by the midday sun, was not lack or barrenness, not fear of want, but a sense of abundance, as if the land hid some secret spring within itself. No matter how harsh the conditions, how poor the vegetation, how arid the climate, how fierce the sun, here there would always be enough. Enough food, enough drink, enough light. *Enough love*. Greece was a promise of sanity. Even then I could feel some thread in my fate being plucked.

As I twist my way down the rocky spine of the Peloponnese, I pass through a landscape that is largely deserted, except for tiny villages looming up in the headlights – three, four whitewashed houses, squat and tiled, low doorways, animal pens and the occasional wild-eyed dog caught in the headlights – and then I am out again in the darkness, the rocks and olive groves spooling past my peripheral vision.

Hour after hour I keep myself awake by recalling Alexis's instructions: "You do understand there's no electricity, don't you? Just candles and some gas lights." For a moment he had looked uncharacteristically anxious, as if having second thoughts about his offer.

"That's fine," I had reassured him. "It sounds romantic."

"There's a gas cooker, a gas fridge. You'll have to fire them up, I'm afraid. There's… water from a cistern that collects the rain off the roof, a cleaning lady from the village who probably never comes. So it may be dirty…" I was beginning to get the point. "And it's very isolated. You can only get to the house by boat." Again that flicker of concern. "Of course," he added with a meaningful look, "if you take someone with you, it could be idyllic."

I smiled. "No. Just me – and some books."

He shook his head in wonder. "Christ, you must be a closet hermit! Personally I go crazy after twenty-four hours. After thirty-six I take the dinghy and go to the village just to talk to the fishermen, and after forty-eight I'm on my way back to Athens. I guess I'm not cut out for the monastic life. But it *is* beautiful," he had added, as if to reassure me. "And you'll get a complete rest. That's for sure."

Alexis told me of a naval battle fought in one of the bays beside the house during the Peloponnesian War in four hundred and something B.C. Dozens of boats sunk, hundreds of people drowned in the bay right beside the house. Sometimes fishermen pull things up in their nets: iron swords, bronze spear points, that sort of thing… I had felt an odd stirring at the base of my neck. "Because of that, local legend has it that the island is haunted."

"Ever seen any ghosts?"

Alexis harrumphed dismissively. "Only the ones staggering home late from the *taverna* after too much ouzo." Then he added again, as if for assurance, "You do understand there's no light?"

Why was he so worried? It sounded Spartan, romantic. No light was fine by me. At least for a few days.

It is nearly midnight by the time the car coasts down the rough slope to a flat, open parking space. The swivelling headlights illuminate a stand of poplars and a small white chapel, barrel-roofed with a tiny cross on top.

"It's less than a mile from the mainland. There are a couple of boats; they call them sea-taxis. Actually they're converted fishing caiques." The way to signal was to open the church door; then someone would come across from the island to fetch you. "If you arrive in the dark, of course, you can try flashing the headlights, but if it's late there may be no one around – and there's no hotel for miles. So you'll need to arrive in good time, or else be lucky…"

I take my case and the few bags of provisions I had bought at the airport and walk in the direction of a faint orange glow I can see. As it happens I am lucky. The glow turns out to be a small boat with the roughly painted words, WATER TAKSI illuminated on the side of its cabin. A heavy dew has come down and my feet slither on the wet timbers of the rickety jetty. My senses are hit by the first sharp tang of the sea. From below me comes the soft suck and slap of the water, interspersed with the deep even growl of someone snoring contentedly.

A dark figure lies stretched out in the stern of the little boat, asleep. I cough theatrically, but he stays motionless. So, lacking other options, I drop my bag noisily onto the deck and step aboard. Slowly the figure uncoils itself, sits up and rubs its eyes. In the dim light I can just make out his face, long and thin, harlequin-like, with heavy brows and a thick mat of black hair.

I point into the darkness. "*Conchili*," I try, naming the house. He looks blank. This could be difficult. "*To spiti Koromilas*." Alexis's name seems to register. He nods and, without a word, clambers uncertainly to his feet. He unties the rope and tosses it on the deck, then disappears into the wheel house. A moment later there's a cough and shudder as the engine kicks into life, the light snaps off and we are moving out into the open sea.

Across the water the lights of a small village appear, then vanish behind some invisible headland. I turn to look back, but there is nothing behind us now but darkness. Only the pale wash fanning out marks our passage in the void. For several minutes we seem to float, as if suspended in space. I have the strange sensation of sliding, directionless, slipping across the surface of the oil-smooth sea. Aware too of an acute sense of separation. Strangely I remember the ancient Greek belief that the souls of the dead cannot cross water.

Then, without warning, the sweet, sharp smell of pines comes through the dark at us. Instantly the driver cuts back the engine. The boat slows, then rocks gently forward on the stern wave. He stoops and picks something off the deck. The beam of the powerful flashlight sweeps right and left. I can see only an expanse of rocky shore stained by tides, and above it a sharp rise dense with pines and a thick tangle of undergrowth. A tiny, white chapel flanked by cypresses, stands on a low promontory to our right. The boatman angles the flashlight down. The water dissolves, leaving us suspended, as if on a sheet of glass. Below us is a strange lunar world of sand and jagged rocks, studded with dense black and purple spiny urchins. A startled crab, caught in the beam, scuttles for safety and buries itself in a soft swirl of sand. Slowly the driver guides the boat up against the shore with his outstretched foot. I clamber out unsteadily and he unceremoniously tosses my bags after me.

"*Posso?*" I ask.

He holds up eight stubby fingers.

"Where's the house?"

He shrugs and gestures up the slope with a curt lift of his chin. I look around. There's no sign of any habitation. He might as well be dumping me on a desert island.

"Where's the house?" I repeat. "*Pou eine to spiti?*"

He eyes me morosely, as if I've asked him to give up some closely guarded local secret. Then he picks up the torch and flashes it up the slope and, for a moment, I catch a glimpse of roof tiles above the topmost branches of the pines. Satisfied, I hand over the money. Without a word, he reverses, spins the boat around and opens the throttle wide, kicking up a cloud of glowing phosphorous under the stern. The beat of the engine slowly fades until he rounds the headland and is gone and the sound is swallowed up by the silence, leaving me in total darkness.

I stand for a long while trying to orientate myself. And only then I realize it isn't silent at all. It's *noisy*! Noisy as hell. And the noise seems to come from everywhere and nowhere at once, surrounding me with great waves of sound swelling and falling. The sound of a million cicadas. But then something very strange happens. The sound seems to dip, then totally disappear and I am surrounded by a deep, almost subaqueous silence. I suppose it's the same sensation of silence that people feel who live beside the constant booming of the ocean. And I have then the strangest feeling that something of the island's spirit has just entered me. And, despite the heat, I shiver.

Above me the night is clear but moonless. The sky is bitumen coloured, studded with stars. To my left the Milky Way spreads like a huge banner across the heavens. But it's little use to me down here. I can't see a thing. *There's no electricity. No light...* In the safety of London, Alexis' words had conjured up a romantic vision of solitude. But now I understand. No light means no light *anywhere*. Not from the flick of a switch or a crescent moon, not from the orange glow of a distant town, or the window of some isolated cottage. Here is an ancient darkness severing me from the world, so total it feels as if my eyes have been bandaged. As if the darkness is *inside* me. Tentatively I stretch out my hand. *I can't see it!* For a moment an illogical panic flickers and, like a man waking from a nightmare, I touch into some kind of swelling prehistoric fear that this unyielding dark might go on *for ever*.

Then my logic reasserts itself and I begin blundering up the slope, cursing my over-fertile imagination and my failure to bring a torch. At first it seems easy. The rock beneath my feet gives way to a soft mulch of pine needles as the ground begins to rise. But soon I run into a thick tangle of scrub and undergrowth. Wiry brambles tug at my clothes and soon I'm completely stuck, like some animal trapped in a thicket. Thorns as hard and sharp as nails rake my hands as I try to clear a path and I can feel blood begin to ooze. Then finally I'm free and start forward again, but now I catch my foot, stumble and hit my head hard on a low branch, spilling my belongings in the dark. I slide down and lean back against the tree trunk. I can feel the sharp ridges of the bark pressing through my drenched shirt. I sit for a moment, breathing heavily. I feel ridiculous, thrashing around here in the dark like a trapped animal. After all, I can't be more than thirty yards from the house. All the same, I'm aware of a faint, illogical drumbeat of panic in the darkness.

I sit for a while longer, allowing my breathing to slow. Gradually I begin to distinguish the black tree trunks embossed against the faint, light shimmer of the sea. Then the mesh of branches above me comes clear, dotted with stars. Heartened by this fractional return of sight, I get to my feet, gather up my things, and begin again, this time more carefully, one hand outstretched, feeling my way. Gradually the ground flattens out. And then I hit my shin on something hard and sharp. Reaching out, I can feel what must be the edge of a stone terrace. Above me rises the dark outline of the house. I fumble my way to the door.

At first the lock refuses to give. The heavy iron key Alexis had given me in London is rusty and looks as if it hasn't been used for years. As I twist it sharply, I pray it won't snap, leaving me marooned here in the dark. But eventually it grates, the door squeaks open on unoiled hinges and I pass through. Inside, the air is warm and inert, smelling faintly of mould. The place must have been shut up for months. For a moment I think I hear a rustling sound. Surely my imagination? Then the silence crowds around me again, pressing on my ears. Tentatively I begin to inch my way forward until I touch the rounded edge of what seems to be a table. A thick layer of dust feathers my fingertips. It's eerie, this slow-motion apprehension of the world only by touch. Suddenly there's a scuttling movement in the darkness. Instinctively I jump back, my right arm flailing. Something crashes to the floor and shatters. The sound echoes like gunshot in the silence.

Slowly I begin to move forward again, through an open doorway into another room. My outstretched hand explores a smooth stone surface, then a basin, taps. Either a bathroom or a kitchen. I brush against the rough edge of something instantly recognizable. I pick up the small cardboard box and shake it, and heave a sigh of relief to hear it rattle in response.

The first match flares, then snaps and gutters on the stone floor. I try again and the second one yields enough light to show a stack of candles piled at the far end of a wooden shelf. And soon, as the candle wicks catch and blossom, pushing back the enveloping darkness, I see that I am standing in a high-ceilinged room, sparsely equipped as a kitchen. There is a quiet plop as the ancient cast-iron faucet looses a single drop of water into the huge stone sink.

FOURTEEN

When I wake it is as if from a drugged sleep. I lie on my back and allow my eyes to take in the room. It contains only a small blue cupboard, a white table, a battered wooden chair with a rush seat and an indistinct sepia photograph in a black frame. To the right of the bed is a low table. The previous night's candle has cascaded onto its rough surface leaving a generous rosette of wax. There are two large windows, one opposite me, the other to my left. The slatted shutters are letting in hard bars of sunlight that stencil themselves on the wall beside me. Outside the cicadas are already at full throttle. My mind feels strangely fuzzy. Too tired even to undress or find sheets, I had apparently stretched out fully clothed and pulled a blanket over me, and now I can feel its coarse prickle against my bare feet.

Slowly I begin to piece together the events of my arrival. In the clear light of day there's something embarrassingly childish about the way my imagination had so completely outrun the plain facts, like a six year-old turning shadows into monsters. After all, I had simply arrived at a strange house in the dark, stumbled up a wooded slope and had trouble unlocking the door. It's hardly the stuff of nightmares. Yet some of that unease seems to be with me still and the harsh daylight feels less reassuring than it should. I shake myself, sit upright and begin to inventory more details.

Suspended across one corner of the ceiling is an enormous cobweb, liberally studded with black flies. It hangs there like a diaphanous, decorative swag, some huge spider's winter larder. I feel an odd flicker of anxiety. All my senses seem to be on high alert this morning. As a child I had been petrified of spiders. Their black akimbo legs, their malevolent stillness and explosive movements had seemed to concentrate everything that was malign and threatening in my small world. And even now, deep down, some irrational traces of arachnophobia still linger. I throw back the blanket and swing my feet to the floor.

Cleaning the house turns out to be hard work in the building heat. It's like bursting into an undiscovered attic. The place doesn't seem to have been touched for years. Cobwebs and mice droppings are everywhere. As I throw back the shutters and the sun pours in, the light is thickly speckled with dust. Some of the furniture has been shrouded with bed sheets and looks eerily like snowdrifts in the hard light. It takes almost two hours to get the place in order, but once done the house looks surprisingly grand for what Alexis had called a 'hunting lodge'. It is whitewashed throughout, with grey stone floors, generous windows and high, well-proportioned rooms. There are even a few delicate details, like the antique porcelain door knobs and finger-plates on the doors, as if some wife or daughter had been allowed in at the last minute to add a touch of softness. As I go out on to the terrace to empty the battered dustpan of the last filaments of the giant spider's web, I suddenly have the eerie feeling of being watched. It's a feral bristling at the back of my neck. I swing round. Through the pines to either side I can see the sun shimmering on the water. The sky is a deep cloudless blue. Nothing else. I stand there, surveying the landscape, feeling foolish and uneasy.

The house stands on a headland that rises some thirty feet above the sea, clasped between two bays. All around the house, as everywhere that I can see on the island, the land is thickly wooded with pines. The small bay to the west is deep but narrow, ending in a curve of sand and a grove of carefully tended olives, hemmed in by the ubiquitous pines. The bay to the east is much broader and seems to contain two small dwellings. This presumably was the site of the ancient sea battle, the genesis of all the local superstitions. Directly ahead, to the north, across a strait perhaps a mile wide, is the bulk of the mainland, deeply indented with coves and rearing up into barren lavender-coloured mountains.

Eventually I make my way down to the small chapel I had glimpsed the night before. It stands at the tip of my promontory, just clear of the sea. The door gives under my touch. Inside it is cool and dark, smelling of old smoke and incense. A rough wooden iconostasis is decorated with primitive scenes of St. George on horseback spearing a dragon. Saint George looks heraldic and implacable in his silver armour and brightly coloured plumes. The recumbent dragon lies open-jawed and looking understandably glum. A carved wooden lectern holds an open copy of the bible and, beside it, an ornate brass stand supports a tray of sand spiked with slim, snuffed candles. Propped in one corner is a bucket and mop and a green plastic bottle. I stand for a while absorbing the protective silence.

At length, almost reluctantly, I open the door and step outside. Coming out of the darkness, the sunlight is blinding, the shrilling of the cicadas intense. I make my way along the rocky shore. The small house in the centre of the bay seems well tended but bolted and shuttered. There's a deep drift of pine needles against the base of the blue door. It must have been unoccupied for weeks, if not months. The second building turns out to be another chapel, with a small bulging apse and a tall cypress at each end, but this time locked and bolted.

I return to the house, realising that I am quite alone out here. The limpid beauty, the translucent sea, the sun, the azure sky, the silence are exactly what I had craved in the stress of the last weeks, exactly what Alexis had wished for me. But what I feel now, as I stand here surveying my island kingdom, isn't peace or relief at all, but an overwhelming sense of desolation and a huge echoing loneliness.

*

I stayed out at the house for five days. I spoke not a word and saw no one, except the occasional fishing boat setting its nets in the bay below me. The heat, the stillness, the silence, the constant drone of the cicadas seemed to produce in me a kind of trance. Slowly I began to feel as if I was poised between two worlds, not fully at home in either. Again and again, but most especially in the searing light of midday, something would flicker at the edges of my vision. But when I turned, nothing would be there. But still I felt not quite alone. It was as if *the whole place* was alive. And suddenly an archaic world peopled with daemons and nereids, satyrs and wood nymphs didn't seem quite so absurd after all. It felt as if cracks were starting to appear in the walls of my logic and other things were beginning to leak through. Was this what Carla had meant by 'The Other World'? Was there indeed a whole subtext to life that I had always missed? Was Elizabetta right that there are more things between heaven and earth than are dreamed of in my limited philosophy? And thoughts of Carla kept coming back to me.

At night mosquitoes droned in my ears and crawled across my body. By day armies of ants arrived within minutes to carry off any food I dropped. On the second morning I entered the kitchen to find a seething black trail winding its way through the open window, along the edge of the sink and under the lid of the sugar container. I flipped it open with a spoon. Inside a coiling mass heaved and swirled. I leapt back, threw the jar into the sink and turned on the water. Then I seized the broom and frantically battered the trail into extinction, feeling absurd even as I did it.

That night I dreamt of the spider. It crouched at the centre of its web, while I watched, frozen with terror. I woke sweating. And suddenly as I lay there, something surfaced that I knew was not a dream. I was four, maybe five years old, peering round the corner of a doorway, observing the world through the crack of light between door and jamb, listening to footsteps coming up the stairs. It was early morning and my parents were away. I trembled with excitement as the footsteps came closer. Then she appeared, naked, walking down the passage with a teacup in her hand. I was transfixed, terrified, as all the unexpected whiteness of her body contracted into that sprawl of black hair at her centre. It reached out to envelop me. For days I had been ill. And now, as I lay in the darkness sweating, every woman I had ever had, every woman I had ever desired, flooded my mind and crept over me. Every position, every variation and perversion, excited my body and ate at my spirit with a ferocious hyper-adolescent intensity, until I finally found solace in masturbation and drifted back into sleep.

The days continued still and calm, but the silence was oppressive. And my dreams were becoming frighteningly real. Stealthily they began to move beyond the borders of sleep. Whatever mechanism it was that had always separated imagination and reality, dream and waking, past and present seemed to be dissolving and something was starting to bleed through from the other side. There was a sense of quiet malevolence in this strange feeling, like a dry, mocking laugh that came from the woods around me. It was as if I had presumed in my naivety to know what Greece was all about, and now she was showing me a quite different face. *If you would know me*, she seemed to say, *then you must know this too.*

I tried to calm myself with logic – there was *nothing wrong* with the place. I was just tired. But the truth was that I was no longer quite master in my own house. Thoughts came and went now of their own volition, and when memories came, they were not the ones I wanted. Things half-forgotten and long forgotten were beginning to creep out from the shadows.

"Hold the little bugger down! We'll teach him to kick."

Then another voice. "You'll regret it if you fight, you little prick. We've all been through it. Think you're special do you? Get his belt open."

I struggled with all the ferocity of a cornered animal, got an arm free and lashed out. There was a grunt of pain as I connected. Then a hand across my face, trying to pinion me. With coiled force I wrenched my head free, twisted sideways, sank my teeth into flesh, heard a howl of agony.

"Christ, look what he's done. It's bleeding! Only girls bite, you little shit. We'll show you."

"Let's sink him," came another voice. Then a chorus of agreement and the room wheeled as I was carried spread-eagled along a green corridor and down narrow stairs. And half-way down, a frozen moment – my brother, four years older, gazing down at me. An exchange of voices. "He bit Carson. Look at the blood! We're going to sink him." I saw flickers of emotion as I pleaded silently, and then a dismissive shrug of the shoulders. "Oh, well then…" And down we went, along another passageway as terror engulfed me, the terror of a falling man whose last hand-hold has been severed. And then the unmistakable smell of the boot room, the sweat and dampness and the stale stench of rugby boots, the sound of running water, cold flagstones against my face, agony as my arms were forced up my back.

"Why's it called a Belfast sink?"

"Dunno. So's it's deep enough to drown a bloody Mick in, I suppose." A burst of laughter. " Is it full? Right, Tullis, we'll show you what you get for biting."

At first ice cold water pouring sulphurous up my nose and the myopic glassy view of the plughole. Then my ears pounding, my eyeballs swelling, my lungs searing… And then a terror beyond anything imaginable as I realised that no force of mine could sever that grip. I was a prisoner. I knew I was going to die.

I opened my eyes onto a strange white-washed room. A woman in a starched uniform was standing over me, her face creased with worry. The sensation of my wet hair stuck to the pillow. The smell of antiseptic and soap.

"He's come round," she said with a long exhalation of breath. And then the headmaster staring down, his head, strangely disembodied, seemed to float above his tweed jacket. His black hair parted in the centre, black-rimmed glasses like a deathshead. His face devoid of emotion.

"That's all right then," he said at length. "You'll be okay. It was just a silly prank that got out of hand. Those responsible have already been dealt with. So we'll say no more about it, eh? Never complain, never explain. That's how we do things here. You'll be all right," he repeated, almost as if to reassure himself.

But where to go from here? I remembered thinking. I knew what would have happened to those who had been 'dealt with'. And who was going to protect me from their reprisals?

The first person I saw when I emerged from the sanatorium the next morning was my brother, his face etched with guilt, but his manner filled with bravado. "Nothing I could do," he said casually. "It's a school custom for new ticks. And if you bite, that's what you get. The thing is, from now on don't show fear. If you show fear, start to blub, tell the parents – anything like that, they'll make your life hell."

And that was how I learnt to survive. You didn't get brownie points at an English boarding school for being sensitive. So I learnt revenge by being tougher, better, brighter than the thickies who had nearly drowned me, harder on the rugger pitch, quicker on the sprint track. Always hiding what I was feeling. Never trusting, never giving any advantage, always keeping at bay, by force, by cunning, by charm, by intelligence, by treachery or bribery, by any means at all, that overwhelming terror of powerless suffocation.

When I emerged from this vision, I was trembling. All my life I had excised those feelings of panic and terror, of utter helplessness and humiliation. And now they had come back to claim me, as if some separating door had been kicked flat and thirty years later I was engulfed by their chaos, all the darkness I had shut out suddenly roaring back in. Somehow, in broad daylight, I had strayed into the dream world and I couldn't help recalling Carla's warning, "Things you have chosen to turn away from…"

That was when I knew I had to get out, had to make contact with the real world again, to reestablish my own clear identity. Perhaps I was no more cut out for the monastic life than Alexis. Perhaps he too could sense something strange in this place. Perhaps the stories of the haunted island weren't so fanciful after all.

Either way, as the day cooled and evening began to settle, I managed to rouse myself from the lethargy that had engulfed me. I took the small rusty outboard from the storeroom at the back of the house and walked down the pine-needled track to the small cove where the dinghy was riding at anchor. After three pulls the ancient engine spluttered into life and moments later I was chugging out into the broad bay.

As the shore receded, the headland seemed to slide back into its correct proportion. It was after all just a wooded promontory clasped between two bays, with pine-clad hills rising behind and, opposite, the dark mountains of the Peloponnese. Nothing more. And, as my sense of logic began to erase the strange cubist chaos in which I had been engulfed for the last four days, I felt a deep surge of relief.

FIFTEEN

From where I'm sitting at a rickety *taverna* table under a sagging bamboo awning, I can take in pretty much the whole village of Katakolos. It consists of a line of low whitewashed and ochre-tiled cottages, strung along a broad crescent of shingle held between two wooded headlands. The bay is not deep and, to the left, a rough concrete jetty has been constructed to protect the small fishing boats from the northerlies. To add a touch of grandeur someone has placed an antique cast-iron streetlamp at the far end. The island seems to have no real roads, since even the harbour front is paved only by a stretch of loose shingle that disappears at each end into olive groves.

Trusting to local knowledge, I have settled on the better frequented of the two tavernas. The other one, across the bay from here, seems almost deserted and I can see the owner occasionally pop out like a figure from a Swiss cuckoo clock to scan the horizon anxiously for possible punters. But over here the place is quite crowded. The clientele consists entirely of men in their fifties and upwards. They cluster in small groups drinking *raki* or playing backgammon. They are mostly small, wiry figures with deeply sunburnt faces like pickled walnuts and the gnarled, arthritic hands of fishermen. Apparently women are *personae non gratae* in this establishment and the young men must have fled to menial jobs in Athens or

Thessalonika, or to be unskilled waiters in the fleshpots of Mykonos.

I had expected surprised stares when I entered. Alexis had told me that foreigners are a rarity down here. After all, there aren't any hotels and only a couple of houses that will take in visitors. But instead, a few heads had glanced up and nodded in casual welcome and someone had called out "Kosta!" to summon the owner, who came lumbering out from the dark interior. He's a lugubrious but friendly enough giant of a man with coal black eyes and a ragged Mexican-style moustache. And now he has laid in front of me a large glass of ouzo, a plate of grilled octopus, a basket of warm crusted bread and a small cracked saucer containing olives.

The clack-clack of the backgammon has a hypnotic quality. From the far end of the jetty comes the rhythmic slap of an octopus being tenderized on the concrete. With the ouzo moving smoothly through my system, I can feel myself begin to relax. The last few days have been a temporary aberration brought on by too much stress, a bit like being caught in one of those childhood nightmares when you know you are dreaming but struggle to wake. But sitting here now with the taste of anise on my tongue, I sense the nightmare receding until it's nothing more than a distant mirage.

The whole place is a time warp and it's strangely soothing to see how little has changed here since the days of my earliest visits to Greece in the sixties. It's like sitting in one of those painstakingly detailed mockups you see in folk museums, showing what life was like in a crofter's cottage in nineteenth century Scotland. The rough paper tablecloths are snapped in place by enormous elastic bands; the squat glass tumblers look thick enough to withstand a minor explosion; the heavy salt and pepper pots (probably empty) have the usual red and green plastic caps. The chairs are wooden and rush-seated. Their thin rickety legs are precariously splayed and held together with thick industrial wire. The seats are excessively narrow, clearly designed for a generation of small-boned working people on enforced low-calorie diets, long before the arrival in Greece of McDonalds and the take-away pizza. Even with my relatively slim frame I can feel the hard wooden edges digging uncomfortably into my buttock bones.

"They're nearly all plastic now."

The voice, which is deep and heavily accented, comes from somewhere over my right shoulder. Since I'm presumably the only person here who speaks English, this bizarre remark must be aimed at me. I start to turn but, at the same moment, the figure steps into view. He's probably in his late sixties (although it's hard to tell with these weather-beaten, corrugated faces), thicker set than most of the men around me, with a grey stubbled cranium and an extravagant tuft of white hair protruding above each ear like a pair of miniature wings. He's dressed in baggy khaki trousers and a much darned, faded blue shirt. He has a ragged grey moustache and his slender nose veers off to one side, as if it has been broken in a fight. At first sight he looks like another of the local fishermen, with his clothes freshly washed after a night out at sea. But there's something not quite right about him. My obsessive art dealer's eye has already registered that his hands are far too well kept to have spent a lifetime hauling nets, and his eyes are a clear light blue – a rarity down here in the southern Aegean. If anything, with his high cheekbones he looks more Slavic than Greek. Also, of course, he seems to speak English. By now he is standing behind the chair opposite me.

"May I join you?" he asks in that totally unabashed way the Greeks have.

I hesitate, trying to concoct an acceptable excuse; but clearly there isn't one. The Greeks are big on hospitality. It's a code of honour instilled in their chromosomes over millennia. They even have a genial god for it – *Zeus Xenios*, the god of strangers. I have seen anxious and baffled foreigners trying to buy vegetables on remote Greek islands by simply holding out their hands filled with change like importunate children. And the vendor will only take precisely what they owe. Try that kind of naivety anywhere else around the Mediterranean and your palm will swiftly be emptied. On the other hand, I've had big-scale art dealings with Greeks over the years and they are always a nightmare – wily, suspicious and unreliable. But that's a different thing; that's commerce. This is hospitality, and in these small matters the Greeks are scrupulously honest, and that's because you're a wayfarer, a guest. To cheat you would bring dishonour, to refuse a place at the table unthinkable. So what else can I do?

But my complicated deliberations are, in any case, rendered unnecessary, because my mustachioed friend, presumably trusting in the protection of *Zeus Xenios*, is already settling into the chair opposite me. He takes two plastic pouches from his back pocket and lays them on the table.

"I mean the chairs," he goes on as if this were a perfectly normal line of conversation. "They're nearly all plastic nowadays." I stare at him. It's so odd, the way he has started talking about the chairs as if he has been reading my thoughts. "Only Kostas here keeps the old ones. Old Nikos over there," with a jerk of his head in the direction of the nearly empty *taverna* across the bay, "put in plastic ones last year. His son from Athens told him it would be good for business." He shakes his head mournfully and gives a low chuckle. "It was the best favour he ever did to Kostas. We all moved over here.

They're a bit uncomfortable, of course, hard on the arse. But they're what we're used to."

The ancient Greeks invented logical reasoning. But, in my experience, there has been considerable slippage in the meantime. Very few things in modern Greece seem to happen logically. They usually occur spontaneously, randomly, often hilariously and nearly always with a gleeful avalanche of chaos. But even by these standards, this opening salvo is bizarre. Who is this elderly man, who looks like a fisherman but clearly isn't, who has appeared out of nowhere and started on a totally random line of conversation in – despite the accent – nearly perfect English, as if we are old friends who have just been parted for an hour or two?

For a moment I wonder if I'm being set up. As the only English speaker on the island, is he the one who bores and torments any passing foreigner for the amusement of the locals? I glance discretely around, checking for sly grins or the first signs of wizened faces spluttering into their *raki* glasses. But the drinking and concentrated backgammon seem to be going on just as before. So perhaps he's simply the local wino, already high as a kite, venting his random thoughts to anyone who will listen.

At this moment Kostas appears with a tumbler half filled with ouzo and places it in front of my companion, who carefully takes a single cube of ice from the small metal bowl on the table, drops it into his glass, waits until the liquid begins to turn cloudy, then grasps the rim between his thumb and forefinger and swings it towards me.

"*Stiniassas!*" he says as we clink glasses. "*Kai kalos elthate stin Katakolo* – And welcome to Katakolos!" Then he downs half the glass and I get the sinking feeling that this is going to be a long night. He wipes his hand across his moustache and leans back in his chair.

"We Greeks say," he goes on in the tone of a man who has only just briefly been interrupted in the middle of a sentence, "that if you sleep under a fig tree in the heat of the day, the god Pan will come and drive you mad. Did you know that?"

This is getting more unhinged by the minute. Although, given my strange experiences over the last few days, the remark strikes an odd chord.

"No, I didn't. And does the god Pan put in frequent appearances on Katakolos?"

He gives me a hooded look to let me know he's quite aware of my attempted irony. Then he opens the plastic pouches and begins to roll a cigarette. Once licked and carefully sealed, he sticks it into his mouth and lights it. The whole operation has the feeling of being done for dramatic effect.

"The god Pan is supposed to have died in the reign of the Roman emperor Augustus on the island of Paxos." A long drag on the cigarette. "At any rate, that's what the Christians try to tell us. Are you a Christian?"

"Not so you'd notice."

"But you don't believe in the existence of Pan either?"

"Let's say I'd probably be a little sceptical."

"Then you shouldn't be," he says firmly. "Pan, Zeus, Aphrodite, Mars, even old Hades and Saturn – they all exist, you know. It's just that we've got them in our heads now, where we can't see them anymore. More's the pity. We've killed them off and stuffed them inside us, so we think they don't exist. Pah!" He blows out a contemptuous snort.

I'm starting to feel as if I'm caught in the middle of a play by Pinter. I don't really understand the dialogue, but something under the surface is beginning to create a rustling sense of unease; and the references to Hades, Saturn and Aphrodite are stirring uncomfortable memories of Carla. He's crazy, of course, mad as a hatter; but it's clear that, unless I'm going to stand up rudely and leave, I'm not going to get rid of him in a hurry. So, lacking better options, I decide to humour him.

"So you think we should honour the gods by slaughtering oxen and sheep and carving up the thigh bones right here on the quayside maybe? Burnt offerings in the *tavernas* and all that sort of thing?"

He gives me a long, sardonic look to let me know he's got the measure of me and takes a pull at his ouzo before replying.

"The one thing we should never do," he says slowly, "is to mock the gods. It doesn't pay."

I feel a flash of irritation. His apparent craziness has lured me into mocking him and now he's turned the tables. He's the one who's doing the condescending. I search for a suitably sharp response, but my wits seem to have deserted me. Probably the ouzo isn't helping.

He sits looking at me now with a kind of detached humour in his opaque blue eyes. "Anyhow," he says, "whether we've got the gods inside us or outside doesn't really matter. What matters is that we know they're there." Then he smiles, showing a strong line of uneven teeth, yellowed by nicotine. Two of the side ones, I notice, are missing. Suddenly he picks up his nearly empty glass and brandishes it above his head. "For such a conversation," he declares, "we need more ouzo. *Kosta mou!*" he calls over his shoulder. "*Ena karafaki!*"

He turns back to me. "So – you stay at the Koromilas house?"

"How do you know that?"

For some reason I don't like the idea of being watched in my solitude. And besides, how the hell *does* he know?

He drains his glass, then raises his eyes to mine. "You arrived by boat?"

"Of course. Is there any other way?"

He shrugs. "So I know. Everyone knows. Everyone in Katakolos knows when everyone comes and leaves. Everyone knows the Englishman is here. Everyone knows everything. It's a very simple system. That's why we don't have telephones."

He picks up the plastic pouches, carefully spreads the tobacco shreds into the slither of paper and begins rolling himself another cigarette. The pause gives me just enough time to regain my equilibrium.

"So what else do you know?"

"That you stay at the house alone. That you don't come to the village. The people here wonder about that."

"Oh, do they? And just what exactly do they wonder?"

He shrugs. "It's quiet out there. I know the place. Very quiet sometimes."

"So perhaps you wonder if I go mad sleeping under a fig tree at midday? Is that it?" I pick up my glass and regard him coolly over the rim. I don't appreciate being the centre of village gossip.

He stares back. "There are no fig trees at Conchili," he says. "But still I wonder."

For a moment I am silent. I feel absurdly outmanoeuvered. I had tried to make light of the superstition about the fig tree (and he's right – there aren't any at the house). But now I feel uneasy. It's as if this total stranger has looked into me with those piercing blue eyes and seen my inner swell of chaos of the last five days: the dreams and the alcohol, the fantasies. Even the masturbation. I recall the disappearing figure at the edges of my vision. Suddenly I feel watched.

At this moment Kostas arrives with a half-scale bottle of ouzo and another bowl of ice. My companion glances up at him, then indicates me with an extravagant flourish of his left hand across the table. "*Kosta mou*, allow me to introduce my very good English friend, Bronson…"

"How do you…?"

"And this," he goes on, totally ignoring me, "is Kostas the Bandit. He's Cretan – as you can tell by his piratical moustaches. The Cretans are bad people. Very bad. And all quite crazy." He taps the side of his head with his forefinger. "They drink *raki* like water, beat their women and rape their goats."

It's unclear if Kostas has understood any of this insane diatribe but, in any case, he smiles broadly and claps my companion on the back. "*Kalos anthropos*," he says. A good man. Then he rubs his hands on his well-worn apron and disappears again into the *taverna*.

"How do you know my name?" I insist. "Did you hear from Alexis?"

"Alexis?" For a moment he looks puzzled. "Ah, you mean Alexaki! A good man, but sadly he never comes here now. So now we all know each other's names. Alexaki, Kostas, Bronson and I – allow me to introduce myself – am Dinos."

I realise my persistence is going to get me nowhere, but at least I can start putting some questions back to him. In this crazy conversation any kind of logical answer would be a minor victory.

"Dinos what?"

He shrugs. "Just Dinos. Though people here don't call me that in any case."

"What do they call you?"

"*O psaras*."

"The *fisherman*?" I glance again at his well kept hands and neatly clipped nails resting on the paper tablecloth. "Is that true?"

"Is what true?"

"Are you a fisherman?"

"No." He smiles, then uncorks the bottle and pours us two enormous glasses of ouzo and drops a cube of ice into each.

"How is it at the Koromilas house?"

"Quiet."

"Ah. So that is why you have the Greek disease. I see it."

"And what the hell is the Greek disease, if I may ask?" I can feel the ouzo loosening my tongue.

He takes a long draw on his cigarette before replying. The evening is coming down now. The mountains of the mainland are hidden in shadow. The lights around the bay begin to wink through the darkness.

"Homesickness," he says at length. "The Greek disease is homesickness."

"*Homesickness?* I came here for a quiet holiday, precisely to get away from London and too many people. And what's more, I'm having a good time," I lie. "So I'm hardly likely to be feeling homesick."

"Homesickness," he says slowly, "is not a matter of geography. It is a condition of the soul. A yearning. The ancient Greeks called it *pothos*. They even had statues of it. It may happen anywhere, of course. But here in Greece most especially. Here, in these quiet places, where you can sense the presence of the gods, you always yearn for more. That is why we Greeks are melancholic, even when we appear merry. You hear it in our music. You can sense it in our dances. You see it in our faces." He sips his ouzo, then goes on quietly, "And sometimes even foreigners – special kinds of foreigners that is – feel it too."

Before I can think of a response he's off on another riff.

"Do you know, there's a tribe in Africa who say that we are

born with four eyes?" Christ, this is getting unhinged. "Two are open at birth and two closed, and the closed ones are normally only opened at death. But…" He raises one index finger, slightly crooked with arthritis, and stares at me, "some few people are born with all four eyes open. No one knows why. They are the ones who can see more, because they are closest to the Other World. This can be very dangerous, because then they are also born close to death. So either that person will die young, or they must learn to see clearly with all four eyes open." He sips his ouzo. "Very clever people those Africans," he murmurs almost to himself. "Very clever." He lapses into silence. I notice, even through my fog of alcohol, that he is studying me now with an odd intensity. Suddenly he jabs out a finger.

"Where did you get that scar?"

Instinctively my hand reaches up to touch the white diagonal line above my right eyebrow. "Oh, that… Just a childhood accident."

He nods. Then, without warning, he rises, as if he has just remembered something and picks up the plastic pouches. "I must leave you now," he says rather formally. "It has been a great pleasure. We shall meet again."

And, before I can gather myself, he turns, rests his hand for a moment on my shoulder and vanishes behind the corner of the *taverna*, leaving me staring at the empty chair and the darkness gathering on the waterfront.

*

Not surprisingly I wake with a raging hangover. Ouzo does that to you. Hoping to clear my head, I wrap a towel around my waist, go down to the sea and dive in. The water closes over me. Below, the seabed is glass clear, the urchins an iridescent, purple-grey on the rocks. In that silent place everything is still and calm and, for a moment, I feel at peace. But, as I break surface, my mind is again on a rolling boil. I float for a while, allowing the swell to lift and lower me, the water fizzing quietly in my ears. Then I climb out and lie naked on the rocks in the early sun and try to order my mind.

The little whitewashed village had reassured me with its echoes of the innocent Greece of my youth. At least, at first. But that odd conversation in the *taverna* is reverberating with a force totally out of proportion to its significance. After all, it had been just a casual drinking session with an alcoholic and slightly deranged Greek. It's the kind of random encounter that can happen at any time in these islands. I've experienced such evenings before. They invariably end in jovial back-slapping and protestations of life-long friendship, followed by a bad hangover. But even the hangover doesn't explain the sense of dislocation I am feeling this morning. Who is he anyway, this bizarre fisherman who apparently isn't a fisherman at all, with his self-conscious Greek accent and his near perfect English syntax? He certainly didn't learn that kind of grammar in a fishing boat in Katakolos, or even driving a taxi in Chicago or the Bronx. And what of that odd feeling that he had somehow been expecting me?

Our whole crazy conversation about gods and fig trees and 'the Greek disease' had been totally random, full of non-sequiturs. But still, something in it is jolting my mind. Randomly my thoughts jump to Carla, her clear Italian voice echoing in that Renaissance library high in the hills of *Le Marche*, her references to fate and the Other World. And then Sylvia, leaving me the legacy of her excoriating letter. Each had been saying quite different things. And yet somehow, in some way I can't quite grasp, saying something very similar.

And now my mind, as if with an obstinate will of its own, begins to wander wider still. To my mother lying, plugged in and wired up, in that hospital bed in the last hours of her life, constructing strange fictions, as if all the anchors of time and place and logic had been loosed on the seabed of her mind and random debris floated wildly to the surface, coalescing in stories of events that had never happened in places she had never been. As if, in some crazy way, she was remembering the future. Or Shakespeare's lunatics – Poor Tom, mad Lear raging on the heath, crazed Ophelia – their ramblings incoherent, pure madness. But somehow scratching at some truth below the skin of logic. In a place where the mind doesn't care to go.

And, as I lie there with these thoughts swirling randomly through my head, I realise with shock that I am actually afraid of staying another night out here alone. Not physically afraid, but afraid of my own thoughts. Afraid of where my mind might lead me.

But what did you expect? A mocking voice asks in my head. *What did you expect it would be like out here alone on a wild Greek island, with no light and no company and no noise except for the rustling of the wind? Romantic? Peaceful? Idyllic? No, I'll tell you what it's like. It's like having your brain dumped in a steamer and suddenly all the pores open up simultaneously. You can't choose your thoughts or your feelings any longer. They come and assault you randomly and at will. And all the things you didn't want to know, all the memories you thought you had obliterated, all the fears you had turned away from, start to come back out of the shadows to claim you.*

That crazy fisherman had said that we have the gods inside us now. Is that what this is – suddenly I have the gods rampaging in my head, out of control?

I get up and wrap the towel around my hips. Flight is the obvious course. Pack up, go back to England. Get involved in real life again. Gracefully accept defeat. But there's a streak of obstinacy in my character, probably the legacy of ten stoical years in an English boarding school. Never give up, never surrender. No matter what the cost. No matter how absurd or brutal or self-destructive the process. So, in the end, rather than a humiliating retreat, I settle for a qualified withdrawal.

PART TWO

When an inner situation is not made conscious it will appear outside as fate.
C. G. Jung

O the mind, mind has mountains; cliffs of fall Frightful, sheer, no-man-fathomed.
Gerard Manley Hopkins

SIXTEEN

As I round the last rocky outcrop, the road flattens out. Ahead of me stands a stone monument. The large black cross that rises above it is sharply silhouetted against the gunmetal sky. On an instinct I pull the car over. The wheels thud down from the tarmac onto the loose shingle. I cut the engine and step out.

I am high up and the air is thin and keen. I reach into the back seat and drag out a sweater. As I pull it over my head, I get a sudden burst of claustrophobia. I must have closed my eyes for less than a second as I dragged the wool over my face but suddenly I feel light-headed, as if my blood pressure has dipped then soared. Despite the cold I am sweating. I lean back against the car for a moment and wait for my breathing to steady.

I have spent the last four days in the wild southern Peloponnese, visiting obscure archaeological sites, staying in ramshackle hostels, eating rabbit *stifado* and drinking homemade *raki* with the owners. Above all, trying to regain my sense of the normal after the chaos of the previous days out at the house. And, by and large, I seem to have succeeded. At least until now, for something about this place feels strangely sinister.

Above me the shoulder of the hill is scattered with outcrops of rock and tumbled boulders, speckled with low prickly scrub and clumps of gorse. Within days the early summer will presumably penetrate even into these barren uplands, bringing splashes of colour, scenting the air with rosemary and thyme. But today there is only cold and grey.

Feeling slightly unsteady, I bypass the monument and walk to the edge of the escarpment. Far below me a huge plain is laid out like a relief map, the bare slide of upland rock gradually giving way to cultivation: at first olives, the ordered lines of silver green unmistakable, then lower down the darker tones of orange and lemon orchards and the dark spikes of cypresses. Flashes of silver suggest poplars, and a brilliant emerald swathe meandering across the valley floor shows the passage of a river and its lush vegetation. I count three widely spaces villages, suggested only by the blur of ochre roofs. At the far end of the plain, perhaps some twenty miles away, the Tagyetus mountains close in on the valley. The air is still and silent except for the occasional peep of swifts as they arc and wheel far below me. And even further down amongst the tumbled rocks, I can see the tiny brown flecks of goats moving between clumps of vegetation. The mournful, hollow clatter of their bells floats up to me. A bus, like some tiny insect, is making its way up the spiralling mountain road in my direction.

I turn and go back to the monument. I'm hesitating and I don't know why. To tell the truth, I would rather not go at all. A ball of melancholy seems to have lodged itself in my stomach. But having got this far, it would be absurd to get back into the car and leave.

The simple, rectangular structure is surrounded by a low dry-stone wall of grey rocks. As I pass through the opening I feel as if I am entering a sanctuary. But not a sanctuary of peace. The year before I left school, the sixth form had been taken on a two-day outing to visit the war cemeteries of northern France as part of the ritual of Remembrance Day, a trip intended to make us feel grateful for the sacrifice that had been made all those years before on our behalf. I – like everyone else in the party – viewed the whole excursion primarily as an opportunity for cigarettes and alcohol. But, as we clambered out of the coach at the first cemetery, inappropriately noisy and still swapping obscene jokes, the entire party fell silent. I think it must have been the sheer scale of the place there amongst the rolling copse-studded planes of Picardy. Thousands upon thousands of tiny white crosses stretched away in geometric, psychedelic patterns, like some vast pop-art painting gone mad. An unimaginable number of dead. I was stunned by the somber quietness of it. Stunned too by the feeling that, despite the slaughter – I had seen the photographs of the rat-infested trenches and the bodies spread-eagled on barbed wire across the shattered lunar landscape – there was a kind of peace now, a sense of something unspeakable having been laid to rest. But here, in this barren upland I can sense a darkness in the place. I have a sick feeling of foreboding, and a rising fear as if the incident, whatever it was, remains unresolved, the grief still leaching out of the past.

With an effort I begin to climb the steps. As I reach the top, I can see that what I had thought was an altar in white marble is, in fact, a large engraved stone slab. Whatever happened here is obviously not entirely forgotten, for two battered wreaths of wild flowers lie at the foot of the stone. The wind has swept the loose, dry leaves into one corner of the platform. There is something deeply touching about this small gesture of remembrance in this bleak, deserted place.

I am close enough now to be able to read the inscription:

στους πεσόντες....*To the Fallen........*

But after that it becomes long and complicated, far beyond my rudimentary Greek. Below are four columns of names arranged in alphabetical order: Andronikos, Iannis... Astakis, Georgios... None of them is given military rank. All must have been civilians. Slowly I begin to count. I feel compelled to read and mouth each name individually, as though anything less would be disrespectful. All the way through to Zefiros, Dimitris. Below is inscribed the date:

2 February 1943.

At that time of the year the landscape here would still have been locked in winter, deep pockets of snow everywhere under the rocks, the ground frozen hard as iron, fingers numb on the rifle barrels. Was that how it had been? Ill-equipped and outnumbered on that freezing February day, under a leaden sky as now, had they tried, with primitive, ramshackle peasants' weapons, to hold the pass against the advancing Germans?

My chest feels strangely constricted, as if I can't take in enough air. I turn and hurry back to the car. Half way down the spiralling road, I meet the asthmatic bus labouring its way up.

SEVENTEEN

Something moves in the darkness. I know I am awake. I try to rise, but my limbs are blocked as if weighted with lead. I have entered some space between the worlds. In the silence of the room a voice begins to echo softly.

Do not be afraid. I have come now because your soul has summoned me and because you have visited the pass at Stavraki. I am here to tell our story so that you may begin to understand.

There is a long pause, a silence more profound than anything I have ever known, as if we are buried at the bottom of some deep well. Then the voice begins again, the tone slightly different, as of someone who is profoundly tired.

When I woke that morning I was sick with fear. Maria was pressed against my back for warmth. The bed was piled with the few blankets and clothes that we possessed. On the far side of the room two panes in the small window had been smashed the previous year by one of the German soldiers who had been drunk on raki. I had boarded them up, but the wind still howled round the edges of the shutters.

It was still dark. I was wide awake and sensed, even in the silence, that something was wrong. I lay there, listening to Maria's breathing. I felt alone and afraid. The fear was like a shard of ice in the centre of my stomach. Slowly it spread through my whole body. I longed for summer. Maria stirred in her sleep and turned over, pushing herself against me, craving warmth like an animal.

As I lay there in the freezing February morning, I felt utterly and completely alone. Then the noise began. By now the light was seeping round the edges of the shutters. The sounds came from the far end of the village. Muffled, distant shouting, a faint clatter of woodwork. More shouting, then silence. Then again, the same pattern.

Slowly the noise came nearer. There was only one main street in Metana then. The progression was very rapid. I lay still. Maria moved and said something in her sleep. It sounded like "Mercy". My fear had concentrated into a tight frozen ball. I did not go to the shutters to look out. There was no need. I knew I was powerless. There had been dawn house-to-house searches before; but this one was different, faster, more definitive. Maria stirred again. She had always been a heavy sleeper. There was nothing I could do. I knew it had started.

The footsteps paused outside the door. I lay motionless. Then there was a crash and the sound of splitting wood. The door splintered and gave way. Two German soldiers burst into the room. I saw that they wore helmets, which was unusual. Their faces were blank. They both carried rifles with fixed bayonets. Even in the half-light, the bayonets had an odd neutral sheen.

Then it all happened very fast. They grabbed me by the arms and pulled me out of the bed. Maria was sitting bolt upright, her long hair tangled, her black eyes wide with terror. Within seconds I was out in the village street trying to pull on my battered boots. Everything came to me in fragments: the biting cold, the soldiers shouting, my son Dinos standing in the open doorway, his face glazed with fear, the door swinging on one hinge in the wind, the fresh wood showing raw through the place where the blue paint had been split open; the face of old Anna Koutolakis from the doorway opposite, draped in black. Her eye sockets seemed empty. Her husband Manolis, was beside me.

We were given orders to march. There was silence except for the steady tramp of feet on the dusty road. Manolis had been ill all winter, and occasionally a burst of coughing would shake his thin frame and pierce the silence.

We were marching and marching fast.

Slowly the scene settled and came into focus. I was at the back of a column of men arranged in pairs, side by side. It took only seconds to realise that all the adult males of the village were there. At the front was even Stavros Liadis, seventy-nine years of age, the oldest man in the village, limping badly. Just in front of me, and to the right, was Sotiris Larnakos, who was fifteen. His face was twitching violently. Directly in front, ten rows ahead, I caught sight of the long black hair of Pappas Elias, his carriage erect, marching firmly. The village priest! It was an outrage. Till now, even the Germans had treated him with respect. Suddenly fear surrounded my heart and squeezed it, a fear beyond just fear for my own safety. My arms and legs began to shake uncontrollably.

I fixed my eyes on the German soldier marching to my left, slowly noting each detail of him, hoping that this would prevent the rising chaos from overwhelming me. But my mind was playing tricks. Only at the very end did I notice the one really striking feature of his presence that morning. Not the fact that he wore a helmet, not the rifle slung over his right shoulder, not even the ridged bayonet fixed to the end of it. The one thing that my mind refused to see, despite all the messages from my eyes in that early grey light, was the shovel he carried in his left hand, gripped half way up the rough wooden handle, his fingers blue and red in the numbing cold. More than half the soldiers were carrying shovels. Some were carrying two. They must have emptied the village of shovels. Then I started to count. One for each man.

The march lasted over three hours. It was bitterly cold and inside our ragged boots our feet were bleeding and raw. But none of this seemed to matter. We were going up towards the path to the north, over the mountains into central Arcadia. Twice old Liadis stumbled and had to be dragged to his feet. But there was no stopping. My mind wandered over those left in the village, Maria, Dinos, twelve years old, and Sophia who already looked so much like her mother. Where were we going? Were we to dig the foundations for some camp? There was no logic, and my brain refused to focus, always sliding sideways into some other track.

Around midday we were ordered to halt on the plateau just below the summit. There is no settlement there, only a small shrine with a white cross. It has always been called Stavraki – the little cross. We used to take food and go up there on Sundays in the spring because the view is so beautiful. But that day I saw only the blank mountains surrounding us on all sides. The valley was featureless as if covered with a layer of ash. My village of Metana was a smudge of grey on the valley floor. The wind was bitterly cold, and all around were pockets of snow. A few flakes drifted in the wind.

The Commandant ordered each man to take a shovel and dig a trench two meters by one meter. He offered no explanation. Pappas Elias turned to him, his eyes blazing, his hands spread wide. He uttered only one syllable. The nearest soldier hit him in the face with the butt of his rifle. It made a dull thudding sound. A crescent-shaped cut opened along his right cheek, and his eye swelled and closed almost as I watched. No one said a word. We dug.

The ground was rocky and frozen and it was hard work. We had to spread out to find sufficient soil. It took well over two hours before the Commandant was satisfied: forty-three shallow trenches. Then we were ordered to lay down our shovels and stand to attention. I heard the Commandant say in halting Greek:

"*In the name of the Third Reich you will all be executed for the murder of Corporal Stein.*"

Pappas Elias stepped forward, moving towards the Commandant, his face blackened and swollen, raising his hands, shouting out, "No, no. In God's name, not all…" Then everything seemed to happen in slow motion. The Commandant raised his pistol, held it at arm's length. He shot the priest in the chest. He staggered, his eyes frozen wide. Blood was everywhere.

I gasped, unable to breathe. A metallic clatter came from behind me. I spun round. Not two metres away a German soldier was raising his rifle. His eyes were an unnatural pale blue. I struggled to take in one last breath. And then, I heard the sound…

A terrible rattling shakes the room as I suck in a huge gasp of air. I am sitting upright, my hands clutched to my throat, shaking as if I have fever. I climb out of bed, cross to the window and reach for the shutters. My hands clatter erratically against the woodwork. I can hear my teeth rattle in the silence. There is no moon and in the blackness I can just discern the faint outline of a tall cypress.

I grope my way along the wall until my fingers feel out the doorway into the bathroom. Trembling, I find the box of matches and a candle. I hear the sharp grate as the match bursts into flame. For a moment I am blinded. Then the candle flickers into life. I am two feet from the mirror, staring at a face that seems unfamiliar. It gazes back at me from the other side of a dividing wall of glass.

For a long time I stare in wonder. And in recognition.

It both is and is not my face.

*

Later, as I lie in bed trying to sleep, the weather changes. A strong wind blows in from the west and howls round the house, setting up a constant moaning amongst the surrounding pines. I doze intermittently. Bits of my dream keep coming back to me. I am acutely aware of my impending departure, a feeling that I am about to embark on a long, perilous voyage. I feel unspeakably anxious and vulnerable, as if someone has removed a layer of my skin. Shortly after dawn I rise and find the terrace strewn with pine needles and small branches from the night's gale. The wind has dropped now, but the sky is darkly overcast. Between the trees the heaving wind-blown sea is slowly subsiding in erratic and fractured patterns. Steady rain is beginning to fall.

*

"Telephone! Telephone!" Kostas is waving frantically from the doorway of the *taverna*.

I have hugged the shoreline in the little dinghy, but it has been a bumpy ride. Out in the channel the whitecaps are still churning. Only a frantic desire to get away from the oppressive solitude of the house could have driven me to make the journey in these conditions. I tie the bobbing dinghy to the dockside.

"*Telephone?*"

"Yes, telephone. One hour before. Her name Zoe." He pronounces it in the Greek fashion, with the stress on the final syllable. He hands me a scrap of paper with her name and number on it. It takes a moment for my brain to adjust. Then I remember that Alexis had given me the telephone number of the *taverna* – the only one on the island – and I had left it with Zoe in case of emergencies. I nod calmly, but I can feel my pulse quicken. It is early morning in England, the gallery not yet open. What could have prompted her to call at this hour? Kostas beckons me and I follow his broad back into the darkness of the interior.

The telephone is an ancient bakelite affair that feels as heavy as a brick in my hand. It takes three attempts to get through. Then I hear the familiar British ringing tone, followed by the familiar voice.

"Zoe?"

"Bronson? Is that you? Oh, good." Even through the static her relief is palpable.

"What is it?"

"It's Antonio. He called me at home about two hours ago. He's in a lather about something."

"Antonio?" The anxiety ratchets up another notch. I try to keep my voice steady, but in my subliminal system Antonio is triggering danger. "What did he want?"

"I don't know. You know how he is on the 'phone. He just said it was urgent. *Very* urgent."

"Ok, I'll call him. Anything else? I'll be home soon anyway. The line's very bad."

"Yes. I can hardly hear you now. Everything else is fine. Just Antonio…"

In a burst of static the line goes dead. I click down the rest on the archaic telephone. I know Antonio's number by heart.

"*Pronto.*" The voice is unmistakable, the line a little better.

"What is it?" I ask immediately.

"Call me back on this number." Antonio reels off a set of figures, probably for a nearby call box. I jot them down on a ragged piece of paper lying on the bar. This time it takes almost ten minutes to get through.

"*Pronto!*" I can hear voices in the background. I imagine

him in a crowded café, hand clenched around the speaker. "We've got a problem."

"What?"

"They've found the thing."

"Who?"

"The Italian Customs."

"*Jesus!* Which one?"

"Ours." In spite of the secure line Antonio is still guarded.

"The black one?"

"Right. The other one's okay. Already through. But this one got stopped at the border. It was a chance thing." Antonio's voice is hoarse, his anxiety palpable even through the distorted line.

"*The border?* Why didn't it go by air as usual, for Christ's sake?"

"There was a problem. A strike at the airport. We didn't want it sitting around. The transporter said he had a safe way through the Brenner. I don't know what happened."

"What about the driver?"

"The police have him. They're questioning him now."

"Christ!" I can feel something tighten across my chest. I pause, reluctant to ask the question. "Can they trace it back?"

"I don't know. We try to keep things separate. The driver doesn't know. He has just the address of the freight agents in Geneva." He hesitates. "Maybe we lose the statue."

I feel a small surge of relief. That at least would be containable. "Antonio, can you fix it?"

There's a long silence.

"Can you?"

"I don't know!" he shouts, suddenly losing control. "I don't fucking know!" There's a pause while I absorb this. Then he says more quietly, "I'm sorry. It's difficult. Here in Rome it would be no problem. Here, I have friends – in the *Carabinieri*, the customs, even judges, politicians. You know. But up there I'm not sure. It's not my ground. I'm trying to find out." Then he says, "We could have a big problem. This isn't just an ordinary object. They'll make a very big fuss."

"I know that. Do what you can. I'll leave for London."

Without warning, the line goes dead.

I go to one of the tables and sit down. I feel light-headed and sick. The situation could spin out of control. Once roused the *Carabinieri* will be relentless. Suddenly I ache for the protection of London. I feel naked, stripped by events down here. I want to be back in a place where there are proper telephones, proper fax machines, even television. As if these things might somehow shield me from the threat that seems to be gathering.

"Problem?" asks Kostas, stroking his ragged moustache. His dark eyes show concern.

"No. Everything's fine. But I have to leave. Can you call a water taxi from the mainland?"

Kostas nods somberly. "*Kali tyche*," he says, invoking the ancient goddess of luck.

I pay him for the telephone call and go out to the jetty. I need to get back to the house to start packing up. I should be able to get away within the hour.

I take coffee at one of the tables outside the *taverna* while I wait for the water taxi from the mainland. Kostas has told me that out in the channel it is still too rough. I may have to wait a while. I watch the boats rise and fall rhythmically on the swell.

"*Kalimera*, my friend." I turn to find Dinos standing in the doorway with a cup of coffee in his hand. He must have been sitting inside. "I see you are leaving us."

I nod. "It feels like time."

He settles into the chair opposite, takes the battered plastic tobacco pouch from his trouser pocket and drops it on the table. "How was the journey?"

"What journey?" Then I remember that nothing goes unnoticed in the village. "Oh, the journey. It was fine."

He stares at me and frowns enquiringly. "Is something up, my friend? You seem troubled." His tone is unexpectedly solicitous.

I stay silent. The truth is that after Antonio's telephone call and my traumatic night I feel anxious and faintly sick and I don't want to talk to anyone. Least of all to this crazy fisherman with his intrusive questioning.

"You will return", he says inconsequentially. Does he mean to London or to Katakolos?

"Return here? I doubt it. I…"

But I'm interrupted by a sudden cry from Kostas. I look round. A water taxi is rolling heavily as it circles the end of the concrete jetty. Immediately I feel my stomach contract. It's time to leave.

Dinos escorts me to the boat. Before I climb aboard, to my surprise, he embraces me.

"Go well, my friend," he says. "*Kalo taxidi*. You are going on a long journey. We Greeks have a saying: *Light your candle before night overtakes you.*"

Then, before I can ask him to explain, he has turned and is walking back towards the *taverna*.

EIGHTEEN

I decide to take a different road back to Athens, one that avoids the war memorial. The detour seems like an absurd superstition, but I sense that the place holds more darkness than I can deal with at this moment. And my dream – or hallucination, or whatever it was – remains unexplained in a way that seems to erode the boundaries between my waking life and the fantasies of sleep. A crazy fear crouches in me that if I pass that place on this particular day I might enter the dream state and lose the power to return. For a moment I wonder if I am losing my mind.

The other road takes me even deeper into the heartland of Arcadia. The impending threat from the black statue won't leave me. A tight ball of fear has lodged in my stomach. I try to console myself that surely Antonio's street-wise connections will enable him to manipulate the Italian system and we may get away with paying a substantial bribe. And if that fails and the statue is confiscated, we will just have to split the loss, lick our wounds and wait for the next chance. I think of the possible selling price of Carla's sculpture and, for a moment, I feel consoled. But these diversions feel paper-thin, as if I'm dancing on the lip of a volcano, trying to ignore the abyss beside me.

For more than an hour the road climbs and the vegetation

thins. Then finally it levels out. Patches of mist swirl and part to reveal vistas of grey rock and barren scrub. The metal sun glows whitely behind the sealed lid of the sky. I pass not a single car and see no sign of life, except an occasional flock of unattended goats. Startled by my sudden arrival, their bells clatter eerily as they leap from the narrow road and scramble down over lichened rocks.

At a place where a group of dark stones has been piled together to form a cairn, the way divides. There are no signposts. I hesitate, but only for a moment. Then, on an instinct, I swing the car to the left. The road snakes down into a deep defile. Sparse vegetation clings to ledges and fissures. The overhanging rocks are blackened with damp. Down here even the veiled sun feels shut out. Half-way down, something comes for me. Not a thought, not a feeling, but some terror that has been standing in the shadows, waiting for me in this barren defile all my life. Suddenly it steps forward and takes me.

I keep driving, trying to pretend that nothing has happened. I shift the gears very precisely, hoping to keep a fingerhold on reality. But deep down I can see, as if on a cinema screen, the chain of events begin to unroll: the courteous police officers becoming ever more insistent, the documents minutely examined, the charge, handcuffs, imprisonment, the clank of metal doors, computerised details taken by faceless guards, intimate body searches, stripped of clothes and dignity, stripped of all hope or defence. And then the interminable chain of days. Unprotected, constantly at the mercy of unreasoning violence. The whole world shrunk to the space of a prison cell. No escape anywhere.

The thoughts click into one another with terrifying mechanical logic. But as I drive the car through the grey

Arcadian landscape, I begin to sense that even these mental processes are merely a defence, the last fragile barriers of my mind. Beyond here lies only the Underworld, a place where not even death itself can bring an ending. I can feel chaos rising, swelling up like some dark flood from a place I have never visited. I clutch the steering wheel hard and try to concentrate on the road ahead.

As I drive on towards Athens the landscape seems blank, as if the colours have been leached out, leaving everything monochrome. Two hours out from Athens I come to a turning signed to the Theatre of Epidaurus, sacred to Asklepios, the god of healing. I have a strange, atavistic sense that something in that place might help. I turn the car onto the straight narrow road towards the ancient site. It is already midday and crowded. Inside the gates the crowds stream away towards the ancient theatre. I turn left into the deserted sanctuary. Almost instantly the babble of voices dies away. All is silent except for the faint clatter of sheep bells from beyond a distant line of silver poplars.

I sit down in a grove of pines, feeling the softness of the needles under me, the ridges of the trunk against my spine – and wait, hands pressed together, sweating. Silently I begin to pray, praying that something will come to relieve me of this terror. But with a rising wave of panic, I realise that nothing and no-one is coming. For the first time in my life, I am completely and utterly unprotected and alone.

I open my eyes. Somewhere to my right a woodpecker chaffles derisively. I turn and flee the sanctuary, hoping that with the mechanics of the airport and the familiarity of London, all this will fall from me and I will wake from the nightmare and life will return to normal. But when I reach the airport, the simple act of showing my passport has become a terrifying ordeal, a trial at which at any moment my guilt might be discovered. I seem to be in the grip of some kind of panic attack. But surely panic attacks pass quickly. But this feels as if it may go on forever.

On the flight to London I begin drinking heavily; and with the alcohol comes a sense of well-being, as if the other state were some mirage which is now disappearing back into the sands of delusion. In this condition I collapse into bed in London.

Time passes. I am wide awake, the alcohol bled from my system. The euphoria has gone. I am back in the reality of the present, alone. And yet I have the sensation that someone or something has entered the room. Sweat pours from my body. I lie motionless for hours, too terrified to move, knowing only that 'they' have come for me, until light begins to filter through the curtains and at last I fall into some state between sleeping and waking, troubled by strange shapes and movements. Later I drift out of this again, knowing that I have been summoned back to the greyness of the world. The sense of being a condemned man weighs on me like shackles.

*

Thus began a pattern that was to haunt the next six weeks. Time lost its usual markers. The days and nights collapsed into each other. In the day I was a walking deadman, moving through the world without my skin on, red-raw to the simplest encounter, a swirl of chaos lurking just beneath the surface, waiting to break through and erupt at any moment. Every gesture, every action, every sound held unknown terrors. The ring of the telephone on my desk could pitch me into panic. Raising the receiver to my ear was an effort as if it were cast in lead. I knew I was walking the borders of sanity, patrolling a no-man's land between the worlds, held rigid by the fear that at any moment I might stagger over and be gone forever.

The news from Antonio told me nothing. Everything was blocked, waiting. But I knew that what was happening to me had spread far beyond the bounds of the black statue or the police or prison. Something had ruptured between myself and the Underworld and I was in another parallel zone now, where logic no longer served and my mind was bobbing helplessly atop a vast swell of terror. A terror that had neither height nor depth, nor breadth nor beginning nor end. Nor reason, nor reprieve. This was the medieval vision of Hell, a Hell that went on *forever*. Some days I was pinned helpless against a sweating wall of fear. Some days I was suspended in a fraying net above a bottomless chasm. Some days I was clamped to a rock-face a thousand feet above the ground, with no handholds to right or left, or up or down; and no knowledge of how to climb. And night was coming on. Some days I was locked in a prison, or a cave, or a coffin that was gradually shrinking. Only this was not the prison with an entry and a release date. This was the endless, all consuming, inescapable prison of my mind.

These were all metaphors. Some residual part of my old brain ought to have been able to tell me that. But metaphor means different things to different people. When you are trapped inside your own metaphors they are terrifyingly real. And no one can tell you otherwise.

And the nights were always the worst. With enough alcohol I would collapse into sleep, but within an hour I was awake again. In the early hours of the morning, with my already threadbare defences at their lowest ebb, 'they' would come for me. Soon I began to identify them as 'The Dragons'. Silently they came while I lay motionless, too terrified to move. I imagined that each night, Promethean, they ate my liver. I knew this was something that would remain forever incommunicable to anyone who had not undergone such a trial.

It was after six weeks of wandering in this never-ending hell, haunted by a continual sense of dread, exposed to an endless ongoing panic attack, that David appeared unexpectedly one morning at the house. He was, as far as I knew, unannounced. I was startled. And disorientated. And ashamed. And relieved to see him.

He takes one look at me, leads me into the studio and sits down beside me on one of the long sofas.

"Okay, tell me about it."

But the trouble is that I can't. I don't know how to. I'm terrified that talking will only arouse yet more demons. And besides, there are no words for what I am experiencing.

He touches my arm. "It's okay," he says gently. "I know a lot about these things. I've been there too."

And luckily I can imagine that he has. And the thought that anyone could have been in this place and survived is surreal but comforting. So I begin to tell him about the black statue, about Antonio's phone call. Even about my strange dream in Katakolos. For, in some way I can't explain, it seems connected. But when I try to tell him how the earth has opened up in Arcadia and swallowed me into its blackness I can't go on. As if naming it would provoke even more terrifying attacks. He tries to persuade me to talk, even to see a therapist. But I shake my head. If I can't talk about it to my closest friend, what would be the point of sitting with a total stranger? David's eyes circle the room, apparently searching for inspiration.

Suddenly he says, "There are huge plane trees outside in the square."

I stare at him. "So?" What does this have to do with anything?

"It's a beautiful day. They're just coming into leaf. Go and sit under one for fifteen minutes. I'll wait for you."

"What the hell good would that do?"

"Just do it. *Please*. We'll talk again when you get back."

It seems a pointless exercise, but there's an urgency in his voice, so I go anyway. Despite the fine weather the garden is deserted. I head for the largest of the enormous planes. I sit and, as I lean back against its peeling bark, something very strange happens. I don't believe in 'energies', but suddenly, as I sit there, I can feel some kind of movement like a pulse in the tree, as if its vast size and longevity are slowly spreading through me. I can sense its beginnings from seedling to tiny sprig, through to the vast spreading canopy above me. And then I can feel, in a way that has nothing to do with my normal senses, the vast line of trees that it has come from and that it will go back to. And from this beautifully long perspective I see, as if I am viewing myself from space, the smallness of my own life. *This life*. But, oddly, the feeling is not one of diminishment or insignificance, but rather of an unbounded freedom, as if I have suddenly found my rightful place in the cosmos. And there is nothing in the whole world to fear. I remember the Buddhist saying, 'Big mind. Big heart.' Surely, for a blessed moment, this is it.

Terror stalks you in different ways. I have come to learn that during these weeks. But it is at its most cunning and malevolent when it feels you begin to escape its clutches. The moment I move my back from the tree my sense of freedom shrivels. I lean back again immediately, but it is too quick for me, sliding like a steel blade between me and all that had liberated me a few moments before. And I am cut adrift again, floating on an ocean of terror, paying doubly now for my moment of liberation.

David studies me very intensely when I get back, as if searching for clues.

"So?"

I tell him I had felt better. Only briefly better. Only slightly better. But yes, for a moment calmer, not terrified.

"So the clouds were able to part for a while?"

I shrug. "I guess." Though with my insides roiling again it doesn't seem like much of an achievement.

He sits for a moment, hands folded, staring at the ground. "Then I don't believe you're clinically depressed, which is what I had feared. If you were, there wouldn't be any breaks in the cloud at all. Real clinical depression is like a turtle shell that clamps down on top of you and there's just no way out."

"So what is…?"

"I think you're in a spiritual crisis."

"A *what*?"

He's silent for a while. "Do you remember," he says at last, "your Italian astrologer?"

"Carla? Of course."

"Well, I think she was right. I think this is the moment when Saturn and Pluto have erupted from the Underworld into your life in order to claim you. But there's a reason in what's happening. They are doing it for a purpose and just now they have allowed you to see a glimpse of the light. And if there's even just a tiny fragment of light, then you can imagine that there is ultimately a way out. This isn't a chemical imbalance in your system. This is something spiritual. All you really need is time. Time and perhaps a belief that ultimately there is a purpose in all this."

"Time? How long?" It's the one answer I desperately need. If I knew a date, a month, even a year… If I can give this thing a shape, a boundary then I know I can survive. It's the infinity, the limitlessness that is so terrifying. The terror of the astronaut cut loose in space.

David must have seen my need, but he doesn't try to console me. I know now how much courage that takes. Instead he says, "Let me tell you a story."

"A *story?*" David's ideas are getting more unhinged by the minute.

"Yes. It's one of Grimm's Tales. Many years ago it saved me." He shuffles forward to the edge of the sofa and laces his fingers.

"Once upon a time…"

It starts out as one of those northern Gothic fairy tales that emerge from the dark woods of Germany. Frankly I expect it to be banal and, for a moment, I doubt David's wisdom. There are, typically, three brothers. The two older ones are jealous of the youngest who is the naïve, blessed simpleton. One day when they are walking through the forest they come to a clearing they have never seen before. And in the centre of the clearing stands a well.

For some inexplicable reason, at the mention of the well, my stomach lurches with anxiety. It's like some kind of distant warning shot.

They drop down a stone to ascertain the depth, but only a dry solid sound comes echoing back up the shaft. The well is empty. Then the youngest brother is persuaded to climb into the bucket. Naively he accepts and they lower him down to explore.

But the moment the bucket touches the ground and he climbs out, the bucket is hauled back up and the two older brothers disappear. And he is left helpless and alone with just a faint glimmer of light penetrating from the world above. For a long while he is frozen with fear. As his eyes grow accustomed to the dark, he can see that he is standing on loose earth in a large vaulted chamber with rough walls. Then, for no apparent reason – except that there is nothing else to do – he begins to walk up and down, pacing the loose earth flat. Day after day he walks up and down, not knowing why he is doing it, totally lost from the world above. *Up and down, up and down…*

The swelling anxiety has invaded all of me by now, but the rhythm of David's voice has become hypnotic. The story echoes inside me.

Up and down. Up and down….. Until one day, when the sun is at its highest and some faint light penetrates down into the well, he sees that he has paced all the ground flat. And at that moment he sees for the first time that there is a flute hanging on one of the walls. Has it been there all along, unnoticed? Have his eyes failed to see it? Has something been blocking his sight until now? Curious, he takes it down and begins to play. And, as the music fills the chamber, the bucket starts to descend and the spirits of the cave appear. And within minutes he is being hauled up towards the daylight and the world above. Gradually the light at the top of the shaft grows brighter and broader and he can smell the pines and hear the chatter and singing of birds. And eventually he comes up.

"And when he comes up……" David allows a long pause, "*He comes up in another place.*"

There's a long silence. Something strange has happened. Something inexplicable and far below the level of thought. A kind of osteopathic crack in my psyche. In retrospect, I think that story with its ancient wisdom saved me that day. For all

I know it may have saved my life. For the first time in weeks I don't feel like a helpless victim. Something is required of me. Where I am has a purpose. I am pacing the ground flat. I am accepting that I don't know how long it will take. I am, as Carla would have said, for the first time, allowing Saturn and Pluto into my life. I am opening the door for something new to come in. This is the only strategy against which terror has no weapons. Acceptance.

"How do you feel?" asks David.

I start, as if I had been woken from a dream.

"Weird," I say. "Weird but better."

"I think," says David slowly, "that you may have just begun to climb back into the bucket."

*

That night, for the first time in weeks, I don't drink. It's as if David has placed a small, steadying hand against my back. Eventually, despite my sobriety, I fall asleep. But two hours later I am awake as usual. My body has developed its own internal alarm. I can sense the presence of the dragons, can almost feel their breath on my neck. But something is different. There seems to have opened up a tiny pin-prick of space on which I can stand and watch myself lying there frozen in my bed. I am no longer the total captive of my own mind. As I lie there sweating, I see myself standing on rotten boards above an abyss. I try to hold myself up by sheer force of will. Every muscle and sinew aches with the strain. Then suddenly the boards crack and give way. And I go down. All is blackness. Defenceless, I give myself up to the dragons. And sleep.

I am watching a small troupe of dark-skinned musicians, dressed in oriental blue costumes with gold buttons. There is a blind harpist who plays with heartbreaking beauty, his head thrown back, his unseeing eyes gazing at the sky. Then the central figure stands up to play his flute. He is slim and very tall, perhaps ten feet, towering over the scene, commanding it with his surreal presence. With a shock, I see that he has only one leg. All the way up to the hip, the other leg is missing. Yet he stands and plays with such beauty that I know that it is precisely his one-leggedness, his terrible wound, that gives him his power.

The moment I wake I know that something is different. It is…… an absence. A normality. A quietness. I lie totally still, waiting for the terror to return. Waiting for the dragons to begin their work. But nothing happens.

Sunlight is slanting through the gap between the curtains. I can hear the faint hum of London going about its business outside the windows. Slowly, very carefully like someone uncertain after a long convalescence, I ease myself upwards and sit on the edge of the bed. I am intensely aware of the texture of the pile carpet under my bare feet. It's as if my feet have been numb, insensate, all my life.

Carefully I stand up, cross to the window and draw back the curtain. Outside everything is the same. And radically transformed. The fresh green of the young leaves glows iridescent. The sky is a deep cerulean blue, as if it has been enamelled. A stillness lies over everything.

I think of my first sight of Greece, glimpsed from the deck of the ferry. It had this same freshness and clarity. But this is somehow different. More real, more connected to who I now am. I go back and sit down on the bed. And suddenly I am flooded by a sense of gratitude. Not gratitude for anything in particular. Just an overriding gratitude for life. It is the calmest, the most beautiful and most profound sensation I have ever known. A total exploding of the prison bars. It is that kind of quiet, peaceful ecstasy that comes with the ebbing of constant pain.

I have stepped out onto the clock-ice and heard it crack. I have looked down and seen clear through what supports us to the immeasurable depths below. I have walked in the Underworld and paced the ground flat. And I have come up in another place. The long night is over.

*

Two days later Antonio telephones in a lather of excitement. The Italian Customs have released the statue! A 'specialist' from the Instituto delle Belle Arte has finally inspected it and pronounced it a modern forgery! Of no commercial value! *Che cretino! Che stupidita!* Antonio can barely contain his excitement. Or his laughter at the absurdity of the whole situation. He chatters on and urges me to come to Rome so that we can celebrate in style.

As I replace the receiver, I am totally unmoved. It's like receiving news of something you already know has happened long ago. The black statue, the police, the clank of the prison doors were emissaries from another world. Antonio's call has come from a different reality than the terror that had gripped me night after night as the dragons had devoured my liver.

That night I sleep quietly, dreamless. Gradually my sleep pattern returns to normal. Though I sense that that word, 'Normal,' will never have quite the same meaning again. I know that there are medical terms for what I have been through – nervous breakdown, chronic depression, panic attack, paranoid delusion, temporary psychosis… The modern lexicon is generously extensive. But when I think of it now, I think rather of Carla, of her ominous predictions of Saturn and Pluto. Whatever modern medicine may say, I know that something different has happened. An archaic rite of passage, of which modern medicine knows nothing, has taken place within me.

As my life settles down again, I come to see that, in some sense, I'm back to where I was before. Before the Dragons; before Greece; before Dinos; before Sylvia's death; before Carla… Before…

Only, of course, I'm not. Yes, I still have the gallery. I'm still dealing in antiquities, going about my day much as before. Zoe is still trying to keep me in order with her waspish manner. But it's as if someone has twisted the lens and shifted the focus and nothing will ever be quite the same again. The arrival of the Dragons has blown my old life into the air. And now I'm waiting quietly to see if the pieces want to settle down into some new, comprehensible pattern. I'm in the waiting room, wondering what is now expected of me.

NINETEEN

"I think you'll be pleased, Bronson. He looks a whole lot better now that we've got those stupid bloody restorations off him." Ted Jarvis, master stone mason and restorer extraordinary, is wheeling a heavy metal trolley across the hall and into the studio. On it lies a bulky shape wrapped in a thick grey blanket, held in place by two broad webbing straps. "But it was a hell of a lot more difficult to clean than you made out it would be. The front was all right – just soaking, then soap and water. But the back was a real bugger, encrusted as hell. I had to work with those tiny water jets that dentists use and do it inch by inch. Get too close for a second or turn the power up too high and you'll take the whole bloody surface clean off the marble. Right Sammy?"

Sam, his burly young assistant, is kneeling down, unfastening the straps. He looks up and gives me a sly wink. "He's a grumpy old bugger, but put a block of marble in his hands and he knows what he's doing all right. I'll grant him that."

"That's enough of that," says Ted, good-naturedly. "You grip the base, I'll take the top and on the count of three we'll lift him nice and easy into place."

Ted brushes aside my offer of help with a wave of his hand. "This ain't work for you, Bronson. You're a poncey art dealer, for God's sake. You'd bloody rupture yourself. Okay, Sam, one… two…"

There's a moment of silent expectation as the *kouros* rises into the air, then settles on its base. But before I can take it in, aggressive hooting starts up from outside.

"That'll be the first complainer," says Ted calmly. "We had to double-park to unload." He takes a rag from his pocket and polishes away a handprint from the base. "We'd better be on our way. Enjoy your new friend. Beautiful work it is. It's Naxian marble all right. And pure Greek. None of your Roman short cuts. Claw chisel all around, then slow abrasives. Must have taken a bloody age. But you can't beat it. The surface is like silk. Anyway, we'll be off now before our friend out there blows a gasket. I'll send the invoice to Zoe next week. No hurry. I know you're a good payer."

I escort them to the door, where Sam lifts the trolley down the steps and opens the back doors of the van, while Ted gives a genial smile to the middle-aged blonde who sits scowling behind the wheel of her black Mercedes. Then he slides into the front seat and with a casual wave they pull away down the narrow, tree-lined street.

I turn back to the house. The *kouros* faces directly down the broad space of the hall towards me. As I enter the studio a cloud must have shifted, for the room is suddenly flooded with light. It is a strange, frozen moment. One part of my brain is rooted right there, in the light of the studio, stunned by the statue, taking in its perfect balance, the blithe confidence of its striding pose, the luminous glow of the marble. Like silk, just as Ted had promised. But another part of me is falling back in time.

A strong north wind had been picking up since dawn and was

beginning to mound the sea into foam-capped breakers and set up an insistent clatter in the rigging of the small yachts in the harbour of Mykonos. It cost me double to persuade the reluctant boatman to set out on the six mile journey in such conditions. David had left ten days before, called home by news that his mother was dying, and I had moved on from Athens, taking the ramshackle steamers from island to island, stunned by the light and the glittering clarity of everything around me. And now I was headed towards the very heart of the Aegean – Delos, a low, barren outcrop of rock, silent now and uninhabited, but in antiquity a place so sacred, so pure, so totally outside of man's power or time's covenant that no-one was allowed either to die or be born there.

After what seemed an interminable period of pitching and rolling and being lashed by the gale, we finally slid in under the lea of the small islet of Rhenea, sheltering Delos. Soaked and salt-encrusted and feeling faintly sick, I clambered out onto the wooden jetty. For an hour and a half I wandered alone amongst the ruins, circled the Sacred Lake – now a shallow dust bowl – listened to the wind howl down the Avenue of the Lions, watched the enormous iridescent green lizards sunning themselves on the tumbled marble remains of temples and sanctuaries; until, battered by the wind and scorched by the sun, I made my way towards the ugly, squat, concrete museum. A full *meltemi* was roaring out of the north now and I was relieved to step into the shelter of the dim lobby and buy my ticket from the sleepy attendant.

The first room contained only broken shards of early pottery. I passed quickly through to the second, a smaller space where sunlight slanted in through a high, barred window. And stopped, almost winded by the presence of the single sculpture that stood alone there. Nothing had prepared me for the shock of this first sight of a Greek *kouros*. It was in one moment both utterly outside my experience and achingly familiar.

It stood there, a nude youth, one foot slightly forward, arms held stiffly to the hips, the hair carefully braided, a faint smile on the lips. With its blithe confidence and utter stability he was like a messenger from another world, carrying with him a promise of sanity, a blueprint for another life. As I stood there I felt a deep yearning open up inside me, a yearning, I sensed, for something I must once have known and then forgotten. And it was then that the strangest thought entered my head: If I could somehow *inhabit* that smile, then my life would be complete…

The front door clicks open. I glance at my watch. Nine o'clock! I must have stood here for over an hour since Ted and Sam left. I feel unsteady, as if I am waking from a deep sleep.

Zoe puts down her things in the hall. It's a warm morning and she is wearing a thin cotton dress, her auburn hair fastened back at her neck. She is looking at her most attractive. She comes and stands beside me.

"Oh, wow!" she says in a low voice. "Even I can tell that this is something special."

She circles the statue slowly, occasionally putting out a hand to touch it. At length she says, "I take it all back. Your overlong visit to the beautiful, mysterious countess was worth it after all." Then she pauses and raises an enquiring eyebrow. "How much?"

"Buying price?"

"I know that," she says with an impatient toss of her head. "I wired the money, remember?"

"Selling price?"

"Uh huh."

"I reckon… around five million dollars."

A low whistle escapes her and she shoots me an odd, searching look, something I have never seen in her before. "Well," she says, "that should certainly keep you from starving for a while." Then, without a further word, she turns and goes to make coffee.

I turn back to the statue, but now its radiance has vanished. It's like being brought crashing down to earth, suddenly sobered up in the middle of a massive high. Zoe isn't moralistic; she knows the realities of my business, but… something in the sculpture, something in the price has clearly shocked her. And suddenly I feel an uneasy sense of betrayal. Though by whom and of what I can't quite say.

TWENTY

"*Pronto.*"

I recognise Ricardo's voice.

"*Sono il Dottore Tullis. Posso parlare colla Contessa Carla, per favore?*"

There's a long pause, as if he's considering my request. Then he says, "*Un attimo per cortesia.*"

I had expected a warmer welcome. Perhaps he has forgotten who I am. Perhaps this is simply an up-market butler's way of dealing with unexpected telephone calls. In the background I can hear the clack of feet, then distant voices. Then more feet. I imagine Carla walking down the long stone loggia...

"Bronson?"

It isn't Carla.

"Elizabetta?"

"Yes, it's me. What can I do for you?" Something is clearly wrong. There's a brittleness and a distance to her voice that I don't recognise at all from our previous meeting. Could she have discovered the real value of the statue in the meantime?

"Actually I wanted to talk to Carla."

"I'm afraid you can't at the moment." She hesitates. "She's had a slight accident. She's in hospital."

"Is she alright?"

"She is recovering." The voice is deadpan, clearly wanting

to forestall any further questions. I tell her that I want to come to Prosaro to discuss something rather important about our business. She is silent for a moment, obviously trying to penetrate my obliqueness; at the same time registering the need for caution on the telephone.

"But I thought our business was finished."

"It was. But there's something new. Something I want to add. It's rather important."

Again a pause. "I see. Yes, such things are better discussed face to face. If it isn't too much of an imposition, perhaps it would be best if you came here – if you feel it's important enough." Then she adds, "I have things to do in Venice. Maybe it's more convenient for you if we meet there?"

"And Carla?"

"The doctors prefer that Carla doesn't see people for a while. But I can transact any business that is necessary."

Her tone is not unfriendly, just resolute.

*

It is just after twelve when I arrive at the Hotel Gritti and drop my bag with the concierge. It's clear that I am expected and that Elizabetta is *persona grata* at this grandest of Venetian establishments. The *maitre d'hotel* shows me to a table on the terrace that fronts directly onto the Grand Canal and informs me that the *Contessa* has called to say she will be a little late. Meanwhile, would I care for a glass of *prosecco*? On the house, of course.

Left alone I can feel anxiety begin to swell inside me like a balloon being inflated. What I have to say about the statue is awkward but manageable. But, of course, it's to Carla that my mind now goes. Elizabetta's icy manner on the telephone has given me pause for thought. We had parted at the Villa on friendly, almost intimate terms. So what might have happened in the meantime? And what about the 'accident' she alluded to, but was so reluctant to discuss? In some inexplicable way, whatever it is, I feel strangely responsible. Perhaps my escapade with Carla in the *salotto* has had deeper implications than I imagined. If I think about it now, I can see that what we did that night wasn't just sex; it had an eerie quality of ritual about it. And the next morning Carla had seemed so febrile, so vulnerable, so disturbingly adolescent. Have I unwittingly helped to force her deeper into her darkness…?

At this moment my wandering thoughts are interrupted by a movement at the entrance to the hotel, and the next instant Elizabetta is coming towards me, walking with that same easy, athletic gait that I remember from our first meeting. She is wearing a light lavender-coloured dress and broad tortoiseshell sunglasses. For a moment my unruly mind flickers over what is probably in the heads of most of my fellow diners – a young man having an assignation with an older, beautiful woman. Then, to my surprise, she is kissing me on both cheeks and settling into the wicker chair opposite. She seems slightly out of breath. Only when the waiter has brought a second glass of *prosecco* does she push the sunglasses up into her hair and I can see the dark rings under her eyes and the sense of strain in her face. Briefly we exchange pleasantries. Then she slips off the sunglasses, clicks them together and places them on the starched linen table cloth. She looks at me very directly. The look is, to say the least, challenging.

"You said on the phone there was something you wanted to tell me about the statue. I hope it's nothing unpleasant. This wouldn't be a good time."

And suddenly I realise how difficult this is going to be. I had seen myself as the harbinger of good news, a kind of guardian angel arriving from the heavens. But now it seems I'm going to have to pick my way through a minefield of diplomatic ambiguity.

"I don't think you'll find it unpleasant," I counter. "It's just that the situation has changed."

She frowns. "Changed? In what way?"

"Well, when I bought the statue at the *Villa Ducale* it was heavily restored and badly encrusted. At the time it had all the appearance of being a fairly mediocre Roman copy of a Greek archaic sculpture. And I paid an appropriate price for such an object. I imagine you know the sum?"

She nods, her eyes fixed on mine. "Eighty thousand dollars?"

"Right. But now that the statue has been cleaned and the restorations removed, it's fairly clear that it is not, in fact, a copy at all, but a Greek original." I pause. "And that alters the price very considerably."

She looks at me quizzically, but says nothing. There's something unnerving about her silence. So I press on. "I would estimate that a realistic selling price now would be of the order of five million dollars. And, under the circumstances, it seems only fair that I should just take a commission of ten percent – which is still, after all, a very substantial sum – and give the rest to you and Carla when it is sold."

She sits staring at me. Then she cocks her head to one side and gives a wry smile. "And did this realization of the real value come *before* you did the transaction with Carla? Or only afterwards?"

I could lie, of course. But there's something in that look that demands honesty.

"No," I say. "I knew at the time when I bought it." I look directly at her, daring her condemnation. But I see no anger in her eyes. Slowly she nods her head. "It seems that Carla and I are not the only ones who have been forced to change in these last weeks. I see it in you too. Carla said something strange about you when you left. She said, 'I think the Underworld will have to claim him before he can truly become himself.' Does that mean anything to you?"

I nod. "I think it does now."

Then she looks at me gravely. "I realise, of course, that you need never have revealed any of this. We could have taken our eighty thousand dollars and been very content with it. We do need it badly for the house." Suddenly her grey-blue eyes fill with tears. After a while she wipes them away. "There are a thousand things I could say," she goes on. "But none of them seems quite adequate. So let me just say that what you have decided to do is a very honourable and generous thing. It is the act of a man with a generous heart. And I thank you for it from the very bottom of my being." She pauses and looks down for a moment, obviously choosing her words carefully. "I see that things must have changed in you. Otherwise you could not have made that decision. And that touches me. And therefore I am going to tell you the truth about Carla." She dabs at her lips with her napkin and when she resumes, I notice that her voice has thickened. "Carla tried to commit suicide ten days ago. It wasn't just a cry for help. She meant to kill herself. It was pure luck that she didn't succeed. She slashed her wrists in the bath and it was just chance that I found her. She lost a lot of blood and was in intensive care for several days. But she's out of danger now. She's back home recovering."

The last words are barely audible to me. It's as if the air

has been drained of oxygen and for a terrible moment I feel as if I might faint. I remember Carla's strangely adolescent walk when I left her at the Villa and suddenly I recognise that a premonition has been horribly fulfilled. And I am a part of it.

Elizabetta leans forward and touches my hand. It jolts me back to consciousness. "It wasn't your fault," she says gently, as if reading my thoughts. "I want you to know that. In a sense, it had nothing to do with you. You were merely the passing catalyst. It was an event that has long been waiting to happen. There can hardly have been a day in the last fifteen years when the possibility hasn't crossed my mind. And I've always known there would be nothing I could do to prevent it when it came."

"But *why?*" I know the question is banal. Who can answer it? But still I need some kind of explanation, if only for my own peace of mind.

Elizabetta spreads her hands. "Why does anybody?"

"Because they can no longer bear the horror of where they are every waking moment?"

She nods. "Yes. I can see you know something of these things yourself. That I believe is why you have changed."

"I think that when people discuss suicide as outsiders," I say, "never having been anywhere near it, they tend to talk as if the person should have weighed things up logically in advance. 'She had so much to live for'. That sort of thing. But they have no idea what it's like to be so terrified that each single breath contains horror. Then death becomes simply a welcome release. That I can understand. But Carla…"

Before I can go on the waiter comes to take our orders and, for a while, after he has gone, we sit in silence, listening to the boats on the Grand Canal, the metallic announcements as the *vaporettos* come and go at the nearby *stazione*. My mind is filled with questions. At length I say, "You may not want to talk about it, but there's something I just don't understand. When I went to the *Villa Ducale* with Carla to look at the statue, she took me into a library and did some kind of astrological reading with me. You may know about it?"

She nods.

"She was so utterly calm, serene, *wise* then. I just don't understand how someone like that can shortly afterwards…" My voice trails off.

"Try to kill herself? No, of course, it eludes logic. But the psyche isn't built of logic." She pauses. "I would say that Carla is what one calls 'an old soul'. But being an old soul doesn't mean that it makes it any easier to live in the world. In fact, I think it probably makes it a great deal more difficult, because then one sees the world in a completely different way and has quite different values and expectations from most people." She spreads her hands on the tablecloth and stares down at them, apparently searching for a better explanation. Eventually she pulls in a deep breath. I have the sense that she has reached some kind of decision.

"I was pleased when you called because, after Carla's suicide attempt, I wanted to talk to you anyway. What I want to tell you is not about her, at least not directly. She may do that one day, if she wishes, in her own words. It is not for me to second-guess her heart or put words into her mouth. I've tried to do too much of that already. Instead I want to tell you a little about myself. And in that way you may understand Carla better." I'm mystified and she must have seen it in my face. "No one of us is ever separated from our past or our surroundings, you know. That's a myth. The sins of the fathers will *always* be visited upon the children."

"Even unto the third and fourth generations?"

Suddenly her face floods with emotion. "Just one generation is enough, believe me. And it doesn't always have to be just the fathers. We're all complicit in some way."

And so Elizabetta begins to tell her story.

TWENTY-ONE

Elizabeth Denham had been born into a wealthy cotton-spinning family in Athens, Georgia. She was a southern belle and an heiress of some scale. In 1937, at a ball in Washington, she had been introduced to a young attaché at the Italian Embassy, Count Alessandro Ruspolini.

"Sandro was quite different from the earnest young men I knew in Georgia. He was like quick-silver – witty, charming, dashing, aristocratic, and very, very handsome. He literally swept me off my feet. I was naïve, of course, and it probably helped my cause with Sandro that my family owned huge farms in Georgia and all through the Carolinas. The Ruspolinis had grand estates too, of course – and grand titles – but no real money. It was a classic twentieth century merger between moneyed America and aristocratic Europe. And my parents were all in favour. Having a countess in the family would certainly add lustre to the Denham name."

"But weren't they concerned…?"

"About the Fascism?"

I nod.

"Not really. In 1937 it didn't seem so threatening. Also, what people nowadays don't understand is that back then Italian Fascism had glamour. It wasn't born in the sweaty beer halls of Munich, led by a downtrodden angry little man with a scruffy moustache. Even the funny *Il Duce* had a kind of glamour." She gives a small smile. "Even if it was somewhat of the music hall variety. But there was nothing music hall about Sandro. He had a quiet authority about him. I think that's what really hooked me. We were married within six months and left with great fanfare on the Queen Mary. And I was the new Contessa Ruspolini. It was a kind of fairy tale wedding."

Until now her tone has been light, as if the glitter from that courtship more than forty years before has somehow infected her. But suddenly all the lightness drains away.

"If I think about it now, I should have seen right from the start, at least right from the moment we got married and came back to Italy, that something wasn't quite right." She gives a small ironic smile. "A bit like Italian fascism – it wasn't quite what it appeared behind the glamour. But I suppose I was infatuated. I was blinded by my new life, by Italy and by my position as mistress of a grand historic estate."

At this moment the waiter arrives with our first courses. He pours the wine and departs and for a while we eat in silence. Then Elizabetta begins to talk again. Exactly why she is telling me all this is still unclear but I'm fascinated by this sudden unexpected glimpse into her past and – if I'm honest – by the intimacy in which it binds us.

"It was only a year after we arrived in Prosaro that war broke out. At that point I was technically a neutral citizen, of course, though things were very tense right from the start. Long before Pearl Harbour it was obvious that America would eventually come in on the Allied side. I could tell from the letters that were coming from the States, at first nervous, then increasingly jingoistic. I think Pearl Harbour was just the trigger America had been waiting for. It was a kind of relief. It completely swept away any moral scruples we still had." She gives a slight smile. "It gave us the permission we craved to think of the Germans as evil bastards and still hold onto our God-fearing Christian consciences. Only, of course, I didn't feel like that. I was caught in the middle. My parents kept writing, urging me, then eventually begging me to come 'home.'" She etches the inverted commas ironically in the air with her forefingers. "But they didn't realise that by then home for me was Italy. There was no way I could leave and go back to the self-righteous suffocation of Georgia. They also didn't realise with what unseemly haste their early enthusiasm for the glamorous and aristocratic Count Ruspolini had miraculously evaporated as public opinion in America had swung against Italy. I think they wanted me back in Georgia principally because it was a terrible social stigma to have a daughter so intimately associated with *Il Duce*; because by then Sandro was part of his inner circle."

"Did you love him?"

"Sandro? Oh, yes, I loved him. Or at least I thought I did in those days. Have you ever been in love?"

I shrug slightly and spread my hands. "I suppose."

She smiles. "A diffident, macho response. But what I suppose you are already realizing is that the word love means very different things at different stages of our lives."

She lapses into a thoughtful silence. I wait for her to go on. At length she starts again, but seemingly in a different direction.

"The day America declared war there was rejoicing in Italy. It was like a popular holiday. Brass bands playing, people dressing up, patriotic speeches. But two days later – I think as the reality sunk in and people became afraid – the mood turned sombre and ugly and in the afternoon a group of villagers turned up at the house, mostly young bloods headed by the mayor who was clearly drunk and wanted to arrest 'L'Americana'. Presumably it was meant to be a sort of citizen's arrest and, when you saw the kind of mood they were in, it had potentially terrifying consequences." She draws in a deep breath and her spine straightens. "Alessandro was amazing. He went out to meet them on the terrace, but made sure he was standing three steps above them. He listened to their ramblings without saying a word. I was standing just inside the door, absolutely petrified. I thought his silence meant he was going to give me up to them. But then he suddenly held up his hand – I could just glimpse him from behind the curtains – and in about three sentences he dismissed them and sent them back to the village with their tails between their legs. He never even raised his voice. He had that kind of charisma and authority. And arrogance, of course. But his arrogance saved me, because theoretically I should, at the very least, have been interned as an enemy alien. But Sandro knew how to handle the fascist officials and in the end, there was a compromise and I just had to swear an oath of allegiance to *Il Duce*." Unexpectedly she laughs. "I did it in the mayor's office in the Town Hall down in Prosaro. I remember I had one hand behind my back with my fingers crossed like a school girl. But that little deception enabled me to stay free, though my situation, as you can imagine, was not very comfortable. For the rest of the war I hardly left the estate."

At this moment we are catapulted back into the present by the waiter arriving with our main courses – *vitello tonnato* and salad for Elizabetta and grilled sea bass for me – and for a while we eat in silence. Then Elizabetta clears her throat.

"Immediately after the war the Allies put Sandro in prison for being a renowned fascist and someone who had, at least at some point, been closely associated with Mussolini. But he was only inside for about six months. In Italy favours can usually be traded to bend things as trivial as the law. I was technically safe because I had never given up my American citizenship, thank God. But it was still a terrible time. We had almost nothing to eat and I suffered the fate of the vanquished, whilst being treated by most of the locals with a surliness reserved for the victors, because for them I had always remained 'L'Americana'. 1946 was a grim year in Italy. We were trying to shake off our complicity with the atrocities that were coming to light in Germany and old scores were being settled even within families. There was appalling poverty and hunger and hate and shame. And the terrible thing was that it all seemed so at odds with the Italian character, its openness and *joie de vivre*. It was as if the whole Italian spirit had been turned inside out and its shadow lining had been exposed. The sunny southern Mediterranean had suddenly become the dark underbelly of Europe, even as the north was beginning to climb back on its feet.

"But, of course, I had Carla. At times it felt as if she was all I had. And I blame myself now for having depended so much on her child's love to fill the hole in my own heart; as if perhaps I was sucking the soul out of her into my own neediness, instead of just giving as a mother should…"

I start to speak, but she holds up her hand to forestall me.

"I remember she used to have bouts of playfulness, but always slightly frenetic. And then she could lapse into silence for hours like some doll with her soft black hair and her shining dark eyes, just gazing out at the world as if she was totally baffled by what she saw there." She hesitates. "I'm slightly psychic myself, or hyper-intuitive I suppose you would call it, and I was aware even then that Carla was somehow in touch with something beyond. Not just in the make-believe way of children, but in some way that was more profound. And more troubling.

"Then Sandro came back from prison. He didn't talk about it but, of course, he was changed. He had always been a strict man, wanting things to be done correctly." She gives a wry smile. "Not an easy virtue to hold in Italy at the best of times. But now there was an anger in him and he could erupt into furious rages about things that seemed trivial. At the same time he was wonderful in many ways. He got the farm running again. He sorted out the family estates and even, despite his temper, somehow won the villagers round, so that we gradually returned to some form of pre-war normality. I don't know if I still loved him then, but I was grateful. And of course, I was totally dependent on him. My family had cut me off completely and would have nothing to do with me. As far as they were concerned I had fought with the enemy. I can still remember the letter my father wrote after I refused to leave Sandro and go back to Georgia in 1942. He told me with a kind of horrible old-fashioned southern courtesy that I would never be allowed across their threshold again and that he had changed his will accordingly. So I had gone from being a southern heiress into a penniless woman living in a foreign country where she was no longer really welcome and whose husband had somehow become a stranger to her. I sometimes used to wake in the night sweating, fearful that Sandro would throw Carla and I out in the street if I displeased him. And in those days there was nowhere for me to turn."

I look at her in silence, trying to imagine this poised and graceful woman, as some kind of fearful outcast. To our left a *vaporetto* arrives and the holiday passengers stream off into the splintering sunlight and disappear into the dark arteries of Venice. It all seems so impossibly distant from the story Elizabetta is telling me, and from the shadow that I sense lies over it. And suddenly, listening to this story, I can't help feeling how trivial and lightweight my generation has become, unaware – even as we turn these southern countries into our hedonistic playgrounds – that these lands, *within living memory*, were soaked in blood.

"So what happened then?" I ask at length.

"It was during that period that I began to train as a phsychotherapist in Rome with someone called Roberto Assagioli. I had always been interested in psychology and I desperately needed to get away from the house and do something that was purely mine. Assagioli was a wonderful man, small, dapper, a great thinker and writer, but also incredibly compassionate and never in the least condescending, in spite of all his wisdom and learning. Under Mussolini, of course, all forms of psychoanalysis were disapproved of." She gives an ironic smile. "Fascists aren't keen on psychological introspection – for obvious reasons. And Assagioli spent some time in prison during the war. He almost never spoke about it, except to remark that it was the perfect place to think. 'Always bless the obstacle,' he used to say.

"I went down to Rome two or three days a week and then back by train. Sandro disapproved too, of course, and it was agony being separated from Carla; but I just knew that I needed that space, that breath of outside sanity, otherwise I was going to go crazy. Eventually I took a lover in Rome. It was inevitable, I suppose, given how bad things were with Sandro by then. He had become very withdrawn and I had the feeling of the house being slowly invaded by shadows."

She pauses for a moment, apparently lost in the memory. I'm aware that in this small, private revelation a gear change has taken place in our relationship. To our right another *vaporetto* docks, bobbing slightly on the swell.

"All psychoanalysts have models for the psyche, because it's impossible to talk about the workings of the mind without one. Freud had his – the ego and id and so on – and Jung had his. Assagioli's was quite different. It's a beautiful model, deceptively simple at first, but the more you work and live with it, the richer it becomes."

She picks up the heavy silver knife, and begins etching small rings on the table cloth in front of her. I soon see that the rings form a circle.

"What Assagioli said was that we are all made up of various elements which he called 'sub-personalities', most of which are very diverse in character and behave in quite different ways. And some are outright contradictory."

"But isn't that schizophrenic?"

She shakes her head. "Not at all. It's absolutely normal. If you were sitting here with, say, Carla – or any other attractive young woman – or with a potential art buyer, or with your bank manager or a member of the Carabinieri who wants to question you about your involvement in the Italian art world, you would certainly be behaving very differently in each case. Your body language would be different – even if you weren't aware of it. You would be using different turns of phrase and gestures. You would most probably be dressed differently. Each of these is a separate sub-personality and we move between them all day long, normally without being at all aware of it. Assagioli said that what we need to do is to become aware of them and learn how to move gracefully and appropriately between them. It's a very sane, polytheistic way of looking at the world, a bit like the Greek gods – you may be very logical and dominated by Athena one minute, then someone attractive steps through the door and whoosh Aphrodite and probably Dionysus have swept you away. It's how life really is, not that absurdly rigid monotheistic construct that we've been brought up with. Christianity has a lot to answer for in terms of its psychology."

"I think I start to get the point," I say, although I'm also wondering why she is taking me on this long detour.

She nods. "But it's a little more complex than it appears at first sight, because we normally prefer some parts of ourselves to others, we judge them and unconsciously arrange them hierarchically and usually try to avoid the bits we don't like – unsuccessfully, of course. But Assagioli's model is circular and essentially flat. There is no hierarchy. Each sub-personality – every single bit of ourselves – has both strengths and limitations, but none is actually *better* than any other. There's no judgement in it. It's simply a question of understanding each sub-personality and knowing – consciously knowing – which one serves us best in any given situation."

"It sounds rather cool and calculating."

"Not at all. It's just about living consciously. And if we can do that we are far less likely to do damage to ourselves." A slight, deliberate pause. "And to others."

She allows a silence and under her unremitting gaze I can feel a strange shift take place inside me. She is not blaming me for what happened to Carla in that aggressive knife-in-the-guts way that I know so well from Sylvia. But I am somehow being quietly held to account.

Then she goes on more gently, "I don't believe you caused Carla's attempt to take her own life. I do want you to know that. That was an event long waiting to happen and I've lived with the daily fear of it for the last twenty years. At the same time I think you triggered something in her. She was obviously very attracted to you. You have a combination of charm and ruthlessness that's not unlike her father. I know that something happened between the two of you that night and I can guess what it was. It wasn't by any means the first time. But you were different. You touched her soul. Despite all her defences I could see that. You opened her up. But in doing so, you also opened up her darkness."

At this point our coffee arrives, and I'm glad for the respite. I'm feeling faintly winded by what she has said. I might have found it easier if she had raged at me and blamed me for my deception with the statue and what has happened with Carla. But there's something unnerving about her almost detached view of things. Instead of forcing me into defence mode, I can feel her opening up a Pandora's box in me. Somehow I need to explain myself.

"I think I was incredibly confused by Carla," I begin once the waiter has left us. "I thought I was in charge of things, but a lot of the time I actually felt quite at sea. It was as if I never quite knew where she was."

"Carla is a very confusing person. And that's why I started to tell you about Assagioli and the sub-personalities. It wasn't meant to be just a boring psychanalytic lecture. Carla has, for example, a sophisticated, charming woman-of-the-world sub-personality. Then there's a delightful, enthusiastic teenager sub-personality. She also has a very wounded, confused adolescent part too. But one of the most prominent and most unusual sub-personalities is that part of her that I call 'The Seer'. In a sense, of course, it's a gift. She's a genuine clairvoyant who can access knowledge beyond most of us, which is mainly channeled through astrology. But fundamentally it's another – and much broader – way of seeing the world. And when she fully inhabits that part of herself she can be magisterial, totally authoritative. I know – I've seen her do it often enough. And I imagine that's what you witnessed that evening in the library. But that doesn't necessarily make her *wise*. That's a totally different thing. And the problem is that that Seer sub-personality is so powerful that it can sometimes be very hard for her to come out of it. And, at the same time, she can't allow herself to be trapped there, because then she really would – at least in our times – be seen as delusional or possibly schizophrenic. In an earlier age, of course, she would simply have been burnt as a witch. So then one occupies a kind of no-man's land between the two worlds. It's both a gift and a curse. A curse because it puts you outside the normal order of things. It makes friendships difficult and it can leave a terrible longing, because you're in touch with things that are so at variance with the life that you have had to lead. Particularly in her case."

I don't miss the stress on that last sentence. And suddenly a totally different image of Carla begins to form in my mind, and her plaintiff words in the *Castello* come back to me.

"*Sometimes I feel I live in a completely different world to everyone else.*"

"But I still don't understand. Presumably she's not the only psychic in the world. So how do the others…?"

Elizabeth holds up her hand. "There's another part of Assagioli's model that I haven't told you about. The most important part." She pushes aside her half eaten plate and sketches out again the ring of sub-personality circles with the tip of her knife. Then she pauses and draws a larger circle right in the centre. The waiter, mistaking her gesture, comes to remove the plate, but Elizabetta smiles and shakes her head.

"What's that?" I ask. "There in the centre?"

"This is probably the most difficult bit to understand. This is the only part of us that is not a sub-personality. Assagioli called it simply the 'I'. It's where we are when we are utterly calm and truly feel in our centres. It's the still point of the turning world, if you like. Most people have at least some experience of it, although they may not register it as such."

My mind jumps instantly to my first sight of Greece, glimpsed from the deck of the ferry in the dawn light. It had been a moment of absolute calm, a feeling of *'Here I truly belong.'* A glimpse into some Platonic realm far beyond my normal self.

"For some people the 'I' has spiritual connotations, of course. But it doesn't have to be seen that way. On a more prosaic level, it can be simply what Assagioli called 'The Observer'. This is a mature part of us that doesn't get sucked in to things and doesn't judge, but remains completely calm and can see exactly what is going on and which sub-personality would serve us best in the current situation."

"Again, if I may say so, that sounds rather detached, almost ruthless."

"Detached is a cold term, but the 'I' is very benign. It has our – and everyone else's – best interests at heart." She gives a small smile. "If we could all inhabit our 'I's a bit more often the world would be a much less troubled place. Assagioli's term for it was 'Disidentified', which simply means not identified with any of the sub-personalities."

"And everyone has this faculty?"

"Everyone has it in potential, and the wise amongst us cultivate it as we mature. But in some people it can be damaged and then it's extremely hard to access."

"Damaged by what?"

Elizabetta looks down at the table for a long moment. Then she raises her eyes to meet mine and I can see pain there.

"Usually," she says, "by deep childhood trauma."

There is a long silence and suddenly the floodgates of my mind seem to open and I am standing in the loggia of the *Villa Ducale* with Carla, gazing down into the courtyard with the sound of the fountain playing in the distance.

It felt so incredibly safe.

I experience a moment of pure descent, so unnerving that I actually clutch the edges of the table. How could I have been so stupid, so obtuse and self-absorbed not to have noticed what was going on? And I have been a part of it.

Finally it is Elizabetta who breaks the silence, and when she speaks she takes us in a most unexpected direction.

TWENTY-TWO

"Guilt is a terrible thing. It devours you from the inside. You spend day after day begging God to forgive you for what you know is the unforgivable. *Of course* I should have known what was going on. Of course I should! I was studying to be a psychotherapist, for God's sake! If you look at the plain facts it's beyond shocking. I would go down to Rome for two or three days a week to study and see my lover and leave Carla in the care of Sandro, with only the servants around. And each time I came back Carla would be quieter and more withdrawn and the house would be fuller and fuller of shadows. I asked her again and again if everything was all right, but she just looked down and said, "Yes, Mama" and I couldn't get anything out of her. And Sandro too was increasingly strange and withdrawn. By that time all forms of intimacy between us had ceased."

She is looking down at the table now, her hands folded in her lap, her food is half finished. Her shoulders are shaking and I know that she's crying softly. I have a sudden urge to reach out and take her hand, but I know it would be wrong. Off to our right I can see a waiter hovering nervously. I gesture for him to stay clear. Then she dabs at her eyes and looks up.

"And then I came home early from Rome one day because I wasn't feeling well and I found them. That was the last time I saw Sandro alive. That evening he dressed up in his full military uniform. He went into his study and shot himself with his service revolver. Only two things saved me at that point. I knew I had to be there for Carla as she grew up. However much of an inadequate mother I might be, the one thing I couldn't do was leave her parentless. And the other great saviour was that I was able to tell Assagioli about it. I swore I would never tell anyone, but then the next time I saw him, there was something about the allowingness of his presence so that I just couldn't hold it, and it all burst out. I sat in his consulting room and cried for about two solid hours. And then slowly he began to talk. I don't even remember now exactly what he said. I only remember that he didn't judge me. Can you imagine that? I tell him of the most terrible crime that a mother could ever possibly commit – and he doesn't judge me!

"And slowly, over time, he showed me how battered and weakened I had been by the war and by being caught in such a terrible situation between two loyalties, and how Sandro had somehow dazzled and beguiled me and how my whole Puritan upbringing had made such a thing unimaginable, so that I had retreated into a kind of shell of denial. He didn't forgive me. He didn't excuse me. He didn't blame me. Above all, he didn't judge me. He just laid it all out for me to see. *All* of it. Not just from the narrow perspective of guilt and blame and shame. And gradually I stopped thinking of myself as evil and began to see that I had been frightened and naïve and lacking in the kind of courage that that situation needed. I have never forgiven myself, but then I don't think any of us truly has the right to forgive another, because it's just another way of standing in judgement over them. But gradually – I know this will sound like a therapeutic cliché, but it's true – I began instead to see myself with compassion. Without compassion we're all lost and life is worthless. Without Assagioli I don't think I would have survived those years."

For a moment she pauses, then she adds, "One of his favourite sayings was, '*Bless the obstacle*', and one day I challenged him on what could possibly be the blessing in such a tragedy. And his response was very simple. 'Elizabeth,' he said, 'the rest of your life will give you the answer.' I suppose he was talking about atonement."

She lapses into silence. I feel shattered and deeply moved. But strangely calm too, as if all the unnecessary trivia of my life has been burnt away. The world around me – the bobbing gondolas, the faceted light on the Grand Canal, the glittering dome of the *Dogana* – all look unreal, as if they are being projected onto a cinema screen. And suddenly something about her clicks into place. At first you see only what's on show – the elegance, the charm, the house, the life-style, the servants… It all looks so easy. But there was always, right from the start, that sense that here was someone who had not just x-ray eyes, but a much *wider* vision of the world than I had ever encountered before. It was silent, almost imperceptible, but *there*. And that presumably was why I had felt so incredibly comfortable with her from the start, why I had so uncharacteristically opened up within minutes of our first meeting. But now I get it. Behind the façade of elegance and perfection, this is a woman who has suffered, suffered terribly, who has looked down, day after day, into an abyss of despair. And, in doing that, her heart has not shriveled, but expanded. I feel a sudden surge of gratitude that people like Elizabetta exist in the world. People who have been in Hell and come back to flourish, to spread light around them. It's a naïve and possibly childish idea, I know. But still true. What happens in the heart simply happens… Elizabetta's voice summons me back.

"I have never told that to anyone," she says. "Anyone other than Assagioli, that is."

"So why me?"

She gives a small shrug. "Because I trust you." And then an unexpected smile. "In spite of all the evidence to the contrary." Then her face grows grave again. "And it felt like it was time we were honest with each other. I also have an enormous favour to ask."

"Try me."

"You said you would go on from here to Rome."

I nod. "Yes, I have to meet someone there."

She draws in a breath. "Would you come to Prosaro for the night and see Carla?"

"*Me?* I would have thought I was…"

"The last person?"

"Something like that."

"Before I left this morning Carla asked me to ask you. She says she wants to see you."

"Is that a good idea? Can you at least tell me why?"

She spreads her hands. "I'm not sure. But I am sure it would be the right thing. The why is more complicated." She pauses and sips her wine. "I think you will find she has changed." She obviously sees my look of alarm. "For the better. It was touch-and-go for a while when she was in intensive care. She lost a lot of blood. And I think that seeing her life from that extreme perspective has changed something profoundly in her. You were the last real contact she had with the outside world before she tried to take her own life, and I know you are somehow important to her."

My mind is reeling at the thought of what may be hidden in this request. Fragments seem to be floating around in my brain without any order. Uppermost is fear. Fear of the kind

I had felt as I walked down the hospital corridor towards Sylvia's room. Fear of finding something that is beyond my capacities to handle. And a weight of anxiety of what Carla might expect from our meeting. Elizabetta sits looking at me, waiting for my answer. There's a total openness in her face. And a lot of grief. And suddenly my heart feels flooded. Illogically, irrevocably flooded. How could I, who have walked up and down all those days in the Underworld and known its terror, how could I think of refusing such a request?

In the end there is only love and fear. Fear drives out love. But love can also drive out fear.

*

Carla is seated in an armchair at the end of the *salotto*. Beside her the French windows onto the terrace are open. She is clearly unaware of my presence. She sits perfect still, her hands folded in her lap, gazing out in front of her. Seeing her like this, her profile imprinted on the rolling landscape behind, is like looking at a Renaissance painting; so much is gathered into the stillness. Aeons of time seem to separate me from the last time I stood in this room. Clearly the gods – as Dinos would say – are no respecters of human chronology.

On the drive from Venice, Elizabetta and I had talked of other things. And much of the way we had travelled in comfortable silence. It was as if we had said everything – at least for the moment – that needed to be said. But with Carla it's a different matter altogether. What lies between us is uncharted territory. But at least my conversation with Elizabetta over lunch has given me some kind of key to her mystery. All the same, I can feel the knot of tension tightening in my stomach.

As I begin to cross the floor she starts and turns towards me. Without speaking, she gestures to the chair opposite her and for a long while we sit in silence. Oddly it feels an easy silence, like a pause in a conversation between old friends. Closer to I can see – not surprisingly – that she is very pale and she has lost a lot of weight. But I see too that her eyes have changed. They have lost that half-veiled, disturbing quality that had so unnerved me when we first met in London. They seem clearer now, more candid, more like her mother's. And I register too that there's a new quietness about her, a kind of coherence. No longer does she feel like an insect caught inside a glass jar, buzzing frantically from one part of herself to another. Is this the presence of the 'I' that Elizabetta had talked about in Venice? Has it taken this near fatal disaster to instill in her something that has been missing all her life? At length she breaks the silence.

"Thank you for coming. I imagine it wasn't an easy decision."

"Probably easier than you think."

She gives a small smile as if she understands. "And Mama has told me about your offer with the statue. I thank you, and that tells me that you too have changed."

"A lot has happened since we last met – to both of us, it seems. A whole lot of water under the bridge."

"Under all our bridges, I suppose. You know, when we first met you were so obstinately closed," a small smile, "if I may say so. So fixed in your ways, so confident that nothing was going to upset your life. But it was clear from your chart that change, probably violent change, would be swift and inevitable. And I sensed the moment we met that you and I were on some kind of collision course. It was an odd moment when I looked down at the computer and saw it all laid out there. But it also seems that we have both survived our individual journeys to the Underworld. For that was by no means certain, you know."

I nod, remembering those darkest days when death had, for a moment, felt a desirable option. "And have come up in another place," I say.

She frowns.

"It's from one of Grimms' tales about the youngest brother who gets tricked into going down a deep well and has to walk the ground flat until..."

"He comes up in another place." She nods and smiles. "Yes, I understand. They were very wise the strange brothers Grimm. And so perhaps was your Mr Eliot:

...to arrive where we started

And know the place for the first time."

I feel profoundly moved by this strange bond that suddenly seems to have encircled us. "So what do we do now in this new place – you and I?"

She gives a small shrug. "Well, I believe the first thing is that we do not need to talk about what happened before. The past is past. It has served its purpose. Is that not so?" I nod uncertainly. "So we meet, then part and go our own ways. We remain friends, probably life-long friends, although our paths may not cross very often. And above all we honour what we have been to each other – Gateway Guardians."

"Gateway Guardians?"

"Yes, we each held the gate open so that the other could pass through into another place. It's a sacred act. And that is why we will be in each other's hearts for ever. There was an opportunity there from the moment we met, but we were both too blind, too unconscious, too bound to all our old ways and our old wounds. That was why it required so much pain. We are both lucky that we have survived and have been allowed to come up in this different place that you talk about. To have a second chance. It seems the gods must love us after all." She gives a quick, teasing smile. "But you will mock my use of these strange esoteric terms."

"I think I mock them a lot less now than I used to. And that's rather disconcerting."

"Then allow yourself to be disconcerted."

She reaches out and takes my hands.

"I don't regret what we did. It was what the gods demanded of us. I shall remain your shadow sister all your life, the one who brings you messages – and occasional riches – from the Underworld, lest you are ever tempted to forget that the Underworld too is a part of you. And sometimes, at special moments, I will come into your head, even if at first you don't know why. And though we may very seldom meet, our fates are bound together in that special way. And always will be."

Then she leans back as if the effort of talking has tired her. I have noticed on the low table beside her a blue and white Chinese bowl containing several coloured marbles, exactly like the ones we used to play with at school. Absentmindedly she picks some up and allows them to roll through her fingers. She catches my look of enquiry.

"No, I am not regressing totally back to childhood, playing with marbles, in case you were wondering. I have been doing the I Ching, the Chinese oracle and choosing these small objects at random is one of the ways."

"No more astrology?"

"Not for the moment. Right now I need gentleness. And astrology is not always so gentle."

"I think I know what you mean," I say ironically.

She smiles. We are playing with each other again, but not

as we used to, not as a defence, but rather as a kind of openness, a light-hearted way of acknowledging what we share.

"And I have cast the oracle several times for your new future."

"And what's the verdict?"

"Well, because it is gentle it is also sometimes a little obscure. Also sometimes a little strangely Chinese. But one phrase comes again and again."

"And that is?"

"'*Make a sacrifice and you will succeed.*'"

I frown. "A sacrifice? What kind of sacrifice?"

She gives a light shrug and smiles. "Of your old life perhaps?"

TWENTY-THREE

At this time of the morning Perugia's main square is largely deserted. During the night the municipal workers have been out and hosed the place down so that a moist fragrance now hangs in the air. In a little while the shopkeepers will arrive and begin to rattle up their metal shutters, but for now all is quiet and the pigeons have the run of the place. They perch on the rim of the marble wellhead that stands at the centre of the square or stagger about on their scaly, scarlet legs as they peck busily between the damp cobblestones.

Mostly the place is still in shadow. But I manage to find a café in a small wedge of sunlight that falls between the tall ochre-tiled houses. The previous evening I had strolled through the narrow streets and enjoyed half a bottle of Lambrusco on a terrace overlooking the fading Umbrian landscape, before retiring to my hotel to sleep a dreamless sleep of perfect peace. After my underworld existence of the last weeks, I feel like a condemned man set free. And Elizabetta's tragic story and my meeting with Carla, far from having depressed me, seem to have given me new inner ballast. As I look around me now, everything seems benign, slowed down and somehow beautifully glazed, like the shell of an egg. It's the kind of morning when even the most melancholy must feel grateful to be alive.

The waiter arrives with my cappuccino. It is perfectly frothed and liberally sprinkled with chocolate. I unwrap the two cubes of sugar lying in the saucer and carefully drop the first one into the cup. There's a sense of spaciousness about this little ritual, and I take an absurd, childish delight in watching the cube balance for a moment on its cushion of foam before it sinks slowly out of sight. A pale oatmeal stain begins to leach its way up the funnel of froth. I am just about to insert a second lump when a shadow falls across my table, blocking the sunlight. Mildly annoyed, I look up and I'm surprised to see a blonde woman smiling down at me. I take in the very blue eyes, the faint dash of freckles across the prominent cheekbones and the unmissable fact that she is rather beautiful. While I am registering all this, I am staring uncomprehendingly – and presumably rudely – up at her. Her smile begins to fade and two vertical lines of doubt etch themselves up from the bridge of her nose.

"Bronson?" The voice is uncertain and slightly accented, and with its familiar tone she suddenly comes into focus.

"Julia! I'm so sorry. I was miles away."

The smile returns. "So I see. But I'm afraid I'm interrupting a very intimate moment."

Out of politeness I rise, but now it's my turn to frown. "Intimate?"

"Between you and your cappuccino. Shall I leave you to it?"

"Oh, I see. No, of course not. Come and join me. Coffee?"

She nods and settles into the chair I have pulled out for her and I signal to the waiter for another cappuccino.

Julia von Homburg is Austrian and lives in a glittering white stucco house in Belgravia with her tall, impeccably good-looking German banker husband, Bernhardt, and her equally impeccably good-looking blonde teenage daughter, whose name I now forget. On the London social scene they rate as a beautiful couple, and their good looks – and her charm – have propelled them out of the usual Eurotrash circles up into polite upper-class English society. Personally I avoid polite upper-class English society like the plague. It gives me an overwhelming sense of claustrophobia. Nonetheless, our paths occasionally cross at functions laid on by Christie's or Sotheby's, where she appears perfectly dressed and effortlessly charming.

The waiter emerges with the coffee. He runs his eyes over Julia with the kind of silent, expert approval that race-horse trainers reserve for outstanding thoroughbreds. Julia smiles up at him, then tosses her cerise blazer back over her chair, drops a lump of sugar into her coffee and takes a long sip. "Mmm. That's good! I couldn't quite believe my eyes when I saw you. I thought you must have a *doppelganger*."

"Me neither – as you may have gathered."

She smiles. "You're forgiven. It's probably good to have one's ego dented from time to time." She stirs her coffee. "What are you doing here?"

I explain that I've been in Rome on business and just felt like taking a couple of days off in Italy. I don't mention that my business had consisted of a long bucolic lunch with Antonio and Enzo to celebrate our escape from the jaws of near disaster. We had gone to Antonio's favourite restaurant just off the Via Appia, where the owner greeted us like royalty and laid on a gargantuan feast while we sat under a pergola of freshly sprouting vines. Four bottles of Chianti Classico had been consumed, followed by prodigious quantities of grappa. The festivities had ended with Enzo dancing on the table like a performing clockwork monkey while the owner strummed on some kind of miniature guitar. Towards five o'clock I had staggered to the toilets and put my head under the cold tap. A more responsible person wouldn't have driven at all, of course; but by now I fancied a couple of days wandering aimlessly in Italy. And besides, I could sober up on the *autostrada*. So, when, two hours later, the green and white sign for Perugia had come rushing towards me, I had just hit the indicator switch and pulled off onto the slip road. Why not? It seemed a random act of pure instinct. Just what I wanted at that moment.

"And you?"

"I'm here with Gemma. She's doing History of Art for her A levels and I thought it would be good for her to spend some of her holidays seeing Florence and Perugia and a couple of other places. The problem is she knows I studied art history myself about a hundred years ago and she expects me to know all about it! So I sit up at night secretly reading my Baedekker so as not to disappoint her." She taps a thick blue hardback that protrudes from her bag. "That way the next morning I appear suitably full of artistic knowledge."

"Is Bernhardt with you?"

Her right hand, which is in the process of transferring a second lump of sugar to her cup, freezes in midair. For a long moment she just gazes into her coffee. "Oh dear," she says at length. "You're a bit out of touch with London gossip, aren't you?" She obviously sees my look of puzzlement. "Bernhardt and I separated three months ago."

My first reaction is disbelief. It seems so utterly unlikely. Or does it? But before I can speak, she goes on, "I should tell you right away that I was the one who left. It was my decision." There's a sharp note of defiance in her voice, as if she is willing me to challenge her. For a moment we are both silent, neither of us quite sure how to proceed. At length I say, "No, I hadn't heard. I'm sorry."

She lets out a low puff of breath. "It's something of a cause célèbre in London circles. So I thought you'd probably know. People love to talk."

"Is there…?" I stop myself.

"Someone else?" She shakes her head. "That's the last thing I would need at this moment. But, of course, it's the question that everyone wonders about. Or, at least, presumes. But only the very brave, or the very nosy, actually dare to ask it."

"Which am I?"

She gives a dry smile but doesn't attempt to answer. Instead she makes a strange dismissive gesture with her hand as if sweeping crumbs from the table. "I don't think I should bore you with this any longer. I'm afraid I'm not terribly good company at the moment – far too tediously self-obsessed."

I study her more closely now and notice she has lost weight and there are dark smudges under her eyes. I'm guessing that the Italian trip, for all its art history rationale, is actually an attempt at mending fences with the daughter. It must be emotionally exhausting for both of them. I wonder how it is for her to be cut adrift in the savagely gossiping world of London society, suddenly shorn of her exemplary roles of perfect wife, mother, hostess. It must render her perilously close to being a non-person in every way that counts in her circles.

"And I should also say," her voice has the determined tone of someone who doesn't want to leave any loose ends hanging about, "that I've changed back to my maiden name."

"Nothing by halves."

She gives me a small suspicious frown. "Well, I thought it would make things clearer for everyone." Then the firmness wavers and I can see tears welling up in her eyes. She looks down and crumples the paper napkin in her hands, winding it tight around one index finger. "I'm sorry. The last few weeks have been rather a strain."

I feel totally wrong-footed to see this normally supremely poised woman suddenly so vulnerable. I can think of no easy way to comfort her.

"What is it?" I ask, searching for a way to steer us to more neutral ground.

She looks startled. "What?"

"Your name."

"Oh, Larisch."

"Julia Larisch…" I turn it over on my tongue. It has a slightly exotic feel and strangely it suits her. "Is that an Austrian name? It doesn't sound like it."

"Hungarian. My mother was Austrian. That's why I've spent most of my life there. Until London, of course. But my father came from Budapest."

"Is he still alive?"

Her eyes turn down again and for a moment I wonder if I have unknowingly wandered into another emotional minefield; she is obviously extremely raw. Then she shakes her head. "No. I never knew him. He made the mistake of disagreeing with Stalin. Not a good idea in post-war Hungary. Apparently he wasn't a man who was easily deflected from his purposes. My mother used to say I've inherited a lot of his genes." Then she tosses her head as if wanting to shake the air clear. "Anyhow, enough of such things. It's too beautiful a morning to be somber. Let's talk of Italy and all things Italian instead. You're an art expert. What should we see here that one might otherwise miss?"

Her tone is bright, matter-of-fact again – and brittle. Of course, I'm relieved to follow her diversion, but I also register a feint wash of disappointment that we're back on such mundane ground.

"Well, most things here in Perugia will be in your Baedekker. But there's a small, largely unknown chapel in a scruffy area behind the cathedral, which has beautiful reliefs by an obscure artist called Agostino di Duccio. He's the man who did the carvings in the *Tempio Malatestiana* at Rimini. I don't know if you've seen them?"

"Hmm, I clearly am with an expert! I think you're a bit out of my league. I thought your field was supposed to be Roman statues and so on, not Renaissance art."

"I have many loves," I say flippantly.

"So I've heard." She gives a quick teasing smile and a slight lift of one perfectly plucked eyebrow.

"Hmm. Is that what you hear in your scurrilous London gossip circles these days?"

To my surprise she puts back her head and laughs. And suddenly a memory capsule breaks open. The very first time I had met her had been at a cocktail party with Sylvia. I had told a joke and Julia had made this same gesture of throwing back her head and letting out this laugh. Not loud exactly, but a sound of such free, unrestrained delight, that people nearby had turned to stare. It had been like having a peephole briefly slid open to expose some kind of unexpected stowaway. Then Sylvia, as if sensing danger, had murmured an excuse and, taking my arm, moved us on.

But later that night I had a disturbing dream. I was lying on the floor of a room. It was completely bare – no carpets, no curtains, furniture or any form of decoration. It was as if the removal men had been in and done a thorough job. The feeling of the dream was of complete and utter desolation. Suddenly I noticed a green plant pushing its way up through the gap between the ragged skirting and the bare floorboards. In desperation I reached out to take hold of it. Somehow I knew it would save me. But as I lunged, it began to retreat. I grabbed again and again, but with each attempt the plant retreated further until there was only a tiny tendril of it visible. I knew this was my last chance. Desperately I dived forward, but the plant had gone. I started to scream in despair. I woke sweating and wondered if I had really screamed; but in the dark I could hear the faint buzz of Sylvia's breathing beside me. Later that day we left to go sailing in Turkey.

"I'm sorry," she says, putting her hand over her mouth, "I'm an incorrigible laugher. It keeps getting me into trouble. Apparently that's something else I got from my father. The Hungarians used to be known as the gayest and most carefree people in Europe – until they got crushed by Hitler of course, and then by Stalin. But obviously a few drops of Hungarian blood must still run in my veins."

I study her for a moment. The laugh is intriguing; it doesn't seem to fit with the rest of her, and for some reason, I register that this is the first time I have ever been alone with her.

"So…" she says, "what else?"

"Well, we're only about sixty kilometers from Arezzo, so I imagine you'll be going there to see the Piero della Francesca frescoes?"

She nods dutifully. "That's slated for tomorrow."

"And if you go that far you should really go on to Borgo San Sepolcro to see Piero's painting of the resurrection – if you've never seen it?"

She shakes her head. "Afraid not. You mean the one where Christ has his foot on the edge of the tomb? I only know it from photos. But isn't it an awfully long way to go for just a single painting?"

"Not to my mind. It's one of Europe's greatest masterpieces. If Gemma's at all interested in art, she definitely shouldn't miss it." I hesitate. "Look, I'm going up there tomorrow myself. It's one of my favourite paintings. Why don't you come with me?" The lie is out of my mouth before I can check it, so I decide to press on. "One would really need to stay overnight, of course. Otherwise it would be too long a day. But there's a perfectly okay small hotel and *si mangia bene*." I put my index finger to my cheek in the vulgar south Italian gesture for good food. She laughs again, but I can sense a number of conflicting thoughts running through her.

Then, totally unexpectedly, she leans forward, gives a small shrug and just says casually, "Well, why not? Only, of course, I shall have to bring my chaperone".

*

The chaperone turns out to be more difficult – *even* more difficult – than I had anticipated. While Julia sits beside me trying to keep up a flow of light conversation, Gemma crouches in morose silence in the back, arms folded tightly across her chest. She's so closed she resembles a mollusc. The best that Julia can elicit from her is the occasional bovine grunt. There's something exhausting about parents trying to cajole their reluctant children. I wish Julia would just be quiet.

Actually I have considerable sympathy with Gemma. Whatever may have been her take on her parents' marriage, the one thing it must surely have seemed was stable; which is what kids seem to want most of all. So I'm guessing that Gemma would much rather it had continued just as before. Unless, of course, Julia and Bernhardt were beating hell out of each other behind the walls of their immaculate white stucco house

– which is hard to imagine in the Homburg household. So it must have been devastating when her apparently conventional mother suddenly walks out, changes her name and now, to top it all, picks up some stranger in Italy and invites him along to form a threesome. Under the same conditions, at the same age, I would probably have behaved the same way. 'Bolshy' would have been my father's take on it.

By now we have left behind the broad plain below Perugia and have started the long climb towards San Sepolcro. The umbrella pines and olive groves gradually give way to oak woods. Spring hasn't yet fully made it up here and last year's coppery leaves are still clinging stubbornly to the branches. Mercifully Julia has given up her attempts and lapsed into silence.

As the silence lengthens, I begin to ask myself what the hell I am doing here shut up in a car with a woman I barely know and a resentful teenager. I could, of course, think of amusing myself for a while with Julia; but I certainly have no intention of getting involved with a highly emotional woman on the rebound from a failed marriage. If I have learnt anything from my long series of failed relationships, that much wisdom at least seems to have penetrated. And, strangely, with a woman so obviously attractive, the erotic possibilities haven't even really occurred to me before. So why did I make that sudden impromptu offer? We antiquities dealers are supposed to be cunning and considered in our actions – we have to be to survive – weighing the possible consequences of each move. But the truth is that the words were out of my mouth before I had even thought about them. It was as if I had been some passive ventriloquist's dummy, having his tongue activated by an unseen hand. And now I'm paying the price.

I check the mirror and I'm surprised to see Gemma staring back at me. She has obviously been studying me for some time. Instead of looking away she holds my gaze steadily. Then, to my total astonishment, she winks. It's not a brief flutter of the eyelid, but a broad, bold, deliberate, cocky kind of wink. I almost burst out laughing. Instead I wink back, and then, taking this as a kind of semaphore, I break the silence.

"Gemma's an unusual name, isn't it? Is it short for something else?"

At the sound of my voice Julia jumps as if she has been pricked with a pin. There's a long uncomfortable pause while Gemma slowly weighs the merits of giving up the moral high ground of her silence. Then she says, "Gemma's actually a nickname. I was christened Hildegard, which is a horrible name. It sounds as if I'm destined to grow into a crotchety old spinster. And I certainly wasn't going to use my second name, which is even worse – if that's possible."

"What is it?"

She wrinkles her nose. "Ernestina."

I can't help smiling.

"Disgusting isn't it? Who would christen their child *that*?"

"It's a family name," says Julia defensively.

"So where does Gemma come from?"

She shrugs. "Oh, I don't know. I think it was when I was quite small and some teacher at school said I was a little gem and then my friends all laughed and began to tease me about it. And since I didn't like my real name anyway, it just stuck. So even my parents had to give way in the end." She slides another sour glance at her mother.

"I think Gemma's a lovely name," I say.

She regards me suspiciously in the mirror for a while, as if she's trying to assess my seriousness. Then suddenly she shoots her head forward between the front seats and whispers into my ear, "Then I shall allow you to call me Gemma!"

She sits back with a triumphant smile on her face.

TWENTY-FOUR

In my more introspective moments I have sometimes wondered if I am intrinsically unstable. Mercurial, of course, would be a more flattering word, with its overtones of speed and multi-faceted talent. But it's as if I can sense a feint undertow of chaos constantly tugging below the surface of my apparently well-ordered life. And the semi-psychotic episodes of the last few weeks haven't done much to counter that suspicion. I'm good at buying and selling antiquities, of course. Good at making money apparently. But, if I'm really honest, I'm not at all sure I would be useful at very much else. Certainly not at the investment business my father had lined up for me. I imagine myself bringing the renowned firm of Tullis & Branson to its knees by making spectacularly reckless trades out of sheer boredom or deep-seated anarchy. Doubtless my shrewd father would have had the foresight to get rid of me within six months – "Better to part now on good terms" – before I could do too much terminal damage.

Given this inherent flakiness, it's surprising that Piero della Francesca is my favourite artist. By far. His paintings exude a kind of geological solidity, a rootedness, an oaken calm. There's nothing ethereal about his saints or his angels, as they stand there tousle-headed, feet splayed broad as dinner plates on the earth. They're obviously all grown from peasant stock, skilled at cutting corn and shearing sheep and treading knee-deep in the wine press. There's an angel in one of his paintings at Urbino who stares out at you, arms folded, barring your way with the implacability of a night-club bouncer. You wouldn't dream of messing with him. Even Piero's odd UFO-shaped clouds feel more substantial than I am. Compared to them you could blow me over easily. Perhaps it's precisely my longing for his solidity, for that deep calm – precisely the same calm that the *kouros* statues so beautifully embody – that seems to underlie the surface of his paintings and draws me back again and again to his work. Interestingly, the little we know of Piero's life seems to indicate that he was erratic and unreliable too.

His frescoes in the church of *San Pancrazio* at Arezzo are high up, so that you have to crane your neck to gaze up at them like a supplicant. Once, when they were being restored, I bribed a guard to let me climb up on the scaffolding. Face to face with the figures of Adam and Eve, Solomon and Sheba, just inches away, they felt like beings from another world, extraterrestrials who had come down to earth in human form to show us how it should be done. I came down a little dusty from the flaking plaster and deeply moved.

The famous fresco of the resurrection here at San Sepolcro – where I have made my impromptu and probably ill-advised detour with Julia and her daughter – is wedged uncomfortably between two brick arches. It's far too big for the space and seems to overpower the rather small room. Modern taste would say it's all out of proportion. But the Renaissance artists had bigger things on their minds. Christ stands at the centre, one massive foot firmly planted on the edge of the tomb, whose marble lid has slid unceremoniously off to one side. He is about to climb out. To his right the hillside is in full summer bloom, to his left it is still in the barren grip of winter. It is recognisably the country around San Sepolcro. At first sight you think the paint is missing in some places, the dull undercoat showing through, until you go outside and see the strange greyish volcanic hillsides around you. Below Christ the guards are sleeping in hunched and slightly unlikely postures, as if a spell has been cast that has frozen them in mid-action. So deep is their slumber that they are totally unaware of the gigantic event occurring just behind their backs. The figure second from the left, the one with the dark, curly hair and the broad peasant face is a portrait of Piero himself.

In other paintings of the Passion cycle the figure of Christ is emaciated, ascetic, almost anorexic. It's as if he must have been half dead before they even nailed him up on the cross. But the torso of this figure is massive, muscular, hard-abdomened and barrel-chested, like a statue of an ancient Greek god. There's no apology for the flesh here. The small bloody gash in his side is like a trivial insult.

But it's the face that seizes you and won't let you go. He stares directly out, not so much *at* you as straight *through* you. What you know in that very first instant is that this is the face of someone who has descended into the deepest wells of despair that life can offer and has come back a survivor. *Death once dead, there's no more dying then*. After that the world looks different. I have some idea of that already.

I'm aware, of course, of Julia and Gemma cruising at the outer edges of my vision. From time to time they stop and Julia points something out to Gemma. It feels odd to be taking part in this tourist outing with a beautiful woman and her difficult daughter. And now that I'm in front of the painting a large part of me resents their presence. From the corner of my eye I can see Gemma begin to slide in my direction. She comes and stands beside me and for a long time I try to freeze her off, hoping to preserve my communion with the painting. But it's never going to work. And, in my irritation the communion has collapsed anyway. After a while she asks,

"What do you see in it that you can stare at it for so long?"

There's no hostility in the question, just an open curiosity. I hesitate. I might be hard pressed to give an adequate answer to myself, but how to explain it to a seventeen year old?

"Well," I start, "It's one of the greatest paintings of the Italian Renaissance. Technically it's very subtle. If you look at the figure of Jesus you seem to be level with his face, staring straight into his eyes. But if you look lower down we are actually on the level of the ground looking *up* at the underside of the soldiers' chins and the underneath of the cornice of the sarcophagus. This is because – very unusually – the artist has used two separate vanishing points for his perspective….." I hear my voice drone on. "And that's why I think it's such an interesting painting," I conclude lamely. There is a long silence.

"Oh, I see."

Suddenly I feel ashamed of this mean-spirited response. What am I doing standing in front of one of the greatest of all paintings, one that means so much to me, using my erudition to freeze out a seventeen year-old girl? Is that all I have learnt? I look up at the fresco again, as if seeking help, but the eyes of Christ are impassive now, distant. They stare blankly over my head, ignoring my supplication. From the corner of my vision I can see Julia approaching. I have only seconds before she breaks into our conversation – and then this moment will be gone forever. On an instinct I lean down and take Gemma's upper arm in my right hand.

"Actually," I say quietly, "I think the figure of Christ is me."

She looks at me in bewilderment. But her eyes are suddenly bright with curiosity.

"*You?*" she asks frowning. Julia hesitates, then walks away to look at another painting.

"Yes. You see, I often feel that I have several different characters inside me, but there are two main ones. Now if you look at the painting there are obviously several characters in it, but there are two main ones there as well. Can you see which ones they are?"

I hope the question doesn't sound as condescending and pedantic as my earlier ponderous monologue. Gemma stares hard at the fresco. Her profile has all the fineness of her mother's, but slightly obscured by the softness of the flesh, as if it's not yet fully hewn from the block. She wrinkles her forehead. "Well…," she says hesitantly. "Obviously the figure of Jesus is important. And then perhaps the one who's second from the left. He seems more real than the others somehow. But maybe that's silly because he's sleeping just like the rest…" Her voice trails off in uncertainty.

"No, you're absolutely right. We know from other paintings that he's the artist. So it's a self-portrait."

She sniffs. "He doesn't look much like a great artist!"

I laugh. "No, he doesn't, does he? He was an artistic genius, of course, but I also like to think of him as not so different from the rest of us in many ways." I pause and glance at the unruly-looking figure in the fresco. "I'm sure he enjoyed dunking his bread in olive oil and drinking plenty of red wine and chasing the local girls. And I bet he didn't let anyone else grind and mix his colours, because that's what an artist had to do in those days."

"You mean like a master chef who insists on getting up every day at the crack of dawn to go down to the market just so that he can be sure to pick the right fish and vegetables himself?" Suddenly she seems to be enjoying the game.

"Yes, I can just see him flipping open the gills of the fish to check that they're fresh, or sniffing the ends of the melons. Right?" Gemma nods emphatically. "We tend not to think of artists being so practical," I go on, surprised to find that I'm caught up in her enthusiasm, "but I'm sure Piero was exactly like that. I bet you couldn't sell him any second-rate azurite or rose-madda. And he was also incredibly unreliable. I think it's sort of comforting to know that even someone who can paint so sublimely can also be chaotic and unpunctual just like the rest of us."

"How do you know that?"

"Well, we still have quite a number of his letters."

"You mean real five-hundred-year-old letters in his handwriting?"

"Right."

"That's amazing!" She tosses her hair back from her eyes.

"He was a very expensive artist for his day. He knew what he was worth and, like a good peasant, he didn't give anything away for free. He did a whole series of frescoes in the church of a village near here called Arezzo – we'll go there tomorrow on the way back – but half-way through the project he just packed up and went off to Rome for a couple of years to work for the Pope…"

"A couple of *years*!" Her eyes widen in disbelief.

I smile. "Yes, I know. Just like any modern builder who keeps disappearing to do another job elsewhere. And there are furious letters from the town council of Arezzo to his father saying: 'If you don't get your son back here to finish up, we're going to throw him off the job. And, moreover, the bastard has already taken our money!'" Gemma laughs. "Yes, I always enjoy that too," I say. "Sometimes I can really identify with him lying there: tired, lazy, going to sleep on the job, sensual…"

To my amazement, at the mention of the word 'sensual' Gemma cocks an inquisitive eyebrow at me. It is done with such apparent coolness and experience, as if she has played this game a thousand times before.

"I mean enjoying the good things in life," I say with mock severity, but smiling – and wondering if the ability to flirt is hard-wired into the female chromosomes. "If you like, he was just a regular guy."

"So what made him a great artist?"

I pause. This time I want to give her a real answer. At length I say, "Well, I think the fact that he must have been aware of that huge figure standing behind him so much of the time. Which he knew was also a part of him. Just as it's part of all of us."

She frowns. "The figure's Jesus, right? But what does it mean… apart from the obvious?"

"Well," I stop and glance round. Julia has her back to us, bending over to read a label below one of the paintings. She's clearly giving us space. "Like I said, I feel there are two major parts to me. And the one that seems to rule most of the time is the one who's lying on the ground there fast asleep, probably having eaten and drunk far too much. Or just plain lazy. And he's quite oblivious of what's going on just over his shoulder, totally unaware of that incredible renewed life rising up just behind him. But in my case I don't feel I am totally oblivious. At least not all of the time. That's part of the problem. It's more like being uncomfortably aware of something, then closing your eyes again and choosing to ignore it. It's easier and far more comfortable."

"Like turning over and going back to sleep when the alarm clock rings?"

I smile. "Right. But sometimes – just sometimes – I *am* aware of the presence of that figure. At least, a little bit. And then I'm so wide awake and life seems so incredibly beautiful and miraculous that I can't imagine how or why I should ever want to go back to sleep again. But of course I do. And usually pretty quickly too." I pause, wondering if I have lost her, but she is staring up at me, her head to one side, her eyes squeezed in concentration. "And there's something in Christ's face that seems to talk about the suffering of being awake all the time, or perhaps the need for suffering in order to be fully awake at all. I don't know…"

"The need for suffering?" She looks puzzled.

I shrug. "Yes, I suppose I don't really understand it either."

"So does that mean that if you're awake often, you'll be a great artist?" she gestures at the painting with her left hand.

"Who? Me?"

"Yes."

I laugh. "Not with paint I'm afraid."

"Then with what?"

"Perhaps with life," I say. But as soon as the words are out of my mouth, I realise how absurdly pretentious they sound. "I know that probably sounds stupid… and perhaps it is. Obviously, if I can't paint or draw or write or compose – and I can't, at least not well enough, then it's quite true that I'm not an artist and never will be. All the same, if being 'woken up' makes me produce anything at all, I would hope that it might be…" I hesitate, suddenly uncertain where this conversation is leading us, "real friendships, real relationships… perhaps real love." I'm surprised by my own words and, for a moment, I remember David's stinging question in the park that day – *How much real love do you have in your life?* Gemma is looking at me with grave concentration. For a moment there is silence.

"And how much of the time are you asleep?" she asks.

"Me? Oh, pretty much most of the time," I say laughing, relieved to be able to lighten the tone. "And if I have any virtue at all it is that at my ripe old age I finally start to recognise it. And just occasionally I try to do something about it. But not often enough."

"And what wakes you up?"

"That's not a very easy question." She looks disappointed. "And I'm not being evasive. But I suppose... things like this painting, great sculpture, beautiful landscapes like we passed today, some poetry, certain contacts with people. But there's no guarantee that I won't come in here tomorrow and feel absolutely nothing at all in front of this fresco. Perhaps it depends who I'm with."

She smiles, obviously relishing the implied compliment. Then she grows serious again. "And Mummy?" The question isn't hostile, just very direct. "You really like her a lot, don't you?"

"I suppose," I say. "Otherwise I wouldn't be here." I know it's an evasion and somehow unworthy of our conversation. On an instinct I glance up at the painting. "Yes," I say. "I like her a lot."

"I don't think Daddy's ever woken up," says Gemma.

At that moment Julia comes and stands beside us. "May I stand with you?" she says. "You seem to have been having quite a discussion." For a moment Gemma looks annoyed. Then she says, "Bronson was explaining the painting to me. It's really interesting." I'm startled at my sharp fish-leap of pleasure at her simple statement.

"I expect I've bored her quite long enough," I say. "Why don't we take a wander around town before dinner? It's worth seeing."

Outside the sun has set and the temperature is dropping. As we come down the steps onto the cobbled street, Julia slides her arm through mine. "And how was Piero's Christ today?"

"I had the distinct impression that he smiled at me."

"Funny, I thought that too," she says and squeezes my arm. Gemma is already looking into shoe shops.

*

The waiter sets down the three huge plates of pasta on the check table-cloth. Gemma sniffs and wrinkles her nose. She had been wary of my recommendation: the local speciality of spaghetti with a sauce made from wild boar. She eyes me suspiciously.

"Since you enticed my mother and me all the way up here with the promise of great food," she says, "it had better be good." She sticks her fork in the pasta and begins to twirl it energetically. I'm still perplexed by the change that has come over her since we first met this morning. Although her questions are still sometimes spiked with suspicion, they have an ironic tone now, as if it's all part of some new game to keep me on my toes. She also seems suddenly curious about me. On our walk through the mediaeval town she had cross-questioned me in surprising detail about my career as an antiquities dealer. Gemma puts the accumulated spiral of pasta into her mouth, opens her eyes wide and lets out a low purr of appreciation.

"Worth the trip?"

She nods vigorously, finishes chewing and wipes her mouth with her napkin.

"Mummy says you don't have children. Why not?"

"Gemma," breaks in Julia. "Perhaps Bronson..."

"No, it's fine," I say quickly.

Gemma looks pleased with herself. It's obvious that she's trying to bullock her way into adult territory. And why not? She has had more than enough adult condescension from me in the museum.

Gemma turns to her mother, deliberately challenging. "No, really, why not? Of course, there could have been other reasons we don't know about. Perhaps his wife took the pill. Or she was just infertile. Perhaps Bronson didn't fancy her and…"

Julia flushes and is clearly about to deliver a reprimand. I hold up my hand. It's obvious I have to intervene before the evening degenerates into emotional guerrilla warfare between mother and daughter.

"To take your points one by one," I say, ticking them off with the crook of each finger. "No, she didn't take the pill. No technically she wasn't infertile. All the tests showed that. And yes, I did fancy her. At least enough to get the job done."

Gemma beams. Beside me I can feel Julia's anger deflate. She smiles at me in a way that simply says thank you.

Gemma cocks her head to one side. "But do you miss not having children?" Having made it to the adult high ground, her voice is quieter.

I hesitate. "Well, in some ways I think I'm pleased. My ex-wife would have used them after the divorce to make my life hell. And they would have been caught in the middle. It would have been a nightmare."

"But do you *miss* them?" persists Gemma.

For a moment I'm unsure how to respond. I realize that I have never even asked myself this question before. The silence lengthens uncomfortably. Both mother and daughter are looking at me, waiting for an answer.

"Well, to be honest, even though it may sound strange, I've never really thought about it that much." I recall my conversation with Gemma in the museum that afternoon, how deeply I had been touched by her sudden openness and enthusiasm. "But yes, since you ask, I suppose there probably is some part of me that does miss it very much." I meet Gemma's gaze.

"Why don't you have some now?"

I smile. "Well, for one thing the appropriate lady doesn't seem to be around. For another, I think I'm getting a bit long in the tooth for that."

Gemma leans back, dabs her lips with her napkin and regards me with narrowed eyes, as if blatantly inspecting me for stud purposes. "Oh, I don't know," she says with an exaggerated drawl.

*

Back in my cramped bedroom I find it difficult to sleep. The weather is sultry and there feels something undischarged in the day's events. My mind tracks back to Gemma's outspoken questions. Is there something abnormal, even monstrous, about me that I have never missed the presence of children in my life? Never even thought about the subject. And then, years after my marriage has finished, a teenager I hardly know has suddenly surfaced in the middle of dinner an ache that must have sat there in the shadows all my adult life, unacknowledged. It seems I've missed the boat again. For a moment I feel like a man marooned on a narrow spit of sand.

There are more things between Heaven and Earth than are dreamed of in your philosophy...

In these last weeks my life has been unrolling in

unexpected ways, throwing up thoughts, feelings, events that I am totally unused to, as if what is happening now bears no relation to what has happened before. *Before* things had a kind of predictable logic – I got a call, I bought an object, I sold the object, I made a lot of money, I met a woman, I spent the money... I got another call... I met another woman... There was a comforting familiarity to it all.

But now? *Now* things seem to be much more random. Carla arrives uninvited out of nowhere with her *kouros* statue and her crazy astrology... Sylvia dies without warning... A black statue appears in my dream... Then it appears in reality... I have a nervous breakdown (or 'spiritual crisis' or whatever David may choose to call it)... I seem to recover...I drive to Perugia... I meet...

It's as if the present has been severed from the past and everything is happening unexpectedly. And yet.... *And yet?* In some way I can't explain, my life feels more *coherent*, more meaningful than it did before. Is it possible, as Carla has suggested, that there really is some kind of pattern hidden in all this apparent chaos? Something not governed by the laws of cause and effect, but governed by... By *fate* perhaps? Whatever that may mean. By the planets even...? And if so, where might Julia fit into all this?

Suddenly the room is illuminated by a sheet of white lightening that lights up the patch of sky between the shutters. The thunder cartwheels down out of the mountains. Within minutes it is raining torrentially. I feel a sense of release. For once what the atmosphere had promised has been delivered. I lie in bed listening to the rain battering the cobblestones and gurgling in the overcharged drain pipes. Then I fall asleep.

I am standing in a large room looking at the back of a figure wrapped in shawls, like an old crone. As I stare, the figure turns. To my surprise, she is young, dark-eyed and beautiful. She carries a baby, also heavily swathed. She holds out the baby towards me in a gesture of offering. But as I step towards her, the image vanishes and I am standing on a shingle beach beside the sea. An old man is throwing nets into the water.

TWENTY-FIVE

"God, what a storm that was last night! Even the poor cicadas seem to have been stunned into silence. But where has all the water gone? Everything seems as dry as a bone."

"It's this volcanic soil. It just swallows it in one gulp. But it does have its compensations. Sniff the air."

Julia pulls in a deep breath. "Mmm. Beautiful. I get... rosemary?"

"Right."

"And lavender... and sage..."

"And wild thyme."

"I'm not sure I know what that smells like."

I stoop and break off one of the fragile stalks, then crumple the papery leaves between my palms. I hold them out to her.

"Nice. It smells like aromatic dust. Are we headed anywhere in particular?"

"Just to the top of the hill. There's a great view over the town and surrounding countryside from up there that I wanted you to see. Will Gemma be awake soon? I don't want her thinking we've eloped."

She gives an ironic chuckle. "You clearly don't know teenagers! I nearly have to dynamite her out of bed in the mornings. I think she rates sleep – at least late morning sleep – far more highly than Renaissance art."

I laugh and for a while we walk in silence, finding our way between the knee-high clumps of sage and gorse, while I try to unpick my own reasons for wanting to be alone with Julia before Gemma can commandeer the emotional space again. Kant said that we are opaque to our own motives and I'm inclined to agree with him. There's something intriguing about discovering that this woman I have known purely as a social figure is turning out to be quite different from what I had imagined. I don't know how genetically accurate the 'Hungarian blood' thing is, but as a metaphor it certainly resonates. Even her change of name seems somehow emblematic: Julia Larisch is a whole world away from Julia von Homburg. It feels as if she is tentatively reclaiming exiled parts of herself.

At length I say, "You know, I didn't think you would come."

"On this walk or to San Sepolcro?"

"Both, but especially to San Sepolcro."

She smiles. "Well, as a matter of fact, neither did I. I think the words jumped out of my mouth before I could stop them. As you can see, I'm given to occasional bouts of recklessness. Must be that Hungarian blood again. I've managed to keep a pretty tight lid on it for the last twenty years or so, but you seem to have prized it open. For good or ill."

"No regrets?"

"About coming?" She shakes her head. "None at all."

"Just so long as we don't run into any of your fashionable London friends, I suppose, who'll start the gossip wheels churning back home."

She shrugs. "Well, there's not a lot to gossip about, is there? Anyhow, frankly I don't really care anymore. And besides I don't think too many of my SW3 neighbours are going to be shacked up in Borgo San Sepolcro, especially at this time of year. They're much more likely to be lazing on the beaches of the Maldives. It's only crazy aficionados like you who would make the hike all the way up here. But thanks for dragging me along. I'd have been far too lazy to do the trip by myself."

Then she stops walking and turns to me. Her face is suddenly serious. "I also wanted to thank you for yesterday."

Puzzled, I shake my head.

"What you did with Gemma."

"Oh, that. That was just…"

"Nothing?"

"Not exactly, but I don't think I'm terribly good with young people. Insufficient experience, I suppose." I shrug, unsure how to continue.

"But you did the one thing she really needed – you took her seriously. It may have seemed like a small thing to you, but I think it meant a lot to her. Her relationship with Bernhardt has always been difficult. With all his endless travelling and his obsession with work, he's been a pretty distant father. Frankly I don't think he's ever quite known what to do with her. He'd have been far more comfortable with a son – pheasant shooting, mountain hiking, stock prices – all that male stuff is much more his thing. And, to be honest, he'd probably have been a pretty good father in his own way. And then I'd have been the one who felt excluded."

"Is that what he feels?"

Her shoulders lift. "I guess so. I think Gemma's baffled by their relationship. It just isn't what she feels it ought to be. She's grown up semi-fatherless and I think that's left her with a difficult mixture of longing and resentment." She pauses, nodding her head slightly. "And, God, do I know what that feels like! I suppose that's why I could see so clearly that you were giving her something that was quite special for her yesterday."

I am about to demur when she raises a hand to silence me. "I know you think it was nothing. That's because you do it so naturally." That puzzles me too. I genuinely don't think I've done anything unusual and, as far as I am aware, my skill with teenagers is limited, to say the least. "I could feel how she blossomed by being taken seriously by an older man," Julia goes on, "and even flirted with in a nice, safe kind of way." There's a wistful tone to her voice. "And I'm afraid that's probably also what gave her the euphoria to overstep the boundaries a bit last night."

"You mean the bit about the pill and so on?"

"Afraid so. When we went up to bed she asked me if I thought you were impotent! She didn't want to let go of the subject."

I smile. "She can certainly be a bit of a handful sometimes. But that's okay."

"I refrained from telling her about your reputation in London, which would certainly have knocked that accusation on the head."

I glance across and I'm surprised to see a small teasing smile at the corners of her mouth.

"Reputation?" I ask innocently.

"The one that makes you the prime target for all the divorced women in London society. Not to mention half the married ones too."

"But not you," I return.

"Ah." She stops. It's a stupid, clumsy remark and immediately I regret it. But soon she begins walking again and when she speaks I'm relieved to hear that her tone is still light. "I'm a respectable married woman, you know."

"*Was*," I correct her.

"But still married. And still respectable."

"No past affairs even?"

She shakes her head. "I'm afraid not. Not that it's any of your business, by the way. Pathetic, isn't it?"

I'm not entirely surprised by her answer. Hungarian blood or not, she doesn't seem the type for casual affairs. I register a small pulse of satisfaction inside myself. I say, "Pathetic? I think I'd rather call it integrity. What you see is what you get."

She gives a wry chuckle. "Oh dear, that makes me sound like some incredibly frosty ice maiden."

"I'd say less and less so by the minute. Even by the second."

Her face breaks into a broad smile and she gives a mock bow. "Thank you, kind sir. As a rapidly ageing single woman, every compliment – however blatantly dishonest – is very welcome." Then she grows serious again and frowns questioningly. "You're good at deflecting things that deep down you really want to hear, aren't you?" Before I can question that unexpected conundrum, she goes on, "Actually, I'd say you're a bit of a puzzle altogether, Mr Tullis."

"*Me?* From the way you've just been describing me, I would have thought I'm an open book. Just wine, women and song apparently. All too easy to read."

"Hmm. Not that easy. Now let me guess..." She stops again and holds up her right hand. "Highly successful antiquities dealer – right?"

"If you say so."

She nods and ticks off one of her fingers. "Respected art connoisseur. Renowned charmer. Famous seducer of married women..."

"Oh, *please!*"

She holds up her other hand to silence me. "This is my turn, remember? Hard-nosed realist. Maker of prodigious amounts of money. Probably quite ruthless when he wants to be. But surprisingly private and reclusive, not giving much away. A lone wolf maybe? Maybe quite lonely…"

I'm about to protest, but her searching look forestalls me. Instead I say, "Why on earth do you say that?"

She gives a small shrug. "The lonely thing? Oh, I don't know. Feminine intuition, I suppose."

"Great! Do you do this character-shredding bit with all your friends? I'm surprised you've got any left."

She laughs. "I haven't. Not many. Not many real ones, at any rate. Haven't you heard that I'm famous for my waspish comments? They just slip out sometimes. Anyhow, I still think I'm right about the puzzle. In your case – unlike simple me – I suspect that what you see is most definitely *not* what you get. That's how you've always struck me."

I am surprised – and not displeased – to realise that she must have been quietly observing me over the years. But the jibe about lonely has hit a strange nerve.

"So tell me more. Though I'm not at all sure why I should want to hear it."

"Well, I think my intuition was sort of validated yesterday when we were in the museum. It felt as if there was something going on which was quite different from the Bronson Tullis I know from London. And yet, strangely, it didn't surprise me at all."

"Like?"

"Well, firstly, when you were looking at the painting of the Resurrection, there was a…" she hesitates, "a kind of intensity about you. I've been taken to art galleries by men before. It's usually how they think they can start seducing me. Not very subtle really." Her lips turn up in a wry smile. "But with you it was quite different. You weren't trying to impress me with your knowledge, and it was just so obvious how much that painting really mattered to you. And I don't just mean intellectually. I could see it touched something in you. And…" She hesitates. "This is going to sound hopelessly metaphysical; but that feeling spread into the rest of the room. I felt touched by it and I know Gemma did too, even if she couldn't have articulated it. And then you were so incredibly kind with her. I hadn't expected that. Really just kind and thoughtful and unpatronising. I wonder if you know how rare that is?"

"Are you describing anyone I know?"

"Oh, and like I said, very good at deflecting things that deep down you really want to hear."

"Hmm. I'll have to think about that one. I'm not too used to this kind of psycho-scrutiny."

"In that case you should hear some more, because I also think that you have somehow changed since I last saw you."

I frown. "In what way?"

"Oh, I don't know. Perhaps gentler, more considerate."

"Telling an art dealer that he has become gentle is almost an insult."

She laughs and for a while we walk in silence. But in some obscure way, it feels as if she has quietly taken the conversation down an octave and I'm obliged to respond in this new register.

"Well," I say at length, "you're right about the painting. It *is* very special to me. I brought Sylvia here once in our early days together. I suppose I wanted to share it with her. And do you know what happened? She was actually jealous that I gave it so much attention! So she then managed to fabricate a huge row about absolutely nothing just to distract me." I spread my hands in bafflement. "Jealous of another woman – okay, that I can understand. But jealous of a painting! Can you imagine that?"

To my surprise she doesn't answer for a while. Then she says thoughtfully, "I'm not sure about jealous. But I can imagine how a woman might ache for that kind of intense attention herself and then, when she doesn't get it, she might feel quite bereft. I think I can understand that."

I look at her, puzzled. "God, you women are a mystery! Anyhow, after that I made sure that I only ever came here alone."

"Until yesterday."

I hesitate, surprised that the thought hadn't struck me before. "Yes, that's right, I suppose. Until yesterday. I hadn't thought of it that way."

"Which, when you *do* think about it, was actually quite a risk. You didn't know I wasn't going to ruin it for you in my own special way."

We have reached the crest of the hill. The conversation has taken a totally different path from anything I had expected. I turn and gaze out over the valley. The jumbled ochre roofs of San Sepolcro are spread out below us. The sounds of the waking town filter up through the clear air – the splutter of scooters, the rattle of metal shutters, the anarchic crowing of a cockerel. A bee drones its way lazily from bush to bush. And suddenly I feel a strange calm inside me. I turn to her. She is looking at me, her head on one side, brow furrowed, with a slight smile on her lips, as if she's enjoying the task of trying to puzzle me out. Our eyes lock. And there is a sudden, unmistakable fuse of intimacy between us.

In all my adult life I have only ever known one way to deal with such a situation – to cross the small space that separates us and take her in my arms. I sense she won't resist. But, at the same time, I'm aware of some counter-pull. Then, illogically, Carla comes into my mind and I have an odd premonition that whatever I do next will be of huge importance. A kind of silent fulcrum in time.

The seconds pass as we stare at each other, not moving.

Then I say, "If we don't go back now we'll probably find Gemma sitting in the café by herself, drinking Campari and seducing half the waiters."

She smiles and I can sense the relief in her. We walk back in silence but, a little way down the slope, she reaches out, takes my arm and squeezes it. "Thank you," she says quietly. And, for once, I don't need to ask what she means.

*

The narrow cobbled street in Perugia is wrapped in shadow. Their bags unloaded, we stand facing each other, suddenly an awkward triangle. Gemma steps forward, puts her arms around me and kisses me on each cheek. "Thanks," she whispers in my ear. "It was great. I hope to see you again soon." She steps back. "I'll go and see if our room's ready." And in a flurry of white sneakers on the cobblestones she is gone into the darkness of the hotel.

Julia and I stare at each other in astonishment. Then we both laugh. Julia shakes her head. "Well, whatever next?"

"She's certainly full of surprises."

"Yes." She looks down. And suddenly the silence between us is loaded.

"Look," I begin. "I'd be sad not to see you again when we get back to London. Would you like to come to the gallery one day and we could have lunch?"

She smiles. "Yes," she says simply. "I'd like that very much." She raises her cheek to be kissed. Then she turns and follows Gemma into the hotel. And I'm left with an unruly kaleidoscope of feelings. About Gemma. About Julia. But uppermost – and to my surprise – is a kind of blank sadness that I will be travelling alone back to London and an empty house.

TWENTY-SIX

Two days after my return to London a letter arrives, postmarked Italy.

Dearest Friend,

Thank you for coming to see me. I suspect it took more courage than you gave yourself credit for. When we talked after dinner that evening and you told me what had happened to you in these last weeks – your 'descent to the Underworld', as I think you called it – you probably didn't realize what a gift you were giving me. I suspect that whenever we are really honest with someone, when we dare truly to open ourselves, as you did to me, then we automatically give a silent gift to our listener. As the Talmud says, "What comes from the heart enters the heart".

What you will know by now is that I am not at all the person I pretended to be when I first stepped into your gallery last April. All my life I have felt like an outsider, even an outcast. And my gift of 'seeing more' has more often felt like a terrible curse, cutting me off from other people and from the life around me. When I was a child I longed to be normal. I would even pray for it every night. But when you told me how often you thought of my words about Saturn and Pluto when you were in the depths of despair, and how it gave you just the faintest hope of a kind of meaning to hold on to, I felt deeply touched and somehow validated. I think that is what all we who sometimes suffer despair crave most – a sense of meaning and purpose in life. The greatest terror of all, I believe, is that there is no meaning and we are all adrift in the void, with no place to stand.

But just knowing that my words – about which you had been so skeptical when we first met – had helped you in the very depths of your distress, gave me a kind of strength for the future, a belief that my ability to see beyond the obvious can really be a gift and not a curse, a gift that could be grafted onto a more normal life. I know that I shall never be 'mainstream', and I don't suppose I shall ever want to be. But what I do want is to feel at peace with who I am; and then to be able to use what talents I may have to help others. And that is the gift that you have given me. Perhaps that is one of the many things that binds us together.

After you left, I looked again at your chart. I hope I wasn't too harsh with you that first evening in the Castello library. I could see then what was going to happen to you, even if I couldn't see what form it would take, and I was hoping that if I warned you, I might be able to protect you from it. As an astrologer I should have known better than to try to play God. We all have to go through what we have to go through in order to learn. Some of us have to do it several times. (Actually I believe some of us have to do it over several lifetimes, but I won't stretch your credulity too far!) But when I looked again at your natal horoscope, it seemed to me not just a difficult chart to navigate, as I told you that first evening, but also potentially a very rich and beautiful one.

I think that the main difficulty may be that until now you have lived out the fate of your chart too literally. We all tend to do this in some way and then we get trapped in the literalism. For you, your 'descents to the Underworld' until now have taken the form of literally digging in the earth to find antiquities, and the riches of Pluto for you have been just money. At least, this was the case until Saturn and Pluto dragged you down and forced you to see that there are other kinds of depths. And perhaps other kinds of riches than just the bankable ones. And if you ever forget this invitation into depth, then your life will come to feel lightweight and trivial and your soul will wither. And that is the last thing I would wish for you.

There are many ways to stay in the depths that are not as dark and terrifying as you have experienced in your Underworld: periods of silence and aloneness, voluntary withdrawal from the world of doing, meditation, inner quietness. But, perhaps above all, love. Love in all its many varieties. Love is the great deepener. And if you believe that I genuinely am a seer – as you called me – then perhaps you will allow me to say that this is your life's lesson.

Dig deep in love, my friend, and you will surely find riches. If that doesn't sound too pretentiously biblical…

With my love,

C.

TWENTY-SEVEN

In the morning light that slides through the overhead windows, the *kouros* looks at its most radiant. The freshly cleaned marble has a perfect even sheen so that it glows, almost as if lit from within. For a long while Julia circles it in silence, hands clasped behind her back, brow furrowed in concentration. It is exactly a week since we parted in Perugia. A week in which, to my surprise, I have missed her intensely. It must be one of life's great mysteries that you can miss something you didn't even know existed before. I've occasionally missed other women, of course, but usually with a tense, erotic edginess. But this feels different. What I hadn't fully registered in Italy was the easiness of our contact, the absolute lack of strain. Probably I hadn't noticed precisely because it *was* so natural, so normal, like the taking in and letting out of your breath.

"It's very beautiful," she says at last. "Of course, quite a lot of it is missing. Does that bother you?"

I shrug. "I suppose I'm used to looking at fragmentary statues. If you deal in antiquities it goes with the territory. But I guess it bothers you?"

She steps back and puts her head to one side as she studies the statue again. "Not really," she says slowly. "In a funny way I actually find it attractive. It almost makes it like a contemporary sculpture. It gives your imagination room to expand. Where did you find it?"

"It was lying in someone's abandoned cellar in Italy. When I first saw it, it had arms, legs, head – the whole works. All added in the nineteenth century."

She wrinkles her nose in distaste. "It must have looked grotesque, like a piece of Victorian kitsch."

"It's what the travelling aristocracy liked to do back then when they hauled things home from the Grand Tour. They were fixated on the idea of recreating the perfection of classical Greece."

"I should have thought Victorian England was about as far removed from classical Greece as it's possible to get!"

"That's probably why they were so desperate to emulate it. It was a kind of acceptable counter-balance to all that uptight Victorian stuffiness. But, at least with this one, the owner was emancipated enough not to give him a decorative fig-leaf."

She laughs and turns back to the statue. Then she reaches out and runs the tips of her fingers lightly over the torso from the sternum, down over the thorax to the taut belly.

"What a beautiful man." Her tone is abstracted, almost wistful.

And suddenly, out of nowhere, I am assaulted by an absurd stab of jealousy, for all the things I haven't shared with her, all the history of which I am not a part – her lovers, of course, but not just that. Odd, intimate things: what toys she liked to play with, the desk she sat in at school, her favorite pencil, her first adolescent crush… It's so strange this sudden inexplicable ache in the gut that almost seems to wind me. Luckily Julia doesn't seem to notice. She settles down on the arm of the long sofa and pushes a strand of hair back behind her ear.

"How did you first get interested in antiquities? It's an unusual area of the art world isn't it?"

I remember Elizabetta asking me pretty much this same question in Prosaro. And she has some of Elizabetta's intense scrutiny. So I tell her of my first visit to Greece, how the light, the colours, the landscape had so totally intoxicated me.

"And that's where you first saw sculptures like this?"

"Yes. The first time I saw a statue of a Greek *kouros* – that's the ancient Greek word for a youth, by the way – was in a small museum on a tiny uninhabited island called Delos. Everything about it – its poise, its luminosity and confidence, its dignity, its total lack of compromise – was unlike anything I had ever seen. In some strange way it felt like a kind of challenge."

She frowns. "A challenge? That's an odd word."

"Yes, I suppose so. But that's exactly how it felt. At the time I was completely uncertain what to do with my life. I was wondering whether I should drop out of Cambridge. And, as I stood there in front of the statue, I remembered that Rilke had seen a *kouros* in the museum in Vienna – very few had been excavated in his day – and he wrote a poem about it. He called it 'Apollo'. And the ending really resonated for me."

"How does it end?"

"*Here there is no thing that does not see you.*
You must change your life.
That was the challenge, I suppose."

She nods slowly.

"*Denn da ist keine Stelle, die dich nicht sieht.*
Du musst dein Leben ändern."

I stare at her. "You know it?"

She tosses her head. "Even bored Eurotrash housewives occasionally read a book, you know."

"No, really. How do you know it? It's hardly mainstream, even for a German speaker, I imagine."

"Well," she looks down as if she's about to reveal a guilty

secret. "I used to hold a junior lectureship in European literature at the university in Vienna."

"Why on earth did you give it up?"

She gives a small shrug. "I met Bernhardt. I fell in love. His job was based in London, so I moved. Lectureship over. Shit happens, I suppose."

I'm trying to absorb this totally unexpected piece of information. It feels as if I have just finished a jigsaw puzzle to my own satisfaction and then found ten extra pieces.

"So why did you marry him?"

She gives a small laugh. "Instead of sticking to the lectureship, you mean? Well… He was stable. He was steady. I knew he would never be unfaithful. That was important to me. He was good-looking. He had a good upwardly mobile job. He even knew how to ski – *very* important for an Austrian. He was offering security, home, family – all that stuff that I wasn't really used to and deeply craved. In short he ticked a lot of boxes." A brief pause. "That's what we do when we're young, I suppose, without even realizing it – we tick boxes. The only problem is we tend to forget about the soul box. Not so important when we're young."

Then she stops and makes that same odd sideways sweeping gesture with her hand that I remember from our first meeting in Perugia, as if she is trying to sweep away the conversation. "Anyhow, enough of that. Let's talk of more important things. And have you?"

I frown. "And have I what?"

"Changed your life."

"Ah! Well… a lot of things are certainly different from that day in Delos, if that's what you mean. I did drop out of Cambridge and became an art dealer – which was certainly a big departure from what my father had in mind for me at the time. He was horrified. I've sold a lot of antiquities, I suppose. I've made a fair amount of money…" I realise that my voice is tailing off, like an old express train running out of steam.

"Do you think those are the kinds of changes Rilke had in mind?"

Her tone isn't exactly ironic, but it certainly lets me know that my answer isn't adequate. After a while she goes on, "Saint Augustine said that we should rise each morning and plant an apple tree. It's a beautiful image. I've always felt that was probably the kind of thing Rilke was thinking of." She gives a wry smile. "Pretty tough to do though. A whole lot of gardening is required."

If I hadn't realized it before, I certainly do now – just how wrong my original assessment of her as a charming, beautiful, but largely vacuous socialite has been. It's not just the sharp humour or the revelation about her lectureship. There's also a surprising authority about her. I can imagine she doesn't suffer fools gladly. And, after all, it must have taken quite some inner authority to walk out of a twenty-year marriage and change your name overnight. Perhaps Bernhardt, the boring German banker, has had to deal with a lot more than I had reckoned on behind the white stucco walls of their Belgravia house.

She rises and smooths out her skirt. "And now that I've bored you with my history and stung you with my Hungarian irony – which, by the way, doesn't usually go down too well in England – am I still eligible to be taken for lunch? Or have I put myself quite beyond the pail, now that you have seen my …what's that other English expression?"

"Feet of clay, perhaps?"

She smiles. "Ah yes, feet of clay. And not just the feet, by the way."

*

The restaurant is half empty. We settle into our chairs and for a moment we are silent.

"We seem to have talked rather a lot about me," I say. "What about you?"

She wrinkles her nose and pushes back a stray wisp of hair. "Oh, me. Nothing much. In any case, I thought I had already told you quite a lot." She looks down at the table, obviously uncomfortable. But I don't see why I should be the only one to be interrogated. And besides, I'm increasingly curious about her. My 'x-ray eyes', as Sylvia had called them, don't seem to have puzzled her out yet.

"You're not very used to having people ask you direct questions about yourself, are you?"

She shrugs, readjusts the position of her knife and fork to bring them into alignment. "No, I suppose not."

"Is that the result of being so perfect? No-one dares question the perfection?"

"Who me?" She puts back her head and laughs that same laugh that I remember from our last meeting. A couple on the other side of the room turn and look at her with a silent hint of disapproval. She puts her open hand across her mouth and widens her eyes in apology. "I really must get that laugh fixed," she says *sotto voce*.

"But that's the general image isn't it?" I persist. "Perfect wife, perfect mother, perfect hostess, etcetera. And not just in my eyes."

She is silent for a moment. "Well, I wasn't a very perfect wife in the end, was I?"

Before I can respond the waitress arrives to take our order. Julia chooses mixed salad and grilled sea bass. She accepts my invitation to share a bottle of white wine.

"I remember being surprised by your appetite in Italy. I thought you would only eat carrot sticks and drink mineral water."

"It seems there are a lot of things you don't know about me – about my many imperfections."

She opens a packet of *grissini*, extracts one and snaps it in half.

"Why did you leave Bernhardt?"

She stops with the grissini half in her mouth and raises her eyes to look at me. Then very slowly she puts it down on the plate beside her.

"That's a very direct question."

"You don't have to answer."

"No, I know." She pauses, then sits back and regards me gravely. "But I'd like to. Only I'm still not entirely sure of the answer myself; at least not in a way that's easy to articulate. I always thought I was very level-headed, quite considered in my actions. Then I suddenly go and do this. And, of course, everyone is shocked – husband, parents, parents-in-law – oh, my God, yes! – friends. The only one who doesn't seem to be really shocked is the one I most expected would be."

"Gemma?"

"Right."

"And me."

"Yes, that's true. And you."

"Why do you think everyone *was* so shocked?"

She sighs. "I suppose it came as such a total surprise to people. Especially to Bernhardt. I don't think he still really believes it. He told a mutual friend recently that it was just a matter of time before I came to my senses and went back to him. He probably thinks I'm hormonal or something."

"And will you?"

"Go back to him? No. That's the one thing I'm really sure about. I just couldn't any more. At first, at least at some moments, I thought that maybe people were right and that I really had done something appalling as well as stupid. And I certainly felt guilty about it. But somehow even the guilt didn't go deep enough to make me want to change my mind." She pauses. "And, in her own way, Gemma has been very supportive – to my total amazement."

"How?"

"Well, in the beginning I tried to explain it to her as best I could. She was just silent. She looked confused, and frightened – which wasn't very surprising, because I was both of those things myself." She looks down at the table. "And still am a lot of the time." She sighs. Suddenly she looks very tired. "But two weeks later I took her out to dinner. I wanted to try to find out what she was really feeling. I had a whole speech carefully prepared. As the food arrived I launched into it – 'Gemma, there's something I want to talk to you about…' You know the kind of thing. Do you know what happened?" She shakes her head in amazement. "She just reached out and took the fork from my hand. I remember noticing that I was shaking. It was suddenly as if *she* was taking charge. It was bizarre. And then she took my hand in both of hers and just said: 'Mummy, I know something has changed in you. I don't know what it is, but you mustn't go back to Daddy. Please promise me that.' I was completely stunned. But obviously she must have sensed something was going on in me under the surface."

"What happened then?"

"It was very strange. We talk about 'breaking the ice'. But this was more like the ice just giving way under our feet and we both fell through together. And there was a feeling of almost physical relaxation between us. And…" She pauses. Her eyes fill with tears. "In a funny way, our whole relationship changed right there. Ever since we've been much closer. Much more… honest. It's as if there's a new sense of mutual respect. Of course she can still be difficult at times."

"Like the drive to San Sepolcro?"

She smiles and nods. "But we haven't had any more real fights since then, which is amazing." She hesitates, playing with the white napkin on the plate beside her. "And as I was leaving to come and see you – I told her I was having lunch with you – she suddenly gave me a very intense hug and said, 'Enjoy it, Mummy. It's *your* life!' She would never have done that before, been so impulsive, I mean. *Never!* Oh, and she sends her love, by the way."

The waitress arrives with the wine. She pulls the cork and pours a small measure into my glass. I try it and nod. The waitress smiles warmly. She is short and slim with a cascade of dyed blonde hair, a faded beauty from somewhere in eastern Europe. Her complicit smile lets us know that she sees this as some kind of illicit *rendez-vous*, and she is blessing it with her presence.

"Don't you think it's strange," goes on Julia, "that we can live very close to someone, as I did with Gemma for seventeen years, and you think the relationship is fixed in a certain pattern. And then, for no apparent reason, she just touches my hand and says one sentence, and suddenly the whole thing changes. It's such a sudden break. It just isn't logical."

"I wonder if it is such a break. Sometimes I think there are things going on under the surface of our lives, things that are just waiting to happen, and often we somehow block them by not accepting their presence. Or not sensing the right moment to let them come through. Like a snake when it senses that it's time to slough its skin."

"Do you think Gemma was sloughing a skin?"

"It sounds more like she recognised that you were." Julia smiles. "You know, the ancient Greeks had two separate words for time. There was the normal one that we have for day following day. That was '*kronos*'. But they also had the word '*kairos*' to denote a sense of the appropriate moment, those special instances when so many apparently random things seem to come together for a reason – when we seem to have a choice…" I hesitate. "… to affect our fate perhaps? Something like accepting a natural rhythm? I think those moments are vital and yet so hard to recognize, at least in our cultures." Frankly I'm amazed to hear myself talking like this. My mind jumps to Carla. It's as if she has given me some kind of alien transfusion and in Julia's presence this new substance is beginning to pump through my arteries.

Julia has both elbows on the table, cupping her face in her hands. Her brow is furrowed in concentration. I stop and stare at her. And it's as if I am seeing her face for the first time. Not just her obvious beauty, but another quality behind it – a kind of loving generosity. It's a shock that reminds me of the shock of my first sight of Greece, seeing something more profound, somehow *interior* to the visible world, a kind of Platonic imprint of what we normally choose to ignore. And suddenly something seems to fall away from the space between us. I don't know where my next words come from, only that they seem to speak through me.

"To everything there is a season," I say. "And a time to every purpose under heaven." I look directly into her eyes. "And I think that *our* season is now."

Julia returns my gaze evenly, apparently without surprise. "Yes," she says simply. "I think so too."

At that moment the waitress arrives with our food.

The rest of the meal continues quietly, as if nothing at all unusual has happened. Julia talks more about her separation, about Gemma and, with diffidence, about her uncertain future. The nearer I approach her, the more I realise that her mask of perfection isn't so much false as just very incomplete. I feel a swell of shame for having viewed her so superficially. For what seems to be emerging now from between the cracks in her elegant persona is a character far more complicated and unsure than I could ever have guessed. In many ways she still perplexes me. But I also know that beneath the surface of our conversation, some connection has been made between us that, for now, remains ineffable.

We emerge from the restaurant with a final blessing from the waitress. It is after four and we both blink in the bright light of the London afternoon, as if we expect night to have fallen. We stand for a moment, awkward on the pavement.

"Thank you so much for lunch. And for showing me your gallery. It felt like… well… picking up the threads again after Italy."

I hesitate. I'm normally skilled at dealing with this kind of situation, but there's something about Julia, about the strangeness of our whole relationship, that makes me feel like a novice. "I was wondering if perhaps you might like to come to the British Museum with me one day next week," I venture uncertainly. "I could give you a layman's guided tour. Unless you already know it inside out?"

"I'm embarrassed to say I hardly know it at all." She gives me a broad smile. "And yes, I'd love that."

"Next Tuesday?"

She nods.

"I'll meet you on the steps at two o'clock?"

"It's a deal."

The tree-lined street is quiet. We walk for several minutes before a taxi passes and I hail it. Julia turns to face me. "I enjoyed our conversation." She smiles ironically. "So now you have some idea of just how imperfect I really am. Not many people are allowed to see that. It usually feels far too dangerous."

Then she kisses me lightly on both cheeks and without another word steps into the taxi. Within seconds it has turned the corner and disappeared into the London afternoon.

TWENTY-EIGHT

The weather has been hot and dry and the park is showing signs of wear. The white candles on the chestnut trees have faded to a dismal brown and pigeons are pecking busily at the bare patches between the grass.

For a while we walk in silence until the roar of the traffic has dropped to a distant hum. In the shade of a tall lime tree a young couple lie stretched out in each others arms, oblivious to anything except each other. A small brown and white terrier struts up to them and begins to sniff their bare feet. Startled, they jerk up, the girl's auburn hair spilling across her face. Then they laugh and lie down again. The dog, apparently satisfied, wanders off to pee against another tree.

Julia smiles. "It always feels to me as if the park is the innocent side of London," she says. She is wearing a red and white calf-length skirt with a scarlet sash knotted at the hip. As she walks a slit opens on either side of the skirt, exposing a length of leg. Suddenly she stops, stretches out her arms and tosses her head. I remember a similar movement when we had stood in the hills above San Sepolcro. Only this time I notice the bareness of her legs and the swell of her breasts under the thin blouse as she stretches. For the first time I feel a surge of desire. Julia is gazing up at the sun, her eyes closed. Then she drops one arm and shades her eyes. Close by a group of children are playing rounders. She turns to me. "Thank you so much for the museum. It was wonderful. You made everything come alive for me." She hesitates, then gestures towards a chestnut tree.

"Shall we sit down for a minute?" I have the feeling there is something she wants to talk about. Without waiting for a reply, she settles herself against the tree, stretches out her legs and kicks off her flat-heeled shoes. She leans back against the smooth green-grey bark and squints up through the branches. The thick canopy of leaves is fracturing the sunlight.

"Bernhardt and I used to do lots of travelling. Always to exotic places, of course – The Galapagos Islands, Bhutan. That kind of thing. And yet most of the time I was really quite bored." She hesitates. "Even desolate in a funny way." She turns to me. "Isn't that strange?"

I try to picture her in those distant places and feel a sudden stab of jealousy.

"Bernhardt liked to tick destinations off and talk about them to people afterwards. I think it was more about impressing people than actually enjoying the places themselves or learning anything from them. And I suddenly realised in the museum this afternoon just how different I am from that…"

"How?"

"Oh, I don't know… The way you talked about ancient Greece and modern Greece, the people, the culture. It was as if for you the two were still somehow joined, even after two and a half thousand years." She shakes her head slightly. "It really touched me. And it was then that I realised that I need to feel the soul of a place, to get a real sense of its people; otherwise I just feel desolate, as if I'm some kind of alien invader."

I glance at her. She is frowning and looks sad.

"It's a pity just to tick Greece off," I say. "Don't you think? It's…"

Suddenly she smiles.

"What is it?"

"I'm almost ashamed to admit it... I've never been there!"

"Never been to Greece?!"

She shakes her head. "Now you'll think I'm a complete ignoramus. Just exactly the kind of socialite philistine you always imagined I was. I suppose it just wasn't exotic enough in the old days." She pauses. "But now I realise that I'm actually glad. At least it still waits for me."

For a while we are silent, watching the children. It's soothing listening to the occasional plop of the tennis ball being batted away, the whoops of excitement. I turn to her. "Why don't you come with me? This summer? Next week even?"

She stares at me. Then her eyes begin to fill with tears. Perhaps I have pushed her too hard. Perhaps she has misunderstood.

"I'm not propositioning you," I say hurriedly. "I thought..."

"No, it's okay. I know you aren't... It's just... that I can't." She looks down at her lap. Her right thumb scratches at the back of her other hand. There is a pale band on her finger where her wedding ring has been removed.

"Why not?"

She stays silent, gazing out across the park.

"Why not?" I insist. I can feel anxiety, a kind of premonition, gathering inside me.

"I'm going away."

"Where?"

"California."

"That's okay. We can go when you get back. I'm flexible."

"Bronson." She pauses. "I'm going for a long time."

I stare at her. "How long?"

"I don't know."

"You mean you're *emigrating*?"

"I don't know."

"Why not?"

"Because I don't know!" She shouts, suddenly erupting. The ring of children turn and stare at us. Overhead the leaves shift in the first faint brush of air.

"I'm sorry," I say. I'm struggling to keep my voice steady. "I didn't mean to push you."

Julia runs her hand through her hair, then lets it drop limply to her side. "No. *I'm* sorry," she says at last. "I didn't mean to explode like that." She smooths out her skirt. "I made the decision some time ago…" She hesitates, then turns to me. Her brow is furrowed, her eyes look full of pain. "You've been through a divorce. You know what it's like. It's not easy with Bernhardt buzzing around the whole time trying to stir up trouble, blackening me to anyone who cares to listen – which, in my social circle, is most people." She lets out a sigh. Her shoulders slump. "I've just had enough. I've tried to keep everything stable here because Gemma's doing her 'A' levels and I don't want to upset that. I've done enough damage already. But as soon as she's out of school we're leaving. It would be much better for Gemma. And for me. My sister lives there. She's been pressing me to come ever since I broke up with Bernhardt…"

Her voice runs on. But somehow I'm no longer really listening. I close my eyes. I can hear the distant moan of the traffic, the thud of the rounders bat. I feel winded and slightly sick, as if someone has punched me hard in the stomach. I try to gather myself. "Look, I know I've no right to ask this…"

She spins round on one knee to face me, puts her right hand on my forearm. "No. You *do* have a right to ask… I know we could play games and pretend we're just casual friends.

But we both know that's not true." She hesitates, then looks very directly into my eyes. "It's just not the right time. The fact is, you weren't in my plans. Not even a friendship like this. The tickets are bought and I'm going away because I have to. Gemma would be terribly disappointed. We've arranged schooling for her and everything. I can't rethink the decision any more. I just can't!" She clenches her jaw.

"But we can talk on the 'phone at least?"

She stays silent, looking down.

"Why not, for God's sake? That's crazy!"

She is ripping up small tufts of grass with her left hand. I wonder if she is crying. "Look," I say, "something *has* started between us… We don't have to give it a name. But something feels right. Can you deny that?" She shakes her head slightly. It's a gesture that closes me out. "Then what is it?"

"I've filed for divorce against Bernhardt."

I stare at her. "But isn't that exactly what you wanted? Surely that's why you left him."

"Yes. I know." She picks up the loose grass and tosses it in the air. The breeze carries it away to my left.

"Then what is it? I don't see what that has to do with not wanting me to telephone."

She glances up. Her eyes have gone dull. Her face is drained of expression, as if its inner architecture has collapsed. She seems suddenly exhausted.

"Don't you see?" she says in a tired voice. "I just can't take any more goodbyes. I'm not what you think. I'm like one of your broken statues. I'm damaged goods. You just don't know anything about me." She must have seen my frown. "That's not a reproach. But you don't know about my past. My whole life has been one long series of goodbyes. I just can't any more! Not another one. Not now." Her shoulders slump.

"But I'm trying to get us *not* to say goodbye."

She looks down. "I can't do otherwise now," she says stubbornly. "And I can't explain it either. I just know it's right. Not right on your logical level perhaps. But right all the same." She pauses. "It's just that I have things to do which I can only do away from you…"

"Like?"

"Like…" She sighs. "I can't explain it. It's just too difficult." For a long while we are silent. Then she gives a small cough, as if clearing her throat. "You remember what you said to me at lunch the other day… 'To everything there is a season'…?"

I nod.

"I found it in the Bible."

"Ecclesiastes."

"Yes. I read the whole passage. It's very beautiful." She hesitates as if uncertain how to go on. "I'm a person with very little trust. I haven't had much reason to trust people in the past. But when I read that passage, it seemed to connect with some deeper part of me." She lays both her hands flat on her stomach, closes her eyes. It's an odd gesture, like a pregnant madonna in a Renaissance painting. "A time to plant; and a time to pluck up that which is planted. A time to rend and a time to sew." And in a funny way, that I *could* trust. It felt like the kind of certain feeling I had when I was carrying Gemma. I just knew she wouldn't be taken away from me." She pauses. "All my instincts are telling me that we're both still plucking up and rending. And that we need to do that apart from each other. Does that make any sense?" I look at her but don't answer. "And when I read, 'A time to embrace and a time to refrain from embracing… I just knew what I had to do… This is a time to refrain from embracing. For both of us. That's all."

"But I'm not…"

She puts a hand on my arm. "Bronson, don't you understand? It's for you too."

I hold her gaze. And suddenly, totally unexpectedly, I feel calm. It's as if some decision, some decision from beyond my brain, is being silently stitched together inside me. There seems nothing more to say. I want her to be gone now, afraid that her presence may dissolve this quiet sense of resolution that is taking root in me. I rise and hold out my hand.

We walk back towards the road in silence. When we reach Park Lane Julia hails the first taxi that passes. It draws to a halt beside us. For a moment we stand facing each other, uncertain. Then she puts her arms around my neck, presses her cheek to mine and clings to me fiercely.

A moment later the taxi door thuds shut and she is gone.

TWENTY-NINE

When Hades-Pluto came roaring out of the Underworld in his chariot, drawn by a team of black stallions, hell-bent on the abduction of Persephone, who was gathering flowers in a sunlit meadow at the time – an image of virginal innocence if ever there was one – he came armed with the blessing of Zeus, his all-powerful older brother. No great surprise there – Zeus himself was a renowned philanderer and serial rapist. So this was just the older brother giving the younger brother the nod. But the really odd part of the story (which is usually omitted in the telling) is that Demeter also gave her assent. *Why?* Why on earth would a doting mother agree to the rape and abduction of her virginal daughter, particularly by a lover as sinister as Hades?

This is the kind of bizarre thought that is preoccupying me these days as I sit in the London heat. It's as if the whole focus of my mind has somehow shifted. Someone has turned the lens. Where, before, I was thinking only of the surface, the narrative of things, now there seems to be a hunger to look deeper. And one of the places I'm looking, not surprisingly, is in the Underworld.

And what I see – to my shock – is that *I'm* the virgin in this tale. Not literally, of course. I'm a long way from that. But, unlike me, the mythological realm doesn't concern itself with the literal. It has bigger fish to fry. And I (as Carla has so presciently pointed out in her letter) have been stuck in the literal all my life, busy gathering flowers in the sunlight, as it were. It's not that there's necessarily anything wrong with that; the problem lies in what it ignores, in constantly edging around the lip of the volcano, trying to forget that it's there at all. I'm a past master at it. And what I'm starting to wonder is whether Demeter recognised that her daughter was just too lightweight, too naïve, too lacking in experience of the darkness. And that what she required – for her own good – was an immersion in the Underworld to lend her weight and substance and give her the kind of gravitas and wisdom she needed to become a real woman. It's not a story about chariots and rape and pomegranates at all. It's an image of the painful movement of the psyche towards some kind of balance and wholeness. In short, it's a story about me. About Everyman.

It's extraordinary that I'm having these kinds of thoughts at all. Wouldn't Carla be amazed! And now I, who almost never dream, have started to dream night after night of the *kouros*. The dream is almost always the same: the *kouros* doesn't actually *do* anything. He merely stands there motionless in his fragmentary state. But gradually, over time, his missing limbs begin to reappear. It's like watching some cartoon drawing being completed bit by bit. At first the legs, the feet, the arms and hands, the head (not all in one piece) until finally one night the dream is so vivid that it wakes me. What has catapulted me across the boundaries of sleep is the sudden appearance of the *smile* on the face of the *kouros*. It's an enigmatic smile, an indication of some deep inner joy perhaps? I lie awake wondering about it. Just as with my dream of the black statue all those months ago, I have the eerie sensation that the dream *wants* something of me. The *kouros* wants something of me.

But, once again, I have no idea what. Every time I think I have moved forward, I seem to be back at the beginning. Perhaps my life has been planned as some vast game of snakes and ladders where I am is perpetually fated to lose and try again.

And I'm still musing about my sudden mental collapse after the Carabinieri had seized the black statue (now safely in the gallery and about to be sold to a Swiss collector). After all, nothing had actually *happened*. The police hadn't even come. There had been no arrest, no trial. No prison. It had been just a fantasy. And yet something had totally deranged my mind. In modern parlance I had had a nervous breakdown… I was deeply depressed… I had a psychotic episode… Yet none of these diagnoses feels quite right, because in some strange way what had happened to me in those dark weeks feels almost not *personal* at all, as if I have been singled out to look down into a deep oceanic terror that lies just below the skin of *all* our everyday lives, a brief glimpse over the lip of the volcano. *But why me?* I have no idea. But suddenly Carla's talk of the Underworld and Saturn conjunct Pluto starts to make a lot more sense than all the modern diagnoses.

It's more than a decade since I last spent August in London. It's hot and uncomfortable and staying makes no sense at all. I should be lying on a beach somewhere. Yet I take a perverse pleasure in the quietness of the place, the fitful traffic, the heat-drugged tourists, the general sense of *ennui*. It suits my mood. I even enjoy my silent mornings in the gallery, where the telephone never rings, Zoe has left for the month and the postman rarely calls. In August the art world sleeps.

Greece, Carla, all the unexpected events of these last weeks have certainly blown my life into pieces, and they clearly haven't yet decided how to settle down. Is this what David would call 'coming up in another place'? If so, it's a strange and disorientating experience. I'm waiting. I'm walking the ground flat again. Not, thank God, this time in the Underworld; but not yet in the sunlit Upperworld either. I'm occupying some shadowy liminal space between.

Sometimes I feel disembodied, almost like a watcher from another galaxy, struggling to make sense of my feelings. I have heard nothing from Julia, and I know that I won't. On some days she enters my heart silently, without a thought, so that mundane sights like the leaves on a plane tree seen through a café window, or the curve of a young girl's neck queuing in front of me in the supermarket can suddenly open my heart and move me embarrassingly close to tears, right there in the middle of the busy world fluctuating around me. But then there are other times when the thought of her, just knowing that she is somewhere on the other side of the planet, going about her business – *going about it happily?* – without me, can leave me winded with loss, a terrible desolating dull ache in the gut, which feels as if it might go on for ever. If I can make any sense of my situation at all, I would say that, like my stay in the Underworld, what is happening to me is somehow behovely. I am being shriven. Whatever the hell that may mean.

It is on the morning of the twenty-fifth of August that I finally acknowledge that slow gravitational slide that has been silently pulling at me all month. I get up from my desk in the gallery and go out into the street without thinking. I set the alarm, lock the door behind me and walk with a somnambulistic sense of resolution to the nearest travel agent. It is only when I am standing on the heat-bleached pavement, staring at the ticket in my hand, as the buses thunder past along King's Road, that I realise that all summer my destination has never been in doubt. Only the timing.

THIRTY

Kostas embraces me like an old friend. Then he disappears into the dark of the *taverna*. A moment later he re-emerges flourishing a bottle. He points to the label, stabbing at it excitedly with his forefinger: "Johnny Walker! *Black Label!* Just come from Athens. Is the best. Is yours!" Despite the fact that it's only four in the afternoon, he pours me half a tumbler of scotch and retreats inside.

It feels strangely reassuring to be back, drinking neat whisky in the close heat of an August afternoon. I settle into the rickety chair and look out across the strait. The distant mountains of the Peloponnese have almost disappeared in the afternoon haze. A great drowsiness has descended on the little harbour. My absence feels like the merest ripple on the surface of time. It's as if, as far as Katakolos is concerned, the period since my departure has simply dropped out and time here has continued like a seamless garment. Only the fierce, crackling dryness of the heat and the presence of two bearded travellers, their heads tied with spotted bandannas, ruck-sacks stashed under their table, tell me that the island has drifted into late summer.

I have been here for perhaps half an hour, sipping the whisky and feeling increasingly drowsy, when I sense something tugging at my attention. I turn. Dinos is walking slowly along the quayside studying the boats. The limp in his right leg is more pronounced than I remember and he looks thinner. An old straw hat is cocked on the back of his head. I had been expecting him at some point, of course; yet his arrival still carries the shock of an apparition. Suddenly he stops and looks round. When he sees me he raises a hand in greeting and comes slowly towards me. I'm surprised how pleased I am to see him, given the strangeness of our meeting four months ago. He lays the battered hat on the plastic tablecloth and pulls out a chair.

"You don't seem surprised to see me. Did you know I was here?"

"No, but I knew you would come. If it wasn't today it would be tomorrow. Or yesterday. Here in Katakolos time moves at a different pace anyhow. The Arabs say that the soul travels at the pace of a donkey. Very wise people."

I laugh. He's already off on one of his crazy riffs. "It feels like my donkey is still stuck somewhere in the foothills of the Alps." Kostas appears in the doorway and calls out to Dinos. Without taking his eyes from me, Dinos nods. He is staring at me very intensely with his slate blue eyes narrowed, as if weighing me up. "Sooo…" he says slowly, "things have happened, haven't they?"

I avoid his gaze and stare out to the mainland. Then I shrug. "What makes you say that?"

"Is it not so?"

Reluctantly I nod. "Yes. Things have happened all right." And suddenly I have a clear sense of why I have returned to the island. It's more than just the wish to lay old ghosts, to be out at Conchili and not be frightened by the place. I have a need to put all the random bits of these last months into some kind of pattern. Illogically, but instinctively, I know that Dinos can help me.

Dinos raises his eyebrows and leans forward with his elbows on the table. "Well, my friend…" The look is so piercing that I can feel something open up inside me like a trap-door. And then the words come.

For a long time after, Dinos stays silent. Then he takes the plastic wrappers from his pocket and begins to roll himself a cigarette. I feel strangely calm, as if I have talked to some kind of father confessor. When I told him of the dragons devouring my liver he had shown not the slightest surprise, as if such things were an everyday event here on Katakolos. At length he holds up the cigarette and inspects the smouldering tip. He is frowning as if trying to remember something that has just slipped his mind. Then he says musingly, "*Prison*, eh? So that's what set you off on your journey. There are many kinds of prisons, you know. Prisons of habit, prisons of family, prisons of society, of religion. Of desire and need. Of fear and hope. Prisons of belief and memory and of who you think you're supposed to be. Outside prisons – I've been in a few – but the inside prisons are the worst, the prisons of the mind. Particularly if you have a soul that yearns to break out – and can't." Then, without warning, he switches tracks. "But there was something else, wasn't there?"

"*Something else?* Something more than I've already told you! Like what? Isn't that enough?"

"I don't know…" He pauses. I've never seen him this thoughtful before. "It just feels like there's something missing. Something that's not obvious".

For a moment I search my mind. Then suddenly a memory capsule pops. How could I have forgotten? Perhaps it just didn't seem to fit anywhere in the story… Perhaps I hadn't *wanted* to remember it.

"Well, yes, there was something. The night before I left here I had a very odd…experience. I had a dream." I hesitate. "If it really was a dream."

Dinos leans forward and folds his hands on the table. "Tell me."

And so I do. I tell him how that dark figure had stood at the foot of my bed as I had felt paralyzed. How its voice had echoed in the room. As I talk, I'm aware of Dinos's frown deepening. Automatically he rolls himself another cigarette. As he lights it I see that his hand is shaking. When I have finished he is still staring at me. The cigarette is unsmoked. The long stick of ash sags into the metal ashtray.

"What happened the day before you had the dream?"

"Why do you want to know that?"

"What happened?"

There's a special intensity in his stare that I can't ignore. I shrug. "Nothing much. I had been driving around Arcadia for a few days. It was pretty wild country. You could drive for hours without seeing a soul. Maybe I found it a bit depressing. I don't know…"

Dinos nods thoughtfully. "Did you come back over the mountains?"

"Yes, I came down an incredibly steep pass that had some kind of war memorial at the top."

"The memorial had a big stone cross?"

"Right."

"How did you feel up there?"

"At the memorial?"

"Yes." I can sense him homing in on something and suddenly I feel inexplicably anxious.

"Well, it was a great view, but… But what's that got to do with my dream?" I pause, wondering where all this is going.

And suddenly I'm back in all the weirdness of that night, all the feelings of powerlessness and fear.

Dinos doesn't respond to my question. Instead he sits there staring at me.

"To be honest," I say, "I'm not even sure it was a dream. It felt more as if I was wide awake, only I just couldn't move. It was as if I'd been drugged or anaesthetized or something. Let's face it, normal dreams don't happen like that. They don't just come and stand there and tell you stories in perfect prose. That's not a dream!"

Dinos draws on his cigarette. "It's a Homeric dream," he says simply.

"A *what?*"

"A Homeric dream. Iliad Book V. '*And the dream came and stood at the foot of the bed.*' That's exactly how they had dreams in Homeric Greece. The dream comes and stands at the foot of the bed and tells you a story."

"Are you saying I had a *Homeric* dream? Are you crazy?"

"Well, what do you think?"

"But this is the Twentieth Century, for Gpd's sake!"

Dinos is silent. "I'm not sure," he says at length, "that dreams count in centuries."

And he's right, of course. I'm being too prosaic. But still… *a Homeric dream in the Twentieth Century?* There's something here that feels way beyond my competency. Pieces that seem to fit together, but not in any way that my mind can understand. Have I time-travelled? I've heard of such things before, but never believed them, being wormholed back into another time zone. Okay, that might happen to mystics, but surely not to me. At length I ask, "So what did happen up there? I remember the date – the second of February 1943 – but I couldn't read the rest of the inscription. It was too complicated. Was there a battle?"

Dinos takes a deep breath before replying. Then he leans back in his chair and folds his arms. When he speaks his voice has gone monotone, as if he is deliberately bleeding it of emotion.

"That place is called *Stavraki* – it means 'Little Cross' in Greek – because, before the war, there was a small shrine up there, such as we have all over the countryside here in Greece. No, it was not a battle in the normal sense. In 1943 the Germans were in occupation of the entire Peloponnese, and that line of mountains was an important stronghold. Stavraki was one of the few passes where an advancing force could cross. The Greeks were completely crushed by the occupation by then. There were partisan fighters, of course, brave men, but they could do little – just the odd skirmish, a bit of sabotage here and there. There was almost nothing to eat. Men were reduced to digging for roots and eating bark. In 1942 a farmer in the nearby village of Metana managed to raise a piglet in secret, so that it wouldn't be commandeered by the Germans. But, of course, nothing is secret in an occupation. The Germans found it. They hanged him in the village square the next day in front of the big plane tree that you can still see there. They hanged him like a piece of meat. It took him nearly three minutes to die."

I stare at him. "*You were there?*"

"Yes," says Dinos flatly. "I was twelve at the time. I was made to watch along with the rest of my village. Presumably in case I was tempted to raise any pigs myself. It is not something you forget easily. Especially when you are twelve years old." He pauses for a moment and swallows a mouthful of ouzo. Then he goes on. "February that year was bitterly cold, even by the standards of Arcadian winters. On the night of the first, two men of the village murdered a young German corporal who was patrolling that night. They ambushed him and slit his throat from ear to ear. There was nothing special about him. It was just an act such as men will do if you deprive them of their power for too long. The Germans found him shortly before dawn the next morning, lying in a field."

He pauses and looks out to sea.

"The next day, February the second, was the coldest day I can ever remember anywhere. The Germans took forty-three men – the entire adult male population of Metana, together with several teenage boys – and force-marched them out of the village. I remember the Germans were all around them, holding rifles with fixed bayonets. But there was one very odd thing: the soldiers were all carrying shovels. They disappeared up towards the Stavraki pass. The remaining soldiers forced us all into the school house. We waited for hours. There was a terrible hush over everything. Then, in the late afternoon, the Germans returned. Alone. They marched into the village in silence. We never saw the men again. Their remains were only found after the war."

"And that is where the memorial now stands?"

"Yes."

"Was any of your family there?"

"My father. You will have seen his name on the stone: Vernadakis, Giorgios. Another dead Greek."

I feel giddy and drained of blood. Beyond the sheer horror of the story, the memory of my dream is thudding in my head like some insistent drumbeat. *How is it possible that I could dream in a way that people dreamt two and a half thousand years ago? How is it possible that I could dream in perfect detail of an event that took place in a foreign country years before I was born? These things just don't happen. Not in my reality.* I stare at the waterfront, not knowing what to say.

Dinos leans forward and gently prizes the glass from my fingers. "These glasses are very thick," he says. "But I should hate to have you cut yourself by crushing one."

I look down at my hands. The knuckles have gone white.

"So what do *you* think?" I ask finally. "Was it a dream? And if so, why a Homeric one, for God's sake? And how could I possibly have known…?" My voice trails off.

"I don't know, my friend," says Dinos. He must have seen my desperate look. "Really I don't." For a long time he is silent. Then he says, "We Greeks believe that there are some places on the earth where our natural families and our spiritual families cross; where this life and other lives meet, if you like. They are what we call 'Places of Intersection'. It is a very ancient belief. For you Stavraki must be such a place. Some people – perhaps most – will never approach their Place of Intersection. They are the ones who are condemned to live a life of endless wandering. But apparently not you."

"Why? Why *me*?"

"That is what you are here to find out."

And now I'm all at sea. *Homeric Dreams? Places of Intersection?* It's all crazy. The fact is that ever since I first set foot on this island I seem to have strayed towards the dream state, a place where my normal categories of perception have been eroded, wormholing me back into a past I didn't even know existed. I thought I had come back to Katakolos to 'settle' myself, to exorcise the memory of my crazy time out at the house, to make sense of things for God's sake, to feel safely back in my own skin. But now I can feel again a frightening drift towards instability.

"If any of what you say is true, what should I do about it?" I ask, trying to keep my voice steady.

"Do?" Dinos frowns quizzically and sips his ouzo. Then he says calmly, "Wait."

"*Wait?* What the hell am I supposed to wait for?"

Dinos shrugs. "You northerners are too impatient. You want answers, answers, answers!" He waves his arms in the air as if to demonstrate the futility of our enquiring quest. "As if you expect the universe instantly to respond to your demands. You want reasons, explanations! That way you usually miss the point. Sometimes, my friend, the gods simply ask us to be patient. To wait. There is energy in waiting too, you know – if you choose the right time and do it in the right way. This is clearly a time to wait. When we need to know more the gods will inform us." Suddenly he stops and gives me a wink. Then he claps his hands and calls out, "*Kosta mou. Alo ena ouzo!*"

"Not for me! Not ouzo on top of whisky."

"Why not? While we are waiting we might as well have a good time." He leans across the table conspiratorially. "Kostas is very proud of his whisky. His son brought it from Athens. But, you know, that stuff is strictly for the tourists. You and I – *we Greeks* – we drink ouzo."

A moment later Kostas reappears with two tumblers half filled with ouzo. Despite my protests, Dinos tips water into our glasses. The transparent oiliness swirls and eddies and begins to turn a milky white. He picks up his glass between thumb and forefinger and clinks it against mine, just as he did all those months ago. Then he downs his ouzo in one gulp and rises. "I must go now," he says. Suddenly he looks very tired, as if our conversation has exhausted him.

I stand too, then have to steady myself against the table. I can feel the effect of the ouzo on top of Kostas' whisky. "Christ, I can hardly stand! I should be more careful around you. I hope I don't hit any rocks on the way to the house."

Dinos laughs. "There aren't any rocks between here and

Conchili, my friend. All you have to do is not run into the shore. Even you should be able to manage that."

He takes the plastic tobacco pouch from the table and puts it in his back pocket. "Do you like walking?"

"Yes. Why?"

"Good. I will meet you here at nine o'clock tomorrow morning. I will show you something you need to see." Then he slaps me on the shoulder and is gone into the gathering dusk.

The sun has set below the low white houses and the first lights of the mainland are just becoming visible across the strait.

THIRTY-ONE

It is just before nine when I tie the small boat to the dock and cut the engine. Dinos is standing in the *taverna* doorway talking to Kostas. When he sees me he picks up the straw hat from a table and comes towards me. A leather satchel is slung over one shoulder, a heavy stick in his left hand.

"I see you survived the ouzo."

"Just."

"Just is good enough." He stretches out his hand and pulls me up onto the jetty. "No hat?"

"I never wear hats."

"Brave man. Or crazy. We shall see which. Perhaps the god Pan will finally come and drive you mad."

Without another word he turns and starts walking east along the waterfront. As soon as we reach the end of the village, the gravel road fades into a wide dusty track, which winds through lemon groves. Gradually these give way to ranks of olive trees and, within a mile, the cultivation ceases altogether. The track narrows to a rough path, which follows the contours of the shore. The bare hillside to our right has once been terraced. Now it lies abandoned and overgrown with prickly scrub. The terracing has begun to crumble. Dilapidated dry-stone walls snake erratically up from the sea to the hill-top.

I stop for a moment and shade my eyes. "Who built those crazy walls?" I ask. "And *why?*"

Dinos laughs. "You are the first person ever to ask me that question." He shrugs. "They are just walls."

"Well, I've asked lots of you Greeks before, because they are all over the islands, meandering around without any logic. But none of you ever seems to know the answer."

"I too," says Dinos still laughing, "do not know the answer." He spreads his hands in mock despair. "I could say: to mark the boundaries, for example. Although such boundaries can only have been drawn by a blind man with too much ouzo." He gestured towards the hillside with his stick. "Like you last yesterday. Or…" He pauses. "To have somewhere to put the stones when they have been cleared from the land to make room for cultivation. Although we are not always such an orderly people, we Greeks. But…" His voice drops to a whisper. "I personally believe something very different."

"What's that?"

"That they were built by little Cyclopses."

"By *what?*"

"You are a man of archaeological knowledge. You know that the giant stone walls at Mycenae are called 'Cyclopean' because no mortal could possibly lift such huge boulders – only the massive one-eyed giant who trapped Odysseus in his cave. These here are just the same, only smaller. Hence they were built by little Cyclopses. We have them everywhere."

I can't help laughing. I notice how Dinos' accent thickens when his descriptions became fantastical, as if he's some kind of pantomime villain, merrily inviting boos and hisses.

"Aha!" exclaims Dinos. "You laugh at me. I see you do not believe in Cyclopses, big or small. Is that not so?" He smiles, showing the gap in his teeth. We are looking out over the expanse of mirror-flat sea. A grey blur on the horizon and a small white cloud poised above it denote the presence of some far-off island. "Of course, the northern rational man in you does not believe in Cyclopses, does he? Terrifying one-eyed monsters, who shut you up in a cave and eat you alive. Absurd eh?" He pauses. "But the Greek in you knows different. He knows of dragons and such things." He turns and continues down the path, leaving me to puzzle over this conundrum.

For a long time we walk in silence. Occasionally Dinos swishes at the bushes with his stick, sending off wafts of sage and wild thyme and springing loose the occasional startled cicada, which takes flight into the undergrowth. Two gulls wheel lazily in the unbroken blue above us. The sun stings the back of my neck. I turn up my shirt collar and wonder about the god Pan. Even the rocks on the seabed below us look hot. So clear is the light, so scorched the landscape that the whole place seems to crackle in the heat. Suddenly Dinos stops ahead of me. The narrow path has widened out into a broad level platform. "Come," he beckons over his shoulder. "This is what I wanted you to see."

We seem to have reached the southern-most tip of the island. To our right the rocky escarpment gives way to a huge amphitheatre of hills, enclosing two long sandy bays divided by a headland.

"The best kept secret in the Aegean," says Dinos. He puts one arm around my shoulders and gestures with his stick towards a faint dark hump shimmering above the horizon. "There," he says. "Look. The island of Kythera. The birthplace of Aphrodite, goddess of love. If you know anything of Cyclopses and dragons and the Underworld, then it is important that you also know something of her. And respect her. You will need her." Then, without explanation, he starts down the slope towards the beach.

Just where the land flattens out towards the sand is an olive grove, the trees arranged in orderly lines. They are squat and gnarled, crouched like wrestlers. The parched earth between them has been ploughed into small boulders the size of a man's fist. There are no houses anywhere; the farmer must walk from the village. Dinos sits down under an olive tree and leans back against its fissured bark. It is growing in the last piece of cultivation before the hard earth gives way to scrub and dust and then to the white sand of the long beach. I drop down beside him, grateful for the shade. The sun is almost directly overhead now. The line of the horizon has evaporated. Both sea and sky are welded together in a white haze. A distant fishing boat lies becalmed, suspended in the atmosphere. Dinos unhitches the battered satchel from his shoulder.

"How do you like my bag?" He passes it across to me. Something has been embossed across the flap in Greek letters, worn and almost obliterated. Slowly, I trace out the characters with my index finger "*Taksidromeion?* But that's the Post Office!"

"Ha!" Dinos gives one of his short barking laughs. Then he clutches his right fist to his chest. "I," he says theatrically, "am the local postmaster." He opens the satchel and takes out a dark green bottle and some small packages of waxed paper held together by elastic bands. He sets them down on the earth. "About twenty years ago we received a letter from the Central Postal Service in Athens addressed to the Mayor of the Island of Katakolos. There was great excitement, because we don't have a mayor. The whole village assembled and opened the letter in Kostas' *taverna*. It was an instruction to appoint a Postmaster for the island, who would take charge of the distribution of the mail. I was voted in by popular acclaim."

"Congratulations!"

Dinos bows his head appreciatively. "You see, I was 'educated'. In short, I could read. Both Greek and European scripts!"

"So how do you distribute the post?"

"The same way we always did. The boatman arrives and gives the package to Kostas, who opens it and leaves the letters lying on the bar. Everyone comes and collects them as they wish. It's a good system. And I get a pension. And my beautiful bag for free!"

He snaps off the elastic bands from the white packages and lays them open on the sand: a large piece of white cheese, four tomatoes and half a loaf of dark bread. Then he takes a penknife with a black horn casing from his pocket and cuts off a large slice of the cheese, he hands it across to me.

"Graviera," he says. "Goat's cheese from the island. It's good."

I settle back against the tree, kick off my shoes and dig my toes into the sand. Under the surface it's surprisingly cold. I bite into the cheese. Dinos is right: it's strongly flavoured, goaty, but delicious.

"What do you know about Aphrodite?" asks Dinos, returning to his subject.

"Aphrodite...?" I hesitate. The heat seems to have numbed my brain. "Well, she was the goddess of love, of course. The wife of Hephaistos, the mistress of Ares, the god of war."

"Very good" says Dinos, nodding.

"Born over there, on 'Sea-girt Kythera'. At least that's what Homer says. But other myths say that she was also born at Paphos on Cyprus and at Knidos on the coast of Turkey. *Three birth places?* How does that come about?"

"I see someone has wasted a lot of money on your

education," says Dinos. He sniffs. "But these are just dry facts, dead archaeological footnotes. They are of no meaning unless we can worship her still in those places." He pauses and takes a bite from the cheese. "Which, by and large, we cannot. Tourism has seen to that." He uncorks the bottle and hands it across to me. It is made of thick, dark glass and unlabelled. I take a long pull at it. The wine tastes of hot earth and resin. But it's good. I wipe the top and pass it back.

"How often have you felt the presence of Aphrodite in your life?" asks Dinos casually, as if it's the most normal question in the world. But to me it's not normal at all. And suddenly David's question is echoing in my head: *How much real love do you have in your life, Bronson?*

I lean back and sigh. It's such a typical Dinos question. Not one for the mind, yet serious all the same. And it makes me uncomfortable. I settle back against the ribbed trunk and gaze out towards the faint smudge on the horizon that is Kythera. Then instinctively I close my eyes. Face after face, body after body, a storehouse of memory floods back to me. Most of them beautiful. Yet, amongst them all, it's impossible to conjure up the image of Aphrodite.

"I don't know," I say lamely.

Dinos nods slowly. "But now there comes someone quite different."

I stare at him. "How the hell did you know that?"

"Is it not true?"

I hesitate. "I don't know."

"I see." Dinos raises his eyebrows ironically. He picks up one of the tomatoes, rubs it against his faded checked shirt and passes it across. I bite into it. It tastes as if the flavor of all the tomatoes I have ever eaten have been stored up in it. Dinos looks at me quizzically.

"No, really. I *have* no idea. She doesn't seem to want it. In any case, she's gone away."

"And how does that feel?"

The blunt question releases a flood of loss at the thought of Julia somewhere on the other side of the globe, doing... what? I can feel my eyes begin to prickle.

Dinos is silent, observing me. "It seems I touched something." The words are ironic, but his tone is gentle.

"Yes, you did apparently." I'm silent for a while, trying to right myself. "The problem is..." I say at length. Then I shrug. "Oh, I don't know. The problem is... that, inspite of all the difficulties, it still just feels *right*. Being with her feels right. Different from anything I've ever experienced before, different from anyone else I've ever been with. It's almost as if there's something else there, something that's not to do with either her or me. And that somehow makes it right..." I dig my hand into the sand and allow the hot grains to drain through my fingers, frustrated by my lack of words. "I can't really explain it."

"That's the goddess," says Dinos simply. He picks up the bottle and takes a deep swallow of wine.

"But *she* doesn't want it."

"Who? The goddess?"

"No, you idiot. Julia."

Dinos smiles and hands me the bottle. "Are you so sure?"

"Well, she disappeared to California. No address. No telephone number. Apparently no intention of coming back. That seems eloquent enough, doesn't it?"

"Did she say why?"

"She said a lot of things. About her daughter, about her divorce, about being afraid of getting hurt, being abandoned. I don't know..." I stop, hoping Dinos might say something that will make sense of it. But Dinos stays silent, looking out to sea. "She seems to have a streak of incredible obstinacy in her. All those reasons about it being better for her daughter… I just didn't believe any of it. To be honest, I don't think she did either…"

"So you think she's done the wrong thing?"

"How the hell would I know?" I remember the chaotic swirl of emotions as we had sat under the chestnut tree that afternoon in the park. Everything she had said, every excuse for her departure had felt false, invented. And yet, in some odd way, right at the same time.

Dinos cuts off another piece of cheese and passes it over. "Perhaps the lady knows more than you think," he says. "Probably she knows more than *she* thinks."

Suddenly I feel irritated by his opacity. Is he just playing games with me? "What the hell does that mean?"

"You know what it means. You know – if you let yourself think with your heart instead of only thinking with your head." He raps the side of my head with his knuckles. "You'll never make sense of it up there. And nor will she." He pauses. "But she's a woman. She can have a direct connection to Aphrodite, if she lets herself. Even if she doesn't know it in her head, she can think with her womb. That's quite another kind of knowing."

Startled, I suddenly remember how, that afternoon in the park, Julia had laid the palms of her hands over her stomach as she talked. It had been such a strange, archaic gesture. I can see again now her fingers closing over the slight swell of her belly under the thin red and white skirt.

The sky and sea have fused together in a blur of white. The fishing boat has rounded the headland and gone. Nothing moves. "So why did she go? Can you tell me that?"

"My guess..." says Dinos slowly – he seems to be picking his words with unusual care – "...is that somewhere in her instincts she recognised that one does not come before the gods uninvited. It requires preparation. And separation. Separation from our normal lives. All those careful rituals that the ancients knew and practiced and which we have totally forgotten. At our peril."

I stare at him in astonishment. "Do you really think that's why she went away – because she *knew* about that?"

"With her brain, maybe not. But as a woman, deep down, she would have known. She would have sensed that there was a need for space and separation, for respecting the goddess, for not coming before her unprepared." I remember Julia's words before we parted – *I just know that this is a time to refrain from embracing.* And then, *It's right for you too.* She had spoken with such certainty. Not stubborn, but somehow rocklike, something I couldn't shift. She had been in a place beyond either my logic or my pain. She had seen what I could not. And suddenly I feel myself begin to relax as if, for the very first time, I am fully accepting her disappearance, acknowledging that it is bedded in a knowledge deeper than my own.

For a long time we are silent, as if we both know that the conversation is complete. In the heat I begin to doze. Dinos has stretched out and I can hear him snoring against the background drone of the cicadas. Just as I am fading into a deep sleep, he sits up and rubs his eyes. "Wake-up time!" he says. And suddenly he stands, pulls off his shirt, drops his trousers and he is running, limping, naked across the sand towards the sea, his brown back and skinny white buttocks comical on the vast stretch of beach. Laughing, I follow him. The sand is so hot it scorches the soles of my feet. The salt water is achingly cool and astringent as I dive in and feel it close over my head. Afterwards we dry ourselves on our shirts and struggle back into our clothes.

"We should be going," says Dinos. He passes the wine bottle across for one last swallow, then gathers the remains of our lunch into the satchel. Without a word he starts towards the headland.

On the way back we walk in silence. Dinos seems to be wrapped in his own thoughts. I notice that he is limping again. Once or twice he stops to cough violently. It had taken almost an hour and a half from the *taverna* to the beach. Clearly the walk has exhausted him more than either of us have realised. The fragility I noticed when I first saw him on the waterfront the previous evening is visible again.

It is late afternoon by the time we reach the *taverna*. Dinos sinks down into one of the chairs. Kostas looks at him with concern. Then, without being asked, he brings him a glass of water. Dinos begins to roll a cigarette. I'm about to remonstrate with him. Then I stop. It's none of my business.

"Aha!" Dinos winks at me. "You think I smoke too much." He puts the cigarette in his mouth and lights it defiantly. Then he gives a low chuckle. "Well, you're right, of course. But it is of no significance. What is more important is that I would like you to come and dine with me tomorrow night. We shall eat like kings." He fumbles in his pocket and pulls out a pencil stub. Then he takes one of the paper napkins from the metal rack on the table and begins to draw on it.

"I will show you the way."

THIRTY-TWO

The sun is setting as I leave the village. It is a windless evening and the scent of lemon blossom hangs in the air. As the light fades the white houses seem washed with a rinse of palest blue. After about a mile the track divides. In the cleft rises a majestic cypress, its plume an intense black against the bleached evening sky. The lower half of the trunk has been whitewashed. At its base stands a battered *taverna* chair, as if awaiting someone's arrival.

I consult the map. The tree is clearly marked, a small black hieroglyph on the crumpled paper napkin. As indicated, I follow the left-hand path down the slope towards the sea. Tiny donkey hooves imprint the dry soil. To my right a shallow ravine is filled with wild scarlet oleanders, sucking up the buried moisture. Somewhere in the distance a tree frog is sending out the first notes of its staccato cry into the oncoming night. Then, through the olive trees, I catch sight of the house. It is set in the centre of a small shingled bay at the head of a deep inlet. To either side the land is thick with Aleppo pines. The water is stretched like a dark skin across to the mainland, where the first evening lights are just visible. From the far side of the house a thin coil of smoke rises. I pause for a moment, absorbing the silence.

The house is severely rectangular. On the ground floor two

windows are set to either side of a doorway. The green shutters are thrown back against the uneven whitewashed walls. The symmetry is repeated precisely above, but with a fifth window in place of the door. The ochre tiled roof sags at the centre so that it seems to weight the house to the earth. In the slanting evening light the place has a gentle feel, practical, unfussy, workmanlike, built perhaps for a prosperous fisherman in the days when the sea was teeming with fish.

For a moment I wonder if I should go directly round to the seaward side, where the smoke is rising. But there is something about the privacy of the place that makes me hesitate. Instead, I walk up to the door and raise my hand to knock. Then I stop. In the centre of the rough green woodwork is the large ring of a knocker; and directly above it, a cast-iron head of the god Hermes, painted black. Beneath the winged, narrow-brimmed hat, the face is sly, enigmatic, almost diabolic. It gazes back at me with a mocking smile. *In here*, it seems to say, *nothing is quite what you think.*

I grasp the heavy ring and bring it clattering down. The noise echoes in the stillness. For a while nothing happens. Then Dinos's head shoots out from around the corner of the house.

"Ah. There you are! How English! No one has used that door for years. The Greeks just walk straight round to the other side."

He seems in expansive good humour. There is no sign of the previous afternoon's exhaustion. He shakes my hand rather formally as if it is our first meeting. He is wearing baggy khaki trousers and a faded denim shirt with a large patch on the right shoulder. The clothes look old but freshly laundered. The blue of the shirt echoes the startling colour of his eyes. He must have seen my brief scrutiny: "You see, I have put on my best for you." He places his hand on my shoulder. "Come. I will show you my estate."

The seaward face of the house turns out to be identical to the side from which I had approached, except that the door stands open and, to either side of it, a whitewashed stone bench has been built out from the walls. On one of these lies a thin blue and white striped mattress, heavily darned. In front of it is a wooden table and two rush-seated chairs. Halfway down the beach a fire is glowing from within a rough oval of rocks. Piled at each end is a pyramid of flat stones and, suspended between them, a carcass on a metal spit. The spit terminates in three barbed prongs. Clearly a fishing harpoon has been pressed into service. To the left a wooden tray carries a dark green bottle, an assortment of knives and what looks like a bundle of rosemary. I'm surprised by the almost military precision of the arrangements. A sharp, dry scent of cooking drifts in the air.

"Lamb?"

"Lamb. And rosemary. And thyme. And garlic. And oregano. And a few other things besides." Dinos gestures towards the stone bench and pours two tumblers of ouzo, adding water from a glazed earthenware jug. Then he pushes a saucer of olives across the table at me. I lean back against the wall. I can feel the day's heat stored in the stone. Dinos raises his glass "*Stiniyasas – kai kalos elthate!* Welcome!" He takes a long swallow, turns and goes down to the fire to prod the carcass with a long knife. "About another ten minutes," he calls over his shoulder. Then he takes the bottle from the tray beside the fire, raises both arms above his head, and pours a stream of red wine onto the embers. The fire hisses and a black plume of smoke curls up into the evening sky. The air is thick with the sweet, slightly cloying smell of evaporating wine.

"What are you doing?"

"Pouring a libation, of course. Never eat without one." He returns, settles into his chair and lights a cigarette. "'And the sweet savour arose to the nostrils of the gods.'" He articulates the words carefully, then says them again in what I take to be ancient Greek.

"Homer?"

"Correct. The Iliad. Fish was common in those days. The sea was full of them. They hadn't invented deep sea nets and dynamite. No problem. But meat was different. It meant wealth. That's why it was a real sacrifice to offer up the animal's flesh to the gods. Actually, of course," he gives me a broad wink, "they often cheated – a bit like we modern Greeks. They only burnt the bones and the fat as offerings and ate the meat themselves." He shrugs. "Not a lot changes around here over three thousand years."

"So are we to have a Homeric feast?" I can feel the ouzo already threading its way through my veins. It's amazing how quickly this Greek drink works on you, warming the blood, easing the nerves and turning the knees to rubber. And thanks to Dinos, we've already got one foot in the world of the gods. I have the feeling it's going to be a long night.

"Better still!" Dinos refills our glasses, then spreads his arms. "We shall have a feast of the Golden Age. *Stiniyasas!*"

"What's the difference?"

"A big one. For Homer's heroes the gods were up there, detached." He points towards the sky. "Up on the heights of Olympus. Far away. Untouchable. Able to order us around. Often quite vengeful. But in the Golden Age that went before that men sat down and actually ate with the gods. At least that's what Hesiod says." He leans forward, his eyes sparkling, as if present at the feast himself. "Just imagine that!" He empties his glass with one swallow. "That it might still be possible to sit down and eat with the gods around us. What a celebration that would be! But it's an idea we've forgotten."

I can't help smiling. He's like some capsized sailor standing on a rock, defying the oncoming storm. Deluded but majestic. "But *of course* we ignore them," I say mischievously, trying to prod him into a reaction. "It *is* the Twentieth Century, after all. God – or perhaps the gods, if you prefer – is dead, isn't he?"

"Bah! That's a philosophy of fools. And there's plenty of them around. We honour the gods simply by acknowledging their presence and respecting them. You can do that in whatever century you choose – *if* you take appropriate care. Then you can see what else may be going on in an event, other than just the obvious, the material. Which god is hidden in the action?" He pauses and cocks his head to one side, listening. The tree frog has started up again. For a moment Carla's strange statement chimes in my mind: *We must worship at their altars.* "It's the same with everything – eating, drinking, fighting, making love, looking at a cypress tree, eating an olive. It's not the acts themselves that count. It's whether or not you respect the god in the act. That's the great crime of the Twentieth Century – not respecting the gods in what we do."

"Isn't that a bit simple?"

Dinos squints at me from over the rim of his glass. "It may sound simple to you. But it's not easy. It requires time and care and attention. Scarce commodities these days. Take something as ordinary as eating an olive." He picks one from the dish and drops it into his mouth. "You chew. You spit out the stone. You throw it away." He spits it into his palm and tosses it over his shoulder. It lands with a feint plop in the sea behind him. "Job done. Nothing has really happened. *But if you honour the gods, somewhere in your chromosomes* something very different happens, because locked into that tiny, apparently insignificant moment is the knowledge of the picking of the olive, the harvest songs and celebrations, the hot earth from which it grew, the landscape that surrounded it and ultimately the tree itself, sacred to the goddess Athena. So if you honour the gods in your daily life like that, then every single event, every single thing, however small, becomes precious again. Then hunger and scarcity disappear from the soul and each moment is sacred, enough in itself. One breath. One dream. Even…" He stops and cocks an ironic eyebrow at me. "Perhaps even," he says laconically, "one woman…"

He stands up and disappears into the house. I lean back against the rough wall. There is a rattle of plates from inside and the sound of a cork being pulled. The tree frog is obviously sleeping. The silence is total, almost subaqueous, except for the occasional hiss as the fat drips into the fire.

And suddenly I'm back with Carla in that Renaissance library high in the *Castello Ducale*. We're light years away from that here, of course, grilling a lamb over an open fire on a shingled beach, getting smashed on ouzo. But I can't help seeing that they are saying pretty much the same thing – Carla with her planets decorously arranged across the computer screen; Dinos with his homespun pagan beliefs. They're both talking about a need – a deep and urgent need – to honour something *beyond* ourselves. Not *God*. At least not the divisive Christian god that I've grown up with. *That* God is certainly dead. But we're talking here about some kind of polytheistic world peopled by gods and nature spirits and dryads, presences that demand our attention and make everything around us breathe with new life. Six months ago – before I had dreamt of the black Aphrodite emerging from the sea, before Carla had walked unannounced into my gallery, before Sylvia's death, before my stay in the Underworld, before… I would have scoffed at such thoughts. But now? Now I'm not so sure. In fact, now they are starting to make an awful lot of sense.

Dinos reappears, carrying a tray. He sets the table swiftly, places a bowl between us, heaped with Greek salad with a large chunk of feta on top and fills our glasses with red wine. Then he goes down to the fire and carefully slides the carcass from the spit onto a wooden board in one easy movement. He begins to carve it deftly.

For a while we eat in silence; the lamb is delicious. And as we eat I study Dinos. Everything he has been saying – about the gods, the olives, even the last bit of home-spun wisdom about women – could easily be dismissed as ironic chat or just the meanderings of an old man on his second tumbler of ouzo. But I can sense a kind of urgency in him this evening. Everything about him – his eyes, his voice, even his grizzled hair – seems to flicker with vitality. And what he has been saying has an unmistakable edge of urgency to it. It's as if he wants to convey something important to me tonight.

There's no way to gauge or measure this odd friendship. Even the word 'friendship' seems to fit us badly. I know almost nothing about him. Where does he come from? Does he have a family? Where on earth did he learn to speak such perfect English, albeit with a heavy accent? And sometimes our conversations seem to be conducted in a language I scarcely understand. Yet these normal yardsticks feel somehow irrelevant. Beneath them there's a strange, unfathomable closeness. And I'm touched by the care he has taken in preparing this dinner. Despite the irony and occasional roughness I can feel a kind of solicitousness in him.

I pick up my glass, lean back against the wall of the house and gaze up at the sky. The first stars are burning themselves into the darkness. To my left the tops of the pines are etched against the fading white. The tree frog has woken up and found a partner and they are calling gleefully back and forth across the inlet.

"Did you put the door knocker there?" I ask. Something about that strange, enigmatic face is scratching at the back of my mind.

Dinos shakes his head. "No. He was there before I came. And will be after I've gone. But meanwhile he looks after me. I like Hermes. He suits me. He's the patron god of thieves, jesters, tricksters, pickpockets." He spreads his arms theatrically. "Money-changers, merchants, clowns, pimps. Particularly pimps. Everywhere where you need speed, cunning, the skill to slip between the cracks and move fast between the levels of existence, he's there. That's why he's often invisible."

"He doesn't sound very god-like to me."

"You mean not very holy and majestic?" Dinos takes a swallow of wine and wipes the back of his hand across his mouth. "He's majestic alright. In his own way." He stops. "You know what else he can do?"

I shake my head. "We didn't learn about the god of pimps at school."

"He conducts souls to the Underworld. Now that's a serious business. He's the only one who's allowed into Hades' kingdom. None of the other gods can go. Not Poseidon, not Dionysos, not even Zeus himself. And, most importantly..." He pauses and gives me a strange, intense look. "He can *return*. It's one thing to be dragged down into the Underworld as you were. It's quite another to be able to return, bringing something with you, as Persephone did."

Persephone again. For some reason I feel a flicker of anxiety, a distant lightening fork on the horizon. Without my noticing he has taken the conversation down a register and, not for the first time with him, I feel ambushed.

"And the thing about Persephone," he goes on, clearly hitting his stride now, "is that not only did she come back to the upper world, but she was also willing to return to Hades."

"But she wasn't *willing*." For some reason I feel a need to contradict him, as if I'm defending myself against some unspecified accusation. "You obviously know the story as well as I do. In the first place she was *raped*, and then she *had* to go back because she had eaten the pomegranate seeds down there. That was the deal: if she ate anything in the Underworld she would have to return. And, in any case, what did she come back with?"

"Knowledge."

"What?"

"She came back with knowledge." Dinos leans back and folds his arms. "She came back with knowledge of the Underworld. Important stuff. And you're right – she ate and she had to return. But Hades wouldn't have had to drag her down the second time. She would have gone willingly, because by then she knew the importance of returning. She might not like it, but she knew the value of it. That's a very different thing. She knew it enriched her life. She had become *wise*. That's the difference." Suddenly he starts singing in a low, lilting voice:

"*Everything you learn there*
Will help when you return there."

"Christ, now we're really running off the rails."

Dinos, of course, is unphased. "So what did *you* bring back with you, my friend? That's the real question here. Not about Persephone, about *you*. You're an unchanged man, are you? You brought back nothing from the Underworld?"

And once again he's got me. I want to joke my way out of it, but I know the question is far too serious for that.

"No... Not nothing, I suppose. It's just that it's hard... Okay, I know Hades is the god of riches as well as of darkness and death. But frankly it's pretty bloody hard to say I've come back loaded with riches." I'm struggling to articulate some feeling that I know has been lodged in me ever since those long, frightening days of crisis. "Although, yes, I do feel somehow different. More..." I hesitate.

"More like a man?"

I nod in embarrassment. "Maybe something like that. But... it sounds a bit absurd at my age."

"No," says Dinos flatly. "It's not absurd." There's no trace of the usual irony in his voice. "You felt like a man when you returned, because down there in the Underworld you finally faced your dragons. They had been waiting for you long enough – all your life, in fact – but you had kept turning away, hoping you could avoid them. But, of course, you were wrong. It was a rite of passage, an initiation into manhood. I knew it the moment I saw you again in the *taverna*." He lays a finger on his temple. "The mark of Cain. You had eaten of the fruit of the Underworld. It was immediately obvious." He reaches down, picks up the wine bottle that had been standing by his feet and fills our glasses. "Yes, Hades had finally to come and drag you down by the scruff of your neck. That's true. He had certainly waited long enough. You don't dismiss a god like that for so long without retribution. And *of course* it was terrifying. But you *stayed* down. That's the point. You didn't duck out with drugs, or suicide. And when we are down there, there is nothing we can do but pace the ground flat. We have to learn to accept it, to undergo it as a necessary condition of the soul, an inner rite of passage. The ancient Greeks had a word for it – *Katabasis*. It means a 'going down'. They recognised it as a ritual condition, something we have to learn to undertake willingly. It's an act we all need to do sooner or later, if our souls aren't to wither and we live out our lives in silent fear." Something from Carla's letter is reverberating in me. Dinos picks up his glass and takes a long swallow.

For a while I don't respond. I'm still trying to absorb all this. We seem to be running along parallel tracks. Apparently I'm still caught in what Carla called the 'literal' and now I'm trying to switch to Dinos' bizarre, metaphorical way of thinking. At length I say, "What exactly is *katabasis*? I know the word, but how did the ancient Greeks actually do it? You said it was under ritual conditions. But there was nothing ritual about what happened to me. It was chaotic and bloody terrifying."

"That's because you went unwillingly. You were dragged down; so it wasn't part of a ritual. There's a very big difference, my friend." He takes a long draw on his cigarette. "At Eleusis, which is on the road between Athens and Corinth, there was the sanctuary of Demeter, Persephone's mother and the goddess of abundance. At that place people – people who were deemed to be ready, that is – could be initiated into her mysteries. You know about it?"

"I've heard of it, but I don't know much about the mysteries themselves."

"No," says Dinos. "No one does. That's because all those who underwent the rites were sworn to absolute secrecy. But inevitably, over the centuries, a few things leaked out. We Greeks aren't very good at keeping silent. So we know that the initiation was carried out over several days and that it was a terrifying ordeal. *But* it is said that no one who underwent the initiation ever feared death again. So we must presume that they somehow became acquainted with the Underworld and lived through its terror to come out the other side. *Death once dead there's no more dying then.*"

I'm stunned to hear Dinos quoting Shakespeare. How…? But before I can question him, he stops me in my tracks again.

"It seems that Hades has singled you out to become an 'initiate.'"

"*Me?* What do you mean? This isn't classical Greece, for God's sake. There aren't any rites at Eleusis any more. I actually visited the site once. The place was a shambles. People had dumped garbage all over it and there was a stinking oil refinery right next door…"

Dinos shrugs. "It is true. Such sacred places no longer exist. Modern man has seen to that. So you will have to become inventive. To find your own places and discover your own rituals." He pauses. "Or lead a life of fruitless, meaningless wandering."

"But *how?*"

"There is an old Greek saying: *Children go to visit the gods, but adults must make a place for the gods to visit them.* I think you will have to make such a place, my friend. And soon. You have paid respect to Hades once – but unwillingly. Now you will need to find a way to do it willingly. Perhaps this will be a lifelong task."

Dinos stubs out his cigarette emphatically in the hollowed-out stone that serves as an ashtray. In the darkness the drone of the cicadas has started up. What he has just said, for all its apparent obscurity, has struck a deep chord in me. Suddenly he breaks out coughing. He lurches forward, doubled over on the low wooden chair, his shoulders heaving in spasms. I jump up, knocking my wine across the table. "Are you alright?"

"Yes, yes." Dinos sits up and waves me back. "You see, it doesn't suit me to be too serious. Too self-important." He smiles ironically and turns down the corners of his mouth.

He wipes the back of his hand across his forehead. In the flickering candlelight I can see that he is sweating profusely.

I stare at him. And suddenly something strange happens to my vision. It's as if a veil has slid away and I am seeing him for the very first time, but seeing *deeper* than just the image that is coming through my retina. And, in that moment I know, in a place beyond my logic, that I am bound to him by some invisible thread. Then, without warning, all my long-buried feelings of loss and grief and sadness, all the things I have so long tried to excise from my life – all the fears, all the mistakes made, the chances missed, *all the love not given* – well up with a force that leaves me helpless and overflow, pouring across the barriers of my self-control. I jump up and stumble towards the sea. The shingle crunches under my feet. I stand there with my eyes closed.

When I open them again, I see Dinos, mirage-like through the prism of my tears. He is staring at me with a look of great tenderness, his smile devoid of irony. And, for the first time in my life, I know how it must feel to be truly seen by one's father. Not seen as some kind of symbol, or as a substitute for unfulfilled dreams, but seen and loved for oneself, without judgement, without reservation. Then Dinos comes towards me, wraps me in his arms and presses my face against his shoulder. I can smell the tobacco and feel the roughness of his shirt against my cheek. And there's tenderness in his voice, as he says, "Tears too are a way to honour the gods, my friend."

Then he links his arm through mine and we walk back to the stone bench in front of the house. He settles down beside me. "Come," he says, putting an arm around me, while he picks up the half-empty ouzo bottle with his other hand and fills our glasses. "We shall finish this tonight to the very last drop – if we die in the process!"

"You," I say, "are a crazy old pagan bastard."

THIRTY-THREE

The moment I open my eyes I know that something is different. The hangover, which had palpitated so insistently in my head when I woke on the stone bench outside Dinos' house shortly after dawn, has vanished. Somehow, through the fog of alcohol, I must have found my way to the village and steered the boat safely back to Conchili.

I shift my position and stretch. Specks of dust are dancing merrily in the thin shafts of sunlight filtering through the shutters. I rise and open the front door. The blue of the sky is so intense that for a moment I feel giddy, as if I'm staring down into a bottomless well. The iridescence on a spider's web twenty feet away glitters like a rainbow. In the night someone seems to have turned up all the dials of my senses so that everything has become hyper-real. It's as if the fog that has been clouding my vision all my life has suddenly lifted.

I sit down on one of the benches in the shade of the house and rub my eyes. I have known such hyper-intense moments before, of course – my first sight of Greece seen from the deck of the ferry in the dawn light, for example. Or the split second when Carla had playfully pulled her hands away from my eyes and I had gazed out over the virgin landscape of *Le Marche*. Or standing that first time before the statue of a *kouros* on the tiny, sacred island of Delos. But all these had been brief flashes, mere orphans in the flow of time, unrepeatable, leaving behind only a desperate sense of longing for something now vanished and unretrievable. But what this morning, with its feeling of utter peace, seems to promise is that these fragments might somehow be stitched together into some larger fabric and thread my daily life with this kind of quiet intensity.

I lean back against the wall of the house and breathe deeply, sucking in the air. A bee is moving lazily from asphodel to asphodel, the sawnote of its sound gigantic in the still air. The scent of rosemary is almost overpowering. All around me the world seems chiselled back to its original being. For a moment I try to explain what is happening, but my mind spins like a top and collapses. Before and after split away. And I am left in the pure present, where every sound is the first sound, every sight the first sight, every colour the first colour. The noise of the bee fills my head till it roars into silence. And I am gone, dissolved in the landscape. And it in me.

*

I stayed out at the house for five days in a state of wonder. Early in the mornings I went down to the sea and swam naked. There was no wind and the rising sun gilded a network of tiny gold flecks on the surface of the water. Small details swelled to fill my sight: two butterflies greeted me each morning, hovering above the lichened rocks, a precise circle of orange at the tips of their pale grey wings. The fresh new pine cones, perfectly divided into diamond-shaped segments, glowed iridescent green against the sky. A pair of kingfishers settled in the bay. Just before dusk and in the early mornings they criss-crossed the water with their electric flight, lifting their wings to the sun to show their deep russet chests before dipping and disappearing in a flash of cobalt blue. Everything around me seemed to glow with meaning. I could feel myself settling, sinking. Again and again I had the sensation of my heart opening to receive the world. And the world received me back. And I was filled with a profound feeling of gratitude.

When at night I lay on the terrace, gazing up at the stars, I began to sense how all the things that had happened to me in these last months had not been random at all, but were somehow joined in a pattern that was just becoming discernible, like figures emerging from the fog. How each of the decisions I had taken – the 'decision' to buy the black statue, the 'decision' to isolate myself here at Cochili all those months ago, to visit the war memorial at Stavraki, to swing off the *autostrada* at Perugia, even to let Julia leave without protest, and finally to return here to Katakolos had not truly been mine at all. Each time I had been swept along by an invisible current that paid no heed to my mind. Each 'choice' had been a non-choice, which mocked my vain presumption that I was the sole master of my fate. And there was an enormous peace in this realization. It was as if, all my life, I had been struggling, swimming frantically against the tide; and now I could relax and let myself be carried by the current. I had never realised that the world might, after all, be a benign place.

I saw too that, in my crazed terror of prison, I had been saner than I had ever been. For in those moments, as if a veil had suddenly been lifted, I had literally *seen* the prison bars that had kept me trapped in the narrow confines of all my old fears and beliefs and assumptions about the world. Trapped, as Dinos would have said, in a lifeless world without the gods.

I thought often of the *kouros*. Not just of the statue now standing in my gallery, but of all those luminous figures of naked youths with their stiff, hieratic poses and mysterious smiles. And for the first time I began to understand that smile. It was a smile of pure joy, pure gratitude for the gift of life, the simple ecstasy of the here and now. I remembered then the Japanese *koan* that had come to me on the day of Sylvia's death:

Show me the face you had before you were born.

Perhaps this was it. I was an adult being given, for a brief moment, the gift of seeing the world with the wondering eyes of a child.

If the gates of perception were cleansed the world would appear infinite.

I knew even then that this state couldn't last. Certainly not in its present form. But perhaps just knowing that such a vision lay within the broad arc of the possible was enough. Enough to take back to the grey confines of London.

But what had brought about this sudden change? The answer that rose in me was startlingly, almost absurdly simple: *that Dinos had seen me right down to my core and had not judged.* Perhaps he had glimpsed the face I had before I was born?

Often I thought too of Persephone – how, when she came back from the kingdom of Hades, she must have gazed on the exact same flower-strewn meadow from which the god had abducted her. But she didn't look with the same eyes. I knew that now. Once you have visited the Underworld and returned nothing is ever quite the same again. You have come up in another place.

What did the world look like to Persephone when she came back from Hades?

My guess is it looked pretty much like this.

*

On the fifth morning I wake just before dawn. The grey light is slanting through the shutters. I open the front door to find the terrace wet with dew. Each needle of the overhanging pines holds a globe of moisture suspended at its tip, gathering the early light. The roots of the pine trees are sheened with green. In the dry earth around the house wild cyclamen have begun to shoot, pale pink, mauve, lilac. It feels odd that, with the onset of autumn, the world is coming back to life.

I pull on my clothes and start up the hill behind the house. Something is urging me to catch the view of dawn on the strait. Just before the summit I sit down under a pine tree and settle my back against its trunk. The eastern sky is stained white now and, beyond the strait, the mountains of the mainland are humped against the horizon, black, indigo, the colour of crushed violets. Closer to the coast, faint plumes of mist hang in the lateral valleys of the foothills. In the half-light the shoreline looks almost alive, amphibian; it presses forward against the gun-metal sheet of the sea, then recedes to allow the waters to flood into its valleys and coves. From here, the house is barely visible under its canopy of pines. The sea is stretched like a sheet of dark jade between the headlands. But, below me, at its edges, the water is so clear that the grey rocks slip unbroken below the surface, as if the sea has evaporated and its fixed limits have suddenly vanished.

To my right, the distant black shapes of the westernmost islands of the Cyclades are clearly visible, and further south the mountainous form of Kythera. I lean back against the ridged trunk and close my eyes. And suddenly I sense the sprawling form of Greece not as a random scatter of islands, but as a great body spread unseen below the water, emerging here and there to reveal rocky hip and thigh, knee and shoulder at the places which we now call land. And down in the valleys where crabs now scuttle and fishes fret the stone, men once walked and grazed their flocks. Here in Greece there is always this silent promise – that all the disparate parts that lie Atlantis-like below the waters might one day be joined.

And as my mind flutters erratically in the darkness, it suddenly alights precisely on Julia. She is standing in clothes I have never seen her wear – white jeans rolled up below her knees, a faded denim shirt, her blonde hair gathered up in a red and white bandanna. She is walking bare-footed on a long sandy beach, watching the setting sun. I can feel – literally *feel* – her pleasure at the surf ebbing and flowing around her ankles. And I know with an absolute certainty that she was thinking of me.

*

That evening I go to the village and eat in the *taverna*. Dinos doesn't appear. Kostas hasn't seen him for the last three days, maybe four. He doesn't know where he is. He has probably gone to the mainland; he does that sometimes. No-one knows where he goes. The innkeeper shrugs, but I can feel disquiet under that casual shrug.

I wait two more days, but still Dinos doesn't come. The weather holds, but I no longer want to stay. Something is drawing me back to England.

THIRTY-FOUR

"I've got a bit of a surprise for you this weekend."

James leans back with a smile and laces his fingers behind his well-groomed head. In recent years his hair has started to grey and become thin on top, which his expensive barber tries artfully to conceal. He is sitting opposite me on the long sofa. Beside him two Labradors, one sleek black, the other the colour of pale wheat, are lying heraldically nose to nose in front of the crackling log fire. The fireplace is surrounded by an elegant marble mantelpiece bearing numerous embossed and crested invitation cards. Everything here has a baronial look – the high ceiling carries a crystal chandelier that floats above the room like some huge undersea creature. The chintz curtains are heavily ruched and swagged. The long sofas are piled with velvet cushions and the carpet is a dense mushroom-coloured pile. From somewhere in the background comes the muffled clatter of plates being stacked and the discrete aroma of roasting meat. It's English country chic at its most opulent.

James is my older brother, pillar of the establishment, successful senior partner of Tullis and Branson, chairman of his local Conservative constituency, bearer of an OBE and High Sheriff of the county. In short, all the things that I am not. Yet, despite these obvious differences, our relationship somehow seems to works. Blood apparently actually is thicker than water. His predictable right-wing intolerance is – at least in private – only skin deep, alleviated by his sardonic wit and self-deprecation. It's a very English kind of relationship, where we communicate via a safe meta-language – sport, shooting, family gossip – subjects unlikely to suck us into any uncomfortable vortex of emotion. And right now I'm here for one of our oblique bonding rituals – a weekend shooting party. It's hardly my idea of a perfect social occasion, but I have no great objection to shooting pheasants and, on my day, I am even what is considered a 'talented' shot, which is English sporting shorthand for erratic.

"What sort of a surprise?" I ask suspiciously, well aware that James can take quiet malevolent pleasure in tipping his guests into uncomfortable situations.

"I've invited someone you can have arcane intellectual chats with. The sort of thing that mercifully none of the rest of us will understand."

"Who's that?"

"John Kershaw."

"*Lord* Kershaw? The archaeologist? Christ, he'll probably refuse to sit down at the table with me."

"That sounds like fun." James appears unperturbed. "Why so? He seems perfectly affable to me. Very civilized in fact."

"Affable and civilised he may well be with *you*. But he's also rabidly against the antiquities market. He thinks we're all tomb-robbing bandits and should be put in the slammer. In his public pronouncements on the topic – and there are plenty of them – he actually brackets us with arms dealers and drug runners. He'll probably have a cardiac arrest when he finds out I'm in the house."

"Oh, I doubt that." James smiles, but I notice that his fingers have started to drum on his corduroy kneecap. I have obviously sown a seed of doubt in his normally unruffled mind.

"Anyhow, how on earth do *you* know him? I wasn't aware you were suddenly interested in archaeology?"

"I'm not. But I am interested in money." James leaves the ambiguity floating for a moment, teasing me. Then he adds, "And John Kershaw has pots of it. Or at least his college has. St Thomas's is by far the best endowed college in Oxford. In either Oxford or Cambridge for that matter. And we would like to help them invest it."

"I get it. But why has he come to you?"

"It seems Lord K is none too happy with the performance of their present investment people. He's obviously rather more financially savvy than most Oxbridge masters – in spite of being something as totally irrelevant as an archaeologist – and so we are, as they say, courting him. He's a cousin of an old school chum of mine, so I had a convenient way in."

At this moment my sister-in-law, Susannah, puts her head round the door. She is already fully made up, with her long dark hair elaborately gathered into a chignon for the occasion. Although it is hard to believe now, she was once a model. But in the last twenty years her once tall, willowy frame has packed on a considerable amount of weight so that she has become what is generally politely referred to as 'handsome' or 'statuesque'. She has the amiable, forthright, bossy manner and no-nonsense right-wing views that go down well in this part of the world. For what James wants in life he has probably picked himself a winner; although my cynically prurient mind can't help wondering how often they have sex.

"It's nearly seven thirty for God's sake. Can you two boys stop chatting for a moment and come and decant the port,

James, before everyone arrives." She casts a critical eye around the room. "And throw a log on the fire while you're at it."

The head disappears. James rises obediently and begins plumping up the sofa cushions.

"It seems I'm under starter's orders. And you had better start getting changed for dinner." He glances at his watch. "Although the Kershaws did say they might arrive a little late, some college meeting or something."

"I didn't know he was married."

"Oh yes. Charming wife. She just appears a little severe. You've got her next to you at dinner."

"Christ, James, why do you always have to partner me with excruciatingly dull women on these occasions? Can't I, just for once, have someone a bit sexier? Is it malice on your part or just the luck of the draw?"

"Malice, pure malice," says James affably. "Nothing left to chance."

"Well I just hope I don't mess up your carefully laid plans and ruin the weekend for you." I'm aware that the investment contract must be worth a fortune to Tullis and Branson and I'm curious to see if James is going to try and warn me off.

James finishes bouncing up the cushions. "The only way you'll ruin my weekend," he says laconically, "will be if you shoot too many of my precious pheasants tomorrow. But given your known skill with a fowling piece, I think I'm fairly safe. You did bring a black tie, didn't you?"

As I climb the broad oak staircase, I'm aware that the mention of Lord Kershaw has raised an alarm in me. It should be unnecessary. After all, both of us are quite capable of playing the social game over the next twenty-four hours without incident. But still I feel uneasy.

John Kershaw's academic rise had been meteoric. From a double first at the age of twenty-one, he had moved effortlessly through lecturer to become a full Professor at forty. Although archaeology is generally considered an academic backwater, a combination of steely ambition and political know-how had won him a surprise election to the Mastership of St. Thomas's eight years later, soon followed by his apotheosis to the House of Lords.

In his earlier days he had been part of the vanguard of a group of radical young archaeologists who had grown dissatisfied with the ambiguous – and, they felt, demeaning – position that their subject occupied in the academic world, caught uncomfortably between liberal humanism and objective science. So they set about demolishing archaeology's old-fashioned aura of discovery and romance, together with its dilettante image of aesthetic appreciation. Scientific facts were all that mattered now. John Kershaw's weighty publications, packed with pages of carefully crafted statistics, were models of this new discipline. Their aim was to sweep away the subjectivity of archaeology and erect in its place a new empirical science, based purely on careful excavation, statistical analysis and theoretical models, all designed to establish the best possible 'truth' of how ancient societies had been. In the smokescreen of this new precision, it was conveniently ignored that the scientific approach is in itself highly subjective. It had soon become apparent that the old colourful world of maverick dealers and passionate collectors fitted extremely badly into this carefully conceived framework.

By the time I come downstairs most of the dinner guests have assembled. They are standing in small groups discussing the prospects of the next day's shoot. Susannah takes me round and introduces me. The mix is fairly standard for James's shooting parties: two captains of industry who have weekend houses in the area, a local gentleman farmer, one of James's partners at the bank and a pleasant red-faced man who runs a large market garden in the West Country. For some reason I suspect he may once have been a boyfriend of Susannah's. The wives fold themselves effortlessly into this masculine scene.

Lord and Lady Kershaw are the last to arrive. Although I have met Lord Kershaw once before at a round-table conference on the antiquities market – where I had managed to upset him – and he will certainly be well acquainted with my reputation, he affects to be unaware of my identity. He shakes my hand and glances at me briefly. Behind his steel-rimmed spectacles his eyes look dead. Is that their normal condition? Or simply one reserved for people like me that he doesn't want to see?

Contrary to James' warning, Elizabeth Kershaw is a handsome woman with pale skin, soft green eyes and long auburn hair which she had looped up on her head with two black combs. They seem a strangely matched couple. While I make small talk with the market gardener I observe the Kershaws from the corner of my eye. They are moving separately with practiced social ease from group to group. But I can't help noticing that whenever they approach each other, some invisible magnetic current seems to propel them in opposite directions.

Over dinner, despite James' dire prediction, Elizabeth Kershaw proves to be easier company than I had feared. She has an ironic sense of humour and seems unperturbed when I tell her my profession. Whatever she knows of her husband's celebrated dislike of the antiquities trade, she appears not to share his views. Perhaps she is just indifferent. Further down the table Susannah is struggling to engage Lord Kershaw on his own subject. It obviously hasn't been a wise decision to seat her next to a man of such uncompromising intellect.

"But all those gods and goddesses and nymphs and what-have-you besporting themselves, I think they're really rather fun, don't you?" Susannah's voice is shrill; she is obviously clutching at straws. Lord Kershaw stares into his wine glass. Susannah presses on: "Do you actually believe in them?"

Lord Kershaw puts down the glass. He is clearly struggling to be polite. "No, of course not. The mythological figures help to build our picture of what ancient Greece was really like. They provide invaluable information about their customs and patterns of thought, just as the works of art themselves do. They're essential data. But from our point of view we can clearly see them as mere superstitions, primitive ways of explaining their ancestry and the forces of nature around them; all those questions which have now been adequately answered by modern science." He speaks as if he is lecturing a group of retarded undergraduates. "There's absolutely no need to share in these beliefs in order to study the subject scientifically. In fact, to share in them would be absurd – and severely compromise one's objectivity."

Undeterred, Susannah presses on: "But isn't their art supposed to be some of the best ever? I mean, how could they do that when they're still so primitive?"

John Kershaw takes an exaggeratedly long time to finish his mouthful. He puts down his knife and fork. "The art is obviously not primitive in the same way as African or Mexican art. Technically some of it is very sophisticated. But the mythological subjects and the way that the Greeks looked at the world animistically and polytheistically is from an early stage of scientific development. After all, it was two and a half thousand years ago, you know." He smiles thinly. Susannah seems flustered by the word 'polytheistically'. She takes his smile as a signal to change tack and begins to talk about pheasants.

After the pudding plates have been cleared, James politely manoeuvres the women into the adjoining room and firmly closes the door. I am always amazed that, even in this household, the archaic after-dinner custom of dividing the sexes still prevails, and apparently without dissent. Cigars are put on the table in a silver humidor. I am the only one to refuse. James lights his cigar, starts the port decanter circulating clockwise and sits back in his chair. He addresses Lord Kershaw as if opening a business meeting.

"How much trouble do these brigands of antiquities dealers really give you, John?"

I can scarcely believe my ears. James is leaning back with a faint smile on his face. I'm aware, of course, that he enjoys pitting people against each other, as a kind of spectator sport, like cock-fighting, but he clearly has no idea of the depth of feeling that runs through the archaeological debate about dealing. I have an uncomfortable feeling that his joke is about to backfire.

At first John Kershaw appears not to have heard the question. He extinguishes his match by waving it vigorously from side to side. Simultaneously, he sucks in his cheeks and puffs at the cigar, emitting clouds of grey smoke. Then he removes it from his mouth and inspects the glowing tip with studied concern. I notice the perfectly circular stain of saliva at the other end. He lays his cigar in the silver ashtray in front of him, rotates it once between his fingers and looks directly up at me. Even before he speaks I can feel the controlled aggression coming across the table.

"The problem, *of course*, is not with people like you," he says silkily. "But you must admit that there are some fairly undesirable elements working within your business."

I have an odd sense of the man opposite me starting to spin a web. I decide not to be drawn into the game. I smile. "Perhaps I'm undesirable too."

"I'm sure that you take great care to ensure that nothing you sell would have been illicitly excavated."

"What does illicit mean?"

"It means removing any antiquity from the ground that is not in a controlled excavation." He picks up the cigar and draws deeply on it, allowing the smoke to curl up towards the ceiling. "It was all very acceptable and fine in the Eighteenth and Nineteenth Centuries to go treasure hunting, just digging up anything you liked and carting it off back home to your country mansion. But that simply won't do any longer. Our interest now is not just that of the uninformed dilettante. We have moved on from there. I don't deny that collecting may, in its own way, have been an honourable, if thoroughly misguided, passion. But those days are over, just as surely as the days of sticking tiger heads on your wall as trophies are over."

"Do you think that all those who buy ancient art are simply collectors of trophies?"

"I'm sure there has always been a great element of that. A kind of display of wealth and spurious intellect."

"Why spurious?"

"Because the collectors had no serious interest in what the objects really were, their function, their context, what sort of society they were used in. An object without its context is more or less worthless." Lord Kershaw taps the sagging coil of ash from the tip of his cigar. His eyes gleam through his spectacles.

I pause and set down my port glass. I feel a deep distaste for this man with his patronizing self-assurance, for the way he so effortlessly injects rudeness into an apparently civilized academic debate. I know I'm being goaded, and again I resolve not to be drawn – for my own sake as much as for James's. "Worthless?" I ask quietly.

"In any meaningful sense, yes. Although very obviously not worthless in your sense of the word. That, if I may say so, is part of the trouble."

There is a moment of silence. The other conversations around the table have suddenly ceased. James is rolling his port glass between the outstretched palms of his hands, as if in a vain attempt to repot its shape.

"In what way is it part of the trouble?"

"Well..." Lord Kershaw pauses and stretches his hands palms down, spreading his fingers to their maximum extent, like a pianist about to perform. "Very clearly, if there weren't huge rewards being offered on the international art market for such objects by certain unscrupulous collectors and dealers and even – I'm sad to say – museums, no one would bother to go digging for them. And if they were not plundered, looted and stolen in this way they could all be properly and scientifically excavated."

A sudden wave of heat washes over me. "Look," I say, trying to keep my voice calm. "That word 'plundered' is highly emotive. The reality is that most of the objects you refer to as 'plundered' aren't plundered at all. And I wonder what your statements are based on, since I don't believe you've ever had a serious conversation with an antiquities dealer before this. Your need for factual data doesn't seem to extend that far." I pause, realizing that my breathing has become shallow.

Lord Kershaw flushes and opens his mouth to speak, but

suddenly I don't want to stop. "And I'm greatly saddened that university professors and distinguished academics use their intellectual capacities to score points rather than thinking this issue through and trying to find a solution that…"

"In what way, pray, don't we think it through?" interrupts Lord Kershaw. "I should have thought the issue was very clear. These objects are ripped, *plundered*, from the ground so that they lose all their archaeological context. They become useless, stripped of all information. Then they are smuggled out of the country and sold through unscrupulous dealers for exorbitant amounts of money. It seems perfectly well 'thought through' to me."

"Do you really believe that if there were no international art market all these objects that you now see exchanging hands for money would actually be scientifically excavated instead?"

"Well, of course," says Lord Kershaw icily. "What else?"

I can see from the corner of my eye that James's glass-rolling operation is gathering momentum. "It seems to me," I say, "that the accepted archaeological model of the antiquities market is lamentably short of facts. I think that's an area where I may be expected to have a certain amount of information. And from my experience the vast majority of what are termed 'illicitly excavated' objects…"

"Which is precisely what they are," cuts in Lord Kershaw.

The interjection is clearly designed to put me off my flow, but I'm not going to give him that satisfaction. "…and which then turn up on the art market are actually found by accident. By people, often very poor people, digging drainage ditches in their fields or excavating foundations for new buildings."

"Then the people who make these apparent 'chance' finds should report them to the proper authorities," says Lord Kershaw dryly, ironically etching the inverted commas in the air with his fingers. His cigar now lies in the ashtray, the long grey filament slowly crumbling from the tip.

"They 'should', but in reality they don't. Mainly because they know perfectly well that if they do, their land will be confiscated, or their building project will be stopped, while archaeologists take their time, often years, to come and inspect it. And, on top of that, they get no financial reward for their discovery. It's hardly surprising that if they can sell what they find and make some money, they tend to do it. At least in that way they get to eat and the object survives, even if its context may not."

"They could always sell it to the state," says Lord Kershaw drily. "Nearly all countries have legal provision for such purchases."

"That's simply untrue!" Lord Kershaw observes my obvious anger and a thin smile spreads across his lips. I pause and steady my voice. "Yes, there are legal provisions for state purchase in most countries. That's true. It sounds good politically. But are those provisions ever used? No, they're not. That's the reality. The state doesn't pay for those things. They just seize them. That's one mistake. But the really big mistake is this crazy belief that if the finder doesn't have access to a market he will simply call in the archaeologists instead. He won't, because he knows perfectly well that that means no money *and* trouble. The objects don't just lie in the ground patiently awaiting the arrival of the noble-spirited archaeologists. That's a fantasy. And what happens in those cases – if the finder can't sell what he has…?" Lord Kershaw starts to reply, but I cut him off. "I'll tell you what happens: he simply destroys any evidence that he ever made the find, so that the authorities can't attack him later. This means that the statue, or whatever it is, will get buried in concrete in the foundations. Or else deliberately smashed to bits and left at the bottom of the drainage ditch. Or dumped in the Nile. In that way you have neither the object nor its context. And it happens all the damn time! Because that's the situation that the system has created. I can't imagine that that's much of a comfort to archaeologists."

I can feel my heart thumping against my ribs. Lord Kershaw's hands, now laid on the table on either side of the smoking ashtray, are visibly trembling.

"It's clear to me…" Lord Kershaw's voice is shaking. "… That we are dealing with two completely different worlds here. The world of scholarship and the world of greed."

I feel trapped and angry and boxed in. Lord Kershaw has just elegantly and cynically divided the universe into two completely unreal groups. And yet the sense of morality surrounding that word 'greed' seems to render me powerless to reply. I am struggling to control myself. "I've read several of your books, with great admiration for your intellectual skill and erudition," I reply as calmly as I can, "and your ability to order the archaeological data. And yet each time I've finished one I can't help wondering what it is that I've actually gained from it, except some sense of power over the past by being able to order it. A power which is, of course, completely illusory."

"Perhaps we have to consider the possibility that you didn't quite understand the books."

"Perhaps not. So could you maybe explain to me why you wrote them?"

Lord Kershaw clears his throat. "The books were never intended to be best-sellers, surprising though that may seem in a world where profit appears to be the only moving force. They were written to further the study of archaeology, and our understanding of the past in the most precise and objective way possible. The only proper means of doing that is by assembling the maximum amount of correct data. That will always involve careful excavation and the use of statistical analysis. Only then can we arrive at the most accurate possible conclusions."

"What I hear you describing is the methodology. But what interests me is not *how* you do it, but *why? Why archaeology?*"

"I should have thought that was pretty obvious," snaps Lord Kershaw, clearly losing his temper. "By looking at the past we can learn how to do things better in the future."

"Do you really think that your books will enable us to do things better in the future?" I ask raising my eyebrows ironically.

"My aim is to present the record as precisely as possible. Without accurate data we cannot hope to draw the correct conclusions from which to learn for the future."

"And how would you like to see the future?"

"As a world of love, peace and harmony," says Lord Kershaw with biting irony. He stares across the table at me and narrows his eyes.

And suddenly I feel chilled. I know I've been outmanoeuvred by John Kershaw's falsely loaded vocabulary, by his absurd division of the world into good and evil, and by his absolute disdain for anything that cannot be encompassed by the intellect. Suddenly something erupts inside me. "Frankly," I say, leaning forward, "I don't think you could give a fuck about anything that can't be fitted into your statistical tables. I don't think you could give a fuck about ancient Greece, or its spirit, or its art. And least of all could you give a fuck about love or harmony. I don't think you even know what they are, since you can't measure them. Nor could you care less about the utterly boring and soulless legacy of archaeology that you're leaving to the next generation.

Actually I don't think you could give a fuck about anything at all except that dry, tight-arsed feeling of being 'right' that you get when you stare at your completely meaningless statistical tables. You're just terrified of anything that might upset your tiny boxed-in view of the universe…"

I pause. John Kershaw has pushed his head forward like a tortoise. His face has gone livid white. He is staring at me with his eyes narrowed into such an intensity of hate that it feels physical, explosive. Suddenly I remember Giacomino di Simone's face in the warehouse that day when I had dared to tell him the truth about his forged sculptures. The man with the evil eye.

The room is stunned into silence. The diners look frozen, like figures in a tableau. James coughs. "I think we had better join the ladies," he cuts in. He drains his port glass and pushes back his chair. "I can see I had better not put the two of you side by side with loaded guns in your hands tomorrow." There are smiles of relief around the table. Only Lord Kershaw's face remains set.

Last to leave the room, I pass James, who is holding open the door to the dimly-lit drawing room. "I think I just screwed your contract for you," I say.

"Done with the utmost finesse," replies James dryly, but with no sign of malice. There is something majestic about his unperturbability, the way he applies the irony equally to himself. No special cases.

*

I switch off the light and lie back on the covers of the four-poster bed with the curtains open. It is full moon. The silver glow washes over the room, picking out the wood panelling, illuminating the landscape painting on the opposite wall in eerie chiaroscuro.

I am painfully aware that I have ruined the dinner and I regret it for James's sake. I have probably screwed his contract for him. But when John Kershaw had thrown out his challenge about love, peace and harmony, I had felt a savage rage explode inside me. I had wanted to jump across the table and smash him in the face.

I sigh, fold my hands behind my head, stare at the silvery patterns on the ceiling. I had seen in John Kershaw, Oxford professor and peer of the realm, something ugly and inadequate. It hadn't been just the scale of his hypocrisy or his mean-minded arrogance, or the coldness of his disdain for all who cannot match his intellect and share his views that had so chilled and enraged me. But something else hidden behind that smug mask of apparent objectivity and reason, something that felt far more destructive. To John Kershaw and his colleagues, everything that is undiggable, unmeasurable, unquantifiable, everything that cannot be revealed by the spade and examined by the intellect simply doesn't exist. The soul of Greece, her gods and rituals, her passion and wildness do not exist; or exist only as dead historical footnotes, emptied of meaning.

But now I can feel my anger reaching down to deeper roots than just the study of archaeology, down to a rage against all who would strip the world of soul, force it into a narrow monotheism of facts, present their arid observations as the obvious and only truths. And suddenly, as I lie there, something about my irrational fear of prison clicks into place. It hadn't been just the grim reality of incarceration, the loss of liberty that had so terrified me, but something much deeper – a horror of being trapped in the terrible greyness of a world of dead 'reality'. A world of unquestioned laws and structures. A world of received opinions and received religion. A world where two and two can only ever make four. A utilitarian world of facts and money and science, where religion is commandments and liturgy and threats of damnation. A world where God might exist in the catechism and be invoked by politicians, but where the real gods have long ago absconded, leaving the place ash-grey, measurable, quantifiable, usable. Dead. That is the real prison.

I close my eyes and for a moment Giacomino di Simone's face flashes into my mind, his sleek hair and deadened black eyes. Giacomino's blind destruction of the ancient world, rifling through undisturbed tombs, trampling on the remains of sacred burials, discarding everything that is not valuable in his terms feels no different from the destruction that John Kershaw is dealing to the soul of Greece, forcing it into the miserly confines of his scientific system. John Kershaw and Giacomino di Simone are joined at the hip, the one single-mindedly despoiling the fabric of the ancient world, the other, just as surely destroying its spirit.

And suddenly I think of Dinos, of his world still peopled by gods, his reverence before the spirit of Greece. How far removed he is from the mean fundamentalist views of John Kershaw. And how long it seems now since that night out at Dinos' house, and the quiet days that had followed at Conchili. I can sense how, in the months since, back in the sophisticated world of London with all its distractions and temptations, I have gradually, silently allowed the slow vegetative nature of habit to ensnare me again, deadening my own spirit. Is this what Dinos had called 'the prison of habit'? I hadn't only felt enraged by John Kershaw; I had felt polluted. For I now realise that in these last weeks I have silently become enmeshed again in my old life, in the compulsive world of dealing and all its insidious excitements. And in so doing I have allowed something of John Kershaw's deadness to reenter my soul. And suddenly I feel an aching sense of loss and long for the quiet ecstasy of my days out at the house on Katakolos.

*

Shortly before dawn an unexpected frost has snapped in, layering the ground with white and liming the hedgerows. The sky is a perfect unbroken blue and steam rises from the dogs as they weave their way excitedly amongst the guests. I feel utterly detached this morning, like an observer, still bruised from last night's confrontation. To my surprise, Lady Kershaw comes towards me; "May I stand with my table-partner of last night?"

After the suffocation of the previous evening's conversations, I had looked forward to standing alone, gun in hand, somewhere in a quiet wood. But at this moment I have neither the heart nor the will to refuse her. And besides, the unexpectedness of her request has aroused my curiosity.

"Yes, of course," I say, trying to appear gallant. "With great pleasure."

Jane Kershaw is dressed in corduroy plus-fours, green wellingtons and a waxed khaki jacket. A head-scarf decorated with pheasants is knotted under her chin, keeping her auburn hair in check. Her clothes are smart and clearly expensive in an obviously down-at-the-heel kind of way. The jacket is shiny with wear, the pheasants on the scarf have faded to a light tan – all discrete signs that she is a relaxed veteran of such occasions.

"Thank you." She smiles at me. We start out across the field in the direction of a stick planted in the ground to indicate my assigned position. For a while we are silent, listening to the distant rustle of the beaters moving through the wood, the insistent tap-tap of a stick driving the pheasants along the hedgerows back into the cover.

"I hear you had a disagreement with my husband last night."

I turn from my scrutiny of the wood and stare at her in surprise, trying to gauge why she has chosen to raise the topic. I see only an amused, ironic look in her green eyes, the thin lines at the corners crinkling slightly.

"Who told you?"

"He did. He wasn't best pleased."

"Oh, I suppose it's fair to say that we had what the Oxbridge high table might call a free and frank exchange of views." I resume my study of the trees.

"He was royally pissed off." This one has caught my attention. A slight smile wavers at the corners of her lips. She seems to be playing some sort of waiting game – and clearly enjoying it.

"I'm sorry."

"Are you?"

"Not really. Though I probably went too far. I don't think your husband particularly likes people like me."

"You mean antiquity dealers?"

"Yes."

"True." She pauses. "Actually, he doesn't particularly like anybody."

My surprise is interrupted by the harsh chattering cry of a cock pheasant. It rises from the centre of the wood and climbs diagonally away from us with an agitated thrumming of its wings. A single shot punctuates the air. The bird seems to fold in mid-flight, then plummets out of sight behind the curtain of beech trees.

"Oh, good shot!" The voice comes from somewhere behind the wood.

"Did you know that he has a collection?"

At first I think I must have misheard. "A collection? A collection of what?"

"Antiquities."

I stare at her in open-mouthed amazement. A pheasant breaks from the side of the wood and screeches directly over my head. "That's it Bronson. Let the easy ones go!" James's ironic voice comes floating from the corner of the copse of beech trees to our left. Somewhere within the wood, jovial laughter greets the remark. I continued to stare.

"You mean he himself has a collection of antiquities?"

"Yes." She smiles, clearly relishing the impact of her remark. "He bought it years ago, some of it when I first knew him. He was much more relaxed about things in those days. I can't imagine it's particularly distinguished; we didn't have much money back then. I think he just liked to pick things up here and there. Nowadays he doesn't exactly advertise it."

"Why are you telling me this?" I am well aware that she is, for some unknown reason, handing me a piece of political dynamite, free of charge. It's also clear that she knows precisely what she is doing.

"Because I loathe him," she says dryly.

"Yours, Bronson!" James' cry splits the silence. I react instinctively, pulling the trigger even before the gun is at my shoulder. A moment later a brightly-coloured cock pheasant lands at our feet with a massive thud.

"Oh, good shot!" says Lady Kershaw.

*

In the melee of departure on the gravel drive, I can sense John Kershaw avoiding me as he says his jovial goodbyes.

Undeterred I approach him. "Well, goodbye. Hope to meet you meet again before long."

"Yes, of course." John Kershaw is looking ostentatiously past my right ear whilst trying to ignore my outstretched hand.

"Why don't you come and visit me in my gallery sometime? Perhaps I can add to your collection."

I watch the moment of shock in his face. He flushes and his eyes narrow in an animal display of warning. Then, scowling at his wife, he turns, climbs into the dark green Range Rover and slams the door. As the vehicle swings round on the gravel in front of the house, I catch a glimpse of Jane Kershaw through the other window. She raises her hand and smiles.

I can imagine the atmosphere in the car and, for a moment, I wonder if it was unfair of me to have revealed 'our' secret. But deep down I know I would have disappointed her if I hadn't.

THIRTY-FIVE

By the time I arrive the rowan trees are pushing long shadows across the gravel drive. The air is fresh with the smell of damp cut grass and gently rotting vegetation. On this side of the house, beyond the small flagged courtyard, the massive roof plunges almost to ground level. Its faded ochre tiles are encrusted with mounds of dark green moss that sit there like crouching toads.

When I reach the door, I stop and stare in astonishment. There in the centre, above the ring of the knocker, is a head of Hermes, painted black. It is more finely cast than the one at Dinos' house, but recognizably the same. He gazes back at me sardonically from under his winged hat. In the silence I can almost hear Dinos chuckle. I put out my hand to touch it, as if superstitiously for good luck. Then I turn the key, raise the latch and lean against the door. With a feint squeak it gives and I step into the low-ceilinged kitchen.

James had shown only mild surprise when I asked to borrow the house for a week or so. He apparently swallowed my story of needing to do some quiet research. Or perhaps – more likely – he surmised that I would to use it for some more dubious purpose – what we, as hopeful teenagers, used to refer to as a 'shagathon' – and, just for once, decided to be discrete. Either way, he seemed unconcerned. He had originally bought the house when his children were at boarding school in Oxford, but hardly ever uses it now, unless he is invited to shoot in the area. That he still owns it at all is probably due to the fact that he considers prime rural property a good long-term investment.

I move slowly through the deserted rooms, enjoying the sparse puritan atmosphere – the huge open inglenook fireplace, large enough for me to step into without stooping, the narrow, twisting staircase with its creaking boards, the way the uneven whitewashed walls bulge between the rough oak timbers, as if they might burst at any moment. And, as I walk, exploring the silent rooms I am assaulted by the obvious, but unanswerable, questions – *What am I doing here? Why have I come? What do I expect?*

*

Slowly, as day links into day and I sever my contacts with the outside world, the magic of the house creeps over me. I listen less and less to the answering machine. I never turn on the television. My calls to the gallery become infrequent. Zoe's voice grows petulant. She isn't used to this sudden lack of urgency and ambition and it clearly unnerves her. Eventually, after five days, I say, "You're on your own." I replace the receiver with a sense of relief and unhook it from the wall. It's unfair, of course. Yet, in truth, I am the one who is cut adrift now, floating further and further away from the shore. The noise of London is less than two hours away; but that is no longer my reality. My reality now lies within the circumference of the garden and the arc of vision from the topmost leaded window. And within that arc I am totally alone.

I loved the eccentric shape of the house, it's huge barnlike roof to the rear, which plunged so close to ground level that I could remove the damp leaves from the gutter in the mornings without standing on tiptoe. I loved the elegant façade onto the garden, which clad the earlier brick and timber structure with honey-coloured Oxfordshire stone. The large sashed windows, punched through in the Eighteenth Century to gentrify this simple cottage, flooded the south facing rooms with light. I loved the view from the desk in the small study, with the berries on the sloe bush outside pressed against the windowpane. In the afternoons the lowering sun threw spiked shadows from the cypresses across the damp lawn and picked out the colours of the accumulating leaves.

James had never mentioned a gardener and no one came. For the first five days I was quite alone, eking out my simple provisions. When I did finally venture out, I felt oddly slowed down, disorientated, as if I was recovering from a long illness. The woman in the local shop stared at me through her spectacles as I fumbled with the money, almost unable to distinguish the coins. Clearly she thought I was some kind of retard.

The weather held. Time began to lose its accustomed markers. The telephone remained unplugged. Even the books I had brought stayed largely unread, my interest in them gradually fading altogether. I spent more and more time just sitting or walking, observing minutely the details of my surroundings: the precise spacing of the spines on the lavender bushes, the pattern of a blackbird's beak in a fallen apple, the slight distortion from a true sphere of a drop of dew on a spider's web in the early morning sunlight. Everywhere I looked in this damp autumn atmosphere my surroundings seemed to enfold me with a quiet, insistent recognition that they, like myself, would not last. Not in their present form. There was a strange comfort in this realization, a kind of peace.

One day I found a woodpecker lying on its back, dead, unexplained, its feet drawn up, the body hardening. Its long pale amber tongue protruded from its slender beak. I removed two feathers, one brilliant green from its back, one deep carmine red from the crown of its head. I buried it carefully beside the twisted cherry tree on a bed of ferns. I knew I would miss its staccato sweeping flight and its chattering call. For three days it's mate searched ceaselessly, crisscrossing the fields, and then disappeared. I felt the slow decay of the bird's body under the earth.

I was sinking deeper, like a dropped stone descending through water to the invisible bottom. Where once I would have battled this sensation, now I welcomed it. Down here there was another kind of knowing, one not available to the upper world. And in that darkened space memories came to me, their antiphonal voices echoing in my head:

Katabasis – a descent into the Underworld under ritual conditions... You have a great facility for turning away... What kind of a man would descend willingly? A wise man, a man who respects the gods... Each morning we must arise and plant an apple tree... Children go to visit the gods, but adults must make a place for the gods to visit them... There are many ways to stay in the depths...

Was this what I was instinctively doing, following Dinos' admonition to create a place for the gods to visit me? I only knew that I was back in the Underworld, pacing the ground flat day by day. But this time doing it *willingly*, creating my own ritual of seclusion, carving out my own place of silence. To what end I didn't understand. Only that I needed to do it. Increasingly it felt as if the warp and weft of my mind were unravelling, expanding, spreading out, the lack of noise and voices throwing me back on my other senses. Another month of this and I might be able to hear the animals talk! From this strange vantage point, how dry, how hollow all my old concerns, my old desires and ambitions, everything that had held my life together, now seemed. It was as if I had been living in a weightless society, mere dancers on the lip of the volcano.

Day by day I felt things fall away from me – old envies and ambitions, old angers and resentments, old yearnings – leaving me ever clearer, more transparent. My dreams were clear and vivid, spilling over the threshold of sleep, the two worlds no longer severed. I dreamt of swimming deep in the ocean surrounded by blackness. In the day, as I sat in the armchair looking out of the window, strange images came, images of the cavernous silence of the Venetian lagoon in the dead of winter, of a night sea journey, one man solitary in the vastness of the ocean, as if things stored up for decade upon decade were stirring in the darkness. The Puritan atmosphere of the house and its surroundings was so strong as to be almost palpable. Here, all across the bleak Oxfordshire flood plain, a place with few features to comfort the soul, the Civil War had raged. Neighbour against neighbour, friend against friend, fathers against sons. And the unseen ghosts were everywhere, inhabiting every walk of the garden, every room and corner, insistent in their silent presence.

It was after thirteen days of solitude, on a late afternoon when fog clung to the ground like moss, and a thrush came and settled on the stripped branch outside my window; at this precise moment of silence, the presiding spirit of the house returned and entered the garden through the wicket gate into the orchard. I sat quite still, not even surprised. Nothing stirred in the mist, as the tall figure in high boots and a brown slouched hat led a chestnut horse down the flagged path between the withering lavender bushes. He was followed by a woman, upright, dignified and a girl, both dressed in black and white. I could hear distinctly the clop of the horse's hooves on the flagstones.

I closed my eyes. The darkness circled. I could feel the barriers of my mind begin to crumble. Something in the absolute silence of my vigil, in my willingness to descend into the quiet and the darkness had broken the bonds of time and summoned them back.

If the doors of perception were cleansed everything would appear to man as it is – Infinite…

Car wheels crunch on the gravel behind the house. Startled, I shake myself and go to the kitchen, walking unsteadily. I feel like a man who has woken from a deep sleep. I already know who will be there.

When I open the door Julia is standing on the flagstones. She runs her hand through her hair with a quick, nervous gesture. "Zoe said you'd unhooked the phone," she explains hurriedly. She sounds flustered and her face is flushed. "She was worried about you. She wanted to come herself but she can't drive and she wasn't sure exactly where the house was and which was the nearest station – because she couldn't ask you. It all seemed so complicated. So I volunteered to come and find you and see if you were all right…" She raises both gloved hands, then lets them drop. I stand staring at her, uncertain. She hesitates. "May I come in?"

I step aside, feeling boorish that she has had to ask. Standing inside the door, we face each other.

"Well…" I start. Then stop, aware of the strangeness of my own voice. It must be nearly a week since I last spoke, a few brief words on my visit to the local shop.

"Well?" I start again. "What's the verdict?"

Small lines of concentration gather at the corners of her eyes as she studies me carefully. "You look," she says at length, "okay, I suppose."

Behind the banality of the words I can hear her gentleness, an unwillingness to intrude too far. For a long moment we are silent. Then, very slowly, she stretches out her hand and lays it against my cheek. I stare at her. I can feel something rock-like inside me, something that has been gathering there all my life, start to split apart. Unexpectedly my eyes fill with tears.

The heavy oak beam above the ingle-nook fireplace fills my vision. I study the circular knot at its centre. A network of deep cracks radiates out from it. Slowly the picture widens. I notice the uneven white plasterwork above and the large bricked cavity of the fireplace below. A fire is crackling in the grate. Slowly I turn my head. Julia is sitting in the red armchair opposite. She has her legs crossed and in her right hand she holds a glass. She looks very delicate, like a figure in a painting. I feel oddly convalescent, with a sense of life gradually finding its way back into me, like the blood reluctantly returning to a numbed limb.

"Hi." My voice sounds strange.

"Hi. I got myself a drink. I hope you don't mind."

"What happened?"

"You walked in here like a robot, sat down and went fast asleep."

"I did *what?*"

She smiles. "You slept for an hour and…" She looks at her watch. "Ten minutes to be precise. Like a baby. Not moving, barely breathing."

I realise I must have somehow passed out. Had I collapsed here on the sofa? "Weren't you worried that I might have had a heart attack or something?" I ask.

"No." She smiles and shakes her head. "Not at all."

To be honest it feels as if part of me has fallen into the Other World, beyond recovery, somewhere quite different from sleep. And now I am left feeling becalmed and oddly different. My mind grapples to come to terms with what has happened. Have these days of silence and solitude unhinged me at some kind of cellular level, so that I can no longer relate to the 'normal' world?

"You mean you come to visit an almost stranger in a deserted house in the country and he immediately sits down without a word and passes out – and you're not even surprised!"

She shrugs unconcernedly. "No. It just happened. It was what it was. Besides, you're not a stranger."

"No, I guess not. Certainly not after that little episode."

She laughs. "Would you like a glass of wine?" I nod. "I prepared some food while you were snoozing. I thought you'd probably be hungry. It looks like it's been a fairly Spartan regime for some time."

"Was the kitchen in chaos?"

"For a bachelor, not bad. It just didn't look like it had been a high priority." She rises and goes through the open door into the kitchen. I can smell cooking. Suddenly I am ravenously hungry.

"I'm afraid I had to make do with what was there," she calls out. "I just threw everything into one pot and added herbs. If it turns out to be a success, I'll name the dish after the house. Or after you maybe."

Slowly, with exaggerated care, I sit up and lower my feet to the floor. Julia returns with a second glass. "Here. I think you need this. The food will be ready in about ten minutes. I've laid up in the kitchen. Is that alright?"

Throughout the meal I am struck by the matter-of-factness of Julia's presence. It's as if we're an old couple and have sat like this across the kitchen table, chatting, for years. Frankly I'm baffled by my own reactions. Here I am, alone with a beautiful woman in an isolated house with night already closed in, and I feel totally at ease, without the slightest pressure. I look at her as she speaks, taking in her beauty. It's disorientating, this apparent absence of desire. And I'm startled too by the lack of self-consciousness with which I recount my odd world of the last fourteen days. She listens intently, but without speaking. Only when I come to the moment when I had seen the three figures enter the garden I hesitate. Sensing this she says, "Go on." And I tell her quietly, using the word *seen*. Not imagined. Not dreamed, or hallucinated, but *seen*. She nods silently.

I go on to tell her about Katakolos, about Dinos and then, unhesitatingly, about my visit to the Underworld. In the space of one hour, I show her more of myself than I have ever shown anyone before. It feels as if, for the first time in my life, I am using words to reveal myself, not to hide.

In turn, she tells me of her stay in California, how relieved she had been at first to be away from London, and the incessant tug-of-war with Bernhardt over the dismembered scraps of their life together. The distance had brought her perspective and repose. Relieved of the persistent reminders of her past, she had ceased to fret over every uncertain friendship, every look and innuendo, every subtle possibility of rejection. Gradually she had started to let go of the past, to revive her own personality. But California also brought melancholy and homesickness, both for London and for Austria. And eventually for Europe altogether. She could not get used to the strangeness and, at the same time, ordinariness of the place. It was as if she had landed on the moon and found it banal.

In the end she felt the place quietly robbing her of her soul. Her early physical well-being from the climate and exercise turned to dullness and lassitude. Beneath the blandness of the Californian surface something felt sinister. She knew she had to get away, back to London.

We go back into the sitting room and I throw more logs on the fire. It crackles and flares up. When I turn, she is standing just behind me. For a long moment we stare at each other. I have played this kind of scene countless times before. And now I feel lost. Perhaps lost precisely *because* I have played it so many times. And now I want it to be different, to be unstained by my past. I want whatever happens next to be true to what I am feeling. Unexpectedly an image of the black Aphrodite comes into my mind. I stay staring at her, uncertain.

Quietly, not taking her eyes from mine, she says: "*To everything there is a season and a time to every purpose under heaven… A time to embrace and a time to refrain from embracing…*"

THIRTY-SIX

Specks of dust hover lazily in the narrow shaft of sunlight. The whitewashed room feels stripped of all excess, Puritan but merry. Slowly I ease out of the high four-poster bed, cross to the window and part the curtains. The sun is just up. The world outside is layered with frost. The last leaves have been prized free from the trees in the night. Only in the distance a squat oak is still stubbornly in leaf. As I watch, a robin settles on the desiccated branch of wisteria under the window ledge. It stares at me impudently with its round eye.

Julia stirs in her sleep. I turn back to the bed. The sheet is pulled up high, just the top of her blonde hair shows scattered on the pillow. I stretch out a finger and touch it as if to reassure myself of its reality.

"Good morning." Julia is sitting on the edge of the bed, her legs drawn up under her, wearing one of my shirts. The collar is turned up under her hair. Balanced precariously beside her is a tray with coffee cups.

I sit up and rub my eyes. "I must have slept again."

"Again? You were already up?"

"Yes. I looked outside and everything seemed magical. Almost new-made."

She smiles. "I can see I just slept with an incurable

romantic." Then she leans forward and touches my cheek. Slowly she traces the line of my eyebrows. Her finger pauses at the scar above my right eye. "There are so many things I don't know about you yet. But still somehow I do seem to know you."

In the distance, the cackling cry of a pheasant echoes across the fields.

"Why?" she says at length.

"Why what?"

She shrugs. "Oh, I don't know. Just why? Some part of me seems to need explanations, I suppose. Why me? Why us? Why now? Perhaps especially why now. After all, we've known each other socially for, what? Two years at least? And then suddenly it just happens, as if we were somehow fated at this particular moment, drawn together almost in spite of ourselves. Like two sleep walkers in the same dark room." She pours more coffee, then sits back, cradling her right knee in her hands. "You probably won't remember, but about a year ago I sat next to you at one of those boring London dinner parties, the kind that you usually so successfully manage to avoid. I think you were probably only there because some famous art collector was also invited. Anyhow, I was quite pleased to have you next to me because you had the reputation of being a flirt and I thought that at least I'd have some fun with you." She set down her cup. "But I didn't. To my amazement you were completely tongue-tied! I seemed to have turned you to stone."

I sigh. "It's engraved on my memory. I did my best to forget about it afterwards. It should have felt like my golden opportunity – sitting beside the famously beautiful Mrs von Homburg at last. But in reality it was like having my bluff suddenly called. Something in me just wouldn't let me play the usual games with you. And I didn't really know how to do anything else. I felt quite down afterwards, as if I had blown it."

She laughs. "Well, in a way you had. If your aim was to have a fling with me – which, by the way, I suspected – you certainly made a mess of it. In fact you were actually quite boring most of the time – to my utter disappointment. But somewhere in the middle we had a conversation about how it would be to live in New York. And I expected you to talk about all the best bars and restaurants and all the people you knew and how exciting and energizing New York was. What a buzz! All that usual oh-I'm-so-cosmopolitan stuff. But you didn't. What you actually said took me completely by surprise. You said you didn't think your soul could thrive in Manhattan. I don't think I'd ever heard that word 'soul' used at one of those dinner parties before – except possibly to describe the fish. And there was something about the way you said it that really touched me. It was like a sudden flame between us. And then the flame just died. I don't know why."

"I think I changed the subject. I got scared. I felt too exposed."

"Yes, I sensed something like that at the time." She pushes her hair back with both hands, closes her eyes for a moment, as if trying to summon back the memory. "Anyhow, the conversation closed right there. At least on one level it did. But on another level, it didn't at all. On another level it actually started. Because when I thought about it later, especially that phrase 'my soul' – and the tone in your voice – it seemed to open a door for me." She hesitates. "Of course, for a moment, I *was* attracted to you. For the first time, I saw you as more than just a man of ambition and money, racing around the globe buying and selling art and being glamorous, the hot-shot London art dealer. You suddenly seemed *alive*... and somehow vulnerable. And that touched *my* soul." She pauses, and looks down. "But somehow I sensed that the timing was wrong. Something just didn't fit. And I know that if something had happened between us then it would have been just a casual affair." She smiles. "And believe you me, I was ready for it!"

"And did you?"

"You mean have an affair with someone else? You asked me that question before in San Sepolcro. And, believe it or not, I told you the truth." She looks sad and shakes her head. "No. I came very close to it once, but I backed away at the last minute. It felt too frightening. And wrong. Not morally wrong. Just… not right. Not the right person. Not the right time." She pauses. "And I'm glad I did."

"And now?"

"You mean is this just 'an affair'?"

I shrug. "I guess."

She must have caught the look in my face. "What's up?" she asks quietly.

"Oh, I don't know." I cradle the coffee cup between my hands and look out of the window across the frosted fields and lines of hedgerows. "I was just thinking how little I know about you. I don't even really know what happened to you while you were in California. You told me some things last night. But I still don't really know what was going on *inside* you — how you felt about me, if you thought of me, if you missed me…"

She frowns. "Don't you?" I shake my head. "You *really* don't know?"

"Know what?"

She sets down her coffee cup and sighs. "How I ached for you…"

I stare at her. "But you seemed so calm that day in the park when you left, so quietly determined, almost matter-of-fact. You didn't seem..." My voice trails off. I feel at a total loss.

"Sad?" She smiles ruefully. "I think I was numb. The pain only hit me as I sat in the taxi. I started to sob. It was as if something was cutting into my flesh. If it had come any earlier I wouldn't have been able to leave."

"So why *did* you go?"

"Because I knew I had to." She pauses, pushes back her hair with one hand then slides the tray aside and moves over beside me, sliding in under my right arm, letting her head fall back on my shoulder. "It's so difficult to explain. Something in me knew I had to go. And somehow I knew you needed it too. And it was stronger even than the pain of leaving you. She hesitates. "The only thing I can compare it to is being pregnant." The forefinger of her right hand is tracing patterns on the blanket. "I felt like one of those women in the Bible who has to go into confinement before they can give birth. That's just how it was – 'Confinement in California' – just waiting for something to complete itself inside me in its own good time. I didn't understand it. But I did trust it." Her finger stopped. "Without that feeling I couldn't have borne the pain of being separated from you."

I lean my head back, close my eyes and pull in a deep breath, then let it out slowly. There's a huge relief in this knowing. I remember Dinos as we had sat on the long beach on Katakolos – *She's a woman. She can think with her womb...*

"But that day in the park, you seemed so clear, so certain... Beside you I felt almost like a child – panicky, helpless. I wasn't sure you'd ever think of me while you were away. I didn't even know if I was at all important to you."

She sighs. "Oh God! If you had only known..."

For a while we are both silent. "There was only one time..."

I say at length. "I was sitting high up on a Greek island just before dawn and I had a kind of... hallucination." I hesitate. "I saw you standing on a beach with your feet in the surf... There was a big setting sun... you were wearing white trousers and a red and white scarf in your hair..."

She turns and stares at me in amazement. "September the first?"

I frown, then nod. "Yes... that would be right."

She smiles slightly, almost to herself. "Yes. I'd driven to the Big Sur to go for a walk." Her voice catches in her throat, her eyes fill with tears. "It was a beautiful evening. And I *was* thinking of you. Intensely. There was this huge orange sun. And just before it touched the horizon I knew absolutely that you were thinking of me. And suddenly that knowledge just burned right through my body." She pauses, trying to steady her voice. "For a moment I think I almost lost consciousness. And when I came to again, the sun had gone down. But I knew then that we would be okay."

She stretches out her hand and touches mine, running her fingers across my knuckles, tracing the lines of the veins, brushing the small hairs the wrong way. From just below the window a woodpecker chaffles shrilly. We both smile. "She must be back," I say.

"The woodpecker?"

"Yes. She lost her mate."

"How sad. I think I know the feeling." She draws her hand away and looks at me very directly. "Is there one more 'why'?" she asks quietly.

I frown and shake my head, unsure what she means.

"I was wondering if there was a 'Why didn't you come when we made love last night?' that was unasked."

She's right, of course, but I hadn't wanted to ask. At least, not yet. Before I can respond she goes on: "I might have expected myself to explode – I've been celibate for so long. And I'm sure I would have done if I'd felt that this was just an affair." She stops, frowning, then goes on. "I think that with you I've drawn a kind of shell around my body to protect myself. A shell that couldn't be cracked just by sex." She hesitates. "Something else seemed to be needed."

"And that was…?"

She shrugs, shakes her head slightly. "I don't know… Perhaps just this talk… perhaps just for you really to see me. And for me to see you. I know that to *understand* each other takes time. That's different. But not to *see* each other."

Suddenly she moves out from under my arm and kneels opposite me, looking down. The hunched posture of her shoulders opens the shirt, presses her breasts together. Her voice is quiet, but clear. "I missed you in California. I missed you more than I could ever have believed possible. My heart ached for you. My soul ached. My whole body ached." She pauses. "My cunt ached." She looks up. Her eyes look stripped, vulnerable. "I can never be more naked before you than I am now."

I pull her down beside me. Almost without preliminaries I enter her, feeling how ready she is. And immediately I am lost. Lost as I have never been before, engulfed. As much penetrated as penetrating, aware only of the warmth and softness of her, of her urgency, as she cries out repeatedly until we rock each other back into sleep and I am gone again.

PART THREE

THIRTY-SEVEN

The weeks that followed were a time of healing. Not just a superficial skinning over of old wounds, but something that felt more profound; a kind of slow, silent healing from beneath. Sometimes I would wake in the early hours of the morning, half expecting the dragons to have returned. But instead, there was only the darkness and the slow, even breathing of Julia beside me, the warmth from her curled-up body spreading into the sheets around her. At such moments I would sometimes wonder if I wasn't fooling myself, if it wasn't all too good to be true, this almost unnatural ease between us, as if we had known each other intimately for years, not simply months. But I knew that I wasn't. Something new had entered me, something I had never known before: a kind of solidity, a deep animal trust that, no matter what happened, the ground would not give way, the branch would not break and that we were somehow ordained for each other.

Of course, it wasn't all simple. There was always the question of Gemma. Although she was at boarding school much of the time, the bond between mother and daughter was so intense that I often felt excluded. Yet I knew – at least in my saner moments – that the subtle wall they drew around them must have long preceded my arrival in their life. I wondered how much Bernhardt's persistent absences had engendered this fierce, defiant closeness between them. Or perhaps it was the other way around – their closeness had provoked his absence? That I could understand too.

Gemma's attitude towards me followed the same exasperating pattern I had experienced in San Sepolcro, swinging unpredictably from intense child-like affection to periods of resentful silence. Her emotions were like an unruly crowd jostling for position; at any moment a totally unexpected one would elbow its way to the front to seize your attention. It could be disconcerting and sometimes graceless and it was always worst when I wanted to be alone with Julia. Then Gemma and I would clash. It was clear that Julia felt uncertain, caught between the two. It would have been easier if it had been a simple conflict between two competing needs. But the truth was that I was also divided against myself. Whenever I was alone with Julia, my sense of satisfaction was also stained with the knowledge of Gemma's exclusion. I had come to understand, as Julia had suggested in San Sepolcro, that Gemma, in some inarticulate way, actually seemed to need me. But now I was beginning – painfully and to my astonishment – to accept that *I* also needed *her*. And gradually I began to experience something of that strange, ferocious love that a parent feels for their child. I had never understood such a love; it had left me permanently untouched, as if the fate of the next generation was not of my concern. But now, quite unexpectedly, this deep, unexplainable need had opened up in the space between myself and Gemma and I seemed to possess no more skill in handling it than she did.

And there was something else that was troubling me. In one sense everything in my life felt different. And yet, at least externally, everything had stayed the same. I still had the gallery. I was still dealing. I was still ambitious. The black statue had been sold almost immediately; but since then nothing had moved. Most importantly, against all my expectations, the *kouros* was still with me. I had shortlisted six possible clients – four museums and two collectors – all of them likely buyers. But, one by one, they had all come back with refusals: insufficient funds, insufficient interest, insufficient... As Zoe laconically remarked, 'He doesn't want to go yet, does he?' *But why?* There was that odd feeling, just as I had all those months ago when I dreamt of the black statue, that the *kouros* somehow *wanted* something of me, that there was another step to take. *But what?*

*

On a quiet Sunday afternoon, as we are sitting in her apartment reading, with the London rain battering against the window panes, Julia suddenly lays aside her book, very deliberately, as if she has reached a decision. She pushes her horn-rimmed spectacles up into her blonde hair.

"*How are we?*" she asks quietly. Each word is carefully stressed to make it clear that she requires a serious answer.

I turn the question over in my mind. "Hmmm... It all seems rather suspiciously easy, doesn't it? At least most of the time. And I guess neither of us is used to that. Is that what you mean?"

She sighs. "Yes, except when we're with Gemma. But alone it just seems too... I don't know. Straightforward? Doesn't it worry you?"

I think for a moment. "Not really. Though I'm struck by the unfamiliarity of it. That's for sure. Past relationships for me have usually been more about fighting and sex. Not very mature, I'm afraid."

She doesn't smile. "Well, I think it worries *me*."

"Too good to be true?" I raise my eyebrows ironically. We both know what I am alluding to. Two nights previously an argument about Gemma had ended with Julia storming out and slamming the door so hard that I was afraid the ceiling might collapse.

"I think it's the feeling that something may just come and take it all away. And then, when I think that, I get panicky. Don't you feel that sometimes?"

I shake my head. "No. Rather surprisingly I don't. I've never trusted anything very much before. But I do trust *us*. Or it feels more like *it* trusts us… It's like something that's happening *through* me. But no, even if I can't find the words for it, I don't believe it will be taken away. Not even when you scream at me and slam the door. I just put that down to your unpredictable Hungarian temperament." She smiles. "And when you smile like that, then of course I trust."

"Hmm. Are you really so easily persuaded? Then I had better watch out for every woman who smiles at you."

"Perhaps I'm in love." There is a long silence. Neither of us has used this Rubicon word before, as if its abuse over the last two decades of our lives has rendered it taboo. Until now. For a long while we stare at each other. Then quite simply Julia says, "Yes."

The telephone rings. I think of ignoring it but the caller is persistent. I rise and pick up the receiver.

"*Ciao.*" I recognise Antonio's voice immediately. Something in me goes on instant alert. I'm like an animal with a genetic warning system. The episode with the black statue has made me hypersensitive to Antonio's calls.

"Antonio? Is there a problem?"

He laughs. "No, no. *Niente problemi. Niente problemi.*" His tone is deliberately soothing. "No. No problem, my friend. But I have a surprise for you."

"A surprise?"

"*Si*. We've been fishing again."

For a moment I can feel my stomach tighten. Antonio will be calling from a safe telephone, probably a call box, but even so it's unlikely he will speak openly.

"I presume you caught something."

"*Si*. A very beautiful fish."

"Same colour as the other one?"

"*Si*." Antonio chuckles.

"A big fish?"

"Not so big. But *very* beautiful."

"Can you say more?"

"It's better you come. And soon. You know how it is. A fish should be eaten quickly. Otherwise it starts to stink. Especially this one."

"Why?"

"There was more than one fisherman this time."

"Who?" Of course he won't risk the answer over the telephone. All the same, the uncertainty has set my alarm bells clanging.

"It's better you come. I explain everything then."

"Okay. I'll call you." I put down the phone. Even before I turn I'm aware of how much how much Julia's presence has pressed on my conversation with Antonio. She puts down her book and stares at me.

"It was Antonio."

"So I gathered."

"They seem to have found more of the black statue."

"More?"

"Yes. There could be a pair to it. Another statue, I

suppose... Although he said it wasn't so big. So... it could be another, smaller figure, perhaps a statuette of Eros, something like that. That would make sense – Eros is often grouped with Aphrodite. Or... or... it could be the head! It should be lying somewhere close by in the sand." I can feel the excitement surge through me. "Yes, of course, it must be the head!"

"And what did you say to him?" Her tone is ice cold. I'm taken off balance. I can feel my enthusiasm drain away.

"Say?"

"Yes. What did you say to him? Surely you just have to say no after all that you've been through."

"Well, you heard me. I said I'd call him back." I cross to the window and stare out. The rain has stopped and down in the square two girls are throwing a tennis ball for a small brown and white terrier. Each time the dog returns and drops the ball at their feet they jump up and down with delight and clap their hands. Reluctantly I turn.

"What would you have expected me to say?" I ask coolly.

"Well, what do you think?"

I cross the room, "Look, every time I ask you a question you answer with another question." I sink down into one of the armchairs. "It's not particularly helpful, you know."

My feigned composure is like a sudden spark. She jumps up and stands in front of me, shaking. "What do I think you should have said? Does it matter what *I* think? Does it bloody well matter? It's what *you* think is all that counts. And you know what you should have said. You should have said 'No thank you' and put the phone down. You know that! But oh no, you say 'Okay, I'll call you'. We both know what that means! How can you do that after everything that has happened already with that bloody statue? The whole thing nearly landed you in an Italian prison, never mind almost tipping you over the edge of sanity into a nervous breakdown. You told me that yourself!" Her voice is rising. "How can you get caught up in it again? How fucking can you!"

I turn back to the window. I don't want to get involved in any of this. I want to stay with the excitement of Antonio's call. Then I hear her sobbing. I turn. She is hunched on the edge of the sofa with her hands over her face, shaking.

Suddenly I feel numb. "What's happening to us?" I say. I can hear the hoarseness in my voice.

Julia shakes her head silently, her face still buried in her hands. Then she looks up. She looks haggard. "I just felt that you're going to go. You know, down there to Rome again. I know you're going to. And it's so crazy. Even you know it's crazy. It's as if there's a crazy part of you. I've seen it in you before. And I feel so helpless when that happens. Just utterly powerless."

Despite her words, her voice has softened. My feelings begin to flow back into me, as if my heart has been given a signal to pump again. I go and sit down beside her and put my arm around her. She remains motionless.

"Do you think *I* wasn't anxious when I realised what he was talking about?" I feel her faint nod against my chest. "But it's not that simple. I've known Antonio for nearly fifteen years. I trust him and he trusts me. He's always kept his word and he's always stood by our deals, even when things have gone wrong and he's lost money." She looks up at me suspiciously. "He's never let me down. I can't just say: 'No thanks. Fifteen years is over' and put the phone down and walk away."

I feel her relax slightly against me. "That, at least, is something I can understand," she says.

"And there's another thing that's important. If it *is* the head – or any other part that belongs to the statue – I have an obligation to make sure that they're joined together again. Anything else would be a tragedy."

"But wouldn't that happen anyway, even if you didn't buy it?"

"No. Unfortunately the art world isn't that logical. It's driven by money. An object will always go to the highest bidder, no matter what the ethical situation. The world's museums are full of fragments of sculptures that actually join each other, but which stay separated. The way the market operates, if this is the head, it could easily just slip away to another buyer, particularly since there seems to be someone else in the deal this time. It could get complicated."

"Who is it?"

"I don't know. Antonio wouldn't say. But it's bound to complicate things. If only financially."

She pulls away and sits up straight. "And now you're talking again as if you're going to buy it."

Deep down I know she's right. I can feel that familiar surge of adrenalin flooding through me and for a moment I remember Elizabetta's question – *Are all art dealers addicts?* And my reply – *No, but all antiquity dealers are.* Back then it had felt like a light-hearted joke. But now…?

"No. I won't buy it. I promise you that. *And* I can't just walk away from it. I can't just walk away from Antonio."

"You mean you want to tell him face to face?"

I shrug. "Something like that, I suppose." I know the answer is inadequate. "Yes, I shall go. I have to. And I'd like you to come with me."

"*Me?*"

"Yes. We've never been to Rome together. I'd like you to meet Antonio. And…"

"But why? What on earth could *I* do?"

"I'm not sure. I just know I need you there. Perhaps *we* need you there?" She looks doubtful. "I think it's really important."

She stares at me. "Well…"

"And I think we should go through Switzerland on the way down."

"*Switzerland?* Why Switzerland?"

"That's where the body of the Aphrodite is. I sold it to a Venezuelan collector who lives there, just outside Basle."

"But why do you need to see *him* for God's sake? What good will that do?"

"I'm not sure. It's just an instinct. I think it'll be important. In the whole scheme of things."

She starts to say something then stops. There is a long silence. "Okay," she says uncertainly. "I'll come. If you really think it's that important. And you won't buy it. Right?"

"Right."

But I know the conversation isn't over.

THIRTY-EIGHT

I give another pull on the rusted iron chain. From the top of the stone gate-pillar the eye of a surveillance camera peers down at us.

"What now?" asks Julia.

I shrug and tug again, this time more forcefully.

"Perhaps we shouldn't have let the taxi go," she says. "Maybe we got the wrong day. No-one seems to be here."

"Don't worry. We'll get in eventually. It's always like this. The place is rigged out like Fort Knox, but nothing ever works. That's part of its charm."

Julia sniffs disdainfully. A few drops of rain are blowing in the light wind. Suddenly two huge Alsatian dogs surge out from behind one of the outbuildings and run towards the iron gates barking. They are followed by a swarthy man wearing corduroy breaches and a leather jerkin. When he sees us he stops, raises his eyebrows in surprise, then walks suspiciously towards us. We face each other through the railings.

"We've come to see Mr Ortega."

"Are you invited?"

"Yes. My name is…"

The man seems uninterested. He takes a massive iron key from the pocket of his thick trousers and mutters a command to the dogs, who immediately sit panting, their feathery tails lightly dusting the gravel. Then he unlocks the gate. We step through and it clanks shut behind us. The guardian turns and walks away towards the orchard, his job apparently done. The dogs follow at his heels.

"God, what a desperado!" says Julia. "Are we supposed to go with him?"

"I don't think so. The house is over there." I point in the opposite direction. "Thank you!" I call out. The man keeps on walking.

"Are you sure we're invited? This is the weirdest reception I've ever seen! It looks like a billionaire's property all right, but the characters seem to be straight out of central casting for a horror movie."

I can't help laughing. "That's nothing. Just wait till you meet Carlos!" I lead the way towards the wisteria-clad farmhouse and the huge adjacent barn in which Carlos keeps his art collection. As we approach we can hear voices.

We round the corner of the house and instantly Julia's mouth falls open in astonishment. A diminutive man in a dark blue blazer and grey flannel trousers is pursuing a stout figure in chef's uniform down the path behind the house. The small man is shouting curses in French and flailing at the back of the unfortunate cook with a rolled up newspaper. Julia begins to giggle, then covers her mouth with her hand. A door at the far end of the building swings open, and the chef disappears inside. The small figure shouts a final burst of invective and takes a last swipe at the disappearing blue and white leg. Then he turns and casually places the rolled-up newspaper under his left arm, as if nothing unusual has occurred.

"Ah! There you are! How pleasant to see you," he says, coming forward with his right hand extended. His gleaming blue-black hair is matched by the shine of his English brogues.

I introduce them. Carlos eyes Julia appreciatively, then bows low and kisses her hand. "It is an honour to meet you," he says. He pushes open the iron-studded door to the barn and allows Julia to pass in front of us. As he follows, he grips my arm above the elbow and whispers loudly: "My God, but she's absolutely charming! And beautiful too. You lucky bastard."

Carlos Ortega's alert, angular face makes him look like a small, suspicious bird of prey. And his piercing black eyes only add to the impression. He comes from a grand and enormously wealthy Venezuelan family, but his exact parentage has always been shrouded in mystery. The rumours that he is descended, at least in part, from South American Indian stock aren't hard to believe. Although he stands scarcely over five feet tall, there's a force and dynamism about him that give the unnerving impression that, at any moment, he might suddenly explode. Even his permanent state of hypochondria is lived out with a determination that would exhaust most Olympic athletes.

I have known Carlos for over ten years. I enjoy his company, but I also know him well enough to be wary of his moods. He can turn in a second from kindness and generosity to rage and revenge. And, although he may seem randomly explosive, scattering his energies like a hand-grenade, I have always felt that there is something at his very centre that remains cold, impassive, watching. That hidden area, able to both fascinate and threaten, is doubtless part of his magnetic charm. But it also carries with it more than a hint of the diabolic.

Carlos has two great passions: beautiful women and beautiful antiquities. And, of the two, for him the antiquities are by far the more important. Women are dispensable playthings, but he would probably rather die than give up his works of art. Over the past thirty years, he has assembled the best private collection of ancient art in the world. With passionate dedication, he has hunted down and bargained for objects whose value would have been invisible to a less skilled set of eyes. Once he has an antiquity in view, he can be as cunning, implacable and duplicitous as a Renaissance diplomat. It is a combination of talents that has earned him a world-class collection, a formidable reputation – and a formidable array of enemies along the way. Yet whenever he takes one of his objects into his miniature, fine-boned hands and begins to talk about it, he does it with such guileless passion that even those he has tricked will forgive him. At least until the next time.

He is working his magic now on Julia. I watch her face light up as Carlos reaches to a high shelf and pulls down a Greek bronze statuette of Poseidon, striding forward, his trident raised aloft. He enthuses in lyrical language about its beauty as well as the Machiavellian story of its purchase. I can't help smiling as I watch Julia being slowly beguiled by the performance. Alert as a fox, Carlos looks round and catches my knowing smile. "Your boyfriend is laughing at me. How does a beautiful woman like you put up with such a man!"

I walk up to them and put a hand on Carlos' shoulder. "Carlos, I know you far too well. You may be trying to seduce my girlfriend, but your enthusiasm is your only saving grace!"

"My only saving grace!" splutters Carlos theatrically. "It takes a person of true refinement and sensitivity – unlike a coarse brigand like you – to see my real qualities: my kindness, my generosity, my sense of honour and honesty." He turns to Julia. "Is that not so?"

"Oh, absolutely!" Julia beams him one of her special smiles. Carlos holds it for several seconds before spinning round and playfully punching me in the stomach. "God, it's good to see you again, you old bastard! Come and see what I bought yesterday." And he is off across the room in the direction of a Greek marble frieze perched on an oak side table, still surrounded by straw from a packing case.

The tour of Carlos' collection takes almost an hour. From time to time the persecuted chef, now dressed in a butler's black trousers and white jacket, appears and looks anxiously at his master. Each time Carlos growls at him, and the unfortunate man disappears into the kitchen.

"But there's one thing you haven't seen yet. Is that not so?" Carlos' tone is deliberately teasing.

"Is there?" I ask casually.

Carlos smiles. He can obviously sense my impatience and is enjoying his little power play. Then he turns and walks to the tall double doors at the far end of the barn. In front of them he stops with his back to us and turns his head. "My father used to say that in life one should either be, do, or, at the very least, own one thing that is truly extraordinary." He pauses. "I may not have achieved the first two. But the last I most definitely have." With a theatrical gesture he pushes open both doors. Beyond is the library, a long room with heavy oak bookcases on both sides, alternating with high sashed windows. At the very end, directly facing us, in a space where a set of bookshelves has obviously been ripped out, the holes in the wall not yet made good, stands the black statue of Aphrodite.

Julia gasps. The light from the northern windows floods the statue's surface. The broad planes of the marble seem to glow against the pale ochre wall. We all stand in silence. The sculpture is even more beautiful, more majestic than I had remembered. Words seem utterly superfluous. At length I turn to Carlos. "I'm pleased she's here with you," I say. "I know it's the right place." And I mean it.

Carlos nods. "Thank you." He pauses. "Shall we have lunch

now?" He puts his arm around me and escorts us towards the dining room.

"There's something I wanted to tell you about the Aphrodite," I say as soon as the all-purpose servant has finished handing round the dishes and closed the kitchen door behind him.

"I hope you're not going to tell me that she's a fake," says Carlos, chuckling. He raises his goblet of red wine to his lips and holds it there, staring enquiringly at me over the rim.

"No. She's not a fake. But she's incomplete."

"I do know that. Even at my age, one does recognise when a lady has no head. Particularly if she has no clothes as well." He flashes a sly smile towards Julia.

"Perhaps she's not as incomplete as we think," I say.

Carlos narrows his eyes over the glass. "Go on."

"It seems our use of tenses is incorrect." I pause for dramatic effect. "It would appear she *had* no head."

Carlos places his glass down carefully on the oak table. His eyes are sparkling. "How interesting. How *very* interesting..." His tone is as smooth as silk. "Do tell me more."

*

"I'm pleased I came," says Julia, looking out of the taxi window. We are on the five mile stretch of straight road from the city to the airport "Do they always drive this fast here? I thought the Swiss were supposed to be a quiet, introverted, law-abiding people."

"This is what they call the Basle race track. It's where the taxi drivers give vent to their deeply repressed Swiss emotions. It's the Carlos Ortega side of the Swiss character."

Julia laughs. "Yes, well, I certainly know what you mean. He seems to be on a permanent race track! But still, it was fascinating to meet him."

"I see he charmed you. As he does with everyone. At least on the first visit."

"Well, he's a very charming man. Beautiful manners. But tricky too, I imagine."

"Oh, he's tricky alright! A master trickster."

"Then isn't it dangerous to try to do business with him? Won't you get cheated?"

"Not cheated. Outsmarted possibly. That's different. But hopefully not outsmarted too badly."

Julia doesn't respond. I realise that, despite her reservations, she has been drawn in by the clandestine charm of Carlos and his grandiose surroundings. And by the pace of our movements: breakfast in London, lunch in Basle, dinner in Rome. It's the art world. It's seductive. But I guess that even now she is drawing back from that seduction. She has made it very clear that the purpose of our trip is to withdraw gracefully from the situation with Antonio, not to get further entrapped in it. She stays staring out of the window without speaking until the taxi draws up at the curb of Basle's small airport. But once in our seats in the aeroplane, she turns to me. "What exactly were you hoping to achieve with Carlos?"

"I'm not quite sure…" I catch her suspicious look. "I'm not sure because I don't know what's going to happen next. I just wanted to see how the land lies. Because if it is the head that Antonio has – and I can only imagine that it is – then obviously it must go to join the body. Anything else would be a tragedy. Even you must admit that."

She ignores the challenge. "And how *does* the land lie?"

"I would say… complicatedly. The problem with Carlos

is that he can sometimes be too crafty for his own good. He might just end up outsmarting everybody. Including himself. He's capable of that. I've seen him do it before."

"But why don't you just tell Antonio where the body is and let him sell it to Carlos directly? Surely it's not the money that makes you stay involved?"

I sigh. Suddenly I feel heavy, the excitement of being with Carlos and seeing the black Aphrodite draining from me like a balloon expelling its air. "No, it's not the money. The problem is that Carlos would never deal directly with someone illegal like Antonio. At least not these days. It's just too tricky. In recent years this wild South American buccaneer collector has become an almost respectable member of the super-rich Swiss bourgeoisie. He's on the boards of several of their leading companies and museums. So it might be embarrassing if he's caught with red-hot smuggled Italian merchandise on his hands. He needs someone in the middle. Someone experienced in these things."

"And you think it wouldn't be embarrassing for *you* to get caught with red-hot merchandise – especially with your track record?"

The sarcasm is sharp and bitter. I can feel the tension rising between us.

"I already told you I'm not going to get involved…"

"Then why are we going?"

"You know why we're going."

She turns and stares out of the window. The late afternoon sun is shining directly down the lateral valleys of the Alps, throwing every detail into sharp relief, staining the snow-capped peaks. Suddenly I ache to be back in Greece.

THIRTY-NINE

I am just loading the first of our bags onto the metal trolley when I feel something dragging at my attention. Instinctively I turn. Carla Ruspolini is standing a few feet behind me, holding a small overnight case.

"Hi. I just noticed you".

For a moment we stare at each other. Then we embrace and I introduce her to Julia, who eyes her warily.

"What are you doing here?" I ask.

"I'm just spending a couple of days in Rome on family business…"

For a few minutes our conversation floats along on the level of pleasantries, just two casual acquaintances bumping into each other at the airport by chance. But beneath the words I can feel invisible wires being reconnected. When we part we embrace warmly and she whispers in my ear, "Go well, dear friend. Remember what I told you in my letter."

As we wait for the rest of our luggage and watch Carla disappear through the frosted glass doors, wheeling her bag behind her, Julia turns to me.

"She's very beautiful. In a mysterious kind of way. Am I allowed to ask who she is?"

"Of course. Why shouldn't you? She's just an old

acquaintance. I once bought a statue from her and her mother, which they had lying in their house in *Le Marche*."

I turn back to the carousel to gather our second case. Julia's silence is ostentatious and I'm uncomfortably aware of the space between us being filled with things unspoken.

Once through the sliding doors, I look around for Antonio, but he is nowhere to be seen. Perhaps he has been delayed. Only then do I notice the small, nervous-looking man in the dark suit, standing to one side, holding a board with my name on it. I register, not too comfortably, that this is the first time that Antonio has failed to collect me personally.

Julia and I settle into the back of the air-conditioned Mercedes and stay quiet until we hit the *autostrada*. Then she turns to me. Of course, I know what's coming.

"Who was she *really*?"

"Who?"

"You know. Carla whatever her name was."

"Carla Ruspolini. I told you, I once bought something from her, a family heirloom. In any case, what does *really* mean?"

I'm being deliberately obtuse, but I feel annoyed by Julia's persistance. It's so uncharacteristic of her. In any case, how can I describe my relationship with Carla? It's beyond any normal parameters.

"Was it the *kouros* statue?"

"Yes, as a matter of fact it was. Why?"

She stares at me accusingly.

I shrug. "Does it make any difference?"

"Yes, as a matter of fact it does make a difference. To me, at least."

I am about to interrupt, but she cuts me off. "Why are you sometimes so damned secretive, Bronson? It's like this business with the dealing. It's almost as if you're afraid or ashamed or something. It's obvious that there's something going on between the two of you and I just don't understand what it is. Were you lovers?"

I feel cornered and strangely threatened. And I can feel a wave of anger coming up. Then I hear Carla's voice in my ear and remember her letter – *Dig deep in love, my friend…* All my life my love has been shallow, skin deep only.

"Okay", I say, "I'll tell you everything about her."

By the time I finish, we are winding our way through the narrow alleys of Rome. For a long while Julia is silent.

"Are you jealous?" I ask at length.

"Jealous?" She considers this for a moment, then shakes her head. "Not really. At least, not in the normal sense. Perhaps 'excluded' would be a better word."

"But I just told you everything about her. It's not as if we're having an affair. At least, not any longer."

"No, I know. It's not that. It's just… it feels like there's a part of me that wants to have all of you. Probably it's the very young part that has always wanted to hold on to my father for ever and ever, precisely because I never knew him. And, of course, the adult in me knows that I can't and that I can't have all of you either. There will always be other bits, other people in your life outside my orbit. And I'm sort of okay with that." She smiles wryly. "At least on good days. But I suppose what's really important to me is that we're always completely honest with each other. No hiding. No games. No secrets. No matter what happens." She shakes her head. "It's strange – there's a kind of beautiful nakedness in honesty."

"DH Lawrence said that the greatest aphrodisiac is the truth."

She smiles. "Clever man." Then she turns to me. "Look, I don't want to be persistant. Really I don't. And I know that you've told me the truth and that the affair is over. And yet…" She shakes her head. "Oh, I don't know. It's just that there seemed to be such an intense intimacy between the two of you. More than you would just expect even from old lovers."

Of course, I can't deny it. I don't even want to. But how to explain it? At length, on an instinct, I say, "Perhaps the only thing I haven't mentioned is that when we met after her suicide attempt, she said something rather strange to me."

"Tell me."

"She said, 'I'm your shadow sister…'"

"*Shadow sister?* What does that mean? Does it mean she's always going to be in our life?"

I ponder for a moment, remembering David's explanation of the shadow – every part of us that is not in consciousness. Is that what Carla is doing in my life – reminding me constantly to look into my own shadow, lest my life become trivial and superficial again?

"No, it doesn't mean that. She made it clear that we would probably hardly ever meet."

"In your thoughts then?"

"Not even. As far as I understand it, it's something much more impersonal. Perhaps a kind of silent guardian angel. Not one that's necessarily in my thoughts very often and certainly not in my daily life. Just something that's there, warning me off sometimes. Does that make any sense?"

She is silent. "I guess I will just have to chew on it. I…"

At this moment the car draws to a halt outside a tall redbrick building with a grand stone entrance. We are at the end of a cul-de-sac. I have been so busy talking to Julia that I have no idea where we are, but I'm guessing that we are in a side street somewhere off the *Piazza del Popolo*. I climb out of the car and almost simultaneously Antonio appears at the top of the steps. He comes down and embraces me warmly. Then I introduce him Julia. He must be aware that this is the first time I have brought anyone with me on a visit like this and he greets her with due deference, treating her like an old family friend rather than a total stranger.

"Sorry I didn't come to the airport", he says. "I thought it was better I stayed here. I told you I have a partner in this deal."

"Who is it?"

He hesitates, and for the first time I register his nervousness. The faint twitch in his left sheek is always a give-away with Antonio.

"Who is it?" I repeat.

"It's Giacomino."

"*Giacomino*! Christ, Antonio, I thought you never worked with him. He's too bloody dangerous. You've always said so." I glance at Julia. Her eyes are wide with shock and incomprehension. I shake my head at her. "Honestly," I say, "I had no idea…"

"I had no choice," explains Antonio. "We just have to be very careful with him. That's all."

"Why no choice?"

"You know how it is in this business. Giacomino has informers everywhere. He pays people to watch out for him. Sooner or later someone always talks. They get drunk in a bar and boast, or they go out and buy a car they couldn't normally afford."

"One of the fishermen?"

Antonio spread his hands. "I guess. They must have gone out to the same place and tried their luck. Or maybe they took a diver. I don't know. All I know is that when they pulled up this bit they went to him, not to me. So he must have offered them something pretty special."

"Like a ton of money?"

Antonio nods. "Either that, or something less pleasant if they didn't come."

I glance again at Julia. I can see the shock in her face and suddenly I realize it was a mistake to bring her. She is way out of her depth here. I turn back to Antonio. "But then why does Giacomino come to you now?"

"Because they told him that I had the body…"

"Okay, I get it. Of course he knows that the head is worth twice as much to the person who has the body…"

Antonio shrugs. "I guess."

"So I'm being set up to be royally screwed?"

"No! That's why I'm in partnership with him. For protection."

"In partnership with Giacomino! Jesus, Antonio, you'd better eat with a long spoon when you dine with him."

I turn back to Julia. I need her help to steady me. But she is staring away down the cul-de-sac, her face fixed. Suddenly, I feel marooned.

"Come." Antonio takes my arm. "We'd better go and talk to him."

He leads the way up a broad flight of stone steps. On the way up my mind is racing: to have to do business with Giacomino is bad enough, but I'm also aware that my failure to contact him after our chance meeting in Venice and his offer of business will have been taken as a deliberate snub. And that will make him doubly dangerous. It is only when we are halfway up that I realize that I have forgotten about Julia. I turn. She is several paces behind us, walking reluctantly, staring at the ground. At the top we emerge into a loggia overlooking a central courtyard. I glance over the parapet, almost as if looking for an escape route. Below us the court is overgrown, piled with boxes and machinery and lengths of plastic tubing. A striped cat is moving stealthily between some wooden crates. We seem to be in an old palazzo that has recently been converted into apartments. Suddenly a heavy wooden door to our right opens and Giacomino emerges, resplendent in a boldly checked cashmere jacket and crocodile skin shoes. He treats me to a gorilla power-grip handshake, presumably just to let me know who's boss, then bows low and kisses Julia's hand – a compliment which, to judge from the look of distaste on her face, she clearly loathes. Then he puts his arm around a reluctant-looking Antonio.

"Me and my friend, we do good business," he says, presumably trying to set up the dynamic to his own satisfaction before the 'business' starts. "Come. I will show you our treasure." And he leads the way into the apartment. Inside, the walls are newly whitewashed, the floor laid with slabs of grey marble. There is a smell of fresh paint. The place seems completely empty. I follow Giacomino's broad back into a room at the end of the hall. Like the others it is bare, except for a wooden packing case in one corner.

Giacomino crosses to the window, pushes back the shutters and checks in all directions. Then, in spite of this precaution, he half closes the shutters again, returns to the packing case and removes the lid. He leans in and lifts out a spherical bundle of grey cloth. I can see his broad back strain under the tight sports jacket. He lays the bundle on the marble floor, replaces the top of the crate, takes two rough wooden wedges from his pocket and positions them carefully on the flat surface of the lid. Then he crouches down, unwraps the bundle and slowly lifts its contents onto the crate, shuffling the wedges underneath to give stability. He steps back.

The shock is like an electric charge. In the half-light the black goddess stares across the forlorn space of the room directly at me. Her head is half-turned on her graceful neck, her abundant hair gathered up in a chignon, her lips half-parted. Her eyes, inlaid with ivory and shell, glow in the black stone. I feel transfixed by that gaze, utterly stripped. And suddenly I understand: this is not just a decorative statue made to adorn some Roman nobleman's country villa, but a cult figure – a representation of the goddess herself, taken from a temple, where she would have been worshipped in antiquity; the most sacred of all images, washed up here, two thousand years later, in this desolate apartment. I feel a sickening sense of desecration. I remember my conversation with Dinos on the long beach in the south of Katakolos when we had talked of Aphrodite. *'You will need her help. Never betray her...'* A sharp fear twists my insides.

"*Bello*, eh?" rasps Giacomino. "You like?" I don't want to answer. I feel trapped. And angry. Angry with Giacomino and angrier still with myself for having come. I glance at Julia. She is staring at the sculpture. Her face is fixed and drained of colour, her mouth narrowed in a hard line. I cross the room and crouch down beside the head. In the half-light the ivory eyes seem to glow. Instinctively, I reach out to touch the marble; then stop. My hand falls to my side as I try to deal with the chaotic surge of feelings inside me: my fury with Giacomino, a deep sense of awe for the head – I have never felt so moved by a work of art – and an undeniable, furtive excitemement, of which I feel ashamed.

"*Bello! Bello!*" Giacomino's voice grates in the silence. I feel prodded, as if by a blunt-nosed dog. I turn. He is leaning against the far wall, smirking at me. The man who thinks he holds all the cards. The man for whom this sculpture is just a bargaining chip.

"How much?" I ask. I can hear my voice hoarse with aggression. "Just cut the crap and tell me how much."

Giacomino's head jerks back as if he has been slapped. He straightens himself and narrows his eyes. Julia stands motionless. In the distance a police siren wails. Antonio hurries over, takes my arm and guides me out into the hall.

"What the hell are you doing? You know you can't speak to Giacomino like that! He's dangerous."

"I know. I know. I'm sorry. I lost it for a moment."

"You sure did!" Antonio is sweating. He lets go of my arm and wipes his forehead. I can see that his hand is shaking. I hear Giacomino say something to Julia. The voice echoes incomprehensibly in the empty space. "Listen," says Antonio in a hoarse whisper. "Let's not get into the money now. We need to talk first. You and I."

"Yes, I know. I'm sorry. I just don't trust him. He's a pig."

Antonio puts his hand on my shoulder. "Shall we have dinner tonight and talk it through?"

I pause. "Let's meet tomorrow morning," I say at last. "I need to think."

"Think?"

"Yes. Think about the whole thing. I shouldn't have come."

Antonio nods. "Okay," he says uncertainly. But he looks worried. He squeezes my arm. "We'd better go back. Let me do the talking this time."

FORTY

"Where would you like to eat tonight?"

Julia has her back to me, her arms folded on the ledge of the open window of our room at the Hotel Hassler. Below us are the Spanish Steps and the tiled roofs of Rome glowing ochre in the late evening sunlight. In the distance the dome of St Peter's is silhouetted against the fading sky. A huge flock of starlings wheels blackly above it, twisting and spiralling, seeming to turn itself inside out.

She shrugs. "I don't care."

"It's our first night in Rome together and you just don't care!" Even as I speak I know that my attempt at normality is absurd. She turns.

"Listen, Bronson…"

"What?" I can feel her anger and I want to break up her flow before everything spins out of control. The situation feels dangerously explosive, as if we might break something irreparably. And I'm afraid, for us both. "Julia…"

"How could you? How could you?"

"How could I *what*?"

"Ask the price."

I stare at her in incomprehension. "Of course I asked the price. *Of course I did.* Who wouldn't? And I…"

"But don't you see? You're getting involved again. The

moment you do that you're hooked… caught… netted… whatever." Her voice is rising. "I thought you were just going to say 'no' and walk away. I thought that was what we agreed in London. You know we did! But I saw you there. You were acting like a man on a treadmill. Like a fucking zombie. You looked like a hungry wolf."

Now I am angry. I hate the wolf comparison. Hate it because I'm aware it's uncomfortably close to the truth. We're all wolf-like in this business. Me, Antonio, Giacomino. The whole fucking lot of us. We have to be to survive. Otherwise we would just get eaten. "I *am* walking away," I protest. "It's only just…"

"*Oh, for Christ's sake!*" Her face has gone completely blank, mask-like. I have never seen her like this before. It's as if I have touched into some secret area of pain. I sink down on the bed and stare at the patch of grey carpet between my feet. Suddenly I feel exhausted, scattered, unable to find my way, desperate about what may happen to us. I lock my fingers together and squeeze them hard.

"What the hell are we doing to each other?" I say at last, still looking at the carpet.

Julia lets out a deep sigh. She comes and kneels down in front of me. Her shoulders are trembling. Through the parting of her blonde hair I can see the pale gleam of her skull. It looks impossibly defenseless and vulnerable. And suddenly I sense the terrible fragility, the transience of everything – her skin, her skull, her body that will one day decay and crumble into dust. Christ, how fragile we all are! How much we have to lose – and how carelessly we can lose it. A huge sense of waste and sadness floods through me. I reach out and touch the side of her head. I feel the lightest of pressures as she leans into the palm of my open hand.

"Oh, Bronson! Don't you see? Don't you get it?" Her voice sounds weary, exasperated. "I love you. You know that. But when you step into this whole dealing world, something happens to you. You just go away." She looks up and sees my frown of incomprehension. "You do. *You do!*"

"Away from what? Away from *you*?"

"Yes. But not only from me." She pauses. "That's not even the part that makes me desperate."

"Then what?"

Her brow is knitted in concentration. "You go away from *yourself*. From your true self. From your deepest centre. From the you that I love." She sighs, her shoulders slump. "Then I get desperate and feel hopeless and abandoned. Because there I can't reach you. To that place there are no bridges." She is silent. "You know it, don't you?"

I look away. Outside the open window the sky has darkened to deep violet. A flower seller at the street corner is shouting his wares. The fluid sound of the Italian floats up to us. I feel totally lost and don't know what to say.

"Bronson, I don't want to own you. Or constrict you. You know that." I nod. "But when you do this… it's as if you go unconscious. Like a sleepwalker. Then it hurts. It *really* hurts. It's like you wander from your path. And it feels like a wound. A really deep, physical wound." She puts her left hand to her heart, under the swelling of her left breast. For a while she is silent, scratching the floor with the forefinger of her other hand, picking at the tufts of wool. "I don't know," she goes on. "It's so hard to describe. But what's been going on since Antonio called feels like… feels like an addiction. Something that you don't seem to be able to fight."

I get up and cross to the window. Down in the Piazza d'Espagna the shops are illuminated now and people are spilling out onto the streets. The flower vendor's cry is almost drowned in the hum of the city reawakening itself. The dome of St Peter's has become a faint shadow against the sky. Something in her words is right, uncomfortably right. I can't deny that. She has touched into a truth I hadn't wanted to know. And it brings a flash of inner recognition. So much has changed for me in these last months; and yet it's true, something in this whole dealing world – its obsessive excitement, its need for the adrenalin rush, its love of danger, of the clandestine and forbidden – still remains lodged granite-like inside me, filling up some ravenous vacant space in my inner world. It's as if to lose it might be to lose the essence of life itself. "Yes." I say slowly. "Yes I know what you mean. I really do. And yet…"

"And yet…?"

"…There are some parts that do feel right."

"Like?"

"Like when I saw the statue of Aphrodite with Carlos this morning. Or even when I saw her extraordinary black head this evening, in spite of that Neanderthal Giacomino. It touched something so deep in me, something that has nothing at all to do with money, greed, obsession – all that stuff that I know you're talking about. Whatever else happens, the head *must* go to join the body. This is a cult statue, something so sacred that in antiquity no one would even have been allowed to touch it. I can't just stand by and let Giacomino hawk it around the market like some kind of commodity and then sell it to a Texan billionaire to put in his hallway to impress his friends. It would be a tragedy." I pause. "And then there's something else that's even harder to explain."

"Antonio?"

"Right. We have such a strange relationship. We're not really 'close' at all. At least not in the way we normally use the word. It's more based on things like respect, knowing you'll never be let down. In a sense quite distant."

"So you don't want to let him down?"

"I can't. I just absolutely can't!"

"But would not buying the head really be to let him down? Just saying 'no' for once?"

"It wouldn't be just this once. We both know that. It would be for good. The end of fifteen years. And then there's the problem of what happens to the head if I don't buy it. We can't leave it with Giacomino. That would be disastrous."

"But can't somebody else step in?"

I pause, as if reluctant to answer. At length I say, "Maybe…

I can feel something begin to tear inside me. And suddenly I know – know in a place deeper than my mind – that this moment is a fulcrum in time. Whatever I do next will affect the whole of the rest of my life. I look down again at Julia, at the vulnerability of her, at her softness. There has been so much waste in my life until now, so many wrong choices, so much love not given…

In the silence I can hear the world outside going about its business. I stand up, walk round the bed and pick up the telephone. It would be morning in New York. I know David's number by heart. After a moment's pause I hear the long ring tones of America.

"Hello."

"David?"

"Hi, Bronson. That's a terrible line. Where are you? Antarctica?"

"Rome."

"Lucky you. Having fun?"

"David – there's something here for you."

"For *me*?"

"Yes."

Silence.

"What do I need to do?" asks David warily.

"Get on a 'plane and come as soon as possible. *Il piu presto possibile!*"

David chuckles. "Is this for real? What's the catch?"

"There isn't one. Except that there are difficult people involved. But you can handle them." I hear a muffled cough.

"And, to put it indelicately, what do *you* want?"

"Me?" I say, aware of the complete freedom of the moment. "Nothing. Absolutely nothing! This is a gift of the gods."

The line goes quiet.

"David?"

"Yes. Are you sure?"

"Quite sure."

"Okay. I'll try to get on the night flight. I'll call you back."

I give him the number and put down the telephone.

Julia stares at me. "Is that all? He didn't ask any questions? He doesn't even know what it's about! You mean he's going to jump on a 'plane and fly ten hours overnight, just like that?"

"Of course. He knows there's a deal here. He's hooked."

Julia opens her eyes wide in disbelief. "Are you serious? God, it really is an addiction! You're all as mad as hatters in this business!" Then she starts to laugh. I stare at her, bewildered. And then suddenly I begin to laugh too, uncontrollably, my ribs heaving, tears pouring down my face. At the sheer absurdity of it: that David would leave everything and fly five thousand miles through the night just because of a veiled hint on the telephone. And yet I know all too well the excitement he will be carrying with him on that long flight. Something that will cancel the inconvenience and obliterate the exhaustion as he steps off the plane tomorrow morning in Rome. And I know too that it will take a long time for that chemical to pass completely out of my own blood stream.

I cross to the window. The sky is velvety black and even above the glow of the city, a great swathe of stars is visible. Low down, just to the left of the domed shadow of St Peter's, a crescent moon is setting. I feel light. Like a man finally set free from prison. I turn. Julia is standing on the other side of the room. And in that moment I see all the strain, all the anxiety of these last days drain from her face; and there comes instead a look not just of love, but of a total open-hearted generosity. She crosses the room and puts her arms tightly around me.

"Thank you," she says against my cheek. "Thank you."

"For what?"

"For slaying a very, very big dragon. Don't think I don't know what it has cost you. Because I do."

Then she moves back and looks up into my face. She frowns quizzically. "What are you thinking?"

"I was just remembering something Carla Ruspolini once wrote to me."

"What was that?"

"'Dig deep in love, my friend, and you will find riches'. I think I'm finally starting to get the point."

FORTY-ONE

As Christmas came and went and the New Year darkly announced itself, I became aware that some kind of silent sea-change was taking place in my life and with it a subtle shift in my relationship with Julia. No longer did we seem to need to bring to each minor disagreement the vast resources of resentment accumulated over the course of two marriages. It was as if we were finally learning to live in the present. Even Gemma, despite her occasional truculence, seemed to sense this difference and respond.

Then, in late January, something began to chafe at the edges of my mind. Yet when I tried to focus on it, whatever it was would be gone, slipping back into the shadows. My sleep became broken and uneasy.

Some three weeks after I first became aware of this silent presence, I had a strange fragmented dream. It was dawn… I was walking uncertainly across a stretch of dark water between two headlands… in the distance a black gondola was disappearing from view…

Suddenly I was wide awake. I lay in the dark, trying to dredge up lost bits of the dream. Something was missing. I could hear Julia's quiet breathing.

"What is it?" Her voice startles me.

"I don't know."

"Don't you? Whatever it is, it's been quietly eating you for weeks. I tried asking you a few times but you didn't seem to know what I was talking about." She's right, of course, but I hadn't really been conscious of it until this moment. She wriggles across the sheet towards me. I put my arm around her. I can smell the sweetness of her hair, feel the warmth of her body.

"If I knew what it was, I'd tell you."

"Perhaps if you thought with your heart you would know." The echo of something Dinos had once said jolts me. I exhale and close my eyes to shut out the orange glow of the street lights above the curtains.

"Well…?"

"It's crazy…"

"What's crazy?"

"What came to me just now when you told me to think with my heart."

"Well…?"

"I want to go back to Greece. To Katakolos…"

"Then you should go," she says simply.

"But it's winter! It'll be freezing down there. I couldn't stay out at Conchili. It would be like an ice-box. No heating. No electricity."

"With Dinos?"

"That's probably just as cold. And full of tobacco smoke."

She sniffs disdainfully. "Then how about the *taverna*?"

"I don't know. It's probably shut. It *is* crazy. Why on earth should I go there now? The only thing I'd get from it would be pneumonia!"

"If that's what you need to get right now – then you should go and get it." She rolls over and lays her head on my chest, pressing the whole length of her body up against mine.

FORTY-TWO

It is after noon when the car finally coasts down the muddy slope to the wooden jetty at Ormos. I feel exhausted. The long drive, following the sleepless night flight to Athens, has been gruelling and it has rained most of the way. One of the surlier boat drivers ferries me silently across the unmoving black expanse of water to the port of Katakolos. There's no wind and the rain is falling steadily.

As I hurry from the cockpit of the boat to the shelter of the awning of the *taverna*, my bag slung over my shoulder, I catch sight of Kostas standing motionless in the open doorway, his hands behind his back. No-one else is visible. The chairs and the tables from the other café are stacked against the walls, the door fastened with massive padlocks. The whole village seems hushed, as if the rain has enveloped it in silence.

As soon as I breach the curtain of rain and find safe haven under the dripping rush awning, Kostas' face lights up with a flash of recognition. He comes hurrying forward, his hand outstretched in greeting. I have never seen him either so mobile or so effusive. Perhaps it's just the long months of winter solitude and boredom. At such a time, a visitor must feel like an emissary from another world.

"My friend!" says Kostas with undisguised emotion, pumping my hand and simultaneously clapping me on the shoulder: "*Kalos Elthate! Kalos Elthate!* Welcome! Welcome!"

For a moment he smiles. But then the smile dies. He stands looking at me, silently shaking his head as if expecting something. I stare at him, uncomprehending. And suddenly my mind goes into slow motion, aware only of the drumming of the rain on the awning above us, and the enveloping stillness of the port. And something else, unreachable, a kind of premonition.

"We want to write you," says Kostas. "Want very much, *very* much. But we have no address, no house, only London…"

"Write?"

"Yes, and we write Mr Alexis, but never any answer."

"No. He's in California all winter."

"So you no know what happens."

"Know what?"

"Dinos." Kostas spreads his arms wide in despair. "He die."

I stand motionless. I feel numb, unable to absorb this information, aware only of a distant sense of something welling inside me. "Oh my prophetic soul," I say quietly. "Now I understand."

"Understand?" Kostas is staring at me, a pained look on his face.

"Why I came back." I look out across the strait. The mainland is shrouded by rain. How long had Dinos been dead while I was going about my life in London, totally unaware? "When? What happened?"

"Five, maybe six weeks ago. Very bad winter this winter," says Kostas. "Very bad. And Dinos his lungs no good." He taps his chest noisily with his knuckles.

"The smoking?"

"Yes, the smoking, very bad. He smoke too much. But his lungs always bad – from the war."

"The war?"

"Yes. When young boy he spend two winters hiding in Arcadia. He very brave partisan fighter. Then he spend time in prison under the fascists. Very bad. He cough so long as I know him. But this winter, very, very bad." He shakes his head. "He like you very much. He no talk so much, but I watch that day when you first come and he sit down with you. I very surprised, *very* surprised. Po-po-po-po. I never see that from him in my life. Never. I think something funny here. Something I no understand. Very funny." He pauses. "But he good man, brave man, and…" He taps his left temple with the flat of his hand, "Clever man. No clever. How you say?"

"Wise?"

"Yes, wise. He very wise man." He pauses. "He leave something for you." He hurries inside. For a moment all is silent. Then he reappears carrying a battered metal tray on which stand two glasses of ouzo, undiluted, and a brown envelope. As he approaches, I can see my name on the envelope, written in a sprawling hand in black ink.

"For you."

Very gently I pick up the envelope. To my surprise, it's heavy. I open it, trying not to tear the paper. Inside is a large iron key and nothing else. I stare at Kostas. "What's this?"

"The house. Is yours."

"*Mine?*"

"Yes. He give it you. The lawyer come from Stavropolos and do everything. He say he must keep the key and give to you himself. Is correct. But then he have to come back one more time." Kostas winks. "So he leave it me and I give you."

"But doesn't Dinos have family?"

"No. All die. His father, he killed in the war. Very bad thing. His mother, she die soon after. Then two years back his sister and the little one, Katerina, have car accident." He raises his arms in despair. "Everyone around him die. Like he…" He searches for the word.

"Cursed?"

"Yes, cursed."

Cursed? I think of Dinos, of his quality of aloneness. Not loneliness, or isolation, but something less definable. Something, quite apart from his eccentricity, that marked him out. Even at our first meeting, when he had arrived uninvited, pulled out the chair and sat down, I had been aware of it. A sense too that, for some unknown reason, he had singled me out. Unable to frame it in my mind, I had pushed the sensation aside. But now I understood: Dinos had the aloneness of the dying. And the intensity.

Kostas is staring at me as if trying to read my thoughts. "We drink to Dinos?" he says uncertainly, proffering the metal tray. I take one of the tumblers.

"To Dinos," says Kostas. "A brave man and a wise man. The fisherman. *Stiniyasas!*"

We both down the liquid in one movement. Then Kostas reaches back his arm, steps towards the waterfront and smashes the glass down on the pavement. It shatters with a sound like gunshot. I follow suit. The bits of glass lie glinting in the puddles.

I look at Kostas. His face is flushed, his eyes are glittering as if in some kind of triumph. I pick up my bag and make my way out into the rain in the direction of Dinos' house.

FORTY-THREE

Slowly the rain eases. By the time I reach the narrow path that leads down beside the whitewashed cypress it has stopped altogether. The only sound is the faint plop into the puddles from the trees above. The battered chair is still there under the cypress, its legs akimbo, the rush seat saturated from the downpour. It looks surreal, as if just vacated by someone whose presence still lingers.

I have seen no-one since I left Kostas at the *taverna*. I feel quite alone, disorientated, unable to match my feelings to any category that my brain can recognise. It feels wrong to be so detached. I try to think of Dinos as I knew him, but my mind stubbornly collapses. Only my senses seem alive. And my body. The light glints off the puddles. The twisted olive trunks are etched black against the sodden earth. My head aches. I remember that day eight months before when I had first had lunch with Julia and the trees in the park had exploded in my brain with psychedelic force and the roar of London's traffic had gone silent. It feels the same now. Not unreal, but super-real. My senses so sharp they leave no space for thought.

I place my feet carefully going down the path. The dusty summer track has become a sea of mud; I am forced to use the outcrops of rock as stepping stones, holding onto the trailing olive branches for support. Eventually the path flattens out and the house comes into view. I have been here only once, yet it feels strangely like a homecoming.

I go first to the front door and stand for a moment studying the winged head of Hermes. Disparate memories begin to crowd my mind now: the house in Oxfordshire, my first visit to the island, the giant spider's web at Conchili, my meeting with Dinos at the *taverna*, those silent, beautiful days out at the house. I touch the knocker lightly, as if for good luck, then walk round to the sea front. A wooden chair is backed up against the wall at the end of one of the stone benches. Beneath it is a tobacco tin and a half burnt candle in a glass windlight. Water drips through the seat of the chair onto the pavement below. A black circle of congealed ashes on the shingle marks the place where Dinos had cooked. The sea is the colour of slate. Mist is rising from the distant mainland.

The big iron key turns with ease. I raise the latch and the door swings noiselessly open. I stand in the centre of the room and look at the sofa on which I had sprawled that night in a drunken stupor. The air smells faintly of Dinos' tobacco and beeswax. I can feel the cold rising from the flagstones. My breath condenses in the air. I draw my finger along the scrubbed wooden table. Dust.

In the kitchen, plates stand vertically in the wooden rack beside the stone sink, as if the owner has just finished lunch and gone out. On the broad window ledge behind, one of the hollowed-out stones that Dinos used as an ashtray sits empty. Beneath the sink the large blue gas bottle that feeds the cooker has been disconnected. The green pipe lies trailing on the floor. Someone has been in and tidied up, made the house safe.

Slowly I climb the stairs. The steps are shiny with use and slightly slippery. There is no hand rail. Upstairs are two rooms and a small bathroom, which looks out over the olive grove at the back. An old Victorian bath on clawed feet almost fills the space. The smaller of the two rooms is clearly Dinos' bedroom. It is furnished with monastic simplicity. The bed has been made. I walk over and touch the sheet folded down over the faded quilt. It feels cold and freshly laundered, soft and fragile, as only linen can be after countless washings by hand. The shutters have been left open. Whoever has come and made order must have decided not to shutter the house in death.

The second room also looks out over the bay. A plain wooden table and chair are placed in front of the window. It is more a study than a bedroom. A small bed has been pushed up against one wall and is covered with a rug. Books and newspapers are piled on top of it. On the back wall a long bookcase has been constructed from ships' timbers, some of the rivets still in place. It is filled with books from floor to ceiling. I glance at them. Most are in Greek, many with scraps of paper protruding as markers. But lower down are numerous English titles, and, on the bottom shelf, several in French. Could Dinos speak French too? How little I know of him.

I sit down at the table. In the centre lies a large photo album with battered leather corners, and an old tin filled with snapshots. Beside it are Dinos' plastic tobacco pouch and a box of matches. Gently I take the album in my hands. Had Dinos been trying to get his life in order? Yet there are no glue or hinges for fastening the prints. Then a strange feeling comes over me. *The photographs have been put there for me.* It must have been one of the last things Dinos would do. He must have known that I would find them in the house one day. But their presence here, so unavoidable in the centre of the table, seems to urge me to look at them today. *Now.* On the same day that I receive the news of Dinos' death. As if there is something he wants to tell me; some piece of information that can only be passed across the borders of death. *But why? Why*, if Dinos had wanted me to know something, had he not simply told me? Or written a letter? There is something unexplained about the silent key in the empty envelope.

I notice that my hands are shaking. I reach out and take hold of Dinos' plastic pouch. The act of rolling a cigarette calms my trembling. It feels like a ritual and requires all my concentration. By the time I light the misshapen tube my hands are steady. I haven't smoked for years and the sharp taste burns the back of my throat.

Very carefully I open the album. Inside is a pale blue sticker bearing a royal crest: *"Smythson's of Bond Street – Purveyors of Writing Materials to his Majesty King George VI"*. The cream page opposite is blank, except for a dedication written in a bold hand diagonally across the corner. The ink has faded to a rusty brown: *"To Dinos. Happy memories and good luck on your return. Ronald and Marjorie"*. Then underneath in a smaller, more rounded script: *"D. Safe passage. Much love from us both. M."*

I turn the page: a single photograph, black and white, enlarged and slightly out of focus, a dilapidated Greek fisherman's house standing on a shingled beach. I stare in wonder and count: five windows across the upstairs floor. The right-hand one is where I am now sitting. The photograph must have been taken from a boat just offshore. As I look again, almost straining to catch a glimpse of myself in that upstairs window, I feel something strange happen. Something hypnogogic, not from the realm of my waking senses. It's as if time has doubled over and I am suddenly sprung loose into another timeline, sitting here, gazing out at my future self. Then, out of nowhere, a vivid image comes to me: I am standing at the mouth of a cave that leads downwards.

I blink and concentrate on the photograph. Much has changed. The beach is littered with driftwood. Most of the shutters are missing, and those that remain are either broken or hanging from a single hinge. To the right is an ugly lean-to construction of rough stones and corrugated iron. Several of the windows are smashed, the jagged edges glint white against the blackness beyond. On the left, a sapling has taken root in an area where the roof has caved in.

There follow photographs of the interior: rooms filled with rubble from collapsed ceilings, the timbers showing through. Only some familiar markers make the place recognisable: the staircase, apparently intact. And the stone sink under the kitchen window, piled high with debris. Then views of the outside showing the various stages of decay. A close-up of the front door, the wooden paintwork battered and peeling. But the head of Hermes knocker stands prominently in the centre, like a symbol of durability.

I can feel myself being drawn deeper and deeper into the world of the photographs. Post-war Greece. 1945? 1949? What had Katakolos been like then? Suddenly I stop. I feel very cold, concentrated. Dinos is standing in the open doorway of the house staring straight at me. Not just staring out at the camera, but staring *at me*, as if awaiting my arrival. He is perhaps in his early twenties, his black hair brushed to one side. The high cheekbones and slightly crooked nose are unmistakable. Behind him the interior of the house is dark. He is wearing baggy trousers and a rough shirt buttoned at the wrists. He looks relaxed, self-composed. And vulnerable. Vulnerable in the way that those who are dead look in old photographs, exposed to the unseen life ahead of them. Like brief moments of composure; only the subject is unaware of the breaking storm.

Then more prints of Dinos, one of him standing on the beach, arm in arm with a young woman, her black hair drawn up severely. Both of them smiling. Wife? Sister? Lover? The past remains sealed, ambiguous. Perhaps in the end it doesn't matter. Just Dinos standing in front of his house with a woman, both of them happy. On the exact same spot where some forty years later he would stand drunkenly on a chair and pour red wine onto the beach with an Englishman he hardly knew. Had the woman sensed then what he might become?

Then some small square photographs of a town, empty of traffic. Athens? A shot of Dinos leaning against one of the columns of the Acropolis, smartly dressed in grey trousers and white shirt. The landscape behind largely devoid of houses. There follow several shots of the Greek countryside, and one of the empty street of a small village, none of them recognisable. I lay the cigarette down in the stone ashtray and turn the pages faster.

Suddenly another print arrests me. It is clearly earlier, far removed from what had come before. I have the sense of descending deeper into the cave. The photograph is alone in the centre of the page. It shows six men, some standing, some crouching, roughly dressed, all with rifles either propped in front of them or slung over their shoulders. More precisely, five men and a youth. For there, in the centre, unmistakably is Dinos, smaller than the rest, probably no more than fifteen or sixteen. The rifle, held at an angle in front of him, looks incongruously large. Over his left shoulder a long belt of ammunition hangs like a decoration. Most of the men have thick moustaches and very dark eyes. Two have black kerchiefs tied around their heads like bandanas. All are heavily armed. Not just with rifles but also with pistols tucked into their belts. One wears an old-fashioned sash knotted around his waist from which hangs an enormous meat cleaver. None of them is smiling. They stand in front of what looks like the opening to a cave. The rock face is visible above, and the open leaves of a fig tree hang down from the left like a swag.

The figure immediately behind Dinos seizes my attention. He is dressed like the others, but a head taller and less thick-set. He has a lean, intelligent-looking face, close-cropped dark hair and is clean shaven. He seems more angular, less rooted than his companions – possibly not Greek? His left hand is visible, resting on Dinos' shoulder, just beside the ammunition clip.

Then Dinos again, now somewhat older, standing in an open-neck shirt, unsmiling, grave, with a large book under his right arm. Suddenly a cold shaft shoots down my spine. The book is the album now in my hands. The leather corners and lines of gilding are unmistakable. I breathe deeply, holding the album like a talisman. A connection over forty years. But from where to where? The blurred background shows a well-kept lawn, sloping up to a white stucco house. Surely not Greece. England?

Then almost the same setting. Dinos still clutching the album. But now to his right an attractive woman with her brown hair drawn back above her ears, fresh-faced, wearing a white blouse and wide floral skirt. Even in the photograph she seems very present, without artifice. But it is the figure on Dinos' other side that grips my attention. He stands erect in army uniform, wearing a gleaming Sam Brown belt and cross strap. The features relaxed but unmistakable from the earlier photograph. He seems to straddle two worlds.

The three figures stand staring at the camera rather gravely, as if conscious of setting up a marker for posterity. They pose, side-by-side, with English formality. Except for two small details. The man's right hand, surprisingly long and slender, rests on Dinos' shoulder, holding him protectively. On the other side, Dinos' hand is interlinked with the woman's, their fingers locked together. I remember that drunken night out here at the house when Dinos had embraced me. The same man, forty years younger, stares back at me from an English garden. What had he gathered from his surroundings?

There follow other photographs of England. The older couple caught unaware, the man standing incongruously one-legged on a garden chair, the woman behind laughing. Another of them arm-in-arm, smiling at the camera. Dinos reclining on a garden bench in immaculate white flannel trousers holding a tennis racquet. Then the three of them under a plane tree in front of a lake. A distant campanile on the far shore and a paddle steamer with raked funnel off to the right. Then three men standing on a lawn beside another lake. On one side Dinos, on the other the army officer. In the centre a face familiar from countless book-covers. Taller than either of his companions, white haired, holding a book in one hand and an open pair of steel-rimmed spectacles in the other: C.G. Jung. I stare, incredulous. *Had Dinos really known Jung?* I sit back and take a long draw on the cigarette. Then I stub it out in the ashtray.

The album seems to be moving backwards in time, further and further away from the present. The prints are sepia-toned now, slightly faded. There follows a view of the Acropolis taken from the west, three shadowy figures on the top step between the columns, all dressed in black, a family group of parents and a boy. Off to the left a small figure beside a large box-camera on a tripod, waiting to ply his trade. No-one else is visible.

Then a closer view of the same trio, carefully posed,

standing on a pavement in front of a palm tree and some ferns. In the background, a series of elaborate balconies. I recognise the scene immediately – The Grande Bretagne Hotel in the centre of Athens, almost unchanged. The small, anxious-looking boy in the middle, with the slightly crooked nose, is perhaps six years old. He wears a dark jacket buttoned to the neck and short trousers. The woman to his right is also dressed entirely in black, her wide skirt reaches to her ankles; the blouse fastened at her throat in a ruffle, the only concession to decoration. Her mass of black hair is pulled severely back and looped up in a braid, the topmost coil just visible. Her eyes are disturbingly dark, almost too large for their sockets. Her severe face is handsome, high-cheekboned, sensual.

On the other side, the man stands stiffly with both hands by his body. His starched white cuffs protrude several inches from the sleeves of his dark suit. He wears a high winged collar and a broad-brimmed black hat that obscures almost all his features except for his square jaw and the ellipse of his moustache. A pair of incongruously heavy boots protrude from beneath his too short trousers. They stand side-by-side, untouching. A formally posed family group, uncomfortable in their finery. The young boy has an air of bewilderment. In the bottom right-hand corner the photographer has signed his name.

The next page is a studio shot of the woman in the high-necked blouse, probably taken on the same day. Larger than the other prints, it has been trimmed to an oval frame. Even in the softened sepia colours, the face seems implacable. Beautiful but remorseless and unforgiving. I feel chilled. The barren hills of Arcadia come into my mind.

I turn the page. For a long moment the breath freezes in my chest. My whole body feels invaded by ice, as if the top of my skull has burst open and shafts of cold air are pouring in. The face gazes at me across fifty years from its oval frame. The hat removed, clear-eyed, incongruously moustached, a diagonal scar above his right eye. I know I have seen that face before: that night reeling from my dream of Arcadia, I had found my way to the bathroom, and struck the match in front of the mirror. The face had stared impassively back.

I drop the album and spring up. The chair pitches to the floor with a crack like gunshot as the back rail snaps. I clatter down the stairs, out onto the shingle in front of the house. And suddenly, as I stand there shaking, something starts to come up from the ground. I can feel it coming, vehemently wrenching its way free from the centre of the earth, clawing up towards the surface, until it enters my feet. Powerless, I hear a sound start to come from my belly, rifling its way up through my chest, till a terrible cry shakes my body and splits the sky. A cry like the howling of a wolf.

Then the earth turns. And I go down.

FORTY-FOUR

"How you do?"

Kostas is leaning over me.

"How you do?" He repeats.

I try to sit up and look around. I seem to be lying on some bedding in a corner of the *taverna*. There is a rough blanket over me.

"Here. Drink." He holds a glass to my lips. The smell is acrid. I recoil.

"What is it?"

"*Metaxa*. Greek brandy. Is good. Drink."

I take a sip. It tastes of vanilla and burns my throat. For a moment my head seems to fill with blood. Then it clears.

"We call the doctor in Ormos," says Kostas. "But he not there."

"No doctor."

"Is good?" says Kostas.

"No doctor," I repeat. "I don't need him."

Kostas nods, obviously unsure.

"What happened?" I ask.

Kostas pulls out one of the battered chairs and sits down. "I stand outside one, maybe two hours after the rain finish. And I hear a cry. A cry like I never heard. A cry like a wolf, but a big wolf. *Big*! I know you go to Dinos' house. So I take the boat. And I see you lying on the beach! I see you even from far out. I say to myself this winter, this rainy day. No day for sun bathing. So I go look. You no sun bathing," he concludes.

"No," I say, "No sun bathing." Kostas smiles and nods, as if sharing a secret. "You heard the cry from *here?* But it must be three kilometers away!"

"That is what I say to myself. A cry like I never heard. I say: that is not the cry of a man. That is the cry of a big, big wolf, dying. That is a cry from under the ground."

I get unsteadily to my feet and sit down at the table. Something huge, like an enormous wave, seems to have washed through me. I don't know what. Only that I am surprised to find myself alive.

Kostas sits down opposite and looks at me carefully. Then, apparently satisfied, he goes to the kitchen and exchanges the brandy for ouzo. Slowly we begin talking. He tells me again in detail how he had heard the cry and discovered me lying on the beach unconscious. Yet he asks no questions, nor does he treat me with any sense of strangeness. Clearly something had happened out at the house, something connected with Dinos' death; but Kostas seems to have no need to know about it. Perhaps such strange events are quite normal here on Katakolos?

As darkness comes on and with it the chill of night, Kostas shuts the door and switches on the harsh neon light. The village seems deserted. Only once does a shadowy figure pass by on the waterfront. No-one comes into the *taverna*.

"You eat here?"

"*Malista.*"

"Your Greek *very good.*" The ouzo has warmed our spirits.

"Like your English."

"Yes," said Kostas, flashing me a rare smile. I see that fully half his teeth are gold. "Like my English. Both terrible. Very terrible." We laugh. "I have fish. *Lithrini*. Very fresh. The best fish is the winter fish. Cold water is the best. And only you and me to eat it. No tourists. Now the fishermen *love* me when I buy." He touches his heart with both hands in a dramatic gesture.

I smile. "Yes, fish is good."

"*Ne*. Fish very good." He disappears into the small room at the back that serves as a kitchen. A moment later he reappears holding a large red fish by the tail. "See. *Lithrini*. Very good. Very fresh." He indicates the bright bulging eye with his thumb, then flips open the gills to show the red beneath. "The best fish is the fresh fish," he says with satisfaction, then disappears again into the kitchen. I listen to the hiss of gas and the clattering of utensils.

Slowly I sip my ouzo. The ordinary taste of anise sits on my tongue like a novelty. Something has passed through me. Like Kostas I don't want to question it. Don't need to know, to understand with my mind. Not at this moment. Though I have a strange, subliminal memory of Lorca's essay on the *Duende* – that the true spirit of a man enters from the earth through his feet. I sit quietly, enjoying the taste of the drink, listening to the innkeeper whistling tunelessly from the other room. Outside it is now pitch black. I am going nowhere. And it feels good.

I think of Julia. Is she sitting in the house in London? Does she sense what I am feeling? Suddenly I want to call her. I walk to the back of the room, pick up the receiver from the wooden table and wave it enquiringly at Kostas who is busy slicing tomatoes. Scarcely looking up, he nods. I note the numbers on the small meter above the telephone and write them on the notepad lying beside it.

I dial four times before I hear a click, then a pause, then the familiar ringing tones of England. I think of Julia and what she might be doing at this precise moment. But there is no reply. Resignedly I start to replace the receiver.

"Hello." The voice is faint. She sounds strange.

"Julia?"

"No." The voice hesitates. "It's her daughter."

"Gemma? It's Bronson."

"Oh. Hi!" She seems pleased. "Where are you?"

"In Greece."

"I know. But where?"

"On a small island called Katakolos."

"What's the weather like?"

"Foul. It's rained most of the time."

"Oh dear. I'll get mummy for you. She's in the bath."

There is a silence, except for the slight crackling on the line. Then muffled voices.

"Hello." She sounds breathless, uncertain.

"Hello?"

"It really is you!" Her voice rises with excitement. "For a moment I thought Gemma was joking. You got me out of the bath. How are you?" The words are stressed, not just habitual.

"I'm well. We're just about to eat. I wanted to say hello." I think of her standing on the thick carpet, a bath towel fastened round her. It seems a million miles away.

"That's nice. You're going to eat with Dinos?"

"No." I pause, realising that what I am about to say will come as a shock. To me it is already a fact. A completion. "No. Dinos is dead."

There is a long silence. "Oh, Bronson!" Then she is quiet again. "I'm so sorry. Are you all right?"

"Yes... Yes. It's strange I *am* all right."

"You knew it, didn't you?"

"Yes. I suppose so. In a way. There are other things as well. I'll tell you when I'm back. But I'm fine." She remains silent. "Really," I say emphatically, "I'm fine. How are you? What did you do today?"

"Me?" She seems hesitant. "Nothing really. That's not important." I understand her reluctance, but I want to know. I want to place her in time and space, make her more than the distant voice on the end of the line.

"No, tell me. I'd like to hear."

"Well, I had lunch with Gemma and then we spent the afternoon together. She sends her love. I told her you were in Greece and how much you love it there. How much you knew about it and everything. She was very interested. You know what she said? She said she'd love you to take her there one day. Just the two of you."

I'm surprised. And touched. "That's nice. Tell her she's got a deal."

"She'll be thrilled."

We are both silent. There is so much that can't be communicated over distance.

"You're sure you're OK?" she says at last.

"Yes. It's strange."

"Yes. I hear that. Strange. I think I understand…"

"And Dinos left me the house," I say suddenly.

"The house?" She sounds puzzled.

"Yes, his house. He gave it to me in his will. And…" I hesitate. "And I want us to come and live here for a while." There's a long silence. "You don't like the idea?"

"No, it's not that. It's just… But what about the gallery and everything?"

"I'll find a way. This feels more important. The right time

maybe. The *kairos*, remember? Not for ever, but for a while. The right season…"

The line is starting to break up. "Can you hear me?"

"Just."

"When will you be back?"

"Probably in a couple of days."

"Okay. Stay well. I love you."

The line goes dead. I try to picture her standing there with the towel wrapped around her, holding the receiver, but the image has gone with her voice.

"*Efkaristo*," I call out to Kostas.

"*Parakalo*." The broad back is hunched over the stove. I go and sit down.

Even as I sit here I know that the quality of this dinner will stay with me forever. There are no dark corners in me tonight. It is as if the howl of the wolf has somehow drained me dry. And filled me with something I'm only just getting used to – a calmness, a sense of taking my proper place in the world, of being fully present. I relish the sharp taste of the tomatoes, the firm flesh of the fish, the damson colour of the wine in the thick tumblers. For now it's enough.

Over the meal Kostas tells me more of the details of Dinos' death. More of what he knows of his life. I listen, feeling attentive but detached. I am pleased to hear Dinos being praised, his courage, his wisdom, his kindness, his strangeness, how he stood apart. A kind of communal eulogy. But the facts seem unimportant, like reading a diary that is no longer relevant. The real information is in the photograph album. What truth I would ever have of Dinos lies there. Even in death he has left me with questions.

I push back the wooden chair and rise from the table. I know instinctively that I have formed a bond with the strange innkeeper that will never be broken. Across all the differences and all the problems of language we have a friendship. As if sensing my thoughts, Kostas pushes back his own chair, rounds the table, lumbering like a bear, and enfolds me in a crushing embrace. I can feel the rasp of stubble against my cheek, and the smell of garlic.

"You good man," says Kostas. Then, stepping back, he points at my plate, the carcass of the fish picked clean. "And you eat fish like a Greek!" It seems the greater of the two compliments.

"Where you sleep?" asks Kostas suddenly.

I haven't even thought about it. Instinctively I say "At Dinos."

"*At Dinos'?*"

"Yes."

"Is good?" asks Kostas. He sounds unsure.

"Yes. Is good."

"Okay. I take you."

Fifteen minutes later the prow of the small boat grates its way up the shingle. I jump out. The stern wave washes up the shore and covers my feet. I stand with my bag in one hand and Kostas' torch in the other.

"Is okay?" shouts Kostas.

"Is okay. *Efkaristo.*"

"*Kalinichta. Kai kalo ximeroma.*" The old Greek parting – have a beautiful dawn.

"*Episeis. Kalinichta.*"

Slowly the boat turns and disappears round the headland. The silence descends again. There are no stars. I am left alone on the beach.

I pause on the stone terrace, suddenly questioning my swift decision to spend the night here. Might it not feel eerie?

Or unsettling? Or worse? The key grates in the lock and I step in. Immediately, even in the dark, I feel at home.

The house is cold. Cold breathes from the walls and comes up from the stone floor. But with the aid of the torch I quickly find candles and a gas light and within minutes the rough logs that had been stacked in a wooden box are blazing merrily in the open fireplace.

I sit for an hour staring at the flames, my mind becalmed, without thought. Then I take a candle and climb the creaking stairs to Dinos' bedroom. I am surprised to find myself unhesitating. The sheets are cold and the bed feels damp. I know it is going to be uncomfortable. I pull on a thick pair of socks and, without undressing, slide under the covers. Instantly, like a drug, sleep folds over me.

FORTY-FIVE

At this end of the island, the hills are unwooded. As soon as I leave the stretch of pines and olives that skirts the shoreline, I am in a world of bare rock and low prickly scrub. No trees dot the horizon here. The ground is still soft under foot, but all sign of the previous day's rain has gone, except the occasional deep gully carved in the red soil. The scent of thyme, rosemary, oregano, wild garlic explode in the damp morning air.

Towards the summit I find a flat limestone outcrop and sit down facing the mainland. The narrow inlet of Dinos' bay cuts into the land below me. The house is clearly visible, standing alone on the small grey crescent of the beach. To the right, winding its way along the shoreline, is the narrow track I had taken that day with him when we had walked to the long beach in the south. The day we had talked of Aphrodite. In the distance, the path disappears behind the headland.

The dense cloud over the mainland is beginning to part, revealing patches of shoreline: a clump of cypresses, here and there a whitewashed house, and further to the right the indistinct greyness of the town of Panos. A single small fishing boat is making its way from Katakolos towards the coastline. The rhythmical popping of its engine floats up to me.

There had been no strangeness in sleeping in a dead man's bed. As I sit on the high rock now overlooking the strait, I sense the quality of that sleep – dreamless, a sleep of forgetting. The events of the previous day seem far away, the fact of Dinos' death already in the past. But the presence of Dinos surrounds me like an aura. There are endless questions that want to be asked. They seem to float in the morning air. And then evaporate. For I know that they are already answered, in a place where my mind and my speech can never go, in a place below the waters.

For a moment disparate images splinter my mind: lying in another cold, damp bed on another rocky Greek island; the news that my father had died, wired up in a hospital bed. He had slipped silently out of life. I had not grieved. Nothing had changed; nothing had been handed on. I had stayed frozen, growing deeper and deeper into manhood, the years passing, my hair starting to grey. But something inside me had remained unhatched, ungenerous. Suddenly Gemma comes into my mind. Why had she touched me so deeply the night before with her simple wish to come with me to Greece? I remember with shame my frequent annoyance at her requests, her intrusions, her brashness and naïveté. I remember standing with her before the painting in San Sepolcro, how I had lectured her, tried to shut her out.

Dinos' gifts are silent ones, not for the mind, his words obscure, often infuriating. They cannot be weighed or judged, can only be felt. Felt and passed on. Even now I can't really lay my mind on what has passed between us. I know it will be a long time before my brain can come abreast of my soul. Perhaps never.

I look across to the mainland and the dark stretch of unmoving water between. In England it is Good Friday. Obscurely, words from the Bible come into my head:

'And I saw a new Heaven and a new Earth. And the old

Heaven and the old Earth were passed away. And there was no more sea.'

Words written high up on another rocky Greek island overlooking the Aegean, on Good Friday almost two thousand years ago. *And there was no more sea…* What might that mean? I begin to shiver, as if something of the place is passing through me. My whole body begins to shake, my vision blurs.

And suddenly it is as if a veil has been ripped from my sight. And for a moment the world behind sight stands clear. The waters before me roll back. Time rolls back generation upon generation. In the valley between me and the mainland, olive groves stand in neat lines, flocks graze. The mainland is no longer mainland, the islands are not islands but hilltops. There is no shoreline. No above and below. No seen and unseen. All is known. And there is no more sea.

Of all the things Dinos has taught me, this remains unteachable. The knowledge that such a world still exists, present but out of sight. A world where the gods still walk. A knowledge that we are all imprisoned and that separation is an illusion carved out by the human mind; that we need the courage, bit by bit, to chip away until we can begin to break free into another, wider vision. Carla had been right: *Love is the great deepener.* Love of many kinds, a motion of the soul out beyond our narrow selves. It is the one true gift that we can leave to the next generation.

I rise and snap off a sprig of rosemary from the sprawling bush beside me and start down the slope. It is time to be getting back to London.